KNOT YOUR FIRST RODEO

WILD HEARTS RANCH

COZY COWBOY OMEGAVERSE

HARLEY KNIGHT

CONTENTS

KNOT YOUR FIRST RODEO
WILD HEARTS RANCH

I've been pretending so long that I almost forgot what I was hiding from.

Seven years ago, my parents handed me a bottle of suppressants and told me a comfortable lie: *Being a Beta is easier, sweetheart. No one needs to know.*

So I swallowed the pills. Buried the Omega. Built a life in my small Montana town where no one looks twice at plain, boring Beta June.

Then the rodeo circuit blows into town, and a 2:00 a.m. phone call sends me to the local jail to bail out one of its stars, a blue-eyed cowboy who's barely coherent but somehow knows exactly what I am.

He calls me his scent match. Fights my psycho ex in the street. Holds me like I'm precious.

And by morning, doesn't remember my name.

But his pack doesn't forget.

Kai sees straight through my lie with one look. Carter's easy charm makes my suppressants glitch. And Seth watches me like he's trying to remember something important, something just out of reach.

Three rodeo stars. One pack searching for their Omega.

I'm standing right in front of them, choking on a secret that's clawing its way out.

The circuit leaves in a few weeks. My ex is hell-bent on destroying anyone who touches me. And every time these Alphas get close, my carefully constructed life cracks a little more.

I spent seven years being no one.

Now three cowboys are making me want to be *theirs*, and that's the most dangerous thing I've ever craved.

Wild Hearts Ranch (Broncos)
Brutus the Bull
River/
Waterfall
Fire S
Medical C
The P
Hardware Store
BBQ Joint
Moonlight & Magnolias Dance Barn
Craft / Quilt Shop
Toy Store
GAS
Gas Station
Music Store
Copper Canyon Guest Ranch

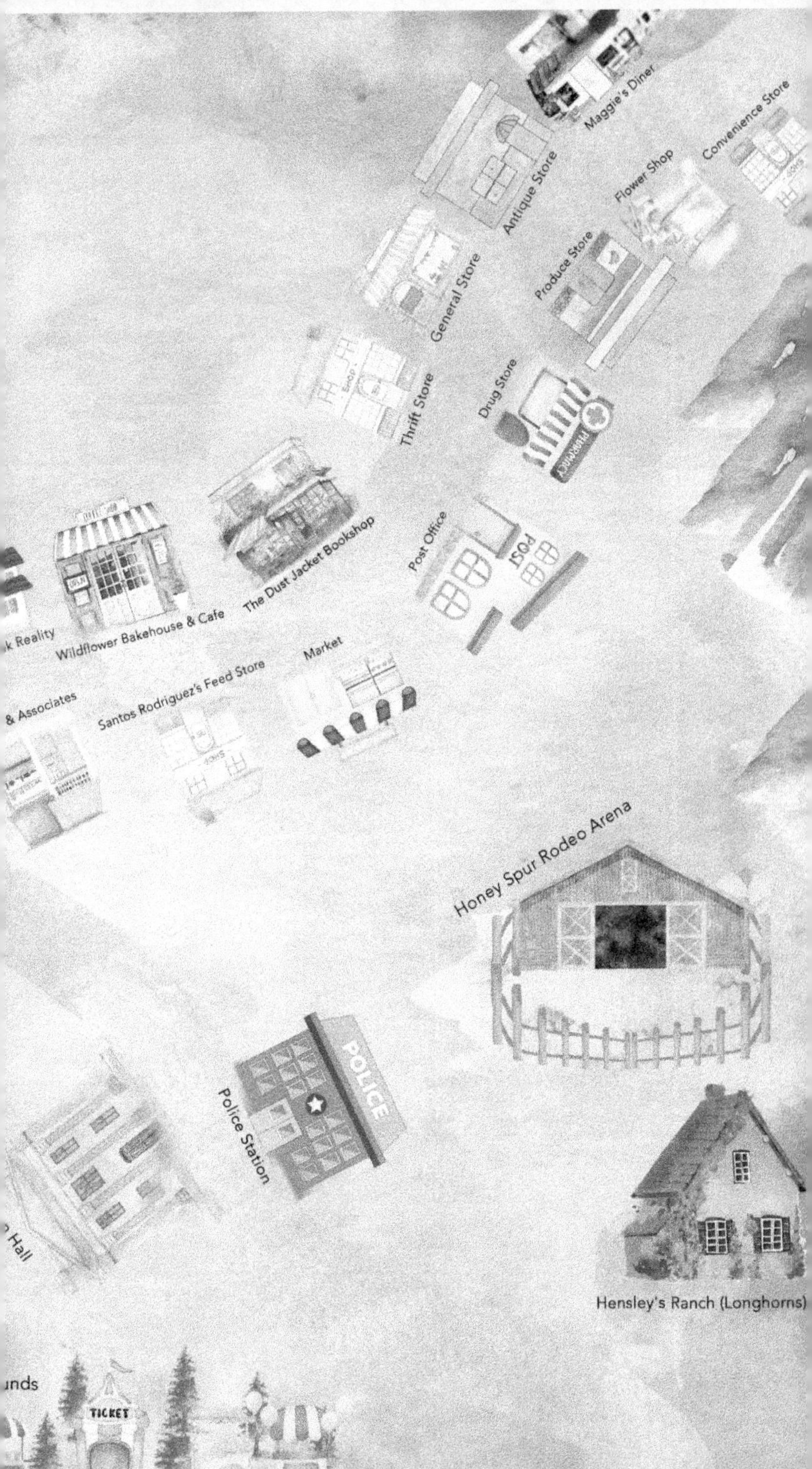

Maggie's Diner
Flower Shop
Convenience Store
Antique Store
Produce Store
General Store
Drug Store
Thrift Store
Post Office
The Dust Jacket Bookshop
Wildflower Bakehouse & Cafe
k Reality
& Associates
Santos Rodriguez's Feed Store
Market
Honey Spur Rodeo Arena
POLICE
Police Station
Hensley's Ranch (Longhorns)
Hall
unds
TICKET

1

JUNE

There's a special place in hell for whoever invented 2:00 a.m. phone calls, and I hope they're seated right next to the guy who thought decaf coffee was a good idea.

My sedan rattles over the one pothole on More Street, the same pothole that's been here since I was sixteen and backed my mom's Buick right into it, and I can't help but smile even as my tires thunk through it. Some things in Honeyspur Meadow never change, and honestly? I kind of love that about this place.

I stifle a yawn and grip the steering wheel a little tighter as I turn onto the main road. This is what I get for joining the town committee.

Actually, no. This is what I get for being the youngest person on the town committee by a solid two decades, and also the only one without a spouse, kids, or a convenient excuse. When Pete called twenty minutes ago, voice gravelly with sleep, asking if I could handle a small situation down at the station, I knew exactly what that meant.

"June, sweetheart, you're the only one who can do this without waking up a whole household."

The details Pete gave me were sparse: Someone from the rodeo circuit in town got into trouble at The Rusty Spur, ended up in a holding cell, and needs to be quietly collected before word spreads. The circuit brings serious money into Honeyspur Meadow every year, fills up our motels, packs our restaurants, keeps the local economy humming, and the committee's job is to keep that relationship solid and drama-free.

So here I am. Barely dressed, barely awake, driving through my sleeping town to bail out a stranger.

I sell houses, running my parents' Sweetwater Creek Realty business. In my spare time, I photograph Honeyspur Meadow, hoping to put together a book of our rural area. So of course I want the best for our town.

I pull into a spot along the curb, right in front of the hardware store, and cut the engine. Farther ahead sits The Rusty Spur, lights still on, music thumping from inside.

Okay, June. Let's do this.

I push open my door, and the cool air hits me. It slides past my coat collar and down my spine, finding every gap between my clothes. I'm wearing yoga pants stuffed into my nice cognac boots, a chunky cardigan that's more holes than warmth at this point, and my coat, which is doing approximately nothing to help. May tends to be the most unpredictable month when it comes to weather in Montana, and tonight's cold.

I lock my car and quickly cross the empty road, and I'm heading up the gravel path that leads off the main road toward the police station. It's a squat brick building with too-bright fluorescent lights visible through the windows.

The glass door sticks when I try to pull it. I stumble into the lobby, catching myself on the doorframe.

Very smooth, June. Ten out of ten.

The warmth inside is immediate and welcome. I take a moment to let the feeling return to my face, then approach the front desk, where a woman sits, staring at a computer screen.

It's Barb. We've met at approximately seven hundred town functions—she brought those dry lemon bars to the last town picnic—but she's looking at me now like she's never seen me before in her life.

Fair. I probably look like a disaster. I didn't even glance in a mirror before I left.

"Hi, Barb." I pull out my best I-am-a-competent-member-of-society smile. "Here to pick up someone. Pete should have called ahead?"

She blinks at me slowly, then takes a long, deliberate sip of her coffee. Maintaining eye contact. Establishing dominance.

I wait.

She sips.

We're really doing this, I guess.

Finally, she sets the mug down with a pointed clink and raises one eyebrow. "Name of the person you're picking up?"

Right. I dig my phone out of my coat pocket and pull up Pete's text from earlier, scanning the message. "Seth Benton," I say.

Something flickers across her face before her expression smooths back to professional boredom. "Wait here."

She disappears through a door behind the desk, and I turn to survey the waiting area. There's one other person here, a guy in the corner who looks like he lost a fight with a hay baler, staring at me with intensity.

I give him my sweetest smile, the one that says, *I will end you if you try anything*, and deliberately turn my back to claim one of the plastic chairs against the wall. I check my phone again. No new messages. The rodeo has been in town for four days now, and every motel is booked, every restaurant packed, and tourists are wandering the streets in brand-new cowboy hats, asking if we have Uber.

We don't. We barely have reliable cell service on a good day.

Finally, a door at the back of the station swings open, and a female deputy emerges.

She's hauling a guy big enough that *hauling* is probably an optimistic description. He's more like...

shambling under her guidance. A slow-moving mountain of a man, head down, dark hair falling over his forehead as he mumbles something that might be song lyrics.

Actually, no. It's definitely song lyrics.

He half sings, half slurs the words to "Sweet Home Alabama," his voice a low rumble that reverberates through the lobby.

The deputy shoots me a look that clearly says, *Good luck with this one*, and adjusts her grip on his arm as they approach.

"You sure you want this big lug?" she asks, sounding like she's offering me a burden rather than a human being.

"Does he have any other options?" I stand up, trying to get a better look at him. He's still not lifting his head, too focused on his private concert.

He continues to sing, seemingly lost in his own little world right now.

"Not at two in the morning, he doesn't, as he's not going back to the bar after the chaos he created," the deputy confirms. "He's all yours if you think you can handle him."

"Lucky me. And yeah, I've reined in bulls before." I approach them, and that's when I finally get a proper look at what I'm dealing with.

He's tall. Six-two at least, maybe more, with the kind of shoulders that look like they were designed to fill doorways. Even slouched and swaying, there's no hiding the breadth of him. He's thick through the chest, strong through the core, with powerful legs. I'm five-six, so compared to him, I'm tiny, but I'm not backing down.

He's wearing jeans and boots. His shirt is charcoal or navy, hard to tell in this lighting, a button-up that probably looked crisp hours ago but has since surrendered to whatever trouble led him here. It's untucked on one side, and the sleeves are rolled to his elbows, revealing forearms that make my mouth go dry.

Holy mother of—

They're ridiculous. Corded with muscle, dusted with dark hair. His hands are big, fingers long and capable, and there's a faint scar visible across his knuckles that suggests tonight's fight wasn't his first.

He's swaying gently, still humming under his breath, head still ducked so all I can see is dark hair, shorter on the sides, longer on top, and that shadow of stubble along a jaw.

The deputy releases him, and he stumbles slightly, catching himself with a grace that seems accidental. Then he lifts his head.

Oh.

His eyes are blue. The color of summer skies and mountain lakes and those perfect cloudless days you remember your whole life. Even glazed and unfocused, even rimmed with exhaustion and whatever else is running through his system, they're the kind of eyes that stop you in your tracks and make you forget what you were about to say.

They find mine, and something in my chest does a lazy flip. He's stunning, with a face made for trouble. High cheekbones, a strong nose with a slight crook, full lips that curve into a slow smile as he registers my presence. There's something almost boyish about his expression despite the sheer masculine size of him.

He grins at me entirely too confidently for someone who's being collected from a jail cell, and I feel that grin all the way down to my toes.

"Hello there." His voice is low and rough, and a buzz runs down my spine. "Didn't know they let angels into places like this."

I arch an eyebrow while the deputy chuckles. "Save it, cowboy. I'm nobody's angel, and you're nobody's prize catch right now."

"That so?" He tilts his head, considering me, and his smile widens. "Because from where I'm standing, you look pretty heavenly to me."

"From where you're standing, you can barely stand."

He laughs at that, and somehow that's worse than flirting. A laugh like that shouldn't be allowed at two in the morning. It's too genuine, too inviting, too likely to make a girl forget her purpose.

"Fair point," he concedes, swaying again. Then he straightens up—or tries to—and attempts a bow that nearly sends him toppling. "Seth Benton, at your service. And you are?"

"June. I'm your ride."

"June." He says my name like he's savoring it, rolling it around on his tongue. "Pretty name. Pretty girl."

"Flattery won't get you home faster. Let's go." I reach out and grab his elbow, my fingers barely making a dent in the solid muscle there. Even through his shirt, I feel the heat of him, the coiled strength. "I've got a bed waiting for me, and it's not going to wait forever."

"A bed?" His eyebrows shoot up, and that grin turns downright wicked. "Darlin', I like where this is going."

"My bed. Alone. While you sober up at the motel. Move it."

I start steering him toward the exit door, nodding my thanks to the deputy as we pass. He comes along willingly enough.

"You're bossy," he observes cheerfully. "I like bossy."

"You won't like it when I leave you on the side of the road in the middle of nowhere."

"You wouldn't do that." He's still grinning.

"Try me."

He laughs that warm, rumbling sound and stumbles into my side. I brace myself, but it's like trying to stabilize a redwood—he's solid, heavy, and entirely too close.

And that's when I catch his scent. There's alcohol there, sure—whiskey, probably—sharp and unmistakable, but it's faint. A top note rather than the main event. Underneath it, there's leather, coffee, and the sweetest chocolate.

Instantly, heat pools low in my belly while my pulse kicks up, just enough to notice. There's a sudden and inexplicable urge to lean closer, to press my nose to his neck and breathe.

What the hell?

I've been on suppressants for seven years, ever since I designated as an Omega at eighteen and my parents marched me through every test they could book, desperate to confirm I was fine. They insisted that I didn't scent right. The results came back clinical and cold: dormant Omega. No distinct pheromones. No cyclical biology. No neat explanation for why my body didn't behave the way everyone expected it to. I hated those words so much that I cried for a week, then learned how to swallow the grief and smile like it didn't matter.

"Being a Beta is easier," my father had said on the drive home, his hands tight on the steering wheel. "People don't look at Betas the way they look at Omegas. No expectations. No assumptions. No Alphas sniffing around like you're a prize to be won."

"You can choose," my mother had added, turning to look at me in the back seat. "You can live as whatever you want. No one has to know."

They bought me my first suppressants that day. Helped me file the paperwork. Never mentioned it again.

And I've been living the lie ever since.

I pull back from Seth slightly, but still loop my arm through his in case he stumbles again. His hip is still pressed against mine, and that smell is everywhere.

"You okay there?" He's staring down at me, those blue eyes curious, and for a moment, he seems almost sober. "You went a little pale."

"Fine. Just tired." I inject as much confidence into my voice as I can muster. "Come on. Door's this way."

We make it through the sticky glass door and out into the cold, which helps. The sharp air cuts through the fog in my head, clears some of that warmth from my system. I take a deep breath, and my heartbeat starts to settle.

"Christ, it's freezing," Seth mutters, hunching his shoulders against the wind. Then, inexplicably, he starts humming again. Different song this time.

"Please don't."

He ignores me completely, his humming transitioning into actual singing as we make our way down the gravel path toward the main road. His voice isn't bad, actually—low and rich, with a natural warmth to it—but the volume increases with every step until he's practically serenading the empty street.

"Oh my God." I tug at his arm, trying to move faster. "You're going to wake up the entire town."

"They should be awake!" He throws his free arm wide. "It's a beautiful night, June. Look at those stars!"

I glance up automatically. He's not wrong because the sky is clear, littered with more stars than you'd ever see in a city, the Milky Way a faint smear across the darkness. It's the kind of sky I've seen my whole life and never gotten tired of.

"Very pretty," I allow. "Now keep your voice down."

"You know what else is pretty?" He spins, pulling me with him in a clumsy twirl that makes me yelp. "You are. Has anyone told you that? You're real pretty."

I stumble out of the spin, grabbing his arm to steady myself. "You're real drunk."

"Am not." He says it with surprising conviction, stopping to face me. We're in the middle of the road we're crossing now, streetlights casting orange pools around us, and he's looking at me with those ridiculous blue eyes like he's trying to memorize my face. "I don't drink. Well, I do sometimes, but not usually, and not tonight, and—" He frowns, visibly losing his train of thought. "What was I saying?"

"That you're not drunk. Very convincing. But on the bright side, you seem like a happy drunk."

"Thank you." He beams at me, entirely missing the sarcasm. Then his expression shifts, curiosity replacing confusion. "You smell nice, you know."

I stiffen. "Stop talking."

"Like lemons. And honey. And..." He leans in, just slightly, nostrils flaring. "Wildflowers."

My heart is flipping again—fluttering, more like it—sending warmth through my chest despite the cold. The only explanation as to why he can pick up my scent at all is that my suppressants must be slowly wearing off, seeing as I took them early yesterday morning and now it's 2:00 a.m. Another reason I shouldn't have taken this job from Pete.

"Come on. You're being ridiculous." I tug at his arm, more urgent now, and we reach the other side of the road. "Car's just up here."

But he's not moving again. He's still looking at me with that soft, wondering expression, head tilted like he's trying to figure something out.

"You smell like my scent match," he says quietly.

I stop walking. Stop breathing, maybe.

"I don't have one yet," he continues, and his voice has gone dreamy. "Never found her. Started to think maybe I wouldn't. But you..." He reaches out, slowly enough that I could stop him if I wanted to, and brushes a curl back from my face. His fingers are warm against my cold cheek. "You smell like I've been waiting for you my whole life."

For a moment, I let myself feel it. The possibility. The pull.

What if he's right?

What if somewhere, beneath seven years of suppressants and careful denial, there's something real? His hand lingers on my cheek. His eyes hold mine.

Then he hiccups.

And laughs.

Then sways so dramatically that he nearly takes us both down, grabbing on to my shoulders for balance and laughing like it's the funniest thing in the world.

"Whoops," he manages between giggles. "Ground moved."

And just like that, the spell breaks.

I let out a breath, shaking my head to clear the fog. He's not lucid enough to recognize his own feet, let alone some cosmic romantic connection.

"Okay, buddy." I hook my arm through his again, more firmly this time, because if I don't stop him, he's going to attempt a heroic lurch and introduce his face to the ground. "You're operating on fumes. Let's get you to the car before you fall."

"I'm... I'm fine. This is my normal walking."

"Sure it is."

He huffs, then leans closer like he's about to tell me a state secret. "June."

"No."

"But, June."

"Nope. Walk now, delusions later."

He attempts a pout. Not a little one, either. A full, bottom-lip-out, wounded-pride pout that should not be possible on a grown man with arms like fence posts. It's frankly unfair. He does it anyway, eyes bright and stubborn beneath the streetlight.

"You can't just boss me around," he mutters.

"Oh, I absolutely can," I say, tightening my grip

and steering him away from the bar, away from the people and the noise in there. "I'm doing it right now."

He lets me guide him for three steps. Four. Then he plants his boots like a dramatic statue and turns his head.

"Stop," he says.

"If you throw up on my shoes, I'm listing you as a fixer-upper and selling you to the highest bidder."

He lifts a finger, solemn. "Darlin'." The word lands wrong. Not bad wrong. Just... too intimate. Too natural in his mouth. It slides under my ribs like it knows the way.

I blink hard. "Don't. Just walk."

He allows himself to be moved again. "You know," he says, voice lowering conspiratorially, "this isn't even the first time I've been arrested."

I laugh before I can stop myself. "That's not the reassuring fun fact you think it is."

"It's a character fact." He jabs a thumb at his chest like he's presenting evidence. "I've got... layers."

"Like in *Shrek*?" I laugh.

"And a record," he adds proudly, ignoring me, then immediately squints as if trying to remember whether that's something to brag about. "Not proud of the record. Well. Depends which one."

"Please tell me you are not about to list your charges like they're belt buckles."

He gasps and sways slightly. "How dare you."

"I'm serious."

"So am I." He leans against a storefront, eyes too blue, too sharp for how unsteady he is. "They made it sound worse than it was."

"That sentence has never been followed by anything comforting."

"It was a misunderstanding." He waves his hand, and the motion takes his whole body with it. I tighten my hold before he can tip. "And I didn't even start the fight."

"Uh-huh."

"I finished it," he states, like that's the important part. "Anyway, my dad would be pissed and even more disappointed in me if he saw me right now. Never can please him."

There it is. The real thing, tucked behind the cockiness. The pressure. The image. The constant invisible audience.

He tries to pull away, jaw flexing. "Where's the camera guy? There's always a camera guy."

"There isn't," I say, though there absolutely could be, which is why I'm walking him like a shield toward my car.

"June, listen. I'm not supposed to be like this. I'm supposed to be... respectable."

My mouth twitches. "You? Respectable?"

He glares at me, then immediately loses the thread and points at my face instead. "Don't laugh at me."

"I'm not laughing."

"You are. I can tell. Your eyes."

"Your eyes are drunk," I remind him. "They're not trustworthy."

He stares at me for a second too long. The air shifts, subtle but noticeable. "You're my scent match," he repeats, quieter now. Not goofy, not teasing. Certain. "I know it. I can tell."

I snort, partly because it's ridiculous and partly because if I don't make it a joke, my throat is going to do something embarrassing. "You can barely tell which direction your feet are facing."

He leans closer, breathing in like he's trying to pull the truth out of my skin. His fingers flex at his sides, restless, like his body wants to reach for me and he's holding himself back by sheer willpower. "It's you."

My pulse kicks once, hard, and I hate it. Not because I want him to stop. But because I don't want my body to betray me. Not now. Not ever.

"I'm a Beta, sweetheart." The lie comes easily, worn smooth from years of practice. "No scent match for you here. Just a very tired woman who wants to go home."

His eyes narrow. "That's bullshit."

"Language."

"I don't care." He tries to straighten again, like he's about to make a speech in front of a crowd. "You're hiding. I know what hiding looks like."

I stare at him. "Okay," I say, deadpan. "We're not doing emotional insight in the middle of the night. We're doing walking. One foot. Then the other."

He opens his mouth, probably to argue, but I tighten my grip and steer him forward again.

He stumbles, catches himself.

We're almost to my car now. I spot it up ahead, when Seth stops so suddenly I nearly plow into him.

"Wait." He holds up one finger, swaying. "I have a very important question."

"Can it wait until we're in the car?"

"No." He turns to face me, and despite the glazed look in his eyes, there's something almost serious in his expression. "Do you believe in fate?"

I blink at him. "What?"

"Fate. Destiny. The universe conspiring to bring two people together." He gestures expansively, nearly losing his balance. "Do you believe in that stuff?"

"I believe you need to sleep off whatever's in your system."

"That's not an answer."

"It's the only answer you're getting at two in the morning."

He considers this, frowning. Then his face brightens. "I believe in it," he declares. "I think sometimes the universe just... knows."

A low whistle cuts through the cold air.

I turn slowly to find Tanner, my ex, striding toward us down the sidewalk, backlit by the orange glow of the streetlamps. He's wearing jeans, boots, that stupid leather jacket he thinks makes him look tough, and there's a looseness to his walk that tells me he's been drinking. His sandy hair is pushed off his face, jaw tight, and even from here, I notice the mean glint in his eye.

"Just fucking great," I murmur under my breath.

We dated for two years, with him tracking my location, checking my messages, showing up wherever I was like it was a coincidence. It wasn't dramatic. It was slow. A steady erosion of my independence that I didn't fully recognize until I was standing in my kitchen one night, asking permission to visit my own parents, and realized I didn't know how I'd gotten there.

I broke up with him fourteen months ago, and he still hasn't forgiven me for it.

"June." He barks my name like a claim, like he has any right to call me that anymore. "Didn't expect to see you out this late."

"Tanner." I keep my voice flat, bored. "Go home. Sleep it off."

His eyes slide past me to Seth, who has gone quiet, watching the exchange with unfocused interest. "Who's this?"

"None of your business."

"Looked pretty cozy from down the street." He takes another step closer. "Walking arm in arm. Cute." He sneers.

"I'm helping a visitor find his motel. That's all."

Tanner's lip curls. "Let me guess. Rodeo trash?"

"Hey." Seth's voice cuts through, sharper than I expected. "That's not very nice."

Tanner's attention snaps to him, eyes narrowing. "I'm sorry, did I ask you?"

"No." Seth smiles, but there's an edge to it now. "But I'm telling you anyway. That's not how you talk about people."

"Seth." I squeeze his arm, warning. "Don't."

But Tanner is already stepping closer, that mean look intensifying. "Big man, aren't you? Coming into town, thinking you can act however you want. Getting handsy with women who don't belong to you."

"I don't belong to anyone—" I start.

"Shut up, June."

I flinch, hating myself for it, hating that he can still make me feel small with nothing but his tone.

Seth goes very still beside me.

"That's definitely not how you talk to her," he says quietly.

"I'll talk to her however I want. She's my girl."

"I'm not your anything," I snap, finding my voice again. "We broke up over a year ago, Tanner. Get over it."

He laughs, ugly. "You think you can just walk away from me? After everything I did for you?"

I shake my head, incredulous. "You didn't do anything except make my life miserable. Now get out of my way. I have somewhere to be."

I try to pull Seth forward, around Tanner, but my ex

moves to block us. His hand comes up, palm flat against Seth's chest, both men similar in height. And there's a moment—brief, charged—where everything goes very quiet.

"You're touching my girl there, asshole." Tanner's voice is low and nasty, the kind that carries even at two in the morning when the whole street is dead quiet. "I don't like it."

Seth glances down at Tanner's hand on his chest, then up at his face. Seth's expression goes flat in a way that tightens my stomach. Not calm. Not relaxed. Empty. Like something just shut off.

"She's not your girl," Seth states, almost gentle. "She told you that. I heard her. You should listen."

The streetlight throws shadows across Tanner's face, and he grins like a lunatic.

"You should mind your own fucking business," Tanner spits. He steps closer, crowding Seth, and me by default, because everything about him is about taking up space. "Go on, rodeo boy. Run along." His mouth twitches like he's amused. "You think you're tough because you can stay on a horse for eight seconds? I can stay on her all fucking night."

My skin goes cold. "Don't," I snap, voice sharper than I meant it. "Tanner, shut the hell up."

He doesn't even glance at me. Like I'm background noise to his little ego performance.

Seth does look at me. Just a flick, but it's enough to

make my pulse jump, like he's checking whether I'm okay, whether it hurt or not.

Then his gaze slides back to Tanner, and the drunk softness in his eyes cracks. He's still swaying slightly, still got that loose, unsteady edge to him, but the look is pure warning. I suspect that when he's not drunk, he'd be dangerous.

"Say that again," Seth demands.

Tanner laughs. "What? You gonna cry?"

And Seth releases this short laugh like Tanner just did him a favor. "Oh," Seth says. "Okay."

I wedge myself between them, palm pressing to Tanner's chest. "Stop it. Both of you. Just stop."

Tanner's arm sweeps out like he's swatting at a fly. It hits me in the face hard enough that I stumble, my boot catching on the uneven edge of the sidewalk, and I go down.

My palms scrape against the cold concrete as my hip slams down, and pain blooms hot and immediate. I sit there for half a second, stunned, breath knocked out of me, pride taking the hardest hit of all.

The street is silent except for my sharp inhale and Tanner's rough chuckle.

"That," Seth growls, low and lethal, "was a mistake."

2

JUNE

Tanner throws the first punch, wild, sloppy, aimed more at Seth's pride than at his face. Seth sidesteps, not graceful, not clean, but fast enough that Tanner swings through empty air.

Seth surges forward and slams Tanner back against the brick wall beside the closed storefront, hard enough to rattle the metal gate over the window. Tanner grunts, but he grins.

"Yeah," Tanner spits. "There you go. Show me what you got." But he swings first again—dirty and fast—catching Seth across the cheek. Seth staggers a half step, boots scraping, and for a heartbeat, he just stands there, tasting it, eyes brightening like someone flipped a switch.

Seth's fist connects with Tanner's jaw even faster.

Once.

Tanner's head snaps sideways, shoulder thudding

into brick. He blinks, then laughs like it's the best thing that's happened to him in weeks.

"Hit me again," Tanner taunts. "C'mon, rodeo boy. Let her watch."

Seth's face is tight, eyes bright and wild. He swings again, messier this time, anger bleeding into the hit. Tanner stumbles forward, catches Seth in the ribs with a heavy punch that makes Seth grunt and fold for half a second.

They collide.

No more wall. No more space.

They're grabbing shirts, shoving shoulders, boots scraping on concrete. Tanner tries to bulldoze Seth into the street, and Seth, half drunk and furious, fights like a man who's been in too many brawls for his own good.

"Stop!" I scramble to my feet, palms burning, voice cracking. "Seth—don't! Tanner, you psycho!"

Tanner swings again, catching Seth across the cheek. He spits to the side, wipes at his mouth with the back of his hand, and the glare he gives Tanner is pure promise.

Then Seth drives into him, tackling him low.

They hit the pavement hard, rolling right there on the sidewalk in front of the dark shopfront, grunting and swearing as elbows and fists and knees land wherever they can. Tanner claws for Seth's collar like he wants to choke him, like he's not satisfied unless he's hurting someone.

"You think you can touch what's mine?" Tanner snarls, breath ragged. "That you can take her from me?"

"She's not—" Seth grits out, and he headbutts Tanner.

The crack is sickening.

Tanner jerks back with a curse. Seth twists, hooks a leg, flips them with rough force, and suddenly Tanner is pinned beneath him on the concrete, Seth's forearm across his chest, fist drawn back.

For a drunk man, he also looks like he might not stop.

Tanner coughs a laugh, eyes glassy and vicious. "Do it," he taunts. "Bet she likes you better when you're violent."

My stomach turns.

"Seth!" I shout, stepping closer, limping slightly. "Look at me. Seth!"

His head jerks, just a fraction. His eyes flick to my scraped hands, the way I'm standing wrong.

Something shifts. Not soft. Not gentle.

Focused.

His fist loosens a little. His breathing stays heavy, chest heaving, but his gaze drops back to Tanner. "You put your hands on her again," Seth warns, voice low and rough with restraint, "and I'll break something you can't fix with a wrench."

Tanner spits blood onto the sidewalk and grins like it's a prize. "Look at you, ridin' in like some damn hero," he slurs, eyes mean and glossy. "She ain't yours, rodeo boy. She don't want you. Hell, she—"

Seth hits him.

It's one hard, ugly punch right to the mouth. The sound snaps through the quiet street like a firecracker. Tanner grunts and goes slack for a second, head turning with the impact, jaw working like it doesn't know what to do anymore. I flinch because it's brutal... and then my stomach twists with a guilty little jolt of satisfaction, because Tanner finally shut up.

Seth stays over him for a beat, breathing hard, still a touch unsteady from the booze, eyes bright and wild like he's fighting the part of himself that wants to keep going. Then he shoves off of him and stands, swaying slightly. He looks down at Tanner like he's something he scraped off his boot, and he delivers a sharp kick to Tanner's ribs—enough to make the point without turning it into a trip to the hospital. Tanner curls in with a pathetic wheeze, hands clutching his side, and I have to press my lips together to keep from grinning.

"Learn some fucking manners," Seth blurts out, brushing off his jeans like Tanner was a mild inconvenience. His voice has that slow cowboy bite to it, even now. "'Specially around women. You hear me, or you need me to spell it out?"

Then he turns to me, and it's like a switch flips. The cold violence drops away, and what's left is plain concern, the kind that flutters in my chest. He's at my side in two strides, one hand gentle on my elbow, the other hovering at my back like he's ready to catch me. "You all right, darlin'?" he asks, eyes searching mine. "You hurt? Let me see them hands."

"I'm fine," I lie, because my palms sting and my hip throbs, but the bigger problem is that a rodeo star I barely know just stood up for me like it was the easiest decision in the world. I swallow, trying to keep my voice steady. "We need to go. Right now."

Seth glances past me, just once, toward Tanner trying to drag in breath through his own ego. His jaw tightens, then he nods and shifts his body so he's between me and the mess, guiding me down the sidewalk like it's the most natural thing in the world. "All right," he murmurs.

I unlock the car with shaking hands and yank open the passenger door. "Get in."

Seth folds himself into my little sedan, squished in, his head brushing the roof, but he manages. I slam the door and run around to the driver's side, my heart pounding. One last glance at Tanner, and I grin as he groans in pain. Then I hop inside.

The engine catches on the first turn. Thank God. Thank hell.

I yank away from the curb like the devil himself is reaching for my bumper, tires squealing as the truck lurches forward. My hands are still shaking on the wheel.

That fight was a really, really bad idea.

I blow out a breath that comes out half laugh, half

sob. "Okay. I shouldn't say this because it makes me a terrible person and I'm supposed to be mature now, but... thank hell you punched that asshole."

"You're welcome, darlin'," he says.

"I'm serious," I keep going, because my mouth is running faster than my brain can catch it. Adrenaline does that to me, turns me into a talking sprinkler. "I mean, I'm not *thankful* that you got into a fight in the middle of the main street at two in the morning, because that is... criminal behavior, but he deserved it so much." I glance at Seth.

His jaw tightens, and his gaze flicks to my scraped hands, then back out the windshield, and for a second, he looks sober enough to scare me.

"And now," I add quickly, because the fear is catching up, "now it's really bad. Because Tanner is... he's Deputy Tanner. Sheriff's department. And he is absolutely going to make this a problem."

Seth blinks slowly. "Deputy?"

"Yes." I nod too hard, because panic needs somewhere to go, and apparently it's going into my neck. "Like, badge. Gun. The authority to ruin everyone's week. He's gonna wake up tomorrow and decide that he didn't lose a fight but got 'assaulted.' And you're gonna be the villain, and he's gonna be the poor wounded public servant."

Seth frowns like he's trying to hold the thought in his head and it keeps sliding off. "He didn't feel like public service."

"No," I snap. "He felt like a restraining order with legs."

I swallow, eyes flicking back to the mirror even though Tanner is already gone from view. "But... you'll be fine," I say, trying to convince myself as much as him. "You're out of town in, what, a few weeks? The circuit packs up and disappears like a traveling circus. And your dad's got friends. And sponsors. And the town council practically rolls out the red carpet for anything that brings money in, so they'll protect you because—" I take a breath, words tumbling. But for me...

Seth hums, distracted.

I glance over and realize he's not listening. Not really. He's digging through my center console with the determination of a raccoon breaking into a cooler. Then he pulls out my stash of Oreos like he just found gold.

"Oh my God," I groan. "Those are my emergency cookies."

"Mm." He pops one open with his thumb, then shoves half into his mouth. Crumbs scatter onto his jeans. He doesn't care. "Smart woman."

I stare at him, half horrified, half relieved that he's acting normal. "I am literally spiraling, and you're looting my car."

"Want one?"

"No."

He eats another anyway. "More for me."

I hate that my mouth twitches into a smile.

The road hums under the tires, the town falling away behind us until the streetlights thin out and the dark starts to feel wider. My heartbeat finally eases down from a sprint to something closer to a speed walk, but my hands are still tight on the wheel, knuckles pale, palms stinging every time I shift my grip.

Beside me, Seth goes quiet. I glance over and find him with his forehead pressed against the passenger window, mouth slightly open. He's asleep so suddenly it's almost impressive. One hand is still curled around the Oreo, and there are crumbs scattered down his shirt and into his lap.

I stare at him for a long beat, equal parts annoyed and, against my will, fond.

"You are so weird," I mutter, like it's an insult. It doesn't land like one.

He just exhales softly, a little puff of breath that fogs the glass near his temple.

The Ridge Motel comes into view a few minutes later, squatting at the edge of town like it gave up trying to be charming sometime in the late nineties. One flickering sign. A row of doors facing the parking lot. Nothing around it except dark fields and a stretch of road that disappears into nowhere. No cute shops. No cozy streetlamps. Just the kind of place you end up when you've run out of options.

Pete insisted we put him up for the night to sleep it

off instead of taking him to the Copper Canyon Guest Ranch, where some of the rodeo stars are renting for the duration of their stay in town.

I pull into the lot, park crooked because my nerves are still buzzing, and kill the engine. The sudden silence is loud.

For a second, I just sit here, hands resting on the wheel, listening for sirens that aren't coming.

Then I glance at Seth again. He's still out cold. I lean over and nudge his shoulder. "Seth."

Nothing.

"Seth," I try again, firmer. "C'mon. Wake up."

He makes a sound that's more disgruntled than human and shifts his cheek against the glass.

I sigh and reach for his arm. "Do not make me drag you. I will drop you. On purpose."

That gets a reaction. His eyelids flutter, slow and stubborn, and he turns his head just enough to blink blearily at me.

"Darlin'," he mumbles, like it's a greeting and a complaint all at once. "Why's it so... loud in here?"

"It's not. You're just dramatic."

He squints around the dark parking lot as if he's trying to figure out where he is. "We home?"

"This is The Ridge Motel. You're staying here so you don't end up asleep on the sidewalk again."

He frowns like he's trying to argue. Then he stares down at his hand as if he's just discovered the cookie.

He lifts it slightly toward me, solemn. "I saved this for you."

"Oh my God." I'm laughing.

I open my door and step out, cold air biting through my clothes. Quickly, I walk around to his side and open the passenger door, and he sits there for a second, swaying a little, blinking at me like I'm a concept.

"All right," I say, holding out a hand. "Up you get."

He takes my hand, and his grip is warm and heavy. He stands too fast and wobbles immediately, knees going soft, shoulders tipping toward me like he's about to fold. I catch him by instinct, one hand on his forearm, the other bracing his chest.

"Easy," I warn.

He makes a pleased noise at that, as though he likes being a problem.

Inside the office, the front desk attendant is a bored-looking kid who barely glances up from his phone when we walk in. Pete has already arranged everything, so in moments, I get the key and head to room 107.

The room is... exactly what I expected. Two beds with floral comforters, a TV that's probably older than me, and a bathroom. The carpet has a suspicious stain near the dresser that I choose not to examine too closely.

Seth doesn't seem to mind. He stumbles through

the door, takes one look at the nearest bed, and collapses onto it face-first with a groan of pure relief.

I hover in the doorway for a second, making sure he's not about to roll off the mattress and take out the nightstand with his skull. When he stays put—muffled, boneless, breathing like he's just fought a war—I step fully inside, and the door clicks shut behind me with that automatic motel latch that always sounds louder than it should.

"All right," I mutter, more to myself than to him. "You're alive. You're horizontal. No more crimes tonight. Fantastic."

The blinds are still open, which means anyone wandering past the window could get a free show of the rodeo star passed out in a floral hellscape. I cross the room and start tugging them down, slats clacking as they lower. They fight me, and I tug several times to get them loose.

Behind me, Seth shifts. The bed creaks. I hear fabric rustle, then a soft, satisfied sound like a man making peace with the universe.

"Interesting meetin' you," he says, voice thick and lazy. "But—"

I turn, ready to tell him good night and leave before he decides to confess his life story again. And I nearly swallow my tongue.

Seth is standing there.

Naked.

Like he's stepped right out of a sinful calendar I absolutely did not order.

For a full second, my brain does that blue-screen thing where everything freezes and the only thought left is *Oh, hell!*

My gaze drops because apparently my eyes are traitors.

He is... insane. Not turned on, not doing anything, just existing, yet his package is so huge, not to mention all the muscles, broad shoulders, that stupid V at his hips, and solid thighs. And I'm staring at that trunk between his legs again.

God!

June. Stop. Immediately.

Seth sways a little, blinks like he's trying to find the floor again, then flops onto the bed on his stomach. "Ohhh, glorious bed," he mumbles into the pillow like he's proposing to it.

I stand there in the middle of the room, cheeks on fire, clutching the cord on the blinds like it's a weapon. "Seth."

"Mmh?"

"You can't just... take your clothes off in front of people."

He rolls his head on the pillow, cheek pressed into the floral comforter, voice muffled and smug. "It's my room."

"I'm still in here."

"Mmh." A pause. Then, very clearly: "I know you're checkin' me out."

I make a sound somewhere between a cough and a strangled laugh, staring at his butt. "Am not."

"Darlin'," he murmurs, like he's smiling into the bedding, "you were starin' so hard I could feel it."

"I was ensuring you weren't going to injure yourself," I snap, which would sound more convincing if my voice weren't slightly squeaky. "You're drunk. People fall. People... forget... gravity."

Seth hums again, low and pleased. "Sure."

I drag a hand down my face and turn toward the door before my eyes betray me a second time. "Good night, Seth."

I get two steps.

"June."

I pause with my hand on the handle. Because of course my body listens when he says my name like that —quiet, rough, not teasing.

"Yeah?" I ask, trying for annoyed and getting something softer.

There's a beat of silence behind me. The bed creaks like he shifted, maybe rolled onto his side. "I meant what I said earlier," he murmurs. "You're my scent match."

I close my eyes. Of all the things that should not squeeze my chest right now, that is at the top of the list.

"It's highly doubtful," I say, forcing a lightness I

don't fully feel. "Tomorrow you won't remember a single thing from tonight."

"I'm gonna remember," he admits, stubborn even through the pillow.

"Mm-hmm." I twist the handle and pull the door open. "Get some sleep. And for the love of God, put pants on if you decide to wander outside."

His laugh is quiet, warm, and it follows me out into the cold motel walkway like a hand at my back.

I step out, letting the door click shut, and then I stand there for a second too long with my face on fire.

Because the worst part is...

For one terrifying moment, I almost wanted him to be right.

3

SETH

The phone won't stop ringing.

I crack one eye open and immediately regret it. Sunlight is stabbing through some gap in the blinds, and my head feels like someone stuffed it with cotton and then set it on fire.

The phone keeps ringing. Loud. Obnoxious. Relentless.

I groan and fumble for it on the nightstand, knocking over something—a lamp, maybe, or a glass—and finally get my hand around the damn thing.

"What?" I groan.

"Where the hell are you, son?" My father's voice cuts through the fog in my skull, sharp and cold as wind. I pull the phone away from my ear, squinting at the screen. 9:47 a.m.

Fuck.

"Dad." I push myself up to sit in bed, and the room

spins for a second before settling into something that's still too bright and too real. "I'm—"

Where am I? I glance around. Floral bedspread that belongs in a grandmother's guest room. Wood-paneled walls. A TV so old it still has knobs on the front.

Some motel. No idea which one or how I got here.

"Everyone's already at the ranch," my father continues, his Texas drawl doing nothing to soften the edge in his tone. "Photo shoot starts in an hour. You plannin' on joining us, or should I tell the photographers to just work around the empty space where my son should be?"

I run a hand through my hair, greasy, needs washing, and try to piece together what the hell happened last night.

The bar. I was at The Rusty Spur. That part I remember. Drinking soda because today was a big day and I needed to be sharp. Someone was playing country music too loud. Carter and Kai were there, being their usual troublesome selves.

Then... nothing. Or not nothing, exactly. Flashes. A brawl at the bar, fists flying, someone's head hitting a table. The back of a police car, maybe? And then...

Hazel eyes.

The image hits me out of nowhere, sharp and vivid despite everything else being foggy. Looking up at me with a mix of exasperation and something softer. Curly brown hair. A face that squeezed my chest.

And a scent.

Lemon zest. Honey. Wildflowers.

Even now, sitting in this shitty motel room with a head full of broken glass, I can almost smell it. Like the fragrance has been imprinted on my brain. Like it's the one thing my body refused to let go of.

Who the fuck was she?

"Seth." My father's voice snaps me back. "You even listening to me?"

"Yeah." I swing my legs over the side of the bed and stand up. The floor tilts, then steadies. "I'm coming. Don't worry about it."

He scoffs. "That's what you said last time. And the time before that."

I don't answer. There's nothing to say that won't start a fight, and I don't have the energy for one right now.

The silence stretches. Then my father sighs—that long, disappointed exhale I've been hearing my whole life. "What were you thinking last night, boy?"

"I wasn't drinking."

"I don't give a damn if you were or not. I had the sheriff show up this morning, telling me my son got into it with the town deputy. That you were arrested and spent half the night in a holding cell." His voice rises, then drops to something colder. "And now they're talking about pressing charges."

I close my eyes. Flashes again—someone shoving me, fists connecting with bone, rolling on asphalt. The deputy. Right. Some asshole on a sidewalk who looked nothing like a cop.

What the hell happened?

"I didn't start it," I mutter, even though I'm not entirely sure that's true.

"Doesn't matter who did. What matters is how it looks." I can hear him pacing, the creak of floorboards under his boots. "You want to be the face of Wildfire Star Rodeo? You want your name on the posters, your face in the ads? Then you need to damn well act like it. Not brawling in the streets like some dumb kid with something to prove."

My jaw tightens. I run my tongue over my teeth, tasting copper. Someone got me good at some point— there's a throb along my jawline that says I took at least one solid hit.

"I'll handle it."

My father lets the silence sit for a beat. "We've got major sponsors lined up this year. Big money. The kind that keeps this whole operation running. And this town—" He makes a frustrated sound. "It's been hit or miss for us. Profits aren't what they used to be. I've been talking to Holden, the finance guy from the town committee, and he insists that we're going to make less this year than our last visit." He sighs heavily. "Maybe moving the circuit to the next town over, Cedarstone, is the better solution. They have a real company running events, unlike this town, which leaves it to a bunch of volunteers.

Cedarstone also has better facilities, bigger crowds, more—"

"Cedarstone's not a real town." The words come out sharper than I intended. "It's a tourist trap with a cowboy theme park. Our core audience is rural. Small towns. Places where rodeo actually *means* something."

"Our core audience is whoever buys tickets."

"No. It's people who grew up with this and who remember what it feels like." I'm pacing now. "Towns like this one, like the one we grew up in. Where you and Mom had me. Where she—"

I stop myself. Too far.

The silence on the other end is different now. Heavier.

I was twelve. Just a kid running wild through the streets, spending summers at the local rodeo grounds, watching the riders with stars in my eyes. Mom was still here then. Still laughing. Still the center of everything.

A year later, she was gone. The car accident took her fast, and after the funeral, Dad couldn't stand to stay in that town anymore. "Too many memories," he'd said. So he packed us up, hit the road, and started the circuit. Been moving ever since.

Mom never saw any of it. Never saw what Dad built in the years after she died. Sometimes I wonder if she'd be proud of us or if she'd hate what we've become—always running, never stopping long enough to feel anything real.

"Just get to the damn ranch," my father says finally. "We'll talk about this later."

"Fine."

"And, Seth?"

"Yeah?"

"Fix your mess before it becomes mine." The line goes dead.

I stare at the phone for a long moment, then toss it onto the bed. My head is still pounding, my mouth tastes like something died in it, and apparently I'm a wanted man in a town I barely know.

Great. Fantastic start to the day.

I stare around the room, trying to find something that might explain how I ended up here. There's a key on the nightstand—room 107, The Ridge Motel—and a piece of paper with the motel's address printed on it. Nothing else. No note, no wallet, no phone number scrawled on a napkin.

Just the memory of hazel eyes and a scent I can't shake.

"You smell like my scent match."

Did I actually say that to someone last night? Sounds like exactly the kind of thing my drunk brain would decide was a good idea.

Except I wasn't drunk. I *know* I wasn't drunk. I had one drink at the bar—a Coke, because I'm not a fucking idiot. Someone must have slipped something into it. That's the only explanation that makes sense.

But then how did I get here? Who brought me to

this motel? And who the hell was the woman with the hazel eyes?

I grab my phone and pull up my contacts. Carter's name is right at the top.

Me: *Need a ride. The Ridge Motel. Out front.*

The response comes in less than a few seconds.

Carter: *Holy shit, you're alive. Whose bed did you end up in last night?*

Me: *Fuck off and just pick me up.*

Carter: 😂😂😂 *On my way. 20 min.*

I toss the phone on the bed again and head for the bathroom. The mirror confirms what I already suspected: I look like hell. There's a bruise forming along my jaw, purple and angry, and my eyes are bloodshot. My hair is a disaster. I smell like sweat and stale beer and something else—something floral and sweet that doesn't belong to me.

Wildflowers.

I turn on the shower, letting the water run until it's hot enough to steam up the tiny bathroom. The pressure is shit, but it's better than nothing. I stand under the spray and let it pound against my skull, trying to beat some clarity into my brain.

Last night.

The bar where Carter and Kai were... We were celebrating the start of the circuit, or pre-celebrating, since the real festivities don't kick off until the weekend. I was being good. Sticking to soda. Watching the crowd.

There was a woman. Dark hair, pale ice-blue eyes,

almost white around the edges. She was pretty, in an obvious kind of way. She kept finding excuses to touch my arm, lean close, laugh at things I didn't say. I wasn't interested, but I wasn't not enjoying the attention either. Ego is a hell of a thing.

And then...

Nothing. A gap. Like someone took scissors to the film reel of my memory and cut out the important parts.

I punch the shower wall, and the pain in my knuckles helps. Grounds me.

What the fuck happened last night?

By the time I get out, I feel marginally more human. I don't have a change of clothes, so I pull on last night's jeans and button-up, trying to ignore the wrinkles and the faint smell of perspiration on the fabric.

The lobby is empty except for an older guy behind the desk who's maybe sixty, balding, and reading a newspaper like it's still 1985. He glances up when I approach, expression neutral.

"Hey." I lean against the counter. "You remember me coming in last night?"

He shakes his head slowly. "Just started my shift an hour ago. Night guy's already gone home."

"You got cameras? Anything that might show—"

He cuts me off with a look that's seen a thousand guys like me stumbling through his lobby. "This is the kind of motel where we don't ask questions about who you bring to your room. No cameras. No records. That's the whole point."

I groan, rubbing a hand over my face. Great. So much for that lead.

"Thanks anyway," I mutter and push through the front door into the morning.

The parking lot is mostly empty. The motel is old, run-down, the kind of place that peaked decades ago and has been slowly dying ever since. Beyond it are just trees and rolling mountains. The road into town stretches out in the far distance, leading to the main part of town. It's quaint streets, wooden storefronts, the kind of main drag that looks like a postcard.

A shiny red pickup truck rounds the corner and pulls into the lot. Carter is behind the wheel, grinning like Christmas came early. He's got those backcountry good looks the women in town lose their damn minds over—deep blond hair hanging to his shoulders, with a short beard and 'stache kept trimmed so tight it's more threat than fluff. Those green eyes hit the light when he turns his head, sharp and smug.

He's in one of his usual checked button-ups, sleeves shoved up.

I climb into the passenger seat. "Not a fucking word," I warn him.

He holds up both hands in mock surrender, still grinning. "Wouldn't dream of it."

"I mean it."

"I heard you. Not a word. Absolutely silent over

here." He pulls out of the lot, tires crunching on gravel. "Totally speechless. Can't think of a single thing to say about finding you at a motel that looks like it was decorated by someone's senile grandma."

"Carter."

"I mean, when I saw your text, I thought maybe you'd ended up at the Riverside Inn or somewhere half decent. But *this*?" He gestures at the fading motel sign in the rearview mirror. "This is commitment to whatever bad decisions you made last night. I'm impressed."

"Are you done?"

He glances at me, eyes bright. "I feel like I could go on. Really explore the depths of whatever the fuck happened to you last night."

"I will throw you out of this truck."

"It's *my* truck."

"I don't give a shit."

He laughs, the kind of chuckle that makes it impossible to stay pissed at him, and he reaches over to crank up the radio. Some old country song fills the cab, and for a minute, we just drive, windows down, morning air cutting through the lingering fog in my head.

Carter has been my best friend going on eight years now. He joined the circuit when he was twenty-two, fresh off his brother's funeral and looking for somewhere to put all that grief. My dad took him in when no one else would. Gave him a spot, a purpose, a reason to keep getting up in the morning.

We hated each other at first. Or I hated him, anyway. This golden-haired charmer with his easy smile and his sad eyes, showing up in my space and making everyone like him without even trying. I thought he was soft. Thought he was just playing cowboy while the rest of us did the real work.

I was wrong. About all of it.

Carter rides like he's got nothing to lose, because in his head, he already lost everything that mattered. His brother died in the ring, a freak accident, bad luck, the kind of thing that isn't anyone's fault but feels like everyone's, and Carter stayed because leaving felt like letting him die twice. That's not soft. That's the hardest thing I've ever seen anyone do.

"So," Carter says, turning down the radio. "You want to fill me in, or should I just keep picturing the worst?"

"Fuck if I know what happened."

"Come on. You gotta give me something."

"I mean it. I don't remember most of it." I lean my head back against the seat. "I recall the bar. Being smart about it, soda all night. And then it's just... pieces."

"Shit." He whistles low. "That's fucked up. You weren't even that wasted when we left."

"Oh, I saw you two ditching me." I cut him a grin.

"Yeah." He doesn't even have the decency to look guilty. In fact, his grin widens. "We ended up with those two girls. Fucking stunning, both of them. Spent half the night at their hotel. Kai was—" He laughs, shaking his head. "Man, Kai was on fire."

"I don't need the details."

"You absolutely need the details. These are important details."

"Pass."

He shrugs, still grinning like a cat that got the cream. He loves this shit—loves bragging about his conquests, loves knowing he scored while I apparently ended up in a haunted motel with no memory of how I got there.

"Last I saw you," he continues, "you were getting real friendly with that dark-haired chick. The one with the creepy eyes."

"Creepy?"

"Just... intense. Ice blue, almost white around the edges? She was all over you. Practically trying to climb into your lap."

"Yeah, I recall her but not much after that."

"Maybe she roofied you."

The thought has occurred to me. "Maybe."

"Or maybe you just finally learned how to let loose."

"That's not what happened."

Carter shrugs, turning onto the main road that leads out of town. "Whatever you say."

We drive in silence for a minute. The storefronts give way to open fields, fences running along the road, horses grazing in the distance. It's beautiful out here. Quiet. Real.

"Apparently I got into it with a deputy last night," I state.

Carter's eyebrows shoot up. "Fuck yeah, you did. Fighting cops now? That's a new level, even for you."

"Sheriff showed up at Dad's door this morning. Told him I was arrested, spent time in a holding cell, might be facing charges."

"Holy *shit*." He slaps the steering wheel, laughing. "Seth, you crazy bastard. Was he at least a big guy? Please tell me you didn't beat up some five-foot-nothing rookie."

"Hell if I remember. I've got flashes—someone on a sidewalk, a fight—but that's it." I rub my jaw, feeling the bruise. "Someone got me good, though."

"Seems like you got him better." He grins. "Fuck, I wish I'd been there. Kai's gonna lose his mind when he hears this."

"Don't tell Kai."

"I'm absolutely telling Kai."

"Carter."

"He's gonna find out anyway. Might as well hear it from me so I can embellish the details."

I shake my head, but I can't quite suppress the smirk. "Think I found my scent match last night too."

Carter's head whips toward me. "The fuck did you just say?"

"Eyes on the road."

He corrects the wheel but keeps glancing over at me. "Your scent match? You serious?"

"I don't know. Maybe. I can't fucking remember." The frustration boils up. "I've got this image of hazel eyes, curly brown hair, this *scent,* but I don't know who she is or where she came from or if she's even real."

"What kind of scent?"

"Lemon. Honey. Wildflowers." Saying it out loud makes it feel more real. "I can still smell it. Even now. Like it's stuck in my head."

"Fuck yeah." Carter grins, punching my shoulder. "That's what I'm talking about. Pack's finally gonna be complete. Who is she? She local? She hot?"

"That's the problem, asshole. I don't remember."

"Jesus Christ." He laughs, shaking his head. "Only you, man. Only fucking you."

"It's not funny."

"It's fucking hilarious."

I flip him off, and he just laughs harder.

The road curves, and the ranch comes into view up ahead—Cooper Canyon Guest Ranch, where the three of us have been staying. It's a two-story wooden structure with a wide wraparound porch, painted white with dark green trim. A big red barn sits off to one side, and beyond that, rolling hills dotted with cattle and horses stretch toward the mountains in the distance. There's a stable complex to the right, and enough land between them that you could forget the rest of the world exists.

It's a good setup. Private. Away from my dad, his new wife, and the rest of the circuit crew. A place to decompress when everything else gets too loud.

Vehicles are parked everywhere today, trucks and SUVs crowding the gravel drive. People milling around near the horse pen, where the photography setup is waiting. Two photographers, lighting equipment, and what looks like half the circuit crew standing around.

My dad is by the fence, arms crossed, talking to someone I don't recognize. Even from this distance, I can feel his disapproval radiating off him like heat.

"How's Kai doing this morning?" I ask, changing the subject because I can't think about mystery women and scent matches anymore without losing my mind.

Carter chuckles. "For once, he's doing better than you. Which is saying a damn lot."

"Fuck off."

He grins. "Don't forget, there's the town fair tonight. Give him time, and he'll outdo both of us. Plus, they have a live band, some dancing."

"I'm not going."

"Come on—"

"Not after last night. Not with whatever the fuck is going on with the deputy situation."

Carter glances at me but doesn't push. "Fair enough," he says. "But if you change your mind—"

"I won't."

"—I'll save you a dance."

"I'd rather eat glass. You know me. I don't dance, don't sing."

He pulls up near the house, and I'm already reaching for the door handle. "I need to change," I say. "Tell them I'll be out soon."

"You got it."

I climb out of the truck, and Carter's voice stops me. "Hey. About the scent-match thing."

I turn back.

"Go make yourself pretty. You look like shit."

I flip him off again and head for the house.

The front porch wraps around the entire first floor, white railings and hanging flower baskets filled.

A faint laugh that sounds familiar comes from the group.

Instead of going inside, I move along the porch, boots quiet on the wooden boards. The wraparound design takes me past windows and rocking chairs until I reach the corner where I can view the backyard.

There's a small group gathered near the horse pen, photographers setting up equipment, some of the circuit crew, and a few people I don't recognize. Local press, maybe, or sponsors. My dad is there too, talking to a woman in a blue dress who's taking notes on a clipboard.

The laugh comes again, and my eyes track the sound.

She's standing near the fence, one boot propped up

on the lower rail, talking to a photographer. Her back is partially to me, but I can see enough.

Tight jeans that hug every curve. Cowboy boots. A Western shirt in rust-red, fitted close through the waist. Her sleeves are rolled to her elbows. Brown hair is up, piled on top of her head in some kind of messy twist, but I can see the curls trying to escape.

She laughs again at something the photographer says, her head tipping back, and even from this distance, something about it calls to me.

I can't even see her face, but she's really fucking cute. I don't know her. At least, I don't think I do. But that laugh...

She turns slightly, gesturing at something in the distance, and I catch a glimpse of her profile. Absolutely stunning beauty, big eyes, and a bright smile.

Who is she?

4

JUNE

The sun is deceptively cheerful this morning, bright and golden. The breeze cuts cold across the ranch, sharp enough to make my nose run, but I'm not complaining. After last night's adventure in bail-and-babysit, I'll take any excuse to be outside instead of lying in bed staring at the ceiling and replaying every embarrassing moment on a loop.

"You smell like my scent match."

Nope. Not thinking about that. Or blue eyes, rough voices, the way my traitorous body responded to a stranger's scent like it had been waiting for him my whole life.

I'm here to help out Belle. She's currently crouched near the horse pen, checking the equipment. My gear is with her too. Her purple hair flutters in the breeze, buzzed short on one side, the rest sweeping on the other side and down her shoulder in a dramatic wave that somehow looks effortlessly cool instead of ridiculous. She's wearing a green floral dress with thick black tights and black boots, a leather jacket thrown over top.

Meanwhile, I'm in my favorite rust-red Western shirt, jeans that I'm pretty sure have a coffee stain on the thigh from this morning, and boots that have seen better days. My hair is piled on top of my head to get it out of my way.

"Okay, here's the plan," Belle begins. "I'm handling action shots, horses, movement, all the dramatic stuff. Once I'm done with all the guys, they're yours for headshots. Shoulders and up. You can watch me work the action shots if you want some insight."

"Sounds good." I set down my bag and start checking my own equipment. Everything is there and ready. I love that I can do part-time photography gigs, as I don't see myself working forever in real estate. "Any particular look we're going for with the headshots?"

"Rugged but approachable. Sexy but wholesome. The kind of face that makes women swoon and sponsors write checks." She winks. "Basically, just make them look like the fantasy cowboys everyone wants them to be."

"So, lie with a camera. Got it."

She laughs and heads toward the corral where the crew is setting up lighting equipment. I follow, leaving Belle's assistant to care for the cameras, while I take in the scene of a gorgeous chestnut mare being led into position, handlers fussing with her mane, a cluster of cowboys gathered near the water station looking like they stepped out of a Western romance novel.

And somewhere among them, probably, is Seth.

Not that I'm looking. Not that I care.

I'm scanning the crowd anyway when I turn and walk straight into something solid.

"Whoa there, careful!" I stumble backward and find myself in front of a wall of muscle carrying a horse saddle in one arm.

"I saw you there," the wall says, and there's laughter in his voice.

I look up.

And up.

And—*oh.*

He's tall, six-one, six-two, with a broad chest and powerful arms and legs that look like they could run through walls. His dark brown hair sits just above his shoulders, pulled up into a messy knot with loose strands falling around his face. He's clean-shaven, which makes his features stand out more than I'd expect—thick eyebrows, long lashes, and eyes that are a pale gray.

There are piercings. Multiple in his ears. One through his eyebrow. And when he shifts the saddle to his other arm, I catch a glimpse of his right arm, covered entirely in a full sleeve of tattoos. Bold tribal patterns, dense and intricate.

He grins down at me, and it's pure sin.

"Name's Kai," he says. "You shooting us today?"

"That's the plan." I find my voice somewhere in the vicinity of my dropped jaw. "I'm the assistant, so don't expect miracles."

"Miracles aren't really my thing anyway." He tilts his head, studying me with open curiosity. "What do they call you, angel?"

"They call me someone who doesn't fall for cheesy pickup lines."

His grin widens. "That wasn't a pickup line but an observation. You've got a face like heaven."

"And that mouth of yours is a straight-up hazard."

"Guilty." He shifts the saddle again, biceps flexing in a way that's absolutely intentional. "But it's the fun kind of hazard. I promise."

The breeze shifts, and the world tilts sideways.

His scent smothers me without warning—sea salt, toasted coconut, and underneath, it's tropical, like fresh, sweet pineapple.

For a moment, I'm not standing in a cold Montana field. I'm floating in warm water, sun on my face, waves lapping gently against my skin. I'm somewhere far away, somewhere beautiful, somewhere I never want to leave—

My foot catches on a rock.

I pitch forward with a yelp, arms flailing, the ground rushing up to meet my face. This is how I die.

Face-first in the dirt in front of a hottie, with horse manure probably inches from my—

Kai moves.

It happens so fast I barely register it. One second he's holding the saddle, and the next he's setting it down in a controlled drop while simultaneously lunging toward me. His hand catches my stomach, the other wrapping around my back, and in one fluid motion, he's hauling me upright, pivoting to catch his own balance, turning so that somehow, impossibly, I end up pressed against his chest with my face buried just below his collarbone.

I gasp.

Which is a mistake.

Because inhaling means getting a lungful of that scent again, so strong and overwhelming that my entire nervous system glitches out.

My face is pressed against warm cotton and solid muscle. My hands are splayed across his chest, feeling the hard planes beneath the fabric. His arms are wrapped around me, one across my back, one still at my waist, and he's so much bigger than me, surrounding me completely, and I can't breathe, can't think, can't do anything except drown in the smell of him.

My heart slams against my ribs. There's a buzzing between my thighs, insistent and alarming, and my whole body is trembling like I'm standing in a hurricane instead of pressed against a stranger's chest.

What is happening to me?

This isn't normal. This isn't how I react to people. This is—

Kai pulls back slightly, his hands still warm on me, and looks down at me with an expression that's shifted from playful to something more focused. More intent.

"You all right there, doll?"

I open my mouth to respond. What comes out is something between a wheeze and a moan.

His eyebrows shoot up. And then that grin returns, slower this time, knowing, like a cat who's just spotted something interesting.

"Did you just sniff me a second ago?"

"I—what—no—"

"Because I'm pretty sure you just buried your face in my chest and took a big ol' breath." He leans closer. "Naughty girl. But if you ask nicely, I'll let you do it again."

Oh my God. My face and whole body are on fire. My brain has completely abandoned ship and left me here to die of embarrassment. Who in the world is this man? My heart is thundering so fast, so loud.

"I think," I manage, my voice coming out strangled, "I'm having a heart attack."

His expression flickers—genuine concern breaking through the flirtation. "Wait, seriously?"

"I don't know." I press a hand to my chest, feeling my heart hammering against my palm. "My heart is doing weird things. Is this what dying feels like?"

He studies me for a long moment, those pale gray eyes searching my face. Then he steps close enough that I catch another wave of that scent, and my knees actually buckle. He catches me again, keeping me upright.

"Is that the impact I have on you?" His voice is softer now, but there's still that teasing edge. "Because I've been known to have that effect on women, but usually not this fast."

I let out a breathless laugh that sounds slightly hysterical even to my own ears. "Are you seriously flirting with me right now? While I'm having a medical emergency?"

"Is it a medical emergency, or is it just me being devastatingly attractive?"

"I hate you."

"No, you don't." He grins, and it's infuriatingly charming. "You're blushing too hard to hate me."

He's right. My cheeks are burning. I'm probably visible from space right now, a beacon of mortification glowing red across the Montana landscape.

"So tell me," Kai continues, tilting his head, "how come I can barely scent you? You're an Omega, right, to have such a reaction?"

The question lands like a bucket of ice water thrown over me.

"I'm a Beta," I blurt out, too fast, too defensive. "Definitely a Beta. One hundred percent. Totally normal, boring Beta."

He stares at me for a beat too long. Those eyes narrow slightly, and there's something knowing in his expression that says he's not quite buying what I'm selling.

"You sure about that?"

"Positive. This is just..." I wave a hand vaguely. "Low blood sugar. Or altitude sickness. Or a delayed reaction to the trauma of almost face-planting in front of you."

"Altitude sickness." His lips twitch. "In Montana."

"It's a very high altitude."

"We're at around three thousand feet."

"That's high for some people!"

He laughs, and the sound rolls through me like I'm too close to a campfire I didn't mean to step into. "All right," he says. "Beta it is."

He lets go of my waist, but he doesn't give me the space back. He stays right there, close enough that his scent floods me and feels unfair coming from a man who knows exactly what he's doing.

"But just so we're clear, doll," he adds, voice dipping like we're sharing a secret. "I don't do favorites. I appreciate the whole damn menu."

"How inclusive of you."

"I'm a man of the people." He closes one eye in a slow, shameless little gesture that should not work as well as it does. "You sure you're steady? You went real quiet on me."

"I didn't."

"You did." His grin turns sharp at the edges. "Like your brain hit a fence post."

"My brain is fine."

"Doll, your words are saying, *Fine*, but your face is saying, *Oh, no*." He tilts his head, studying me like I'm a new toy he's already decided to keep. "And I've gotta tell you, watching a pretty girl lose her composure over me? That's the kind of thing that makes a man sleep well at night."

"I did not lose my composure."

"You sure?" His eyes flick to my mouth, then back up like he's testing how easy it is to rattle me. "Because you looked like you forgot what your own name was for a second."

"In your dreams."

"Mm." That grin deepens. "Whatever. I'm still counting it."

"I wasn't swooning."

"You were."

"I was tripping. There's a difference."

"Sure there is." He leans in a fraction, like he can't help it, like he's testing what I'll let him get away with. "Whatever story you need to tell yourself so you can look me in the eye again."

I open my mouth to fire back something clever...

"June! Get over here! We're about to start!"

Kai's eyebrows rise. "June, huh? Gorgeous name."

"Don't wear it out."

"Wouldn't dream of it." He picks up the saddle he

dropped earlier and hoists it back onto his shoulder like it weighs nothing. "Looks like it's our turn to shine. See you in there, June."

He saunters toward the corral, and I watch him go, trying to remember how breathing works.

What the *hell* was that?

My body is still buzzing, and my hands are shaking. His scent is lingering in my nose like it's been permanently imprinted there, and I'm suddenly craving pineapple.

Check your pills when you get home, I tell myself. *Something's wrong. Something's off. This isn't normal.*

Last night with Seth was weird too. The way my body reacted to his scent. And now Kai.

"You're an Omega, right?"

How did he know? How could he *possibly* know?

I shake off the thought and hurry toward Belle, who's already positioned near the corral fence with her camera ready.

"You look flustered," she observes out loud, glancing at me sideways.

"Nah, I'm... warm. From the sun."

"Uh-huh." Her lips twitch. "Careful there. These rodeo stars only do temporary. Don't go falling for them."

"I would never."

"Sure you wouldn't." She laughs and turns back to the corral, where Kai is leading the chestnut mare to the center of the arena. "Come on, *Juliet*. Let's get to work," she says to me.

Juliet. Right. Because I'm definitely not playing the romantic lead in some tragic love story. I'm the sensible one who doesn't lose her mind over pretty cowboys with captivating smiles and scents that make her want to drown.

Keep telling yourself that, June.

Kai swings onto the mare with fluid grace, settling into the saddle like it's an extension of his body. Belle starts shooting immediately, her camera clicking in rapid succession as he guides the horse through a series of movements.

He's incredible up there. Wild and fearless, pushing the mare into sharp turns, sudden stops, a full gallop that ends in a controlled slide. There's an energy to him, a reckless joy, like he's doing this purely because he loves it and doesn't give a damn about anything else.

"Give me something dramatic!" Belle calls out.

"Dramatic is my middle name, boss!"

He clicks his tongue, shifts his weight, and suddenly the mare is rearing up on her hind legs, front hooves pawing at the air. Kai throws one hand up, perfectly balanced, and holds the pose for three heart-stopping seconds before bringing her back down.

A cheer goes up from the cowboys gathered along the fence. Someone lets out a whistle.

"Show-off!" one of them yells, and I glance over to see who's calling out.

The speaker is leaning against the fence with confidence, blond hair falling to his shoulders, windblown and golden in the morning light. He's got a short beard, closely trimmed, and green eyes that crinkle at the corners when he grins. Checkered button-up shirt, jeans, boots, nothing flashy—but somehow he looks like he should be on the cover of a magazine anyway.

He's ridiculously attractive. Not in the wild, dangerous way Kai is gorgeous, but in an approachable way. The kind of guy who looks like he'd be fun at parties and even more fun in private.

"Jealousy doesn't look good on you, Carter!" Kai shouts back, and the blond one—Carter—laughs.

"Nothing looks bad on me! That's my whole brand!"

"Your brand is being second best, and you know it!"

"In your fucking dreams!"

The banter makes everyone laugh, including me. Belle nudges me. "Too distracting for you?"

"Nope." I fan my face with my hand, not even bothering to hide it. "Not at all."

She grins. "Right."

Kai finishes his set of shots and brings the mare to a stop, patting her neck affectionately. "How was that, boss? Magical enough for you?"

"Perfect," Belle says. "Carter, you're up!"

Handlers move forward to lead Kai's mare away while others bring in a new horse, a gorgeous black stallion with a glossy coat. Carter pushes off the fence and approaches him, running a hand along his neck, murmuring something too low to hear.

"That's Shadow," Belle tells me. "Carter's horse. They've been together for years."

The bond between them is obvious as the stallion nudges Carter's shoulder, and Carter scratches behind his ears with affection. When he mounts up, it's seamless, one fluid motion, like they've done this a thousand times.

He guides Shadow in a slow circle around the corral, and Belle starts shooting. Carter moves differently than Kai, less flashy, more controlled, but there's a quiet confidence to him that's equally captivating. He doesn't need to show off. He knows exactly what he's capable of.

"Looking good out there!" Kai calls from where he's now positioned along the fence. "Try not to put everyone to sleep!"

"Sleep is what happens when they watch you!" Carter fires back.

"That's called being hypnotized by my beauty!"

"You mean bored to tears!"

More laughter. More banter. It's easy to get lost in their charm.

Carter finishes his shots, poses for a few stills, and then guides Shadow toward the fence. As he dismounts, his gaze catches mine, green and warm, lingering just a moment longer than necessary.

Don't, I tell myself. *Don't read into it. Don't be pathetic.*

The shoot continues. More cowboys cycle through—local riders, younger guys who are clearly new to this, a few grizzled veterans who know exactly how to work the camera. Belle directs, I watch and learn, and the morning slides by in a blur of horses and clicking shutters and masculine energy.

A commotion near the gate interrupts my thoughts. Murmurs ripple through the crowd, and a smattering of applause breaks out.

Belle lowers her camera, glancing over. "Ah. The last one. Always someone who runs late."

I turn.

And my heart stops.

He's walking toward the corral with that same unhurried confidence I remember from last night—long strides, shoulders back, like he owns every inch of ground he covers. He's wearing a cowboy hat today, pulled low over his face, casting shadows across his features. Dark button-up shirt, sleeves rolled to his elbows. Worn jeans, scuffed boots, a belt buckle catching the light.

Seth.

He enters the corral, and the crew parts around him automatically—respect or fear, I can't tell which.

His horse is already waiting, a beautiful bay with a white blaze, and he approaches it without hesitation.

My pulse is racing, palms are sweating. Every cell in my body is suddenly, intensely aware of his presence, tuned to him like a radio picking up a frequency.

"Sorry for the delay, ladies," he says, his voice carrying across the space, not even glancing our way. Low and rough, just like I remember. "Got held up."

He mounts the bay in one smooth motion, settling into the saddle with easy authority. Belle raises her camera.

And then he's moving.

Where Kai was wild and Carter was controlled, Seth is something else entirely. Raw. Powerful. He rides like he's channeling anger, maybe, or frustration, every movement sharp and deliberate. The bay responds beautifully, and together they move through a series of maneuvers that make my breath catch.

A dead sprint across the corral, hooves thundering against the packed earth. A sharp turn that sends dust flying. A sliding stop so precise it looks choreographed.

He's incredible. There's no other word for it.

"Damn," Belle murmurs beside me. "He's intense today."

I don't respond. Can't do anything except watch him.

He brings the bay to a stop near the center of the corral, chest heaving slightly. The bruise on his jaw is visible even from here, purple and furious, a souvenir from last night that he's making no effort to hide.

Belle finishes her shots and lowers her camera, looking satisfied. "All right, that's a wrap on action! June, you're up for headshots."

I nod, grateful for something concrete to focus on.

"Gentlemen!" I call out, moving toward the crates Belle indicated earlier. "Let's get this done so you can all get back to your terribly important rodeo and cowboy lives. Who's first?"

Kai's hand shoots up immediately. "Me! Do me first, doll!"

"Eager, aren't we?"

"Always." He drops onto the crate, legs spread wide, and angles his face with a look that's half smolder, half mischief. "How's this? Good enough for the camera?"

I peer through the viewfinder. He looks like a cologne ad, all sharp cheekbones and bedroom eyes and that tattoo sleeve catching the light.

"You don't have a bad side," I admit. "It's actually annoying."

"I know. It's a blessing and a curse." He adjusts his angle slightly. "Mostly a blessing."

"How about something that doesn't look like you're trying to seduce the lens?"

"But seducing things is my specialty."

"I'm shocked."

He grins, and I catch it on camera. "Got what you needed?"

"That'll do. Next."

Carter takes his place and gives me a smile that probably devastates women across multiple states. "Any special requests?" he asks.

"Just try not to make the camera fall in love with you."

"No promises."

I snap a dozen shots in quick succession. The camera loves him, and he knows exactly how to work it without looking like he's trying.

"Perfect," I tell him. "You're done."

He stands, and as he passes me, he pauses. "We'll see you at the fair tonight, then at the photo booth?"

"Yep, for sure," I say, aiming for noncommittal, though part of me is already slightly excited to spend more time with these rodeo Alphas. Of course, that's the wrong thing to be admitting to myself when it will only end one way... and that's with my heart broken.

I wave the next cowboy forward, and one by one, they cycle through. I fall into a rhythm, adjusting angles, coaxing expressions, capturing something real in each face.

And then there's Seth, who is standing at the edge of the group, arms crossed, watching me with a sharp expression. Those blue eyes are searching for something.

"Your turn," I say, keeping my voice steady. "Have a seat."

He approaches slowly. Sits on the crate. Doesn't pose. Just stares at me.

My heart is racing, pounding out of control again. *Stop it,* I tell myself. *Be professional. Be normal.*

"You look familiar," he finally says.

My pulse gives a hard, stupid kick, like my body heard his voice and decided logic could take the day off.

His brow furrows slightly, eyes narrowing the way they do when he's lining up a ride, focused, searching. "Have we met before? Something about you..."

Yes, I want to say. *Last night. You called me your scent match. You fought my ex-boyfriend in the street. You fell asleep telling me you'd remember me.*

But the truth tangles in my throat.

What's the point of handing it to him? He's staring right through the memory like it's fogged glass. And even if I forced it back into focus for him, what would it change?

He's a rodeo star passing through. And he'll remember when he needs to. I don't need his kind of complication.

He keeps watching me, waiting, those blue eyes combing my face like he's hunting for the missing piece.

I open my mouth—

"Seth Benton." The name cuts in from behind me,

deep and masculine, the kind of voice that doesn't ask for attention but takes it.

Seth's head snaps toward the sound, and I follow his gaze.

A uniformed deputy stands at the edge of the driveway, then starts toward us like he's got all the time in the world. My stomach knots so hard it hurts.

Of course last night didn't stay buried.

"Seth Benton," the deputy says again, voice flat and official, "you're coming with me. You're under arrest for assaulting a police officer."

God damn it, Tanner.

My stomach drops.

This is my fault.

5

JUNE

"Seth Benton." Deputy Jones stands at the edge of the corral, one hand resting on the cuffs at his belt, looking like he'd rather be anywhere else on the planet right now.

I've known Leo since he was twelve years old, stealing candy from the general store and thinking nobody noticed. He's twenty-four now, with dark hair cropped short and a face that still hasn't quite hardened into the cynical mask most cops develop after a few years. Right now, that face is tight with discomfort as he addresses the cluster of cowboys in front of him.

"You're under arrest for assaulting Deputy Tanner Rook," Leo continues, his voice carrying across the suddenly silent space. "I'm going to need you to come with me to the station."

My insides freeze up. Someone gasps. A few of the

crew members exchange wide-eyed looks while Belle lowers her camera.

And Seth's whole body goes rigid. "This is bullshit." His voice is low, dangerous. "That asshole struck me first. I was defending myself."

Leo's jaw tightens. He pulls the cuffs from his belt, the metal glinting in the morning sun. "That's not what Deputy Rook's report states. According to him, you initiated the physical altercation while intoxicated. We have a record of you being arrested for drunk and disorderly conduct last night."

"I wasn't drinking." Seth's hands curl into fists at his sides. The bruise on his jaw, the one I watched Tanner put there, stands out, purple and angry, against his skin. "Whatever was in my system, I didn't put it there."

Murmurs ripple through the crowd, but most of my attention is fixed on Seth. On the way his shoulders have pulled back, his chest expanding as he draws himself up to his full height. On Kai and Carter moving at his sides like they materialized from thin air, flanking him with expressions that have gone hard and cold.

And it's my fault.

If I hadn't been standing on that sidewalk when Tanner showed up. If I hadn't—

Stop it, June. This isn't helping.

Seth's father pushes through the crowd, silver threading through dark hair, those same sharp blue eyes fixed on Leo with irritation. He's carrying himself like he expects people to get out of his way. It helps that he's a big man.

"Officer." His voice deepens. "Surely we can handle this somewhere more discreet. The circuit has a reputation to maintain."

"Sir, I'm going to need you to step back."

He huffs loudly. "Are cuffs really necessary? My son is cooperating."

"Sir—"

"He's telling you he didn't start the fight. And that he wasn't intoxicated by choice. The least you can do is show some discretion until—"

"Back up. Now."

His father's mouth thins, but he steps back. Leo moves closer to Seth, cuffs still in hand, and the tension ratchets up another notch. Kai shifts his weight, muscles coiled. Carter's easy grin has vanished entirely, replaced by something sharp and watchful.

And I'm just standing here.

Do something.

My heart is hammering against my ribs. My palms are slick with sweat. I think about last night. Seth swaying on his feet, barely coherent, but still stepping between Tanner and me without hesitation. Still taking that first punch. Still making sure I was okay before he let himself fall apart.

He doesn't even remember doing it. And now he's going to be arrested for it.

Screw this.

"Leo, wait," I say.

Every head turns toward me.

Seth's gaze finds mine too, and something flickers across his face.

"I was there last night, during the incident," I say, walking forward until I'm standing near the group. "I hadn't had anything to drink, and I was completely sober." I meet Leo's eyes, willing him to believe me. "You can check with the officer at the station, and Barb was on duty when I picked Seth up. Tanner approached us on the street. He was drunk. Aggressive. Verbally abusive. And he threw the first punch."

Silence.

The kind of quiet that presses against your eardrums and makes you hyperaware of every tiny sound. The horses shifting in the pen. The wind rustling through dry grass. My own blood pounding in my ears.

Leo's frown deepens. "June, this is a formal arrest. I can't just—"

"I'm telling you what I saw. Tanner shoved me to the ground and then went after Seth. Seth was defending himself. Defending *me.*"

More murmurs from the crowd and wide-eyed stares.

Seth's gaze on me intensifies. His blue eyes are wide, intense, boring into me with an expression that makes my breath catch.

"It *is* you," he breathes. "From last night. You—you were the one who—"

He breaks off, brow furrowing, like he's trying to grab hold of something slippery. Trying to piece together fragments that don't quite fit.

My face heats. I remember last night, him against me, his face inches from mine, that low voice telling me I was his scent match. The way he looked at me in that motel room, like I was something worth remembering.

And now he's staring at me the same way.

I tear my gaze away and focus on Leo, because if I keep looking at Seth, I'm going to combust right here in front of everyone.

"I'm willing to come down to the station and give a formal statement," I state. "But I'm telling you the truth, Leo. Tanner started that fight. Not Seth."

Leo hesitates. His gaze darts from me to Seth to his father to the crowd of onlookers, all watching with interest.

"I still have to bring him in," he says finally. "Formal procedure. But if you want to make a statement, it'll be taken into consideration."

"You have a witness confirming he didn't strike first," Seth's father cuts in. "Surely that means restraints aren't necessary."

A muscle ticks in Leo's jaw. But he glances at the crowd, at the phones I'm now noticing in several hands, probably recording every second of this.

"Fine." He clips the cuffs back onto his belt. "But you're coming with me voluntarily. Any trouble and this gets a lot worse for you."

Seth nods once, sharp. "Understood."

Leo steps back, gesturing toward the patrol car parked near the entrance. Seth starts to follow, then stops. Turns back to stare at me.

Those blue eyes hold mine, and there's so much in that gaze—gratitude, confusion, intensity.

"I'll see you at the station, then," he confirms.

I nod.

He holds my gaze for one more moment that stretches like taffy, that feels like it contains entire conversations we haven't had yet, and then he turns and walks toward the patrol car. The crowd parts around him and Leo, the deputy's hand hovering near Seth's elbow like he's not entirely sure the *voluntary* part is going to stick.

Carter and Kai move to follow, but Leo holds up a hand. "You can meet us at the station." Leo's voice has fallen flat. "But right now, it's just Mr. Benton."

Carter puts a hand on Kai's arm. "Fine."

The patrol car doors slam, the engine starts, and then they're pulling away, kicking up gravel, disappearing down the road toward town.

For a moment, nobody moves.

Then the whispers start. The stares. The general chaos of people trying to figure out what the hell just happened.

"Hey," Kai says next to me. "You okay, doll?"

"Yeah." The word comes out clipped. Tight. "I'm fine."

He doesn't look convinced.

"Thanks for standing up for Seth," Carter says. "I'm going down to the station. You need a lift? I'm Carter, by the way, one of Seth's pack members."

I nod. "Would love that, as I came in with Belle."

He nods toward the parking area, where a shiny red pickup truck gleams in the morning sun. It's huge, with chrome details, extended cab. "Okay. We can make sure Seth's got people in his corner."

"Yeah," I hear myself say. "Okay."

Carter nods to Kai. "Stay here and help Belle wrap things up and deal with the crew and other guys so they all head on home."

Kai sketches a lazy salute, but his eyes are still on me. "You got it." That grin spreads across his face. "Don't have too much fun without me, June."

My stomach flips despite everything. "No promises," I joke, knowing there's no fun to be had at the station.

He laughs as Belle joins me. "You okay, June? You need me to come with you?"

"Nah, I've got this." I try for a reassuring smile. "Just need to give a statement. Make sure the record's straight."

"This is about Tanner." Not a question. Belle knows my history with him, the controlling behavior, the constant monitoring, the way he made me feel like I was slowly disappearing. She was one of the people who helped me see that I deserved better.

"When isn't it?" I say bitterly.

"Hey." She grabs my arm, her grip firm. "Don't let him get under your skin. You know what he's doing. He's trying to drag you back into his orbit, make you feel guilty, make you small. Don't give him the satisfaction."

"I won't."

"I mean it, June. You're stronger than he gives you credit for." She glances toward Carter, who's waiting by the truck. "I'll take your camera with me. Pick it up from my place later, okay?"

"Thanks." I pull her into a quick hug. "You're the best."

"I know." She squeezes me back, then releases me with a gentle push. "Now go. And text me later."

The truck is even more impressive up close. Deep red paint polished to a mirror shine. Carter opens the passenger door for me, and I haul myself up into the cab, settling onto the leather seat.

He rounds the front, gets into the driver's seat, and starts the engine. Being in closed confines with him...

Oh God.

His scent floods the enclosed space. Sweet and sharp all at once, like someone poured cola over a cinnamon roll and then opened the windows after a summer rainstorm. It curls around me, slides into my lungs, makes every nerve ending in my body sit up and pay attention.

My skin goes hot. My pulse kicks into overdrive. There's a tingling sensation spreading from my chest down to between my thighs, and I have to grip the edge of the seat to keep myself from leaning over the center console and burying my face in his neck.

What's happening to me?

I jab at the window controls, rolling it down and sticking my head out into the cool May air. The wind whips against my face, sharp and bracing, and I gulp it down like I've been drowning.

"You all right over there?" Carter's voice is tinged with amusement.

"Yep." I keep my face turned toward the window. "Just needed some cool air."

"Uh-huh."

He pulls out of the ranch, gravel crunching under the oversized tires. I keep my face toward the window, watching the familiar landscape slide past, trying to get my body under control.

This is insane. I've been on suppressants for seven years. Muted responses, dulled instincts, a designation buried so deep I sometimes forget it exists. My body does not react to Alphas like this. It's not supposed to. That's the whole point.

And yet here I am, practically panting because a good-looking cowboy smells like dessert and rain.

Maybe my pills are expired, or I need to double the dose.

"I'm sure everything will work out fine," Carter says, breaking into my spiraling thoughts. "At the station, I mean. Seth will be okay."

"Oh, I'm not worried about him, as I know he's innocent." I pull my head back in, keeping my face angled away. "He seems like the type who can handle himself."

"That he is."

"I'm just not looking forward to dealing with Tanner." I grimace. "My ex."

Carter glances over, one eyebrow raised. "Seth mentioned bits and pieces this morning about last night, but whatever happened to him, it scrambled his brain pretty good."

"Well, he was definitely out of it when I picked him up." Despite everything, I smile at the memory. "Swaying all over the place and singing 'Sweet Home Alabama' loud enough to wake the entire town."

Carter barks out a laugh. "No way. Seth? *Singing*?"

"Off-key too."

"Oh, man." He shakes his head, still grinning. "I would have paid good money to see that. Seth is usually so... intense. Seeing him actually let loose? That's like spotting a unicorn."

"Well, he was definitely loose. Nearly fell over about six times."

"That's amazing. I'm filing that away for future blackmail material."

I find myself relaxing slightly, some of the tension draining from my shoulders. There's something easy about Carter's energy that has the conversation feeling natural.

And the wind through the open window helps, carrying away some of that intoxicating scent before it can fully saturate my lungs. I take shallow breaths, focused on the cold air, trying to keep myself grounded.

I try very, very hard not to notice the way Carter's forearms flex as he grips the steering wheel. The thick muscle, the golden hair, the veins running beneath tan skin. His sleeves are rolled to his elbows, and every time he turns the wheel, I notice the way his biceps shift under the fabric of his shirt.

He's big. So much larger than me. Broad shoulders, solid chest, thighs that strain against his jeans. I wonder what it would be like to climb into his lap. To wrap myself around all that strength and let him hold me up.

Stop it.

My eyes drift lower before I can stop them, to where his jeans are stretched across—

"If I had to guess," Carter blurts out, "you're trying really hard to picture me naked right now."

I choke on nothing but air and my own mortification.

"Excuse me?" I manage, once I've stopped coughing.

He's grinning, that charming golden-boy grin that probably devastates women across multiple states. "You had the look. Eyes traveling south, lingering in certain… regions."

"I was staring at the road."

"The road is that way." He points through the windshield. "Your eyes were definitely going a different direction."

"Maybe I was looking at the gearshift."

"Is that what you're calling it?"

My face is on fire. I'm going to spontaneously combust in the passenger seat of this ridiculously expensive truck, and they'll never be able to explain to my mother how I died.

He winks and somehow makes it charming instead of sleazy. "But don't worry. I'm used to women checking me out. It's a burden I bear with grace and humility."

"I wasn't checking you out."

"Sure you weren't."

"I was *spacing out.*"

"Directly at my crotch. Very convenient spacing."

"Oh my God." I cover my face with my hands. "Can we please change the subject?"

"Absolutely." He's clearly enjoying this way too much. "What would you like to talk about instead? The weather? Local politics? The fact that you're blushing so hard I could probably toast marshmallows on your cheeks?"

"I hate you."

"No, you don't. I'm delightful." He grins wider. "Ask anyone."

Despite myself, my lips twitch. There's something infectious about his humor with the way he teases without being mean, and he seems to genuinely enjoy making people laugh. It's a sharp contrast to the tension of the morning, and I find myself grateful for the distraction.

"Does this routine work on everyone?" I ask, dropping my hands from my face.

"Define 'work.'"

"Do women actually find this charming?"

"You tell me." His green eyes glow with mischief. "Is it working on you?"

"Absolutely not."

"Your smile says otherwise." He laughs, and the sound is like a spell he's placing on me. Damn him.

We drive in silence for a moment, the tension between us settling into something almost comfortable. I keep my face toward the window, watching Honeyspur Meadow slide past, the familiar buildings and quiet streets that I've known my whole life.

"So," Carter says, breaking the quiet. "Seth mentioned something interesting this morning."

"Oh?"

"He said you were his scent match."

Everything in me goes still. "He was out of his mind last night," I say carefully. "He didn't know what he was saying."

"Maybe." Carter glances over, and there's something more serious in his expression now. "But here's the thing. Kai said something similar after he met you this morning. Said there was something about you he couldn't figure out. Something drawing him in even though he couldn't get a clear read on your scent."

I force a laugh. "I'm a Beta. That's not how it works."

"That's what you keep saying." He's quiet for a moment. "But I'm feeling it too, June. There's something about you that's... different. Like I'm looking at a picture that's slightly out of focus. Can't quite make out the details, but I know there's something there."

My hands are trembling. I press them flat against my thighs, trying to steady them.

I know what they're sensing. Know what's calling to them beneath the chemical fog of my suppressants. But I also know what the doctors told my parents when I was eighteen, that my Omega was dormant, defective, that I'd never go into heat or form a proper bond. That I couldn't give an Alpha pack what they truly required.

What's the point of letting them get close? They'd just figure out eventually that I'm broken. That I can't give them the connection they're searching for. And then they'd leave, and I'd be left behind with nothing but rejection and a secret I should never have let slip.

Better to stay hidden. "Maybe you guys are over-thinking it," I say lightly. "Looking for something that isn't there."

Carter studies me for a long moment. I can feel his gaze on the side of my face, assessing, questioning.

"Maybe," he says finally. "But I don't think so."

He doesn't push further, and I'm grateful for it.

We pull onto the main road a few minutes later, and Carter parks along the curb in front of the hardware store. The police station looms up ahead on the small side street, and I realize with a sinking feeling that I've been here more times in the last twenty-four hours than I have in the entire past year.

"Ready?" Carter asks.

"As I'll ever be."

We stroll up the gravel path together, our footsteps crunching in the quiet morning air. The lobby is busier than last night, a few officers milling around, phones ringing, that low hum of activity that says the rodeo has officially made the local PD's life more complicated.

The woman behind the desk, young, dark-haired, someone I vaguely recognize from around town, looks up as we enter.

"I'm here to give a statement," I say. "Regarding the charges against Seth Benton."

She nods and picks up her phone, murmuring something I can't hear. A moment later, she gestures toward a hallway.

"Sheriff Cade will see you. Second door on the left."

I glance at Carter. "You should probably wait here."

"You sure?"

"Yeah."

He nods, but there's concern in those green eyes. "I'll be right here if you need me."

The words settle warmly in my chest, and I have to push down the flutter they cause.

"Thanks."

Sheriff Cade's office is cluttered with files stacked in little towers, and coffee rings on the desk. You can tell he spends more time at work than at home. He's rugged and a man who's seen too much, but he's only in his forties. His wife went missing years ago. Not all the details are known, but it involves an escaped prisoner.

"June." He rises as I enter. "Close the door. Have a seat."

I do, settling into the worn leather chair across from him.

"The team is swamped with rodeo business," he says, "so I'm handling this personally. I understand you were present during the altercation last night."

"Yes, sir."

"Tell me what happened. Your own words."

So I do. I explain about receiving the call from Pete.

Picking Seth up from the station. Walking toward my car and encountering Tanner on the sidewalk, visibly intoxicated, aggressive, looking for a fight. I describe the verbal abuse, the way Tanner shoved me to the ground, the punch he threw at Seth before Seth ever lifted a hand.

"Seth was defending himself and me," I finish. "Tanner started the whole thing."

Cade makes notes, his pen scratching against paper. "Anyone else around who might have witnessed this?"

"I don't know. It was two in the morning, and the street was mostly empty. I was focused on trying to stop them." I pause. "But Seth gave as good as he got once Tanner started swinging. I won't pretend otherwise."

The sheriff grunts, setting down his pen. "All right. Let's go sort this out."

He leads me down another hallway toward a room that I can hear voices coming from. My stomach tightens with every step.

The room is small and harsh, all fluorescent lighting and metal furniture. Seth is there, sitting at a table with his arms crossed, tension radiating off him in waves. Leo stands near the door, looking uncomfortable.

And Tanner is pacing like a caged animal.

He looks even worse than he did last night. The bruise has spread across half his face, purplish black and ugly, his lip split and swollen. His uniform is rumpled, his hair disheveled, and there's a manic energy in his movements that sets my teeth on edge.

When he spots me walking in, his expression twists into something vicious. "What the hell is she doing here?"

I force myself not to react. Not to shrink back into the invisible girl he always wanted me to be. "I'm giving a statement," I state evenly. "About what actually happened last night."

"Oh, *right*." He laughs, harsh and bitter. "You're here to protect your new boyfriend. To spread your legs for—"

"*Tanner*." Sheriff Cade's voice cracks like a whip. "That's enough. One more word and you're suspended."

Tanner's jaw snaps shut, but his eyes stay fixed on me. Burning with hatred. With that same possessive entitlement that made me run from him in the first place.

I hold his gaze without flinching.

"We have a witness statement," Cade continues, his voice clipped and professional, "indicating that you, Tanner, initiated the physical altercation while intoxicated. That you approached the defendants aggressively and threw the first punch." He turns to Seth. "Based on this statement, we're not filing assault charges against Mr. Benton."

Seth's whole body sags with relief, tension

draining from his shoulders. He catches my eye across the room, and the gratitude in his expression makes something warm bloom in my chest.

"However," Cade continues, "there's still the matter of the drunk and disorderly charge from last night. That'll need to be investigated separately. If it's found to be accurate, we may revisit the assault charges."

"That's completely—" Seth starts.

"That's the procedure," Cade cuts him off. "You're free to go for now, Mr. Benton. Don't leave town."

"Wasn't planning on it."

The sheriff turns to Tanner, his expression hardening. "My office. Now."

Tanner's face goes red, but he doesn't argue. He shoves past Leo on his way out. The door slams behind him, and suddenly the room feels twice as large. The sheriff follows. Leo mumbles something about paperwork and disappears, and then it's just me and Seth.

He stands slowly, unfolding from the chair, and God, I forgot how big he is. How much space he takes up. How those blue eyes can make me feel like I'm the only person in the world.

"Hey," he says.

"Hey."

We stare at each other for a long moment. The silence is heavy with everything unspoken—last night, the fight, the way he's studying me.

"Thank you," he says finally. "For standing up for me. You didn't have to do that."

I shrug, aiming for casual. "Just telling the truth. Seemed like the right thing to do."

"Still." He takes a step closer, and I have to tilt my head back to meet his eyes. "Most people wouldn't have gotten involved. Not against a deputy. Not for a stranger."

You're not a stranger, I want to say. *You fought for me last night. You called me your scent match.*

But the words stick in my throat.

"Yeah, well." I manage a small smile. "Never been great at minding my own business."

Something shifts in his expression. "It really was you last night," he says softly. "I remember pieces. Your eyes. Your voice. The way you smelled."

My heart stutters.

"Fragments. Like looking through frosted glass." His jaw tightens with frustration.

"You should get out of here," I say, stepping back before I do something stupid. Like reach for him. Like let myself want things I can't have. "Carter is waiting in the lobby. He'll be worried."

Seth's eyes search my face for a moment longer. Then he nods, something like disappointment flickering across his features.

"Yeah. Okay."

We head out together, down the hall toward the

lobby, where Carter is leaning against the wall, scrolling through his phone. He glances up as we approach, relief washing over his features.

"There he is." He claps Seth on the shoulder. "You good?"

"I'm good." Seth's voice is rough. "Thanks to June."

Carter's gaze finds mine, warm with gratitude. "We owe you one. Seriously."

"It's all good." I shift my weight, suddenly aware of how close they both are. How their scents are mingling in the air, and how my body is burning up, buzzing, responding in ways I desperately need to get under control. "Anyway, I should get going. I've got things to do. Work stuff."

"Let me give you a lift," Carter offers. "Home, or wherever you need to be."

"Nah, really. I'm fine." I take another step back, putting distance between us. "I've got some errands to run in town, and I should probably check in at the office. See if any new listings came in."

It's a weak excuse, seeing as the whole town is booked solid with rodeo tourists; I personally made sure of it. But they don't call me on it.

"Thanks again," Seth says.

I force a grin. "Just try to stay out of jail from now on, yeah? I'm not making a habit of two a.m. rescue missions."

His lips twitch. Almost a smile. "I'll do my best."

I turn and walk out before I can change my mind.

Before I can let myself get pulled deeper into whatever this is. Outside, the cold air hits my face. I take a deep breath, then another, trying to clear the cocktail of Alpha scents from my lungs.

My phone buzzes. I pull it out to find Pete's name on the screen.

"Hello, Pete."

"June! Good, I caught you." He sounds harried. Stressed. "Listen, I just got off the phone with the head of the rodeo circuit, John Benton, and he's... not happy."

"I can imagine."

"He says we're painting them in a bad light by pressing charges against his son when Seth maintains he wasn't drunk voluntarily. Says if we want to keep their support for future circuits—which we do, June, because the town depends on that revenue, and half our businesses survive on rodeo season, including yours—we need to sort this mess out."

I close my eyes. "Well, I did my part and got Seth out of being arrested."

"We need more," he says. "I convinced John that what would help is having a local liaison. Someone to keep an eye on the rodeo stars while they're in town. Show good faith. Make sure there are no more incidents." Pete clears his throat. "The circuit needs a chaperone, June. And I want you to do it."

My eyes open wide. "Are you insane?"

"The job pays really well. And it comes with accommodation at the ranch if you want it."

"I have a house."

"Then it's extra income. Lord knows real estate is slow right now, what with you booking out every available room in town." He sighs. "Look, I know it's a big ask. But you've already met them, you handled Seth last night, and frankly, you're the only person I trust not to make things worse. I was going to ask Norm's nephew, but he got completely plastered at the Spur last night, and I can't rely on him."

"Pete—"

"The town needs this rodeo circuit, June. The restaurants, the shops, the motels, everyone counts on rodeo season to get through the rest of the year. If we lose their support, if they take the circuit somewhere else..." He trails off. "Please. Just consider it. It's only for two or three weeks."

I press my free hand to my forehead. Three Alphas whose scents cause my carefully suppressed Omega to want to claw her way to the surface. And Pete wants me to chaperone them.

I exhale loudly. "I'll think about it."

"That's all I'm asking. Just let me know soon."

He hangs up, and I'm left standing in the cold Montana air. This is completely, utterly insane.

I shove the phone into my pocket and hurry down the main street, my mind spinning. It's almost funny, in a horrible way. Doing Pete a favor is exactly what got me into this mess in the first place.

And now he wants me to dive in deeper.

Three cowboys. Two weeks or more. One secret I've been keeping for seven years.

I let out a groan that startles a passing bird.

What the hell am I going to do?

6

"I heard Kai has a piercing somewhere very interesting," Hazel says, standing there with her pink sunglasses propped up on her head.

I nearly inhale my hot cider wrong. We're at the Honeyspur Meadow Spring Fair near our *Take A Photo With A Rodeo Star* booth, waiting for the guys to turn up while the event is in full swing.

"Oh my God, where?"

I scan the nearby crowd out of reflex, then snap my attention back to her. Hazel's grin turns wicked. "Down there." She flicks two fingers vaguely down her body. "Apparently there's a whole Reddit thread dedicated to speculation about what these rodeo boys are packing under those Wranglers. And Kai allegedly has some... hardware."

"You're telling me there are people online discussing his..."

"Penis jewelry. Yes." She takes a sip of her drink, unbothered in a way that should be illegal. "There are diagrams."

"There are not!"

She's nodding, smirking. "Very detailed ones." Her mouth twitches like she's trying not to laugh. "Someone did research."

"Oh, damn."

Hazel leans in closer to me. "I can show you."

I gasp, because my body reacts before my brain catches up. "We shouldn't."

Hazel is already giggling, fishing her phone out like she's been waiting for this exact moment. "You say that, but your face says you absolutely want to."

"Haze—"

"Shh. Educational purposes."

She taps a few times, then tilts the screen toward me. I lean in despite myself, and the two of us press shoulder to shoulder like we're sharing state secrets. The image that pops up is not a photo. It's worse.

It's a drawn sketch.

A very committed, very enthusiastic sketch—hips, thighs, the line of Wranglers pulled low like the artist has a personal vendetta against modesty. And right there, rendered with horrifying confidence, is a Jacob's ladder.

I stare. Hazel stares. The world narrows to the screen and my own shocked breathing.

"Oh my..."

Hazel makes a tiny strangled sound that might be laughter or reverence. "Look at the size of it," she whispers, like we're in a museum.

I don't even have words. My brain just stays static and scandalized. "That's... that's a lot."

"And huge," Hazel agrees, utterly delighted. "Who has the time to draw shading on hips like this? This is art."

From somewhere close, a shout cuts through the air, like they're calling out a name.

Hazel and I freeze, then she suddenly yanks the phone down so fast it nearly slips, and I choke back a laugh while my heart does a full sprint. We both glance up, wide-eyed, trying to look innocent. Casual. Normal. Two respectable women at the fairgrounds with absolutely nothing filthy happening on a screen.

Only... it's no one. Just a ride operator hollering at a kid to step back, the noise already fading into the general chaos.

Hazel looks at me. I stare at her. And we both lose it with breathless giggles that make us bend over the table like we're fourteen again, wiping tears from our eyes while the fair carries on around us.

When I finally catch my breath, I shove her arm with the heel of my hand. "Delete it from your brain."

Hazel snorts, tucking her phone away like it's contraband. "Too late. It's branded in there. Permanently." She tips her chin toward the fair around us, all lights and noise and people wrapped in sweaters, chasing warmth and deep-fried sweet treats.

The Honeyspur Meadow Spring Fair is a carnival of food and spinning rides, country music from the live band, and carnival games.

"I see them," Hazel sing-songs, not even pretending to be subtle, and I follow her gaze to see Kai, Carter, and two local rodeo guys heading this way through the crowds. "Oh God, June, Kai is even hotter in person than he looked in those photos. And Carter..." She fans herself. "I might actually die."

"You're being dramatic."

"I'm being *accurate*." She flips her long blonde-and-pink hair over one shoulder—the pink bottom half catching the fairy lights like cotton candy. "The whole town has been buzzing about the three main rodeo stars from the circuit. You know they were here, like, three years ago? I barely remember seeing them. I was too busy with that disastrous boyfriend phase, but apparently they caused quite a stir. Broke hearts left and right."

"Shocking. I don't even recall, but I was dating that asshole Tanner."

"And now they're back, and every single woman between eighteen and eighty is on high alert." She pulls out her phone again, scrolling through something, her bold pink nails clicking against the screen. "The online chatter is *intense*. I've seen at least six TikToks about strategy for getting their attention tonight. One girl made a whole video about what perfume to wear to attract an Alpha."

"That's concerning."

"That's *competition*, babe." She grins. "Good thing you've already got a head start."

"I don't know what you're talking about."

"Sure you don't." She pockets her phone and gives me a knowing look. "You definitely didn't spend ten minutes this morning telling me about how one of them caught you when you tripped and held you against his very muscular chest."

"That was an accident."

"Yeah, where you buried your face in his pecs and inhaled like he was a fine wine."

I open my mouth to argue, then close it. She's not wrong.

A gust of wind sends a shiver down my spine, and I wrap my sweater tighter around myself, grateful for the heat lamp positioned near our booth.

"Speaking of things going wrong," I say, desperate to change the subject, "my shower is completely broken. Lost all pressure this morning and the water was ice cold. I thought I was going to freeze to death just trying to wash my hair."

Hazel winces. "Yikes. Probably the water heater. You should call someone."

"With the rodeo in town? Everyone's booked solid."

"I know someone who owes me a favor. I'll text you

his details." She glances up. "Oh, hey." Hazel snaps her fingers, her chunky gold rings catching the light. "You never finished telling me about the chaperone thing. Pete actually wants you to babysit the rodeo stars?"

I groan. "Apparently. Something about showing good faith to the circuit after the whole arrest situation."

"So you did him one favor, and now you're the designated babysitter?"

"That's basically it."

"And the favor was bailing out the hot, grumpy one at two in the morning?"

"Seth. Yes."

"And then his pack showed up at the photo shoot, and they were all immediately obsessed with you?"

"That's an exaggeration."

"Is it, though?" She raises an eyebrow. "Because the way you described it, two of them were looking at you like you were their last meal."

Before I can respond, the group of cowboys finally reaches our booth.

Kai is wearing a black button-up shirt open at the collar, sleeves rolled to his elbows, that full sleeve of tribal tattoos on display. His dark hair is pulled up in its usual messy knot, loose strands framing a face that belongs on a magazine cover. The eyebrow piercing catches my attention as he tilts his head, and his grin is pure, undiluted trouble.

Carter is in a red-and-black checkered flannel that

strains across his shoulders in ways that should require a permit. His blond hair is windblown and golden under the fairy lights, that short beard framing a jaw I want to trace with my fingers. And green eyes that find mine immediately.

No Seth.

I'm not sure if I'm relieved or disappointed. Probably both. The other two locals are lingering nearby in jeans, cowboy boots, and shirts.

"Evening, ladies." Kai's voice is like warm honey. "Heard this was the place to be."

"You heard right." Hazel steps forward, confidence radiating off her like heat. "I'm Hazel. I'll be helping June run things tonight."

"Kai." He takes her hand, but his eyes slide to me. "And this is Carter, Don, and Connor."

I wave to the guys, yet having Kai and Carter watching me burns me up. It's annoying how easily these two can make me lose my composure. I've spent years building walls, perfecting my poker face, and they're dismantling it with nothing but grins and compliments.

Hazel is watching this silent exchange with undisguised glee. "Oh, I like them," she announces. "June, I approve."

"I didn't ask for approval."

"You're getting it anyway." She claps her hands together. "All right, boys. We need to do some test runs before the crowd shows up. Get the positioning right, figure out the lighting."

"Test runs?" I narrow my eyes at her, as we hadn't discussed this.

"I've never worked with *these* particular subjects." She gestures at the guys. "Different energy. We need to calibrate."

"That's not a thing," I say.

She grabs my arm and starts pulling me toward the photo area. "June, Kai, Carter, let's see what we're working with."

The photo area has several backdrop options, a green screen for digital backgrounds, a rustic wooden fence with hay bales, a starry night sky, and a classic Western sunset. Hazel selects the green screen.

"Simple for practice," she says, positioning herself behind the camera. "June, you're in the middle. Boys, make her look good."

"That won't be hard," Kai murmurs, stepping up to my left.

"She already looks incredible," Carter adds, appearing on my right.

Suddenly I'm very aware of how close they are. How their body heat cuts through the cold air. How their scents are curling around me like they're trying to pull me closer.

"Remember," Hazel continues, adjusting her settings, "you want to look approachable but also... cowboy-ish. Make the fans feel special."

"Cowboy-ish," Kai repeats, amused. "Technical term?"

"It is now." She points at Don and Connor. "You two, pay attention. Take notes on how to make a woman feel like she's the only person in the room." Hazel turns back to us. "All right. Show me something."

Kai's arm slides around my waist, not my shoulders. His hand settles on my hip. He draws me into his side until there's no space left to pretend I'm unaffected. The solid heat of him at my flank turns my thoughts soft.

"Like this?" His voice drops low, meant for me, not the audience.

"Good start," Hazel says, snapping a photo. "Carter, get in there."

Carter steps in close behind me, all broad chest, his presence filling the air at my back. His hand finds my other hip, fingers spreading like he's claiming a right to the shape of me, and suddenly I'm held between them. Framed. Pinned in the sweetest way.

I'm breathless.

"How's this?" Carter asks, his mouth near my ear, his breath warm where my skin is already too sensitive.

"Perfect," Hazel chirps, snapping another shot. "Now let's try something more... intimate."

"Intimate?" My voice comes out rougher than I want.

"Trust me," she says, grinning behind the camera. "Kai, put your hand on her stomach. Carter, lean in like you're about to tell her a secret."

They do it without hesitation.

Kai's palm presses flat to my belly, warm through my shirt, steadying me and undoing me in the same breath. Carter leans closer, the brush of him almost a touch, almost a kiss, and the *not quite* is what makes my knees threaten treason.

"You smell incredible," Carter murmurs, so soft it feels like he's speaking directly into my bloodstream.

I inhale, then forget what I meant to do with the air.

"Good," Hazel calls. "Now, Kai, turn her toward you. Carter, stay close behind her."

Kai's hands guide me, slow and deliberate, until I'm facing him. His gaze locks on mine, pale gray and intent, like he's taking count of every reaction I'm failing to hide. Carter stays right there, chest to my back, crowding my space in a way that makes me feel sheltered and owned at the same time.

Kai's thumb strokes my hip. "You're blushing."

"Just feeling hot," I answer.

Carter's quiet laugh ghosts my ear. "You are."

Kai's smile turns sharp, satisfied. "We should do this more often."

"Keep talking like that and I'll step on your foot," I assure him out loud.

"Promises, promises."

Hazel snaps photo after photo as we cycle through poses—Kai dipping me slightly while Carter steadies my shoulders, both of them leaning in like they're about to kiss my cheeks, Carter lifting me off the ground while Kai pretends to be jealous. Each position presses me closer to one or both of them, and by the time Hazel calls for a break, I'm flushed and breathless and my heart is doing things it absolutely should not be doing.

"That's perfect," Hazel announces. "Don, Connor, *that's* the energy we need. Make every fan feel like the most important person in the world."

The guys nod, looking slightly intimidated.

"All right." Hazel checks her phone. "We're about to open. June, help me with something in back."

I follow her behind the backdrop, still overheated, still trying to pretend I'm normal. The second we're out of sight, Hazel grabs my arm.

I huff out a laugh. "What now? You want to take another hundred photos? Maybe keep going until my face freezes like this?"

Hazel's grin goes bright. "Oh my God. June," she whispers, urgent. "June."

"What?" I say, glancing toward the front like someone might be listening.

"You were glowing out there," she says. "I've never seen you like that."

I shake my head. "We were just posing."

She leans closer, eyes sparkling. "And you can't tell me you didn't feel it."

My cheeks heat again. "I felt you being extra."

Hazel gasps, delighted. "Me?"

"You did that on purpose," I accuse, jabbing a finger at her. "You kept moving them closer. 'Hands here, hips there, lean in.' Like you were directing some... porno."

Hazel's laugh is quiet but wicked. "And?"

"And," I mutter, "it was unnecessary."

"Mmm." She squeezes my arm like she's proud of herself. "My strategy worked."

I glare at her. "Hazel."

"I'm serious," she says, still buzzing. "You were glowing. You didn't even realize. You were smiling like you forgot how to brace for impact. And they were gone for you. The way they looked at you? That wasn't camera focus. That was want." She tilts her head, studying me. "And you liked it."

My throat goes tight. "They're Alphas, Hazel."

"So? Who cares?"

I care, I want to say. But I can't explain why without revealing secrets I've kept for seven years from everyone.

"They're only here for two or three weeks," I say instead. "Then they're gone."

"So make the most of it." She squeezes my arm again. "Any woman would kill to have men look at her like that. Like you're the sun and they've been living in darkness. Don't overthink it."

"I always overthink it."

"I know. That's why I'm here to tell you to stop." She releases me. "Now get out there and take some photos. And try not to murder any of the fangirls who throw themselves at your men." She's already walking away, flipping the *OPEN* sign on the booth.

A line forms immediately.

It's insane, a snaking queue of women clutching tickets and checking their reflections in phone screens. Some are dressed like they're going to a club, clearly hoping to catch attention. Others are more casual, just excited for a fun photo. All of them are staring at Kai and Carter like they're made of gold and wishes.

"Welcome to our reality," I mutter, positioning myself behind the camera.

Kai catches my eye and grins. "Don't worry, doll. I only have eyes for one woman tonight."

"Save the charm for the paying customers."

"The charm is infinite. There's plenty to go around."

Hazel directs the first group forward, three college-age girls who look like they might actually faint, and I focus on my job. Take the photos. Capture the moment. Don't think about how Kai's arm wraps around the first girl's waist the same way it wrapped around mine.

Except it's not the same. I can see that now. With

the fans, he's polished. Professional. The smile reaches his eyes, but there's a distance there, a performance.

With me, there was no distance at all.

The next hour passes in a blur of poses and flashes with the four cowboys and strangers pressing themselves against them like they're claiming territory. Some are subtle about it. Most aren't.

One woman—blonde, poured into a revealing dress—actually tries to slide her hand down Carter's chest toward his belt buckle. He catches her wrist smoothly, redirecting it to his shoulder, but she just laughs and presses closer.

Something hot and sharp twists in my chest. My jaw is tight, and there's a possessive growl building in my throat that has no business being there.

During a brief lull between groups, Carter slips away from his position and appears at my side.

"You okay?" His voice is low, private.

"Fine. Why wouldn't I be?"

"Because you've been gripping that camera like you want to strangle it for the last twenty minutes." His gaze searches my face. "You're jealous."

"Am not—"

He chuckles and moves back to his position, leaving me flushed and flustered and way too aware of my own heartbeat.

Kai catches my eye from across the booth. He's supposed to be smiling for the camera with a pair of women who are practically climbing him, but he's looking at me. Through me. Into me.

I see you, his expression says. *Only you.*

Finally—*finally*—Hazel calls the last group forward, and then it's over. The crowd disperses, the booth empties, and I can actually breathe.

"You were amazing," Hazel says, bouncing over. "These shots are incredible. But I've got to run. I have a date."

"Oh?" I grab her arm. "Since when? With who?"

"Since this morning. And I'll tell you everything tomorrow, promise." She's already backing away, phone in hand. "Love you, bye!"

And she's gone.

I'm left standing with Don and Connor, who immediately start packing up the signs around the booth.

"Well." Kai strolls over, hands in his pockets like he has all the time in the world. "Looks like you're free."

I force my face into something neutral, even though my body is still remembering where his hands were earlier. "I should probably head home."

"Or," Carter says, sliding in beside Kai like he belongs there, "you could stay. Enjoy the fair. Let us return the favor for being such a good sport tonight."

My stomach tightens, not from nerves exactly, but from the way his voice lands low, right under my ribs. "What favor?"

Kai's grin turns sharp and delighted. "I may have put our names down for something."

I narrow my eyes, because the sparkle in his gaze is never innocent. "What exactly?"

"The Cowboy Carry race. You and me." He tips his chin toward the main area where people are gathering. "It'll be fun."

"A piggyback race." I stare at him.

"I knew you'd say no if I asked." He shrugs like it's the most reasonable thing in the world. "This way, it's already done. No backing out."

I should be annoyed and tell him that signing me up for something physical without checking is presumptuous at best. But Kai is staring at me like he already knows I'm going to cave, like he's watching my willpower wobble. Carter is close enough that it's hard to concentrate.

I lift my chin, trying to drag control back where it belongs, reminding myself that I did enjoy the photo shoot with them, their company. Then I cave... "One race."

Kai's brows lift, pleased. "Done."

"Then I go home." I shift my weight, forcing myself to focus on the noise around us instead of the warmth at my sides. "Just give me two minutes," I tell them. "I need to take this stuff to the office and lock it up before someone walks off with these expensive lenses." Before either of them can argue, I duck away and into the staff area, past the guard there. Then I slip into the tiny office by the lockers and tuck my gear away, snapping the lock closed.

I return, and in no time, we're up near the races where they hold lots of games. Locals love them, but I rarely participate. There is a roped-off track about fifty yards long. A dozen teams are already lined up, some bouncing on their toes, some laughing, some already arguing about who is going to drop whom.

I manage one full second of normal.

Then I spot Tanner.

He's near the starting line, wearing that smug expression I know too well, like the world was built to applaud him. The moment our eyes meet, his face twists into something ugly.

He detaches from the woman beside him and starts toward us with purpose.

"June." His voice cuts through the fair noise like it owns the air between us. "Didn't expect to see you here."

Kai's arm tightens at my shoulders, subtle but unmistakable.

Carter steps closer behind me, close enough that my back almost brushes his chest.

And I have to fight my own body all over again, because fear and heat are a messy mix, and I refuse to let Tanner see either one.

"It's a public fair," I say, keeping my voice flat.

Tanner's gaze flicks over me, then past me, sharp

and sour. "Public fair," he repeats like it tastes bad. "Including the men you've been hanging around with?" He jerks his chin at Kai and Carter. "Working your way through the whole pack now? What are you trying to prove?"

I feel Kai shift at my side, his posture going still. Carter doesn't move, but the space around him tightens anyway, like he's suddenly taking up more room without trying.

Tanner holds my stare for another second, like he wants a reaction he can use. Then his eyes dart past us to the people nearby. A couple of heads have turned. Someone at the starting line is openly watching. A volunteer in a bright vest is staring like this is better than the race.

Tanner's jaw works. He swallows whatever he was about to say.

Because he must be thinking of last night and how fast it went wrong today. How close it came to becoming something he couldn't smooth over with a badge and a story.

His gaze snaps back to Kai and Carter, and for a heartbeat, the bravado falters. Not fear exactly. Calculation. The kind that knows the consequences.

He straightens, forcing his expression into something hard and dismissive. "Whatever," he mutters, like he's bored, like this is beneath him.

But he takes a step back. Then another.

"She's not worth it," he spits, louder, for the audience. He turns and stalks back to the woman beside him, shoulders tight, pretending he didn't just retreat.

Carter watches him go with narrowed eyes. "Fucking asshole."

"He's not worth thinking about," I mutter.

Kai exhales through his nose, the tension easing out of him. "Agreed." Then his grin slides back into place like he's flipping a switch. "Let's go beat his ass in this race. Now, get on my back."

He's tall and solid, and when I jump, his hands catch the backs of my thighs immediately, big palms warm against my jeans, fingers curling around muscle as he hoists me up. My chest presses against his back, arms wrapping around his shoulders, and my face is inches from the curve of his neck. This close, his scent is overwhelming, flooding my senses until I feel dizzy with it.

"Comfortable?" His voice vibrates through his back into my chest.

"Define 'comfortable.'"

Kai laughs like I've entertained him. "Are you gonna fall off?"

"Probably not."

"Great." He bounces once, settling me higher, and his hands slide up my thighs with zero hesitation, like he's adjusting cargo he intends to keep. "Hold tight, doll. I don't lose."

Carter is hooting.

"I'm starting to think this is less about winning and more about you getting to manhandle me in public."

"Multitasking," he says smoothly. "I'm talented."

I open my mouth to hit him with something biting, but the starting horn blares and my entire body forgets how sarcasm works.

We launch forward, and now I understand why they call it a race. Kai moves like he was built for this. Long legs eating up the ground, shoulders steady under my hands, muscles flexing beneath me in a rhythm that feels indecent. Every stride bounces me against his back. My thighs clamp around his waist on instinct. My breasts press into his shoulders, and I hate that I can't decide if I want to apologize or do it harder.

"You doing okay up there?" he calls over his shoulder, still not even slightly winded.

"I'm trying not to die!"

"That's the spirit."

"Kai," I gasp, "I swear to God, if I face-plant in front of this whole town, I'm going to haunt you."

His laugh is all heat and arrogance. "You'll be fine. I've got you."

His hands squeeze my thighs like punctuation, like he wants to make sure I believe it, and my insides flip with a tinge of arousal.

Around us, other teams are running, stumbling,

laughing. Someone wipes out spectacularly to our left, and the crowd roars. A kid near the rope line yells, "Go, cowboy!" like this is the Olympics. I catch a glimpse of Hazel in the distance with a tall, dark-haired man, phone held high, and I don't know whether to be grateful or furious.

"She'd better not be filming," I wheeze.

Kai doesn't even look. "She's filming."

"I'm going to kill her."

"She'll post it with a caption," he says, dead serious. "'Local girl discovers cardio and sin.'"

I choke on a laugh and tighten my grip. "Stop talking!"

"Can't," he says. "I'm in my element."

And then Tanner appears beside us.

He's running hard, face red with effort, partner bouncing on his back, but his attention isn't on the finish line. It's on us. He drifts closer, deliberate, angling in like he's trying to clip us without making it obvious.

My skin goes cold. "Kai, watch out."

Kai's head tilts, like he already felt it. "I see him."

Too late.

Tanner's shoulder slams into Kai's side.

We lurch. My scream rips out before I can stop it, my arms locking around Kai's neck as the world tilts and my stomach drops. Kai stumbles two steps, boots skidding in the dirt, and for one horrible second, I'm sure we're going down.

But Kai plants his foot in the ground, catching his balance, and his hands clamp my thighs like a promise.

"Hold on," he states, voice suddenly like steel.

"I *AM* HOLDING ON!" I shriek, half terrified, half furious.

Kai glances sideways at Tanner.

"Oh," he says, almost cheerful. "So that's what we're doing."

And then he surges forward again, stronger, faster, like Tanner just gave him permission to stop playing nice.

"Oh my God, I'm going to die!" I call out. "Kai, do not make this worse."

"You mean don't make it fun," he calls back.

Tanner sticks close on our right, breathing hard, drifting in like he's lining up another hit. I tense, clutching Kai's shoulders.

Tanner crowds in, shoulder angling toward Kai's side again, and Kai cuts toward the center of the track where an orange cone marks the lane, then whips around it at the last second with a sharp pivot that makes my body swing.

I squeal, gripping tighter.

Tanner tries to follow the turn, boots skidding in churned-up dirt. He clips the cone. It goes flying.

The crowd roars.

Someone yells, "FOUL!" like this is professional sports.

I'm laughing so hard I can barely breathe. "Kai, that was evil!"

"It was all strategy," he says, not even winded.

Tanner snarls and pushes harder, catching up again, and this time, he commits to the shoulder check like he's determined to send us down.

Kai slows for half a second.

Just enough.

Then he slips sideways and surges forward, letting Tanner's momentum carry him past. Tanner stumbles over his own feet, fighting for balance, his partner shrieking as they wobble.

Kai takes the opening and accelerates, hands clamped on my thighs like a promise. "We got this, doll."

The finish line is right there, lights and cheering and Carter somewhere yelling our names. Tanner lunges once more, but he's a step behind now, too late.

Kai drives us through the line first.

The announcer hollers, the crowd erupts, and I slide off his back on shaky legs, laughing like I've lost my mind.

"You're insane," I gasp.

Kai is howling with victory. "And you loved it."

"I did not," I lie, and Carter's laugh carries from nearby like he doesn't believe me for a second.

Carter is there immediately, lifting me off my feet and spinning me in a circle before setting me down. His hands linger on my waist.

"That was incredible," he says, grin spread wide.

"I thought we were going to eat dirt when he hit us," I state.

"Please." Kai appears at my side, barely winded. "I never lose. Especially not to assholes."

Tanner stalks past without looking at us, his face a mask of fury. His partner trails behind.

I really, truly don't care.

"And now..." Kai announces, going over to the organizer to collect our prize. Then he's back in moments, cradling a plush horse nearly as big as his arm, electric blue with a glittery mane and the most ridiculous cross-eyed expression stitched onto its face. I love it instantly.

"For the champion," Kai says, presenting it with a dramatic bow.

"It's hideous." I clutch it to my chest. "I'm naming him Glitter Bastard."

"Glitter Bastard," Carter repeats. "A noble steed."

"The noblest." I stroke the sparkly mane. "He's been through a lot."

Kai grins. "We won you one prize. But I think we can do better."

"What do you mean?"

He exchanges a look with Carter. "We are *very* competitive."

"Dangerously competitive," Carter confirms. "It's basically an illness."

"By the end of the night," Kai continues, "you're going to need a truck to haul everything home."

"That's not necessary—"

"It absolutely is." He grabs my hand, pulling me toward the game booths. "The competition begins now."

The first game they drag me to is one of those milk bottle pyramids where you throw balls to knock them down. Simple in theory. Impossible in practice. The bottles are weighted, the balls are too light, and the whole thing is designed to take your money and crush your dreams.

Kai goes first, rolling up his sleeves like he's preparing for battle. His first throw is good, solid contact, but only two bottles fall.

"Rigged," he announces.

"It's not rigged," the booth operator says tiredly. "You just missed."

"I don't miss." But he hands over more tickets for another try.

Carter steps up beside him. "Move over. Let me show you how it's done."

What follows is the most intense ten minutes of carnival gaming I've ever witnessed.

They take turns throwing, each one trying to outdo the other. Kai adjusts his stance, calculates angles, treats each throw like a precision military operation. Carter goes for pure power, hurling the balls with enough force that I'm surprised they don't punch through the back of the booth.

Neither of them wins.

"This is definitely rigged," Carter says.

"Maybe you both just suck," I offer.

They turn to look at me with identical expressions of offense.

"Excuse me?" Kai presses a hand to his chest. "Did you just question my athletic abilities?"

Carter nudges Kai. "She's got a point. We've thrown, like, thirty balls and won nothing."

"We haven't won *yet*." Kai turns back to the booth, a dangerous glint in his eye. "We're just warming up."

Twenty more minutes and a frankly embarrassing number of tickets later, they finally win. Kai's throw catches the bottom corner of the pyramid at exactly the right angle, and the whole thing goes down in a cascade of clattering bottles.

The booth operator hands over a stuffed cow with a dopey expression, and Kai presents it to me like it's the crown jewels.

"For you, my lady."

"You spent probably fifty dollars winning a five-dollar cow."

"The prize is priceless." He grins. "Because I won it for you."

We move on. Balloon darts. Ring toss. That basketball game with the hoops that are definitely smaller than regulation. At each booth, they approach with the intensity of Olympic athletes, trash-talking each other constantly while I watch and laugh and accumulate an increasingly ridiculous pile of prizes.

The bumper cars are next.

Carter draws me into his car, a battered blue thing that's seen better days, and suddenly I'm pressed against his side, his arm around my shoulders, his thigh warm against mine.

"Ready?" His voice is low, close to my ear. "For me to defend your honor against any and all attackers."

I snort. "My hero."

Kai is in a car across the rink, grinning like a maniac. When the buzzer sounds, he immediately guns for us, but Carter spins us out of the way at the last second, sending Kai careening into the wall.

"HA!" Carter crows.

"This is war!" Kai yells back, reversing.

They chase each other around the rink while I hold on and laugh until my stomach hurts. Carter's arm keeps reaching for my thigh when we take hard turns.

When the ride ends, I'm breathless and giddy and my cheeks hurt from smiling.

"That was amazing," I manage.

"Just the beginning." Carter helps me out of the car, his hand lingering on mine. "We've got hours yet."

They weren't kidding about the competition.

As the night goes on, the pile of prizes grows absurd. I've lost count of who won what stuffed animals, inflatable swords, a poster of a horse that

Carter insisted on because it reminded him of me, and I'm still not sure if that's a compliment. We made several trips to the car already with the prizes.

And somewhere along the way, the touches start to linger.

Kai's hand on my lower back as he guides me through the crowd. Carter's fingers intertwining with mine when we're walking between booths. The way they lean in when they talk to me, close enough that I can feel their breath, smell their scents, count their eyelashes.

It's intoxicating. Overwhelming. Every brush of contact sends sparks across my skin, and I keep having to remind myself that this is just a fun night. Just a fantasy that can't last.

But God, I don't want it to end.

By the time the fair starts shutting down, our arms are overflowing and my face hurts from smiling.

We stroll back to my car one final time, a slow meander through the emptying fairgrounds, and the mood shifts. Softer. More intimate. The fairy lights overhead cast everything in a golden glow, and the cold air makes me press closer to their warmth.

We reach my car, and I pop the trunk, then open one of the back doors, adding more prizes to what's already there.

"This is insane," I say. "I'm going to have to strap things to the roof."

"Worth it," Kai says, also loading things in. "Every single one."

When everything is packed, barely, I turn to find them both watching me. Standing close enough that their scents mingle in the air between us.

"Stay," Carter says softly. "Come out with us. The night doesn't have to end."

My heart pounds, and every instinct is screaming at me to say *yes*, to let them take me wherever they want, to stop fighting whatever this is.

"I can't." The words come out breathier than I intended. "It's late. I should go."

"Should?" Kai steps closer. "Or want to?"

"Both." I force a breath into lungs that don't seem to want to cooperate. "This was the best night I've had in... I can't even remember." My voice goes softer despite me. "But I'm tired, and I feel a little off, and I think I need to go home and... process everything before I do something stupid."

Kai's mouth curves like he appreciates my honesty. Carter's gaze lingers on me, steady and careful, as though he's reading the parts I'm not saying out loud.

They exchange a look, something quiet passing between them, and then they both nod.

"All right," Carter says, and the disappointment is there, but he doesn't try to hold me hostage with it. "Go home." His voice drops, gentler. "But don't disappear on us."

Kai steps in close enough that I catch his scent

again, that warm, addictive pull my body keeps reacting to before my brain can veto it. "Text when you get home," he says, like it's not a request. Like it's the kind of thing that matters. "So I know you're safe."

My chest tightens, not from fear, not exactly. But from something tender that makes me want to turn defensive, makes me want to pretend it doesn't hit. "You don't have to—"

"I want to," he cuts in, easy but firm, and it lands right in the middle of me.

Carter's hand brushes my elbow, barely there, but it anchors me. "Tonight was good," he says, quietly enough that it feels like it's just for me. "You were good. Don't let your head talk you out of that."

I should say no. Should keep that barrier in place. Should remember every reason this is dangerous.

But my fingers are already pulling out my phone.

Numbers are exchanged. Kai watches me type. When my screen lights up with their names, it feels like a line I can't uncross.

Then I'm climbing into my car, surrounded by plush animals and ridiculous prizes, barely able to see out the back window, and they're still there in the parking lot, watching like they're reluctant to let the night end.

Kai lifts two fingers to his mouth and flicks me a kiss like he's cocky enough to believe I'll catch it. Carter raises a hand in a slow wave, his smile soft in the fairy lights.

I drive away.

This is a terrible idea. Getting close to them, letting them in, pretending I could ever be what they're looking for.

But as the fair lights fade in my rearview mirror, as I replay every touch, every grin, every quiet moment where I felt... chosen, I can't bring myself to regret any of it.

Not even a little.

7

CARTER

June's taillights disappear around the corner, and I'm still standing in the parking lot like an idiot who forgot how legs work.

Kai bumps my shoulder. "You gonna keep staring at that road like it owes you money, or are we leaving?"

"Shut up."

He hums, pleased with himself. "That's a yes."

We climb into my truck. Kai drops into the passenger seat and immediately acts like he pays the registration, one boot propped up like he's king of my damn dashboard. I pull out of the fairground lot and aim us toward the ranch.

The night is cold and clear, stars scattered across the sky like someone got reckless with a handful of diamonds. The road stretches out empty ahead of us, dark and quiet, the kind of silence that makes thoughts louder.

I should be thinking about tomorrow. Circuit prep, as the rodeo kicks off the day after.

Instead, I keep replaying June. The way she laughed when Kai nearly ate dirt at the ring toss. Her eyes lit up every time we handed her another stupid prize. How addictive she smelled when she was right there between us.

Kai glances over. "You're doing it again."

"What's that?"

"Where you go real quiet and your jaw gets tight." He points at me like a prosecutor. "You're thinking about her."

I don't bother denying it. I flick my eyes toward him. "So are you."

Kai snorts. "Yeah, but I'm not the one pretending I'm above it." He shifts in his seat, restless energy rolling off him. "You were real composed back there. Mr. Calm. Mr. 'I'm just here for the community.'"

"One of us has to look semi-functional in public," I mutter.

"Functional is overrated." Kai rakes a hand through his hair, loosening it like he's trying to shake the night off. It doesn't work. "You see the way she looked at us? Like she was two seconds from making a bad decision, then she'd pull herself back."

"I saw," I say, unable to stop thinking about it.

Kai's gaze narrows, like he's watching me carefully now. "That didn't mess with you?"

I tighten my grip on the wheel. "What do you want me to say, Kai?"

"I want you to quit acting like you didn't spend the whole night one breath away from losing your mind."

I stare out at the road, jaw working once. "Fine. Yeah." I swallow, irritated at myself for even saying it. "Every time she smiled at me, I wanted to close the distance. When she got close, I had to tell my hands to behave. And then she left…" I exhale hard through my nose. "I'm not thrilled about it."

Kai's grin turns sharp and satisfied. "There we go. That's the truth."

"Don't make it weird."

"I'm making it better." He leans back, smug. "You're welcome."

I glance at him. "Go fuck yourself."

Kai laughs like he's already planning how to do exactly that and call it a team activity. "After we figure out what June's hiding."

His fingers are drumming against his thigh, that endless energy looking for somewhere to go. I know the feeling. My whole body is humming with it, restless, unsatisfied, wanting something I can't have.

"Here's the thing," Kai adds, and the playfulness drops out of him. "I can still smell her."

He glances down at his shirt. "On my clothes. My

skin." His throat works once. "It's... bad in the best way. Like she got under me without even meaning to."

I return my attention to the road. "You want me to pull over so you can rub your face on your own sleeve?"

Kai lets out a short breath that might be a laugh. Might be a growl. "Don't start." Then he sobers again. "But her scent. It wasn't steady. You caught that, right? It got stronger as the night went on."

"Yeah." My grip tightens on the wheel. "Early on, I barely got a trace. Later, after the games, after she stopped bracing every second... it hit."

"Exactly." Kai shifts in his seat, restless. "Like there's a lid on it. And when she relaxes, it slips."

Silence stretches for a beat. The kind that means we're both hearing the same thing in our heads.

Kai says it first. "She's not a Beta."

"My instincts clocked that the second I saw her," I admit. "They haven't backed off once."

"Betas don't do that to Alphas," he says, voice rough. "They don't make your whole body go alert. Like you're on duty. Like you're... owned."

I exhale slowly. "So why pretend? Why hide?"

Kai shrugs. "Because somebody told her to, or she's hiding something?"

I think of the way June answers too fast when designation comes up. The way she redirects. The way her scent flares for one breath, then vanishes like she shoved it back down.

"If she's masking," I say, "it's not new. That takes

discipline. Constant attention. You don't keep that up unless you're scared of what happens when you stop."

Kai nods once. "Fear or experience."

I glance at him. "And then there's her ex, who's a problem."

"Fucking dick," Kai states. "I doubt he knows, or he would have revealed it. I don't think she's hiding it because of him, as he's only a Beta."

"Which means it's bigger than him," I murmur.

Kai's voice goes quiet, dangerous. "Pack. Family. Somebody who didn't protect her when they should've."

The thought lands heavily in my chest. "Or somebody who convinced her hiding was the only way to survive."

Kai stares out the windshield, eyes hard. "That's not survival. That's a cage."

My fingers flex on the steering wheel. "And cages make people bite."

Kai finally looks at me. "So we don't corner her."

"No," I agree. "We don't push. We make it safe. We let her choose."

Kai's mouth twists. "And if somebody made her believe she had to disappear... they're going to regret it."

I don't argue. I just keep driving because my instincts have already decided one thing.

June isn't just a girl we met at a fair. She's ours.

We drive in silence, the road empty and dark

around us. I should be paying attention to where we're going, but my mind keeps circling back to June. The fear underneath her smiles. The loneliness she tries so hard to mask. The way she stared at us like she wanted to believe in something but couldn't quite let herself.

"You know what doesn't make sense?" Kai says suddenly.

"What?"

"The pull I feel toward her." He gestures vaguely. "It should be fading. We left her. We're driving away. My brain should be settling down, moving on to other shit."

"But it's not."

"It's getting worse. Like the farther we get from her, the more I want to turn this truck around and go back. Find her. Make sure she's fucking safe and ensure no one else gets close to her."

I know exactly what he means. My foot keeps twitching toward the brake. Some primal part of me is howling that we're going the wrong direction. That we should be with her. That she belongs with us.

Belongs with us.

That thought should scare me. We've known her for barely two days. But it feels like something that's been building for years, just waiting for the right moment to explode.

"Why does this road feel wrong?" I frown into the darkness ahead. The landscape doesn't match what my muscle memory expects.

Kai leans forward, squinting through the windshield. "Because you're driving like a man who's been hypnotized. And you missed the turn by a mile, Romeo."

I shoot him a look. "Fuck off, it's not a mile."

Kai digs his phone out and taps the screen a few times, then his mouth twists. "Okay, it's... more than a mile." He lifts the phone toward the windshield like better signal might magically appear. "And there's spotty reception out here. Montana really said, 'Good luck, idiots.'"

I slow the truck. The road is narrow, dirt edged, flanked by black fields and fencing that disappears into the night. No lights anywhere. Just stars and the sound of my tires on gravel.

Kai exhales, annoyed. "If GPS is catching up, it shows us way the hell off. We missed the turnoff, like, way back."

I grip the wheel tighter. "How did we miss our turn?"

Kai points at me without looking up. "Because neither of us was thinking about the road. We were talking about June." He snorts, shaking his head. "We're gonna end up on the local news. 'Two grown men disappear into the wilderness. Authorities confirm the last thing they talked about was a girl and her smile.'" He glances over, smug. "Cause of death: terminal lovesick stupidity."

"I'm turning around."

"Please do," he says, voice suddenly serious.

I ease the truck down the narrow road, looking for a spot wide enough to turn around without ending up in a ditch. The fields are dead quiet.

And then the headlights catch something.

Big.

Still.

Too solid to be a shadow.

Kai goes silent in a way I don't like. "Uh."

"What?"

He leans forward, one hand braced on the dash. "Tell me that's a cow."

I follow his stare, and my stomach knots.

About thirty yards out, standing in the middle of the field like it owns the dark, is a bull. Black as pitch. Horns that look like they could forklift this truck for fun. Eyes that glint in the light and flash back at us, bright and wrong.

"What the hell is that?" Kai whispers, as though volume might provoke it.

"That," I say, deadpan, "is a beast with horns."

Kai's voice tightens. "That's a demon wearing beef."

"Stop."

"I'm serious," he says. "Look at the size of it. That thing pays taxes."

I slow even more, because my brain is doing a fast audit of every bad decision I've made in the last ten minutes. "Why is it just standing there?"

Kai swallows. "Because it's deciding if we're worth the effort."

"Don't say that."

Kai points. "It's staring at us, Carter."

"I know," I blurt out.

Kai's mouth twists into a nervous grin. "Maybe it's June's spirit animal."

"Don't bring June into this."

"You're right." He nods solemnly. "This is what happens when you think too hard about a woman. The universe sends a monster bull to humble you."

I stare at the animal. It stares back. Neither of us blinks. The truck idles like it's holding its breath.

Kai whispers, "If it charges, I'm not getting out. I'm letting it take the truck. You can explain it to your insurance."

"You think insurance covers demonic livestock?" I snort, then immediately regret it because the bull shifts its weight. Slow. Heavy. Like a threat that took its time.

"Okay," I say, voice suddenly calm in a way that means I'm not calm at all. "We're leaving."

Kai nods fast. "Yep. Great plan. Love that plan."

The bull takes a step toward us. Then another. Then it drops its head.

My stomach goes cold.

"It's charging," Kai says, and his voice goes weirdly calm, like his brain has accepted our deaths on principle. "Carter... it's fucking charging."

I slam the truck into reverse. Gravel spits. The tires scrabble like they're trying to climb out of the earth.

The bull launches anyway.

It moves way too fast for something that must be Satan's cattle. Hooves hammer the ground. The sound is a drumbeat that hits my spine.

"Go go go go," Kai barks, suddenly all panic again. "Go, go, go!"

"I AM," I snap, throwing the wheel to get us angled around, but the road is narrow and the truck is long, and the bull is closing in like it's got a personal grudge.

Thirty yards.

Twenty.

Fifteen.

I can see the steam of its breath blowing white in the headlights. The shine of a horn. The thick neck. The shoulders bunching like a wrecking ball in motion. Fuck me!

"It's gonna hit us!" Kai says.

"Kai," I bite out, "shut up and pray."

"Don't tell me to pray," he yells, twisted around in his seat. "God can't save us now!"

The tires finally bite. The truck jerks, traction catching, and I punch the gas.

We shoot forward just as the bull hits the edge of our light.

There's a violent scrape along the side of the truck. Horn against metal. A hard jolt that vibrates through the door like a warning punch.

"That—" Kai chokes, eyes huge. "That thing just tried to open my door!"

"I felt it," I grind out, heart trying to kick through my ribs as I floor it down the road. The truck fishtails once and straightens. "Hold on."

He's grabbing the handle above the window like he's hanging off a cliff. "Carter, I do not want to be taken out by a demonic bastard! Fuck, it looks like one of those territorial Chianina bulls but with a black coat."

In the mirror, the bull keeps coming for a few terrifying seconds, pounding after us like it can't believe we're getting away.

Kai watches it, breath coming fast. "It's still running. Why is it still running?"

"Because it hates us," I say flatly.

"This is the universe going, 'Stop talking about June and drive the damn truck.'"

The bull finally drops back, slowing to a heavy trot, then to a furious stop in the field, head high like it's offended that we didn't die properly.

Kai stays twisted around, staring until it's just a shape in the dark.

Then he exhales, long and ragged. "Holy shit."

"Fuck."

"It felt like that horn was an inch away from coming inside this truck.."

"Don't talk about inches," I mutter automatically, still riding the adrenaline.

Kai whips his head toward me. "Not the time."

I let out a breath that turns into a laugh I didn't plan on. "Where the hell did that thing come from?"

"I don't know," Kai says, still half shouting, "but it had murder in its eyes. That wasn't a normal bull."

"Maybe it was trying to tell us something," I say, hands tight on the wheel.

Kai nods hard. "Yeah. 'Wrong neighborhood, assholes.'"

He laughs, short and shaky, and then it catches in his throat like he can't decide if he's going to laugh again or throw up.

"Christ," he says. "That was the closest I've ever come to being gored."

"We're adding this to the list of things we never tell anyone," I say.

"Agreed," he says immediately. "This goes to the grave. You could torture me, and I'd still deny we got chased by a demon bull."

We drive in tense silence for a minute.

Then Kai starts laughing again. That slightly hysterical edge that comes from almost dying. It's contagious.

I try to hold it back, and fail, a bark of laughter tearing out of me as the adrenaline crashes.

"I can't believe that just happened," Kai manages between breaths. "We almost got murdered by cattle."

"That would've been an embarrassing obituary," I say, still laughing.

"The most embarrassing," Kai agrees. "Taken out by horny driving and satanic livestock." Kai wipes his eyes with the back of his hand, still grinning like an idiot. "And the last words would've been me screaming about June."

The laughter fades in slow waves, leaving the night quiet again.

We find the right turnoff eventually, and the ranch appears ahead, lit up warmly against the dark Montana sky. But there's a figure on the porch, Seth, sitting on the steps with a mug in hand, staring at the stars like he's waiting for them to tell him something useful.

Seth glances up as my headlights sweep the yard, and even from the truck, I catch the smirk forming. We park, then climb out, and Kai immediately runs a hand over the passenger door where the horn scraped it, finding only a shallow dent.

"We got off lightly," he mutters. "Little buff, little polish. Your princess will live."

I snort a laugh as we head for the house like nothing happened, and Seth watches us cross the drive like he's been waiting, all quiet patience and judgment. He doesn't say a word until we're close enough to smell the coffee in his mug.

"You two look like you've been through something."

"We're fine," I say on instinct, because it's the only answer a man is allowed to give.

Seth's eyes flick over us, slow and unimpressed. "Uh-huh." He tips his chin. "How'd the photo booth go?"

Kai drops onto the porch steps beside him with a heavy exhale, elbows on his knees like he's trying to wring the night out of his bones. I stay standing, leaning against the railing, one boot hooked on the bottom step, still keyed up from the fair and the drive and the fact that June is now lodged in my chest.

"It went well," Kai states. "Too well. June got her shots, and she looked…" He trails off, mouth twitching like he hates how much he means it. "She looked fucking incredible."

"And then we didn't stop there," I add, because if I don't say it out loud, it'll keep buzzing in my head. "We ended up staying. Games. Rides. That stupid race."

Kai lets out a short laugh. "Carter bought out half the carnival tickets like he was trying to win the whole fair."

"Don't exaggerate." Yet, I can't help the grin. "She kept lighting up every time we handed her something. Like it mattered. So yeah. We kept going."

Seth watches us a second longer, then takes a slow sip of his coffee like he's savoring this. "You two sound smitten."

Kai's head drops back against the porch post. "That's not a word I'd use."

Seth's smirk deepens. "Seems accurate, though."

I scratch at my jaw, glancing out at the dark

pasture like it has answers. "We got close to her. Spent hours with her. And her scent..."

Kai's posture shifts immediately, all humor fading into something sharper. "It got stronger as the night went on."

"Much stronger," I confirm. "Like whatever's muffling it was slipping."

Seth's eyes narrow, that same look he had last night. "I told you."

Kai nods once, jaw tight. "Yeah. You were right."

"It's not just attraction," I say, because that's the part that keeps catching in my throat. "It's... obsessive. Possessive. Like my instincts decided something before I did."

Kai's laugh is short and humorless. "No Beta has ever done that to me."

Seth sets his mug down, the sound soft on the wood. "Because she's not a Beta." He looks between us. "I'm sure of it."

Kai's gaze cuts to mine, then back to Seth. "We agree."

"So, what now?" Seth asks, like he's testing if we're going to be idiots or men.

Kai spreads his hands. "This means she's ours. And we need to make it clear."

Seth's expression doesn't change, but his voice drops a notch. "Or she already knows. And she's scared."

That lands hard.

I straighten a little, the night air suddenly colder. "So we don't push her."

Kai opens his mouth to argue, then closes it. "We don't push," he grudgingly agrees, "but we also don't just sit back."

"Exactly," I say, relief and frustration tangled together. "We move smart. We stay close. We give her reasons to trust us as we figure out what she's hiding without cornering her."

Seth studies us for a beat, then nods once, slow. "Good."

Kai blows out a breath. "And if someone made her hide…"

Seth's eyes go flint hard. "Then we handle that too."

I stare out into the dark again, thinking of June's smile, her laugh, the way she kept one hand on the edge of the world like she might need to bolt.

"We're not losing her," I say, more promise than statement.

Kai's voice is quiet beside me. "No."

Seth's smirk returns, faint and knowing. "Then we treat her like she's already ours."

8

JUNE

"I woke up to water all over my downstairs, and I have no idea where it's coming from."

Hazel sets down her latte, dark eyes widening. "Define 'all over.'"

"Like a thin layer covering everything. The storage room, the bathroom, the garage." I slump back in my chair. "I turned off the main water supply, but the damage is already done. And I can't even find the source."

She sighs. "Eek, that's a nightmare."

"It gets better." I take a long drink of my coffee. "The plumber came within an hour, took one look, and told me to leave because he's going to have to start punching holes in my walls to find the leak."

"Shit. How many holes are we talking?"

"However many it takes, apparently." I gesture vaguely. "My house is becoming Swiss cheese as we speak." And I'm so stressed that I might have nowhere to live, and I know Hazel has a one-room studio, super tiny, so I can't impose on her.

Hazel winces sympathetically. "Insurance?"

"Called them. They're 'processing' my claim." I make air quotes. "Which means sitting around while my house slowly transforms into a disaster zone."

"I'm so sorry, babe." She reaches over the table to hold my hand.

"Nothing I can do until they fix it, I guess." I glance around the Wildflower Bakehouse & Café, which is warm and bright around us, all honeyed wood and mismatched vintage furniture that somehow works together. Mason jar lights hang from exposed beams overhead, casting everything in a golden glow. A chalkboard menu stretches across one wall, the daily specials written in looping script that changes with the owner's mood. This place always calms me.

Kitty emerges from the kitchen carrying a plate, coming our way. She's twenty-four, with dark hair piled in a ponytail and an apron that's a patchwork of cats, donuts, and what appears to be a bedazzled croissant. Her white blouse is buttoned all the way up.

"Chocolate croissants, warmed." She sets the plate between us. "Rough morning?"

"The roughest."

"That calls for extra chocolate, then." She winks and heads back to the counter.

I tear into my croissant with more aggression than

the pastry deserves. The chocolate is warm and melty, the layers shattering under my teeth. At least something in my life is going right.

My phone buzzes. Pete's name flashes on the screen.

"Speaking of things I don't want to deal with," I mutter, then answer. "Pete. Hi."

"June! Just checking in. Have you had a chance to think about what we discussed?"

"I'm still thinking."

"It's been almost twenty-four hours."

"That's... not that long, Pete."

"The circuit leaves in less than two or three weeks. The sheriff is breathing down my neck. The rodeo coordinator keeps calling me and asking if we've 'resolved the situation.'" He sighs heavily. "I need an answer."

"I just need a bit more time to consider—"

Knock.

I glance at the window beside our table. Nothing there.

"—consider whether this is really the best use of my—"

Knock.

"June."

The voice is muffled through the glass. I keep my eyes firmly on the table, saying, "Is it the best use of my skills, given that I have a real estate business to run and—"

Knock.

"June."

Hazel is staring out the window, a grin spreading across her face. She presses her lips together, clearly trying not to laugh.

"—clients who need my attention, and frankly, Pete, I think there might be someone better suited to—"

Knock.

"June."

Hazel snorts. Her shoulders are shaking.

Knock.

"June."

I refuse to look. I am a professional. I am having an important phone conversation. I will not be distracted by—

Knock.

"June."

Hazel has her hand clamped over her mouth, tears forming in the corners of her eyes.

"Pete, maybe there's another committee member who could take this on."

"Told you before, no one else is suited."

Knock.

"June."

"You're the only option," Pete continues, oblivious. "Word is the rodeo stars already like you."

My face heats. "Where did you hear that?"

Knock.

"June."

Knock.

"June."

Hazel is wheezing now with giggles.

"The rodeo circuit coordinator mentioned it. Said his boys haven't stopped talking about the local girl who helped at the photo booth."

Knock.

"June."

Knock.

"June."

I finally glance up.

Kai is standing outside the window, face pressed against the glass like a kid at a pet store. When our eyes meet, he breaks into the most devastating smile I've ever seen and gives me a little wave. "Hey, June."

I can't help it. I laugh. "Pete, I have to go."

"But—"

"I'll call you back. Soon." I hang up before he can protest.

Kai then disappears from view.

"He's insane," I say.

"He's completely obsessed with you," Hazel corrects, wiping her eyes. "Did you see his face? He looked like he'd just found buried treasure."

"He looked like a man who doesn't understand personal boundaries."

"Same thing." She grins. "So. You going to tell me what happened after I left last night?"

I fill her in on the fun night of carnival games and the mountain of prizes, the way Kai and Carter competed to win me increasingly ridiculous stuffed animals. The way they looked at me when they said good night. The way I couldn't stop thinking about them the entire drive home.

"And then," I add, "I got home and felt like absolute garbage."

Hazel frowns. "What do you mean?"

"Fever. Body aches. This weird... buzzing under my skin." I shake my head. "It's gone now, thankfully. Probably just a bug. Or exhaustion."

"Or." Hazel leans forward, her voice dropping conspiratorially. "Your body is trying to tell you something."

"Yeah, to get more sleep."

"So are you going to see them again?"

"At this point, I think they've installed a tracking device on me." I glance toward the window where Kai appeared. "I'm starting to wonder if I should be concerned or flattered."

Hazel laughs. "Definitely flattered."

I roll my eyes, but I'm smiling. "Okay, your turn. How was the date?"

Hazel's expression shifts into something wicked. "The date was... educational."

"Okay, that's unusual."

"I learned several things about myself. And about

him." She takes a slow sip of her latte. "Turns out, I really enjoy being in charge."

"Go on."

"In charge of *everything*." Her grin widens. "He was very... accommodating. Willing to follow instructions."

"Hazel."

"I may have left him tied to his bed this morning."

I choke on my croissant. "*What?*"

"He asked for it! Literally begged me." She drinks her coffee. "I used his own neckties. Very secure. He said I needed to come back later and 'finish what I started.'"

"You tied a man to his bed and just... left him there?"

"I untied one hand so he could free himself eventually. I'm not a monster." She grins. "But I might make him wait a few more hours."

"You meet the strangest people."

"I attract them. There's a difference."

My phone buzzes. A text from Pete: *Don't forget to call me back. This is urgent.*

I sigh, setting it facedown on the table.

"The man is desperate. The whole town depends on that rodeo circuit." She sets her phone aside too. "Speaking of things that won't give up... you know what they say about plumbers."

"What?"

"Big pipes." She waggles her eyebrows. "And they're not afraid to get dirty."

"You're terrible."

"I'm hilarious." She nods toward the window.

I turn to look, and my brain goes completely offline.

Seth is across the road outside, bent over near the bed of a pickup truck, loading something heavy. And bent over means... yeah. Low-slung jeans. A strip of tan skin where his shirt has ridden up. And an ass that belongs on a museum pedestal.

"Well," Hazel says appreciatively. "That's a view."

I can't actually form words. My mouth dries.

"That is a man who knows how to fill out denim." She tilts her head, studying him like a work of art. "So firm."

"I bet he squats," I say. "You don't get glutes like that without serious dedication."

Seth straightens up, wipes his forehead with the back of his hand, and I watch the movement with embarrassing intensity. The sun is warm today, and he's clearly been working hard enough to build up a sweat.

"He can bend over for me anytime," Hazel murmurs.

"Naked would be preferable."

"Or maybe you bend over for him."

"I am not having this conversation."

Seth bends over again, and we both lean even closer to the window like plants toward sunlight.

"Oh, look at me with all these muscles," a male

voice says from directly beside us. "Sometimes it's so hard carrying all this raw, masculine energy around. But I wear my jeans tight on purpose so everyone can admire my—"

I turn around and shriek.

Hazel nearly knocks over her latte.

Kai is sitting at the end of our table, elbows propped up, chin resting on his hands, staring out the window at Seth with an exaggerated expression of longing.

"—admire my incredible work ethic," he continues in a terrible imitation of Seth's voice. "I'm Seth Benton. I brood professionally. My jawline could cut glass, and my ass was sculpted by angels."

"How long have you been sitting there?" I demand, my heart hammering.

"Long enough to hear the 'naked would be preferable' part." He grins, utterly unrepentant. "Which, for the record, I'll be passing along to Seth later."

"Don't you dare," I gasp.

"No promises."

Hazel is doubled over, face buried in her hands, shoulders shaking with silent laughter.

Outside, Seth straightens up and rolls his shoulders.

"Oh, no," Kai says in that fake-Seth voice. "I seem to have pulled a muscle from being too handsome. Better flex dramatically for the ladies watching through café windows."

"Stop," I wheeze. "That's mean."

"It's accurate." He switches to his normal voice. "The man poses in his sleep. I've seen it."

Hazel lifts her head, tears streaming. "I officially approve. He's a keeper."

"You don't get a vote," I tell her.

"I'm taking one anyway." She gathers her bag, still giggling. "And on that note, I've got a man tied to a bed who's probably getting impatient."

"Go. Be free. Traumatize your conquest."

She blows me a kiss and disappears out the door, leaving me alone with Kai.

"Coffee," he announces, standing up. "I need caffeine. Want anything else?"

I gesture at my mostly empty cup. "Another latte would be amazing. And…" I eye the display case. "Surprise me."

His grin is blinding. "Challenge accepted."

He heads to the counter, and I take the opportunity to compose myself. My pulse is still racing from his sudden appearance, and there's that familiar warmth spreading through my chest that I've been trying very hard to ignore.

When he returns, it's with Kitty trailing behind him, both of them carrying enough food for a small army.

"One latte," Kitty announces with a sly grin, setting a fresh cup in front of me. "And…"

Kai slides into Hazel's vacated seat as Kitty unloads

the tray: two Portuguese tarts, a slice of chocolate torte, a fruit tart, something that looks like a cream puff, a cinnamon roll the size of my fist, and what appears to be half the croissant selection.

"Enjoy, you two," she says, and we both thank her, then I turn to Kai.

"You planning to feed everyone in town?" I ask.

"I wasn't sure what you'd like." He's already reaching for a Portuguese tart. "So I got a bit of everything. We can try them together, rate them, and then I'll know your favorites for next time."

Something flutters in my chest. "Next time?"

"There's always a next time with you." He takes a bite, making a sound of pure appreciation. "Oh, that's incredible. Try this."

We work our way through the pastries, rating each one. The torte is an eight. The fruit tart is a seven. The cream puff is a nine and a half. The Portuguese tart is a solid nine.

Somewhere along the way, his foot finds mine under the table. Not accidental—deliberate. His boot pressing against my ankle, sliding up to my calf, then back down. A constant point of contact that sends sparks up my leg.

I try to focus on the cinnamon roll. Try to focus on anything except the way his eyes crinkle when he laughs, or the way his fingers brush mine when he hands me a fork, or the way he's looking at me like I'm more interesting than any pastry could ever be.

My phone rings.

"Sorry," I say, checking the screen. "It's the plumber."

"Take it."

I answer, and my morning gets significantly worse.

"Miss, I've got some news." The plumber, Eric, sounds apologetic. "We found the source. Bad news is, it's been leaking longer than we thought. There's significant water damage to the subfloor, and we found mold in the walls."

"Mold. Of course there's mold."

"And before we can do repairs, we need to test for asbestos, as the house is old enough that it might have some in the insulation."

I close my eyes. "What does that mean for the timeline?"

"Minimum two weeks. Probably closer to three."

"Damn, three weeks."

"I'd recommend finding somewhere else to stay. Between the gutted downstairs, the draft, and the mold... it's not safe, not to mention it's illegal to stay here, seeing as we found mold."

"Right." I rub my temple.

"Insurance should cover alternative accommodation."

"There *is* no alternative accommodation. I booked every spare room in town for the rodeo tourists."

Eric is quiet. "That's... unfortunate. I'll send you a

quote for insurance and rush those asbestos tests. But you really shouldn't stay there."

"Understood. Thanks, Eric."

I hang up and sigh.

"Everything okay?" Kai asks, concern replacing his playful expression.

"The opposite of okay." I reach for another croissant, because if I'm having a crisis, I might as well have pastry. "Mold. Asbestos testing. Three weeks before I can move back in. And I have nowhere to stay because I was too good at my job and booked out every rental in town. I mean, my office has a couch. It's terrible, but—"

The café door opens, and Seth strides in, drawing everyone's attention.

He's still slightly flushed from whatever he was loading, those blue eyes scanning the room until they land on our table. Something shifts in his expression when he spots me.

He orders at the counter, then makes his way over, sliding into the seat beside Kai.

"Morning," he says. His voice is low.

"Morning."

"What's going on? You look stressed."

I give him the abbreviated version of recent events.

"Easy, you move in with us," Kai says immediately.

I stare at him. "You can't be serious."

"The ranch has plenty of space." He stares at Seth. "Right?"

"More than enough." Seth's gaze hasn't left my face. "Your own room and bathroom."

"I can't just move in with you guys."

"Why not?"

"Because—" I struggle for a reason that doesn't sound insane. "Because we barely know each other and it would be weird, and—"

"Look," Seth cuts in, his voice quiet but firm. "You did me a favor. A big one. You stood up for me when you didn't have to. Let me return it."

I open my mouth to protest, but nothing comes out.

"Just until your house is fixed. We've got the space, you need a place to stay, and honestly?" Kai grins. "We'd love the company."

I think about my options. The office couch that will destroy my back. Begging friends for rooms they don't have. Sleeping in my car.

And then I think about waking up in a ranch house with three Alphas whose scents make my carefully suppressed instincts go haywire.

This is a terrible idea.

My phone buzzes. Pete again: *Please call me back.*

The universe is really not being subtle today.

"Fine," I hear myself say. "Okay. I'll stay with you."

Kai's face transforms with genuine excitement. "Yeah?"

"But just until my house is fixed. And I'm not going to be a burden."

Kai is already standing, practically vibrating with energy. "I'm going to get your room ready. Make sure it's perfect. You need anything specific? Extra pillows? Blackout curtains?"

"Something small and simple. It won't be for long."

"Right." He grabs a few pastries for the road. "See you later." He's gone before I can respond, leaving me alone with Seth.

The silence stretches between us. Not uncomfortable—just weighted.

"So," Seth says finally. "Pete called you about the chaperone thing."

"So you know about it?" I sigh.

His jaw tightens. "My father wants someone to keep us out of trouble. Like we're children who can't control ourselves."

"To be fair, you did get arrested."

"Yeah, the jury's still out on that."

"I know." I meet his eyes.

Something shifts in his expression.

"What actually happened that night? At the Spur? You keep saying you weren't drinking, but you were acting like..."

"Like I was wasted." He runs a hand through his hair. "I've been trying to figure it out. Last thing I remember clearly is ordering a cola. Place was packed, people everywhere, guys wanting to shake my hand, women trying to sit in my lap. Then nothing."

"Someone might have drugged you."

"That's what I think. And when I find out who, they're going to regret it. And I'm going to clear my name."

I think about that night. The way he could barely stand. The singing. "I believe you," I tell him.

Something in his expression softens. "Yeah?"

"You were definitely out of it, but not drunk-drunk. It was different. Like something had hijacked your system."

"That's exactly what it felt like." He reaches across the table, his fingers brushing mine. Just a touch. Just a moment of contact. "Thank you for believing me."

Then he tilts his head, gaze cutting over my face. "You're nervous."

"I'm not."

He gives a short, amused exhale. "You are. But it's not about what I'm saying."

Heat crawls up my neck because he's right and he knows it.

I can smell him every time he shifts, clean and warm, with a sharpness underneath that calls to me. I shouldn't be thinking about it or noticing how his scent changes when he's amused.

If I end up living with them, it's going to be everywhere. In the halls. On the furniture. In my sheets if I'm not careful. And my control isn't made for that.

Seth's mouth twitches like he can read the direction of my thoughts. "You keep doing that."

"What's that?" I ask, too fast.

"Looking at me like you're trying to decide if I'm going to bite." His gaze glides down, slowly, to my mouth and back up. "I might. Depends how you behave."

My breath catches, traitorous. "Is that a threat?"

His smile sharpens. "That's a promise I haven't decided to keep yet."

I swallow.

"Mm." He leans forward just a little, forearms on the table, closing the distance without touching me.

My fingers tighten around my cup.

His gaze holds mine, intent and almost lazy. "You're right about one thing. If somebody did that to me, if somebody messed with my head..." His voice dips, and the fun drains out of it. "I'm not letting it go."

The shift in him is sudden. Not louder. Just... colder. Controlled. Like there's a line inside him and once you cross it, you don't get to walk back.

I force myself to breathe. "So, what now?"

Seth's attention flicks to my hand on the cup, then back to my eyes. "Now I find out who." A beat passes. "And you stop looking like you're going to bolt every time a man looks at you like he wants you."

I give a little laugh. "You don't get to tell me what to do."

"No," he agrees easily. "I get to tell you what I'm going to do." His voice turns soft again, dangerous in a different way.

He reaches across the table then, not grabbing, not

trapping. Just a deliberate brush of his knuckles against my fingers, like he's testing the edge of my restraint.

The touch is brief. But it lights me up like a match. My pulse jumps. My skin tightens. And I hate how badly I crave more.

Seth's gaze moves to my throat. His mouth curves, satisfied.

My chest tightens, a sharp ache of truth I don't want to give him.

He watches me, then lets his smile turn slow. "Living with us," he adds, like he's testing the words on my reaction, "is going to be... nice."

My breath catches.

His phone buzzes on the table. Seth glances down, and the shift is subtle but immediate, the heat in his eyes tightening into focus. His brows draw together as he reads whatever popped up on the screen.

He exhales once, then stares back at me. "I gotta go."

Disappointment flares through me before I can hide it.

He stands, but before he moves away, he leans in just enough that his voice hits my ear like a promise. "See you later." His gaze holds mine. "At our place."

I watch him walk away, heart thudding, and all I can think is, *Am I really doing this?*

9

KAI

I take the corner into the ranch driveway doing about forty, tires screaming, gravel spraying, and I'm grinning like an idiot the whole time.

My electric-blue Mustang fishtails beautifully before I straighten her out, music still blasting through the speakers of some old rock song about wild hearts and open roads. I kill the engine and sit here for a second, drumming my fingers on the steering wheel, trying to contain the energy buzzing through my veins.

June is moving in.

June is moving in.

I've been repeating it to myself since I left the café, and it still doesn't feel real. The woman who's been driving me crazy since the moment she face-planted into my chest is going to be sleeping down the hall from me. Eating breakfast at the same table. Existing in my space. Our space.

The universe finally decided to cut me a break.

I climb out of the car in the late afternoon just as Carter appears on the wraparound porch of the ranch house, arms crossed, watching me with that knowing smirk he wears so well.

"You're going to destroy that transmission one of these days," he calls out.

"She's *my* car. And she loves the abuse."

The ranch house looms behind him, a gorgeous beast with enough land surrounding it that you can't see another building in any direction. I've stayed in a lot of places over the years of traveling with the circuit, but this one feels different. More like home than most.

When we're not on the road, the three of us have a place out in Colorado, in the middle of nowhere, just us and our horses and the kind of silence that lets you actually hear yourself think. We've got a team that takes care of things when we travel, which is more help than I usually want, but it's necessary when you're gone as much as we are.

Years of this life. Barely staying anywhere long enough to remember the street names. Never putting down roots because what's the point when you're leaving in several weeks anyway?

But fuck, I'm ready for something different. Something permanent.

And I'm starting to think June might be the key to all of it.

"You going to stand there staring at the sky, or you

going to tell me why you look like you just won the lottery?" Carter descends the porch steps, boots crunching on gravel.

"Better than the lottery." I pop the trunk. "Come help me with this."

He rounds the car and stops dead when he sees the contents.

The trunk is stuffed. Shopping bags crammed into every available inch, some of them overflowing, fabric and packaging spilling out in a riot of colors. Mostly pink. A lot of pink. Also some cream and white and soft lavender, but definitely a pink emphasis.

"What the hell did you buy?"

"Everything."

"That's not an answer."

"Everything that will make June smile." I start grabbing bags, loading up my arms.

"Everything that will make her feel like this is her place. Comfortable. Safe. Wanted."

Carter stares at me for a long moment. Then he starts laughing.

"You've lost your mind."

"Probably, but she's agreed to move in with us for a few weeks while the plumbing at her place is being fixed. And I'm making the most of it." I shove a bag into his arms. "Plus, there's a method to the madness. If she feels at home here, she'll relax. And if she relaxes..."

"Her true nature might slip out."

"Exactly." I wink at him. "See? Strategy."

"I see a man who spent what looks like too much money on throw pillows." He peers into one of the bags. "Pink fluffy cushions. And is this a faux-fur blanket?"

"Three with different textures. Women like options."

"They also like men who aren't completely unhinged."

"They like those of us who pay attention to what brings them happiness." I grab the last of the bags and click the trunk closed. "Now stop judging me and help me get her room ready."

We head toward the house, arms full of shopping bags, and I can't stop the grin spreading across my face. Carter notices, because he notices everything.

"You're really excited about this."

"Are you not?"

"I didn't say that. But I just learned about it."

Carter follows me up to the second floor, his boots heavy on the wooden steps. "I'm cautious."

"Bullshit. You're thrilled."

"I'm... interested."

"You're over the moon and trying to play it cool because that's your whole brand." I stop at the door to the best bedroom on the floor, the corner room with windows on two walls, an attached bathroom, and enough space for a king bed plus a sitting area. "But I saw your face at the fair and how you looked at her. You're just as gone as I am."

Carter doesn't deny it. He drops his bag with a thud and scans the room like he's assessing a stallion, or a fight, or both.

"This is Seth's room."

"Was Seth's room."

Carter's brows lift. "He's going to lose his shit."

"He'll survive." I step in and start unpacking without hesitation, pulling out cushions and blankets like I'm setting up camp in enemy territory. "June gets the best room. End of story."

Carter follows, slower, eyes narrowing as he takes in the details. "You moved his stuff."

"Sure did, without telling him."

Carter lets out a low sound, half laugh, half warning. "That's how you get buried."

I toss a pale pink cushion onto the bed, then another in cream. "He'll want to act civilized in front of June."

Carter steps closer, voice dropping. "You're doing this because you want her to be comfortable."

"Yeah."

"And because you're staking your claim," he adds, blunt as a hammer.

I pause, then keep arranging the cushions like I didn't just get called out. "Call it whatever you want." I continue decorating. The bed gets the full treatment—Egyptian cotton sheets in soft white, a fluffy duvet in pale blush, and then layers upon layers of blankets draped artfully across the foot and sides, just as I saw on Pinterest. The cushions pile up against the headboard in varying sizes and shades. I even bought some with little tassels because they looked cozy.

The sitting area in the room gets attention too, with a cream-colored throw for the small couch, a few more cushions, and a soft rug I found that looks like clouds. The bathroom already has towels, but I bought new ones in pink-and-white stripes because the ones Seth had were boring as hell.

"You got snacks too." Carter states the obvious, pulling items from another bag. "A lot of them."

"Quality over quantity. Or in this case, both." I take the snacks from him and arrange them on the chest of drawers. Fancy cookies, good chocolate, sea salt chips, gummy candies, a selection of nuts and dried fruit for when she wants something healthy. Mountain spring water in glass bottles because plastic is tacky.

"You've thought about this way too much," Carter says. "What happened to training for the rodeo?"

"I've thought about it exactly the right amount, and this is more important."

We step back and survey my work. The room has been completely transformed—what was once a perfectly nice but somewhat bland space now looks like something out of a magazine.

"It's very pink."

"She'll love it."

"You don't actually know that."

"I know she deserves to feel special." I cross my arms, satisfied. "And this room screams, *You are special, and we're thrilled you're here.*"

Carter opens his mouth to respond, but I hold up a finger. "Wait. Almost forgot. The pièce de résistance."

I grab the last bag and pull out my masterpiece. It's a body pillow. Full length. Custom printed. With my face on it. Well, my whole body, technically. A photo from one of our promotional shoots, printed life-size onto pillow fabric. I'm posed in full cowboy gear, with a hat, boots, jeans slung low on my hips, and a shirt unbuttoned all the way down, showing a good portion of my torso. The expression on my face is somewhere between smoldering and playful.

It's glorious.

Carter stares at it for a full five seconds before he loses it. "What the *fuck* is that?"

"It's me." I hold it up proudly. "In pillow form."

"Why does that exist?"

"So she won't miss me too much when I'm not around." I carry it to the bed and arrange it lovingly against the cushions. "See? Now she can cuddle with me even when I'm not here. Problem solved."

Carter is bent over, hands on his knees, laughing so hard that no sound is coming out. His whole body is shaking.

"You—" He gasps for air. "You actually—"

"Same-day rush order, as I had the photo on my

phone already. The print-shop guy nearly passed out when I told him I needed it in three hours."

"That is the wildest thing I have ever seen in my life."

"The most *thoughtful* thing you've ever seen." I adjust pillow-me's position so he's looking extra inviting. "She's going to love it."

Carter finally straightens up, wiping tears from his eyes. He walks over to the bed, stares down at the pillow, and then—without warning—grabs it and starts dancing with it.

"Oh, Kai," he says in a high-pitched voice, clearly meant to be June. "You're so handsome. I can't believe I get to hold you every night."

"Very funny."

"I just love your smoldering expression." He dips the pillow dramatically. "And the way your shirt is open. So mysterious. So sexy."

"Give him back."

"His name is Flat Kai. And he's mine now." Carter spins Flat Kai around, then looks at the pillow's face with exaggerated adoration. "We're going to be so happy together, Flat Kai. You understand me in ways Real Kai never could."

"You're disrespecting both me and my pillow self right now."

"Flat Kai doesn't mind." Carter holds the pillow at arm's length, studying it. "Actually, Flat Kai is pretty hot. Look at those abs. Did they airbrush these?"

"Those are my real abs, asshole."

"Sure they are." He runs a hand down the pillow's torso. "Hello, muscles I've never seen in real life..."

"I will end you."

"Flat Kai would never threaten me." He hugs the pillow close. "Flat Kai doesn't drive like a maniac or buy a hundred dollars' worth of pink throw rugs."

I lunge for the pillow, and Carter dodges, cackling, holding Flat Kai above his head like a trophy.

We're both laughing now, circling each other around the bed like idiots, when we hear it.

A car pulling up outside.

We freeze. Exchange a look. Then we're both diving for the window, shoving each other out of the way to peer through the glass.

June's sedan is parked in the driveway, and she's climbing out, stretching her arms above her head like she's been driving for hours. She's wearing a blue dress, fitted, with a belt at the waist, hitting mid-thigh, and cowboy boots. Her hair is loose around her shoulders, catching the late afternoon light, and from here, I study how low the neckline of the dress swoops.

"She's here," I breathe.

"I have eyes."

"She looks incredible."

"Again. Eyes."

She moves to the trunk of her car and starts pulling out bags, and Carter is already heading for the door, tossing the pillow back onto the bed.

"I'll help her with the luggage. You clean up the shopping bags so it doesn't look like a craft store exploded in here."

"Good call."

He's gone, boots thundering down the stairs, and I scramble to gather all the empty bags and packaging. I shove everything into the closet and then pause in front of the mirror to check my reflection.

Hair's a mess. Shirt's half unbuttoned. Good. I flex experimentally. Okay. Acceptable.

I hear voices drifting up from downstairs, Carter's easy laugh, June's lighter response. They're getting closer.

I position myself in the hallway outside her room, leaning against the wall in what I hope is a casual, effortlessly attractive pose. Then I reconsider and try a different angle. Then I cross my arms. Uncross them. Try one hand in my pocket, the other braced against the wall.

This is stupid.

Footsteps on the stairs.

I settle on leaning with one shoulder against the wall, arms crossed, head tilted slightly. Confident but approachable. Sexy but not trying too hard.

June appears at the top of the stairs, and I forget every pose I've ever practiced.

She's even more beautiful up close. The blue of her dress brings out those hazel eyes that have been haunting me since the moment I first saw them. The fabric pulls across her bust in a way that makes it very difficult to know where to look, and her legs in those boots go on for miles. She's got her hair tucked behind one ear, showing the curve of her neck, and I want to press my lips to that spot more than I've ever wanted anything.

Carter is behind her, carrying two roller bags, and the smug look on his face tells me he knows exactly what I'm thinking.

"Hey, doll," I manage, and my voice comes out rougher than I intended. "Welcome home."

Her lips curve into a smile. "You're having way too much fun with this, aren't you?"

"Absolutely zero idea what you mean." I push off the wall and gesture down the hallway. "Come on. Let me show you to your room."

"*My room.* That's still so weird to say."

"It won't be weird for long." I lead the way, hyper-aware of her presence behind me, the soft sound of her boots on the hardwood floor. "Fair warning, we may have gone a little overboard with the decorating."

I push open the door and step aside so she can enter.

She takes three steps into the room and stops dead. "Oh." Her voice is small. "That's... a lot of pink."

"Too much?"

"It's like a flamingo had a really productive day." But she's smiling as she says it, her eyes sweeping over the cushions and blankets and carefully arranged luxuries. "You did all this?"

"Wanted you to feel at home."

She moves farther into the room, trailing her fingers over the throw blankets, examining the snacks on the dresser. Then her gaze lands on the bed. Specifically, on Flat Kai.

Her laugh is sudden and loud, bright enough to light up the whole room. "Is that—"

"A body pillow. With my image on it. For your convenience."

"For my *convenience.*"

"When you're lonely and can't have the real thing." I wink. "I've got you covered, doll."

She walks over to the bed and picks up Flat Kai, holding him at arm's length. Her cheeks are flushed, her eyes sparkling with amusement and something else. Something warmer.

"This is hilarious and thoughtful. It's the most absurd gift anyone has ever given me."

I move closer. "Do you like it?"

She looks at the pillow. Then at me. Then back at the pillow. "I love it," she admits. "It's insane, but I love it."

"Then my work here is done."

Carter is standing in the doorway with her bags and a raised eyebrow. "Where do you want these?"

"Anywhere is fine." June sets Flat Kai down gently, arranging him against the pillows like he belongs there. "Thank you. Both of you. This is... way more than I expected."

Her voice is steady, but her hands aren't. She smooths the edge of the blanket twice, then touches her bag strap like she's checking that it's still there, like her body doesn't quite believe she's allowed to put things down. Her gaze keeps flicking to the door, the windows, the hallway, even while she's smiling.

"You're pack now," I say, and it comes out heavier than I meant. "Or at least, you're ours to take care of for the next few weeks. We don't do things halfway."

Something crosses her face. And under it, that aching little want she tries to swallow.

"I'm not—" She stops, throat working. Tries again, softer. "I don't want to be a burden."

"You couldn't be a burden if you tried." Carter sets her bags by the closet, then pauses like he's choosing his words carefully. His voice drops, steady and sure. "And you're safe here."

June blinks at him.

Carter doesn't look away. "Safe," he repeats, like he's planting it in the ground. "No one comes onto this property without us knowing."

Her breath trembles on the exhale, tiny and sharp, like her body has been holding it for years.

"Consider this your space," Carter adds, easing the edge off with a hint of humor. "Do what you want with it. Rearrange the furniture. Decorate. Throw out the creepy body pillow—"

"Hey," I protest automatically.

"—and make yourself at home."

June gives a small, helpless laugh, the kind that sounds like relief trying to disguise itself. Then she nods, more to convince herself than us, and some of the tightness slips out of her shoulders.

"Okay," she whispers. She inhales, then lets it out like she's stepping off a ledge. "Okay. I can do this."

"Take your time," I tell her. "Come down whenever you're ready. No rush."

We leave her there, surrounded by pink cushions and faux-fur blankets and one very handsome body pillow, and head downstairs.

The moment we hit the living room, I start pacing.

"She's here," I say, mostly to the walls. "She's actually here. In our house. Upstairs. Right now."

"I'm aware." Carter drops onto the couch, but his leg is already bouncing, fingers tapping the armrest like he's trying to bleed off energy. "What are we supposed to do now?"

"I don't know." I drag a hand through my hair. "Act normal."

Carter's mouth twitches. "What's normal for you? Because I'm pretty sure your normal is 'punch first, flirt second.'"

I glare at him. "Helpful."

My pacing slows for a beat. Then I start again, because my body doesn't know how to handle this much want and responsibility at the same time.

"I've never felt like this before," I admit.

Carter's gaze lifts to mine, and for once, he doesn't tease. "Me either."

We're both staring at the staircase like it might spontaneously combust when the front door opens and Seth walks in.

He takes one look at us and rolls his eyes.

"So she's moved in, then."

"She's upstairs," Carter confirms. "Getting settled."

"And you two are down here losing your minds."

"We're just... processing."

"You look like two kids who ate too much candy." But there's warmth underneath his sarcasm. "How is she? Did she like the guest room?"

"She loved your room," Carter says. "Said it was perfect."

Seth goes still. Just for a beat. Like his body has to decide whether to laugh or start swinging. "Say that again."

"Your room." I don't bother hiding my grin. "It was bigger. Nicer. She needed it."

"You gave her my room," Seth says, flat.

"I gave her the *best* room," I correct. "It just happened to have your stuff in it."

Seth stares at me for a long moment, then shifts his gaze to Carter like he's confirming that this isn't a hallucination.

Carter lifts a shoulder. "She liked it."

Seth exhales through his nose, slow and controlled.

"You're both lucky it's for June," he says at last. "If it were either of you pulling that move for yourselves, I'd drag your mattress outside and let the horses decide what to do with it."

"She really did like it," Carter adds.

Seth's expression shifts at that to something calmer. "Good."

"She laughed for five minutes when she saw the body pillow," I say, because I can't help myself.

Seth's head turns slowly. "The what?"

Carter's tone is dry. "Don't."

I grin wider. "Don't ask."

Seth holds my stare for a second, then decides he doesn't want that information in his life. He turns and heads for the kitchen. "If we've got a guest," he says, opening the fridge, "we feed her." He starts pulling things out, setting them on the counter like he's laying out tools. Efficient. No wasted motion. "Steaks," he says. "Potatoes. Salad."

"Sounds perfect," Carter replies and steps in, rinsing potatoes without being asked.

I grab a knife and a cutting board, grinning because, for the first time in years of traveling and never putting down roots, I'm starting to think the chase might finally be over.

Now the fun part begins.

10

Three ridiculously attractive cowboys are staring at me across a table loaded with enough food to feed a small village, and I'm trying very hard to act like this is normal.

Except, it's not. Nothing about my life right now is.

I'm seated at a large square table. Seth sits directly across from me with those intense blue eyes, Kai to my left, Carter to my right. The arrangement feels intentional, like they wanted to surround me, like I'm the center of their lives.

I'm definitely not complaining.

"The food smells incredible," I say, inhaling the aroma of perfectly seared steaks, buttery mashed potatoes, roasted vegetables, salad, and fresh bread. "I love home-cooked food more than anything, but living alone makes me lazy. Most nights it's scrambled eggs or whatever I can microwave in under three minutes."

"That's tragic," Kai says, already loading his plate like he hasn't eaten in weeks. "Food is one of life's greatest pleasures."

"Easy for you to say. You have a personal chef." I nod toward Seth, who's cutting into his steak.

His lips twitch. "Someone has to keep these two from starving."

"He's being modest," Carter adds, passing me the bowl of mashed potatoes. "Seth's the only reason we eat actual meals on the road. Without him, Kai and I would survive on gas station burritos and energy drinks."

"I resent that." Kai points his fork at Carter. "I can cook."

"You can burn things, which is different."

"I set a pan on fire once, and suddenly I'm banned from the kitchen forever."

"You set the *ceiling* on fire."

"In my defense, the smoke alarm was broken, so I had no warning."

"The warning was the flames shooting toward the ceiling."

"Details." He snorts, which turns into a chuckle.

I laugh, spooning more mashed potatoes onto my plate. They're impossibly creamy, rich with butter and garlic, and I could probably eat the entire bowl by myself. Except, I'm feeling a bit off where there's a low heat simmering under my skin that's been building since dinner started, but I figure some iron from a good steak and proper food is exactly what my body needs.

"So," I say, cutting into my meat, "the rodeo kicks off the day after tomorrow. When do you guys find time to train with everything else going on?"

"We make time," Seth answers. "Early mornings, sometimes late at night if we run out of time."

"You should come watch us sometime," Carter offers. "See what goes into it before the actual show."

"I'll definitely be at the rodeo. Already have my ticket." I take a bite of steak, which is perfectly cooked, pink in the middle, and have to stop myself from moaning out loud. "God, this is incredible."

"Just incredible?" Seth raises an eyebrow.

"Fine. Life-altering. I may never eat my own cooking again. You've ruined me for all other food." I fan myself dramatically. "Is it warm in here, or is it just the steak?"

Nobody answers, but I notice Kai and Carter exchange a quick glance.

"I went to a bull-riding event last year," I continue, ignoring whatever silent conversation they're having. "Local riders, nothing as big as your circuit, but it was amazing. The energy in the crowd, watching those guys hold on..."

"You'll have to introduce us to the local riders," Kai says. "Always good to meet the brave ones."

"Brave or crazy. Fine line in your profession."

"We prefer 'calculated risk-takers.'"

"I bet you do."

The conversation flows easily as we eat. I'm hyper-aware of the warmth spreading through my body, not just from the food, but from something deeper, like a low fever that keeps building. I take a sip of juice and try to focus on the meal, but there's a flush creeping up my neck that has nothing to do with the temperature of the room.

The guys keep reaching across the table, refilling my glass before it's empty, pushing dishes toward me, making sure I have everything I need. It's unspoken but obvious that they're taking care of me. Looking out for me.

I'd forgotten what that felt like.

The last time someone truly looked after me was years ago, when I was young and my parents handled everything. Now it's just me, navigating life alone, making my own decisions, and dealing with my own problems. Having three people actively invested in my comfort is... cozy and reassuring.

I'm about halfway through my steak when Seth asks, "So what is there to do in this town? Besides bars, cafés, farming, and rodeos."

"That pretty much sums it up." I grin, dabbing at my forehead with my napkin—when did I start sweating? "Though, more people have been moving in lately. Younger crowd. The town's growing, but at its core, it's still rural Montana."

"Any hidden gems?"

"Well, there's a book club at the local bookstore. Meets monthly." I shift in my seat, trying to get comfortable despite the warmth pooling in my stomach. "I usually go with my friend Sophia, who inherited a ranch last year when she moved here. Along with three cowboys, actually." I smirk at them. "Seems to be a pattern in this town."

The guys are watching me with varying degrees of interest, and I remind myself that I'm not chatting with Hazel. I need to filter.

"What kind of books?" Kai asks, leaning back in his chair with that troublemaker grin.

"Romance, mostly. We rotate through different subgenres."

"And you sit around discussing the men's... narrative structure?" He waggles his eyebrows. "Their character development? Their *butts*?"

Carter nearly chokes on his drink, laughing. "Okay, I need to hear more about this book club. Are applications open?"

My face floods with heat, and not just from the fever-like sensation that's been building all evening. Across the table, Seth just grins at me, slow and knowing and infuriatingly smug.

"Oh, I knew you and your friend were checking me out today," he says casually.

"You did not."

"Why do you think it took me so long to pick something up?" He takes a leisurely sip of his drink. "I could've been done in two seconds. But I had an audience, so I figured I'd give you something worth watching."

I stare at him. The quiet, brooding cowboy who barely spoke at the photo shoot is sitting across from me, looking like he just won a prize. So much for mysterious and reserved.

"You're shameless," I manage.

"I'm aware of my assets." He lifts his chin slightly, and there's a cockiness there I haven't seen before. "We're used to being watched. Might as well make it memorable."

I remember the night I picked him up from jail and how different he'd been with his guard down. Sweet and vulnerable and absolutely adorable. Right now, he's all confidence and control, but I've seen underneath that armor. I know what's really there.

"You're all used to the attention, aren't you?" I tease, pushing vegetables around on my plate. The heat under my skin is getting harder to ignore. It's spreading from my core outward, making my clothes feel too tight, my skin too sensitive. "All that practice being gawked at by adoring fans?"

"It's really not that much attention," Carter says modestly. "A few fans here and there."

"And the Reddit posts?" The words escape before I can stop them, and I immediately want to crawl under the table and die.

Kai's eyes light up. Seth chuckles under his breath. Carter looks surprised, then delighted.

"Well, shit," Carter says, grinning widely. "Sounds like someone's been doing research. Should I be jealous that Kai's getting all the online love?"

"So you saw the posts," Kai says, practically glowing with pride. "All of them?"

"I... heard about them."

"She's lying," Seth observes. "Look at her face. She saw everything."

My mind flashes to the image Hazel showed me, the very detailed illustration of Kai's cock with the Jacob's ladder piercing that apparently has its own devoted fan following. I'm blushing so hard I might actually spontaneously combust, and the heat already building in my body isn't helping.

"Fine," I admit, unable to meet anyone's eyes. "I may have seen one illustration."

"Of what, specifically?" Kai is preening now, leaning forward with obvious delight.

"Oh my God, stop. I'm not discussing this at the dinner table. Or ever. Can we please talk about literally anything else?"

"But you brought it up—"

Carter kicks him under the table. "Let her eat in peace. You can interrogate her later."

Kai laughs, holding up his hands in surrender.

The ache that's been simmering in my stomach sharpens, and I press a hand to my abdomen without thinking. The heat is constant now, waves of warmth rolling through me, making my skin feel too tight for my body. I pick at my remaining vegetables, trying to act normal, but there's sweat beading at my temples and my hands aren't quite steady.

What is wrong with me?

"You okay?" Carter asks, studying me with sudden concern. "You look flushed."

"Just full." I wipe my forehead with my napkin, trying to play it off. "Think I'm going to sit on the couch for a bit."

"Do you want dessert?" Seth offers. "There's apple cobbler. Ice cream."

God, that sounds amazing, but my stomach twists at the thought. The ache is deeper now, pulsing with each heartbeat. "Maybe later. I just need to rest."

I push back from the table and stand, and the room tilts.

My legs feel like they're made of jelly. There's a tremor running through my whole body, and the heat has spread everywhere now. My skin and insides are burning. I feel like I'm running a fever and freezing at the same time.

I make it to the couch and sink into the cushions, pressing a hand to my forehead. Definitely burning up. The ache in my stomach is intensifying, radiating outward into my limbs, and I have to close my eyes against another wave of discomfort.

What is happening to me?

I hear the guys moving around, dishes being cleared, water running, the sounds of cleanup. I focus on breathing, trying to will the strange symptoms away. It's probably just exhaustion. Stress. The chaos of the last few days catching up with me.

Except it felt like this last night too. And a bit the night before.

Footsteps approach. When I open my eyes, Seth is there with a cold, damp kitchen towel. He presses it gently to my forehead, and the coolness is such a relief that I actually whimper.

"This should help," he says, his voice softer than before. "Are you feeling sick?"

Carter appears with a steaming mug. "Chamomile tea. Thought it might help."

Kai is hovering behind them, his usual playfulness replaced by genuine worry. "What can we do? Tell us what you need."

I stare at the three of them, surrounding me with care and attention, and something in my chest aches for entirely different reasons than my body.

"The last couple of nights," I admit, "I've had these sharp pains. All over. And I keep getting really hot, like I'm running a fever that won't break." I shake my head. "But I'm sure it's nothing. Probably just exhaustion from everything that's been happening."

"You should rest," Seth says firmly. "In a bed. Not on a couch."

"That's what I'm trying to—"

I start to stand, and my legs buckle.

Carter catches me before I hit the floor, his arms wrapping around me with surprising gentleness. And then he's lifting me, scooping me up like I weigh nothing, cradling me against his chest.

"Come on," he says. "I'll carry you up."

"I can walk—"

"You almost just face-planted into the coffee table. Let me help."

I don't have the energy to argue. And honestly? Being held by him feels... incredible. The moment his arms wrapped around me, something in my body settled. The burning sensation is still there, but it's muted now. Manageable. Like his touch is somehow dampening the flames.

I let myself lean into his chest, inhaling the scent of him, and the ache in my stomach eases another fraction. I exhale with relief.

"That actually feels better," I murmur, surprised.

Seth and Kai are watching us with concern etched into their features.

"Don't worry," I tell them, trying for reassuring and probably sounding pathetic. "I'm fine. Really."

Neither of them looks convinced, but they let Carter carry me toward the stairs.

Up in my room, the pink explosion of cushions and blankets and that ridiculous Kai body pillow are waiting on the bed. Carter sets me down gently on the mattress, then shoves the pillow aside with one hand, making room.

The moment he steps back, no longer touching me, the pain returns with a vengeance.

It's sharp, stabbing, deep in my core, and radiating outward like lightning. I gasp and curl in on myself, one hand pressed to my stomach, the other reaching blindly for something—anything—to hold on to.

"June?" Carter's voice is alarmed. "What's wrong?"

My hand finds his, and I grab on, lacing my fingers through his desperately. The contact is instant relief, not complete, but enough that I can breathe again. Enough that the world stops spinning.

"Please don't go," I whisper.

His expression softens. He doesn't pull away. Instead, he settles onto the edge of the bed beside me, his thumb stroking across my knuckles.

"I'm not going anywhere," he says quietly. "I'm all yours."

I hold on to him, not ready to let go, not understanding what's happening to my body but knowing his presence makes it bearable. The burning is still there, simmering under my skin, but it's not consuming me anymore. Not while he's touching me.

"Your company makes me feel better," I admit. "I don't know why. You make the pain stop. Or at least... dim."

He grins, and God, he's gorgeous. All golden

warmth and easy charm, with those green eyes that seem to see right through me.

"I've heard Alpha presence can help," he says lightly. "Touch, proximity... it's supposed to be calming for Omegas. Especially when they're hurting."

"Yeah, very funny." But my laugh comes out shaky because what if he's right? What if that's exactly what's happening?

I press my hip against his on the bed, seeking more contact, and the ache dims further. My body is reacting to him. To his Alpha presence, and Betas don't react like this. Which means...

No. I can't think about that right now.

"Let's not talk about that," I say quickly. "Please."

"Of course." His voice is gentle. No pushing, no prying. Just acceptance.

He sits with me in comfortable silence. I'm trembling from the implications, because if Carter's touch is soothing my body this way, if his presence is putting out whatever fire is building inside me...

Then my Omega isn't dormant anymore.

And that thought terrifies me more than the pain. Because I convinced myself years ago that I'd never be enough for an Alpha pack. Accepted that heats and bonds weren't in my future. Built my entire identity around being a Beta who didn't need any of that.

What happens if it's all been a lie?

"You seem very deep in thought," Carter observes. "Anything I can do to lighten the load?"

I breathe heavily, holding on to him like a lifeline. "Have you ever felt like your whole life was based on something that turned out to be wrong? Like you believed something for so long, built everything around it, and then suddenly it might not be true and you don't know who you are anymore?"

He stays quiet at first. "That's a heavy question for a Wednesday night."

"I know." I laugh shakily. "Let's not unpack it. I'm just... That's where I'm at right now."

"Okay." He doesn't push, doesn't demand explanations. Just sits with me, his presence warm and steady. "You know what I do when I feel like everything's falling apart?"

"What?"

"I write."

I twist to look at him. "Like what?"

"Poetry, mostly." He shrugs, almost appearing self-conscious. "Nothing fancy. Just a few lines here and there when I need to get something out of my head."

"You're telling me a rodeo star writes poetry? No way."

"We all need an outlet." His eyes meet mine, and there's a vulnerability there I haven't seen before. "No one else sees them. It's just for me."

"Tell me one."

"I don't really remember them off the top of my head—"

"Liar. Tell me."

He goes quiet, his gaze drifting somewhere distant. When he speaks, his voice is softer:

"The arena holds its breath for those who fall, but silence doesn't mean forgetting. Some hoofbeats echo longer than the ride, some dust never quite settles, and I still count to eight every time the gates swing open."

The words hang in the air between us. I think about them, the weight of them, the grief buried underneath. Counting to eight. The time a rider has to stay on. Someone who fell and didn't get back up.

"That's beautiful," I say quietly. "And heartbreaking."

"Yeah." His voice is rough. "It helps, though. Getting it out."

I want to ask who he lost, to understand what he's carrying. But this doesn't feel like the right moment, so instead I ask, "Would you write me a poem?"

He looks surprised. "You want me to?"

"Yes. I'm curious what you'd say about me."

His gaze drops to my lips, then back up. The air between us feels electric. Charged.

"How about I think about it?" he says softly. "And I promise I will."

I smile. The pain is still there, lurking, but his presence keeps it at bay.

"Hey," he says after a moment. "Do you mind if I get onto the bed properly? I can hold you better if I'm lying behind you."

I should say no. Should keep some distance. But

the thought of him letting go, of losing that contact, makes my chest tight with something close to panic.

"Okay," I whisper.

Carter stands and kicks off his boots. The moment he breaks contact, the ache sharpens, deep in my gut and lower still, a burning that's equal parts pain and desire. I groan, curling in on myself, squeezing my eyes shut against the intensity.

This is bad. This is really, really bad.

Then the bed dips behind me, and his arms are wrapping around me, one sliding under my neck so my head rests on his bicep, the other draping over my waist. His chest presses against my back, warm and solid. His hips settle against mine.

And God help me, even through the pain, I feel the spark of something hot and wanting that has nothing to do with fever. His body is hard against mine, all muscle and heat, and some primal part of me wants to press back into him. Wants more. Wants everything.

I bite my lip and try to focus on the relief instead of the arousal.

"Better?" His breath is warm against my cheek.

"Yeah." I let myself sink into him, surrounded by his warmth and his scent. "Thank you."

"No need to thank me, June. Sometimes we just need someone to hold us."

I close my eyes, letting myself float in the sensation of being held. Cared for. Protected. The fire is still stirring inside me for him, for this, for things I've been told

I could never have, but right now, I just want to exist in this moment.

"You smell incredible," I murmur, breathing him in deeply. "Like... safety. Like something I didn't know I was missing."

His arms tighten around me. "Get some rest. I'll be right here."

The darkness comes slowly, pulling me under, and the last thing I'm aware of is his heartbeat against my back and the lingering scent soothing me.

11

JUNE

Sunlight pours through the windows like the universe is mocking me with its cheerfulness.

I blink awake slowly, wrapped in the softest blanket I've ever felt, surrounded by approximately forty-seven pink cushions and one very judgmental body pillow I'm currently snuggling. The room and house are quiet. And the space beside me on the bed is empty.

Carter is gone. And so is my pain.

But I remember him staying, the weight of his arm around my waist, the steady rhythm of his breathing against my neck, the way his scent wrapped around me. I recall the pain fading whenever he touched me and returning like a knife whenever he pulled away.

It was the safest I've felt in a long time.

I sit up slowly, testing my body. The ache is barely there, a low simmer deep within me, but it's manageable now. Nothing like the stabbing agony of last night. Maybe sleep helped. Or maybe the suppressants I didn't take this morning could have made everything worse.

I stare at my bag across the room, where my pill bottle is tucked into the side pocket. Every morning for seven years, I've taken those little white tablets without question. Swallowed them down with water and went about my day, pretending to be something I'm not.

But last night changed things.

Last night, an Alpha's touch eased pain that nothing else could. My body responded to Carter in ways that Betas simply don't.

Face it, June. You know what this means.

I force myself to think it through.

If I take the suppressants, I can keep pretending. Keep the walls up, with everyone, including myself, convinced that I'm just a boring Beta with no designation drama. But the pills might be what's making me sick. The cramping, the fever, the feeling like my insides are trying to claw their way out—what if years of suppressing my Omega have finally caught up with me?

My stomach twists. If I don't take them, my scent will grow stronger around Alphas. The guys will notice. Questions will start. And I'll have to face the truth I've been running from since I was eighteen years old.

That I'm an Omega who was told she'd never be enough.

My parents meant well. I know they did. When the doctors diagnosed me as *dormant*—unlikely to ever experience heats or form proper bonds—my mom and dad did what they felt was best for me so I didn't suffer judgment.

And I believed them because the alternative was admitting that I was broken. Defective. An Omega who couldn't do the one thing Omegas were supposed to do.

So I took the pills, buried my designation, and built an identity around being unremarkable.

But these three men don't look at me like I'm unre-markable. They look at me like I'm everything.

And that terrifies me more than any pain ever could.

I let out a long exhale and make a decision. No suppressants today. If the pain comes back around the guys, I'll know for certain what's causing it. And if it doesn't...

Well. I'll figure that out when I get there.

First priority is keeping some distance. I need space to let my body settle without Alpha influence. Space to think without drowning in their scents and their smiles and the way they make me feel like I'm standing in sunlight after years of shade.

I grab my phone and pull up a new group chat,

adding Carter's and Kai's numbers from when they gave them to me at the carnival.

June: *Just heading into town for a bit. I'm sure you three can behave while I'm gone.* 😊

The response is almost immediate.

Carter: *You feeling okay this morning?*

Kai: *She's ALIVE!* 🎉 *Was worried we'd have to send in a search party. Or a rescue kiss.*

June: *Interesting!*

I smirk to myself.

Kai: *It's like a rescue breath but better. More tongue.*

Carter: *Please ignore him. He hasn't had coffee yet.*

Kai: *I've had THREE. This is me at peak performance.*

June: *Terrifying.*

Kai: *You're welcome.* 😇

Carter: *Seriously, though, how are you feeling? You had us worried last night.*

I stare at the screen, warmth spreading through my chest despite my best efforts to stay detached.

June: *Better. Just need some fresh air and normal human interaction.*

Kai: *We're not normal?*

June: *You literally had a body pillow made of yourself.*

Kai: *And you snuggled pillow-me?*

Carter: *That's called "concerning."*

Kai: *You're just jealous that Flat Carter doesn't exist.*

Carter: *I have never been less jealous of anything in my life.*

June: *You two are hilarious. I'll see you later.*

Kai: *Miss you already, doll.*

Carter: *Drive safe.*

I set the phone down, smiling despite myself, and head for the shower.

The hot water feels incredible, washing away the remnants of last night's fever, clearing my head. I stand under the spray longer than necessary, trying not to think about the fact that I'm in the guys' house, using their bathroom, existing in their space.

When I finally emerge, I dig through my bag for something to wear. My hand lands on a dress I packed almost as an afterthought, red with short sleeves, buttons down the front, falling halfway down my thighs, and a belt at the waist. It's pretty without being too formal.

I pull it on, add my cowboy boots, and check my reflection in the mirror. The color brings out the warmth in my skin, and the belt accentuates my waist in a way that makes me feel... good. Feminine. Like myself, whoever that is anymore.

I grab my keys and head downstairs, moving quickly through the quiet house. The guys are probably out training for the rodeo, and I should be able to slip away without any awkward—

I stop dead at the back window.

The view overlooks the horse corral, where a wild bronco is bucking like its life depends on it. And on that bronco's back, one hand gripping the rope, the other thrown up for balance, is Kai.

Shirtless.

Even from this distance, I can see the muscles in his back flexing with each violent movement. The tribal tattoo sleeve rippling as he adjusts his grip. The way his body moves with the horse, wild, fearless, completely in control even as the animal does everything possible to throw him.

Seth and Carter are perched on the wooden fence, looking ready to jump in if needed, shouting encouragement I can't hear through the glass. Seth is wearing a dark T-shirt that stretches across his shoulders, his cowboy hat pulled low. Carter is laughing at something, golden hair fluttering in the breeze.

They look like a photograph, like something out of a fantasy.

And I need to leave before my body decides to betray me again.

I force myself to turn away from the window and walk out the front door. Every step feels like fighting against a current that wants to drag me back to them.

But I can't let myself get swept away when they're leaving in a few weeks. Not when I have a life here, a business, a home (water-damaged as it currently is), friends who depend on me. I've built something in this town. Something that's mine.

Scent match or not, some things just aren't meant to be.

I'm halfway to town when my phone rings through the car speakers. Mom.

I hit Accept with a sigh. "Hey, Mom."

"June, darling! I was just thinking about you." Her voice is warm, familiar, with that slight Texas drawl she picked up after moving to Dallas years ago. "How are you? How's the house? Did you get that leak fixed?"

"Working on it. I'm staying with some... friends while the repairs happen."

"As long as you're okay."

"I am."

"Darling, you know your father and I worry about you. All alone in that little town, so far from family..."

"I'm not alone. I have friends here. A community."

"But no partner. No one to take care of you."

"I can take care of myself."

"Of course you can." Her voice softens. "You've always been so independent. So determined. But, sweetheart, you can't stay in that town forever. You proved you can run a business beautifully, but maybe it's time to think about joining us in Dallas. There are so many lovely Beta men here we could introduce you to. You wouldn't have to be alone anymore."

I grip the steering wheel tighter. "I'm fine, Mom."

"You always say that."

"Because it's always true."

A long pause.

"Darling, I need to tell you something." Her tone shifts—heavier, more serious. "Your father... well, you know he let you take over the business because you insisted. Because you were so passionate about it. But he always planned to sell eventually."

My stomach drops.

"The business, sweetheart."

"Mom, that's my business. I've been running it for four years."

"Your father owns the building, darling. And the company name. Legally, it's still his."

She's right. I know she's right. When I took over, Dad kept everything in his name because I was young and unproven and he wanted to protect me if things went wrong. I was supposed to buy him out eventually, but the right moment never seemed to come, and now—

"I'll buy it from him," I say quickly. "I'll figure it out. Take out a loan, whatever I need to do."

"June, my sweet girl..." Mom's voice cracks slightly. "He can get much more from investors than he could ever ask you for. And we need the money. Your father invested in something that... well, it didn't work out. We're in a difficult position."

My heart sinks. "How difficult?"

"Enough that we need to sell or we lose our home here."

I pull over to the side of the road because I can't drive and process this at the same time. My hands are shaking.

"What about the money I send you every month? The percentage from the sales?"

Mom is quiet at first. "Your father invested that too. It's... it's gone, darling. I'm so sorry."

The betrayal sits heavily on my chest. Years of working, building, sending money to them, thinking I was helping, and he just... gambled it away on some investment scheme.

"So what happens now?" My voice sounds hollow.

"He's going to find buyers for it." She takes a shaky breath. "Think about moving to Dallas, sweetheart. We miss you so much. You could start over here. Fresh beginning."

"I'm not moving to Dallas, Mom."

"I love you, June. More than anything."

"I know, Mom. I love you too." I sigh heavily.

I hang up and sit here in the silence, staring at the road ahead.

Everything is falling apart. My body. My home. My business. The careful life I've built is crumbling around me, and I don't know how to stop it. Shit!

I don't recall how long I've been sitting here, idling on the side of the road, but I start driving again until I find myself parking in front of The Rusty Spur, knowing that Hazel is here most mornings.

So I get out and drag myself in there, spotting her at a table in the middle of the room with an open laptop, her blonde-and-pink hair pulled into a high ponytail.

She glances up at me. "You look like death warmed over," she announces as I slide into the seat across from her. "You okay, hon?" She gets up and gives me a big hug before I can stop her. Then she pulls back, and her brow furrows as she sits down again. "Why does your scent smell different?"

"I need to tell you something." The words come out in a rush. "Please don't be upset with me. I should have told you years ago, but I convinced myself it didn't matter, and this whole week has been chaos, and I think the universe is finally done letting me pretend—"

"Breathe." Hazel reaches across the table and grabs my hand. "Whatever it is, just tell me."

I take a shaky breath. "I'm an Omega."

She blinks.

"Or I was. Or I am. I don't know anymore." The words tumble out faster now, seven years of secrets spilling onto the sticky bar table. "When I was younger, doctors diagnosed me as dormant. Said I'd probably never have heats, never form proper bonds. My parents convinced me it would be easier to just... take suppressants to conceal my Omega side and pretend to be a Beta. Avoid all the complications of a designation that didn't work properly anyway."

"June..."

"I know I should have told you. But I wanted to believe it myself? Wanted to just be normal and uncomplicated and not have to deal with any of it." I swallow hard. "And then those three Alphas rolled into town, and suddenly my suppressants are making me sick and my body is doing things it's never done before, and I think they might have woken something up inside me that was supposed to stay asleep."

Hazel is quiet for a long moment. Then she stands up again, comes around to my side of the table, and pulls me into a fiercer hug. "Oh, hon." Her voice is thick. "I'm so sorry. That must have been so lonely."

I didn't realize how much I needed to hear those words until tears were spilling down my cheeks.

"I didn't know who I was supposed to be," I whisper. "My parents made it sound so easy—just take the pills and live a normal life. But it wasn't easy. It was pretending every single day. Hiding. Lying to everyone, including myself."

She strokes my hair. "I know."

We stay like that for a moment before she pulls back, keeping hold of my hands.

"Okay. Tell me about the guys and how they're impacting you. Tell me everything."

So we take our seats and I let it all out. The way their scents overwhelm me. The pain that flares when I'm near them and fades when they touch me. Last night with Carter and how his presence was the only thing that made the agony bearable.

"I think they're my scent matches," I admit. "All three of them."

Hazel nods slowly. "That would explain a lot."

"But what am I supposed to do about it when they leave? I have a life here, or I did, before everything started falling apart. And even if I told them the truth, what then? I'm a dormant Omega. I might never go into heat properly. And maybe I'll never be able to give them what they need."

"You don't know that."

"The doctors—"

"Doctors are wrong all the time." She squeezes my hands. "Listen, I'm an Omega. I know what this pull feels like. When I found my fated mate at eighteen, it was like the entire world narrowed down to just him. Nothing else mattered. Nothing else existed."

I nod, knowing she's experienced a tragic past.

Her expression flickers—pain, then acceptance. "I told you before he passed away. Car accident. I was nineteen."

"So sorry."

"It was a long time ago." She takes a breath. "It took me years to feel normal again. To want anything. That's why I don't do serious relationships anymore—can't risk that kind of loss again. But I know how intense that attraction is. How impossible it is to fight. And if you're feeling that, then this is the real thing."

"So what do I do?"

"Talk to them." She says it like it's simple. "Tell them the truth. Let them decide what they want. Besides, from what I've seen, those boys are already gone for you. Scent match or not, dormant or not, they look at you like you hung the moon."

"Around them, I lose my ability to think. I just stand there drooling like an idiot. How am I supposed to have a serious conversation when my brain shuts off every time they get close?"

Hazel laughs. "Yeah, that part is hard. The first few weeks with my mate, I could barely string two words together. But it gets easier. The intensity levels out eventually."

"Eventually."

"A few months. Maybe a year."

"Fantastic."

She's on her feet. "Gonna order us something to eat and drink."

It doesn't take long for the simple bar food to arrive, and while we eat, she tells me more about her experiences as an Omega—the good parts and the hard parts, the things no one warns you about. It helps, somehow. Knowing I'm not alone in this.

"Okay," she says eventually, pushing her empty plate aside. "Enough heavy stuff. I need to show you something that will make you laugh."

She reopens her laptop and connects it to the bar's main TV screen—she's friends with the owner, apparently—and starts scrolling through photos.

"These are from the carnival shoot. The official ones." She flips through images of the guys posing with fans, looking professional and devastatingly handsome. "But then I got bored and started playing around."

She clicks to the next image, and I burst out laughing.

It's me, Kai, and Carter standing in front of the Eiffel Tower. We're posed like tourists, Kai throwing up a peace sign, Carter with his arm around my shoulders, me grinning at the camera. Behind us, clearly photo-shopped in, is Seth on horseback, looking stoic and slightly confused.

"Oh my God."

"Wait, it gets better."

The next one shows us at the Egyptian pyramids. Seth is still on his horse, now wearing a pharaoh's headdress that Hazel has crudely drawn in. The photo after that is the Great Wall of China. Then the Grand Canyon. Then what appears to be the surface of the moon.

"Hazel." I'm crying with laughter. "These are hilarious."

She clicks through more. "Look, here you are at the Taj Mahal. And here's one where I put Seth on a surfboard in Hawaii."

I hear the door open behind us. "What in the hell am I looking at?" a familiar male voice calls out across the empty bar.

I spin around. Seth is standing in the entrance, hat

in hand, staring at the TV screen where his photo-shopped face is currently surfing a twenty-foot wave.

He strolls closer, studying the image with an expression somewhere between disbelief and amusement.

"Is that me?"

"No, that's your doppelganger who happens to be really good at surfing," Hazel deadpans.

"I heard you both cackling from out on the side-walk." He slides into the seat next to me, his thigh pressing against mine, and nods at the screen. "Show me more."

Hazel grins and starts clicking through. Seth watches each image with growing amusement, occa-sionally snorting or shaking his head.

"I'm impressed I made it to Egypt," he says when the pyramid one comes up. "On my horse, no less. That's dedication."

"You're a man of many talents," I say.

"Apparently." He turns to glance at me, and I realize too late how close we are. His blue eyes are warm, irresistible. My face heats. Seth's gaze hasn't left mine.

"You smell different today," he says quietly, low enough that Hazel might not hear.

I look away. "Do I?" I say, playing dumb.

"Stronger. Sweeter." He pauses. "Like yourself."

I don't know how to respond to that. Don't know

how to handle the intensity in his eyes or the way my body is leaning toward him without permission.

"Why are you in town?" I ask, changing the subject. "Shouldn't you be training?"

"Had to meet with my lawyer. The sheriff is trying to move my court date to the same day as my main ride next week. We're getting it pushed back."

I should pull away, put some distance between us before my body does something embarrassing. But his closeness feels so grounding and steadying that I can't bring myself to move.

Seth's eyes shift to the bar, then back to me like he's making a decision. "I'm going to grab a drink," he says, low. "You want anything?"

"I'm fine," I manage, which is a lie. I'm not fine. I'm sitting here trying to act normal while his scent keeps teasing me.

He pushes to his feet, and I study him as he goes, because I can't help it. At the bar, the owner leans in, and they start talking like they've got history. Seth laughs once, shakes his head, says something I can't hear, and it turns into one of those conversations that drags on.

I'm still watching when the TV mounted on the wall with Hazel's photos starts flickering.

Then snaps to black-and-white, grainy, security-style footage.

Seth reappears at our table fast, sliding in beside me, eyes already locked on the screen. He leans forward, forearms on the table, and his voice goes quieter than the music.

"That's from the night I was here," he says. "The night I remember up to the first drink... and then nothing."

The air shifts around us. We all go still, attention pulled up to the silent footage.

On the screen, Seth approaches the bar, looking sober and steady. The place is packed, bodies every-where, people pushing to get closer to the circuit star who just walked in.

And there, hanging on his arm like she belongs there, is a woman.

Dark hair. Pale eyes. Dressed in something tight and low-cut. She's pressed against Seth's side, touching his shoulder, his arm, leaning into him with aggressive familiarity. There are a couple of other women behind him.

Something hot and sharp twists in my chest.

You're jealous of a woman in security footage from days ago. Get it together, June.

"She wouldn't leave me alone," Seth mutters, watching his past self try to create distance. "I remember that much."

On the screen, Seth orders his drink. The bartender sets what looks like a Coke in front of him. He turns to respond to someone calling his name from behind—

And the woman's hand moves toward his glass.

"There." The bar owner pauses the footage. "Did you see that?"

We all lean closer. It's not definitive—she could be reaching for her own drink, could be stretching, could be doing a dozen innocent things. But the timing and angle are suspicious.

"She could have spiked your drink," I say.

"That chick looks super familiar," Hazel admits. "I swear I've seen her."

She's hunching over her laptop, scrolling through photos, then turns it toward us. "I knew I'd seen her. She was at the carnival too. I remember her face." We're staring at the same dark hair, the ice-blue eyes, lurking in the background of one of the fan photos. "You guys might have a stalker," she adds.

"She needs to move the hell on," Seth says.

"Who is she?" I ask.

He shakes his head. "I barely remember her."

Then he's already moving, pushing back from the table and heading for the bar with that purposeful stride, like the footage lit a fire under him. He leans in to speak to the owner.

"Can you send that footage to my lawyer?" he asks loud enough for us to hear him this time.

The owner nods without hesitation. "Of course. I can do it now."

Seth pulls his phone out, already typing, already in work mode.

Hazel nudges my side with her elbow, and I look at her, brows raised. She's grinning like a troublemaker. Then she makes an exaggerated kissy face and flicks her fingers toward Seth's back like she's launching me at him.

I clamp my mouth shut to keep from laughing out loud, but a giggle still slips out.

Hazel's eyes sparkle. She mouths, *Talk to him, touch him.*

I glare at her, but it's weak, and she knows it.

A minute later, Seth returns to the table, sliding back into his seat like he never left, only his focus is sharper now, the edges of him drawn tight.

"Just gotta step out and talk to my lawyer," he says. "Then I'm going to swing by the station and get this in front of them."

Hazel nods, all business. Then his attention shifts to me, and for half a second, he hesitates like this part isn't as easy as dealing with footage and police.

"June," he says, quieter, "can I ask a favor?"

"Depends," I tease, trying to keep it light.

He clears his throat. "I came here with my lawyer, and he's gone. Any chance I could catch a ride back to the ranch with you?"

Hazel makes a noise that is absolutely not a cough and absolutely a laugh.

"Of course," I answer immediately. "We were just finishing up anyway."

The corners of Seth's mouth lift, and he's so handsome that I lose my thoughts. "Take your time. I'll wait for you."

Then he rises, phone in hand, and heads for the door to make the call.

The second his back is turned, Hazel leans in, eyes bright. "Oh, yeah," she whispers, grinning. "You'll wait for that piece of candy."

I choke on a laugh. "Hazel."

She laughs too, quiet and wicked, and I can't help laughing with her as Seth disappears outside.

12

She's trying to pretend I can't smell her, and it's the most adorable thing I've ever witnessed.

June walks beside me toward her car, keys jingling in her hand, and I'm fighting not to grin like an idiot. Because something has changed since this morning. Something fundamental. The scent that's been driving me crazy since the moment we met—lemon zest and honey and wildflowers—is stronger now. Clearer. Like someone lifted a veil I didn't even know was there.

"Thanks again for the ride," I say as we reach her sedan. "I owe you."

"You don't owe me anything." She unlocks the doors, and I fold myself into the passenger seat, suddenly very aware of how small this car is. How close we are. How her scent is filling the enclosed space like it's staking a claim.

She slides into the driver's seat and reaches for the ignition, but my hand covers hers on the gearshift, and she freezes.

"Are you okay?" I ask.

"Fine. Why?"

"Because something's different." I study the flush on her cheeks, the way she won't quite meet my eyes. "Since that night at the jail, I could barely catch your scent. It was there, but muted. Like trying to hear music through a wall." I inhale slowly, letting her fill my lungs. "Now it's like someone turned the volume all the way up and it's controlling me."

She swallows. I'm watching her closely, and I see the moment she realizes she can't bluff her way out of this. Her shoulders tense. Her grip tightens on the steering wheel.

And I can't help it. I grin.

"Don't smile like that," she says quickly.

"Like what?"

"Like you're up to something and you know something I don't want you to know."

"Maybe I do." I quirk an eyebrow.

She stares at me for half a second, then starts up the car and lunges for the window controls. All four windows roll down simultaneously, cool morning air rushing into the car like she's trying to air out a crime scene.

I laugh out loud.

"It's okay," I tell her. "I fucking love how you smell. It's everything. I want to drown in it."

"Don't say that."

"Why not? It's true."

"Because—" She cuts herself off. "I have something to tell you, and you saying things like that makes it harder."

We pull away from the curb and head down the main road, wind whipping through the open windows. It's breezy and cool, but I don't complain. If she needs the buffer, I'll give it to her. For now.

We drive for a while, and she hasn't said a word, so I figure I'll try to break the ice. "You know," I say after a moment, "I know almost nothing about you."

"Maybe that's for the best."

"Not really." I shift in my seat, turning to face her more fully. "Tell me something."

She's quiet at first. "My parents live in Dallas. They keep calling, trying to convince me to move down there permanently."

"And?"

"And they want me to sell the real estate business." Her hands tighten on the wheel. "Technically, it's their business. My dad owns the building and the company name. I just... run it."

"But you built it."

"Yeah, I did." She glances at me, then back at the road. "They need money. My dad made some bad investments., so they're selling, and I'm just supposed to... let it go. Move to Dallas. Start over."

"Is that what you want?"

"Hell no." The words come out sharp. Certain. "But what I want doesn't seem to matter much these days."

She exhales hard, like she's been holding her breath, and glances at me again. "God, that was intense, wasn't it?"

"Nah." I shrug. "It was fine."

She laughs. "You're such a bad liar."

"So I've been told."

The tension in her shoulders eases slightly. "Okay, your turn. What did the lawyer say about the video evidence?"

"Well, I ended up on a phone call with him and the sheriff as he watched the footage. And he said they'll look into it, as it's difficult to tell from the footage if she actually spiked my drink or was just reaching for something on the bar. They need more to go on."

"Damn." June frowns, still staring at the road like she can rewind the footage with sheer stubbornness. "We need to find that girl."

"And do what?" I ask. "She's not going to show up and confess out of the goodness of her heart that she drugged me."

"No," she says, warming to the idea. "But we can do some spying. Figure out who she is. Why she targeted you."

I glance over at her and immediately regret it,

because the dress she's wearing has ridden higher than it should from all the shifting. The hem is sitting all the way up now, showing too much skin, and my brain doesn't know what to do with that besides spiral.

I force my gaze back to the road.

I laugh once, low. "I'm in. Always wanted to play detective."

"I'll get you a magnifying glass." Then she grins, and it does something criminal to her whole face. Like she forgets to guard herself for a second. Like she's just... June.

The wind keeps rushing through the open windows, cold enough to bite without being mean about it. It's spring, but Montana doesn't care what the calendar says. It smells like cut grass and wet earth and the kind of air that gets in your lungs and makes you feel too awake.

I clear my throat. "Can we close the windows now?"

"Nope." She doesn't even glance at me. "I like it."

"It's cold."

"It's brisk," she corrects, like that makes it charming.

"My ears are going to hate you."

She finally looks over, eyes bright with mischief. "You'll survive."

"I'm not convinced," I mutter.

June's gaze shifts my way like she's trying not to

smile. "You've got that tough cowboy thing going. I'm sure your ears can handle a little weather."

If she knew what I was actually trying to handle right now, she'd stop teasing. Or maybe she wouldn't. That's the problem. I can't tell with her.

My attention drops again before I can stop it, tracking the line of her throat, the smooth skin where her collarbone disappears under the neckline of her dress, the gorgeous curve of her breasts.

My cock gives a throb, and it's taking every bit of restraint I've got to keep my hands and my thoughts off her thighs.

She shifts in her seat, and the dress rides up another inch.

Then she speaks again, softer. "Do you have time?" she asks. "There's this place I go sometimes when everything feels like it's falling apart." She hesitates like she hates needing anything. "And you seem like you could use it today too."

I glance at her, careful this time, and find her watching me like she already knows my answer.

"Are you kidnapping me?" I ask.

"Maybe." She tilts her head, that spark back in her hazel eyes. "Scared?"

I let my gaze drop to her mouth for half a beat, then back to her eyes. "Of you?" I say, voice lower than it should be. "Yeah. Probably."

Her breath catches, just slightly.

"Terrified." I lean back in my seat, stretching my

legs as much as the small car allows. "I'll gladly let you kidnap me. Want me to tie up my own wrists and ankles? Make it official?"

She laughs. "That's not really scary if you come voluntarily."

"It would be a dream come true."

She stares at me for a beat too long, then returns her attention to the road. But I see the flush spreading down her neck, the way her pulse jumps at her throat. She's affected. Good.

We turn off the main road onto something smaller, rougher. The town falls away behind us, replaced by rolling fields and distant mountains. It's beautiful out here, the kind of wild, open landscape that reminds me of home in my younger years. Of the years before I lost my mom in an accident, when life was simple and the future felt infinite.

I don't think about that time much anymore. Too painful. But something about this place, this town, this woman... it makes me want to remember.

The road narrows into a path, trees closing in on either side, and June finally rolls up the windows. She parks in a small clearing and kills the engine, and the silence that follows is almost startling.

"Oh, you're going to love this," she says, and her excitement is contagious. "Come on."

She climbs out of the car, and I follow, watching her move. The red dress hugs her curves in ways that leave me drooling. The belt at her waist accentuates the dip before her hips flare out. Her legs in those cowboy boots go on forever, and when she walks ahead of me, I can't stop staring at the sway of her ass.

Focus, Seth. Eyes forward. Think pure thoughts.

That's impossible when she's bouncing through the trees like a kid on Christmas morning, glancing back to make sure I'm following, her whole face lit up with anticipation.

We push through a final cluster of branches, and I stop.

A waterfall cascades down a rocky cliff face, maybe thirty feet high, feeding into a crystal-clear pool that mirrors the sky. Moss-covered boulders line the edges, and yellow and white flowers push up through the rocks. The sun catches the mist, throwing tiny rainbows into the air.

It's stunning.

"I found this place a few years ago," June says, moving toward the water's edge. "When my parents first started pushing me to move to Dallas. I was so frustrated, so angry, and I just drove until I ran out of road." She gestures at the waterfall. "This was waiting at the end."

"It's beautiful."

"Right?" She turns to face me, and her smile is radiant. "I come here when things get overwhelming. The sound of the water, the isolation... it helps me think. Or not think. Depending on what I need."

She's talking with her hands, gesturing enthusiastically, and I realize I could watch her like this forever. The way she moves, the passion in her voice, the pure, unguarded joy on her face.

"Do you like waterfalls?" she asks.

I've never really thought about it before. They were just... there. Background scenery in nature documentaries. But watching June right now, the way the light bounces from her hair, how her eyes sparkle with excitement, and the fact that she's sharing something precious with me—I decide at that moment that waterfalls are my favorite thing in the entire world.

They'll always remind me of her. Of this. Of watching her come alive in a way I've never seen before.

"Yeah," I say, my voice rougher than I intended. "I like waterfalls."

She beams at me, and something in my chest cracks open.

We walk along a worn path near the water, the sound of the falls filling the silence between us. She's telling me about the different seasons, how the pool is warm enough to swim in during summer, how the trees turn gold and red in autumn, how she's never actually come here in winter before.

I'm only half listening. Most of my attention is on the way she moves. The curve of her neck. The occasional glimpse of cleavage when she turns a certain way.

I want her in a way that's primal and consuming and completely beyond my control.

She's mid-sentence when her boot catches on a root, and she stumbles forward with a surprised yelp.

I move without thinking. My arm hooks around her waist, catching her, pulling her back against me. But the momentum carries us both sideways, and suddenly I'm pressing her against a tree, my body pinning hers, her back against rough bark and her front against me.

She's breathing hard. So am I.

"You okay?" I ask, but I don't step back.

"Yeah." Her voice is barely a whisper. "Thanks."

We're so close I can count her eyelashes. Her scent is curling around me like it's trying to ensure I know it's her.

Except I've known her since the moment she collected me from the prison cell and I caught her scent through the fog of whatever drug was in my system. Knew she was mine then.

"You don't need to hide from me," I say softly.

She stiffens. "What?"

"Whatever you're scared to tell me. Whatever secret you've been keeping." I brush a strand of hair from her face, and she shivers. "You don't need to hide."

For a moment, I think she's going to deny it. Going to put up those walls again and pretend everything's fine.

But then she takes a shaky breath. "I'm an Omega, not a Beta."

I don't react. Just wait.

"Well, I was, then I tried not to be, and now I am again. Sounds confusing even in my head." She's talking fast now, nervous, her words tumbling over each other. "When I was eighteen, doctors said I was dormant. Said I'd probably never have heats or form proper bonds. My parents convinced me to take suppressants, pretend to be a Beta, avoid all the complications of a broken designation." She keeps explaining.

"You're not broken."

"You don't know that." Her eyes are bright with unshed tears. "I've been hiding for years. Taking pills every day. Convincing myself I was better off without all of the heats, the bonds, and a pack."

She stops, chest heaving, and stares at me with something like desperation. "You're just going to grin at me?"

I am smiling. I can't help it. "I already knew you were mine, June."

"Yeah, you say that, but—"

"I might have been wasted that first night, but the attraction between us, that magnetic pull I felt the moment I saw you, was inevitable. Like the universe had been building toward that meeting my whole life." I cup her face in my hands, tilting her chin up so she has to look at me. "I was just waiting for the pieces to fall into place. This makes so much sense."

"I'm sorry I lied—"

I press a thumb to her lips, silencing her.

"No. You don't need to apologize to me. Not for this. Not for anything."

In my mind, I'm thinking about those fucking doctors who told an eighteen-year-old girl she was defective. About her parents, who convinced her to hide instead of letting her be her beautiful, natural self. About seven years of suppression and fear and loneliness, all because she believed she wasn't enough. That fucking guts me.

She's more than enough. She's everything. And I'm going to spend however long it takes to show her that.

She opens her mouth to say something else, but I'm done talking.

I kiss her.

My lips crash into hers like a wave breaking on the shore, the culmination of every moment that's led to this. She makes a small sound of surprise that melts into a moan, and her hands fist in my shirt, pulling me closer like she can't get enough.

I trace the seam of her lips with my tongue, and she opens for me instantly, letting me in, letting me taste every corner of her sweetness. She's tentative at first, almost shy, but when I deepen the kiss, she matches me stroke for stroke.

Fuck.

The sound she makes, this breathy little whimper, goes straight to my cock. I press her harder against the tree, one hand tangled in her hair, the other gripping her hip, pulling her against me so she can feel exactly what she does to me. She gasps into my mouth and rocks forward, seeking friction, and I nearly lose my mind.

I kiss her like I'm starving and she's the only thing that will save me. Like we have all the time in the world and not enough at once. Like every fantasy I've had since the night we met is finally coming true and I need to memorize every second before it disappears.

She clings to me, arms around my neck, fingers in my hair, body arched into mine. And I love the way she surrenders to this thing between us. How she holds on to me, lets herself want without holding back.

When I finally break the kiss, we're both gasping. I trail my mouth down her jaw, along her neck, finding that spot where her pulse thunders beneath her skin. I press my lips there, then my teeth, gentle but claiming. She moans, and the sound vibrates through both of us.

"Seth..."

I inhale and breathe her in until she's all I can smell, all I can taste, all I can feel. This is right. This is where I'm meant to be—with her.

She's mine. And she's my pack's.

I lift my head as she draws back, and I let her, though every instinct screams to pull her closer. Her cheeks are flushed, lips swollen from my kiss, eyes glazed with desire. And her nipples, fuck, I can see them poking through the thin fabric of her dress, tight and straining against the material like they're begging for my attention.

But there's fear there too. Underneath the wanting.

I tuck a strand of hair behind her ear, gentle now. "Everything is going to be all right, June."

"I really don't have your confidence." Her voice trembles. "Nothing has gone right for me. Not for a long time."

"It will now."

Her eyes flash, pain and disbelief fighting for space. "You can't promise that."

"Watch me." I hold her gaze and don't soften it, don't back down, because she needs certainty more than she needs pretty words. "Give me time. I'll prove that you are exactly where you're meant to be."

She just stares at me, like she is trying to decide if she can afford to believe it. Something fragile moves across her face, hope that scares her as much as it comforts her. Her throat works when she swallows, and for a second, I think she might step closer instead of away.

Then she takes a step back, breaking whatever was building between us.

"We should head back."

I let a slow grin tug at my mouth. "Why? Worried you'll forget how to hold yourself together with me standing this close."

She laughs like it surprises her too, and she turns toward the path. But before she goes, she glances over her shoulder. The look she gives me is pure heat. "Something like that."

I stand there and watch her stroll away. The sway of her hips. The sunlight in her hair. The way she moves through the world like she is just starting to believe she has a right to take up space in it.

My chest tightens with something that feels like purpose.

Fuck.

I'm already in deep.

13

JUNE

The leather couch creaks as I shift, hyperaware of Seth's thigh mere inches from mine. Across from us, Kai and Carter occupy the other sofa, and the weight of what I just revealed hangs in the air between us like morning fog over the mountains.

I'm an Omega.

Three words that change everything.

"I knew it." Kai leans back, arms spread across the back of the couch, looking entirely too pleased with himself. "From the second you bumped into me at that photo shoot, I knew you were an Omega."

"Well, aren't you clever," I tease, arching an eyebrow at him.

His grin widens. "I also knew you were meant to be with us."

I can't stop smiling at his sweet words.

All three men are staring at me now. Seth's intense gaze from beside me. Carter's curious one from across the coffee table. And Kai, looking at me like I'm the answer to a question he's been asking his whole life.

"It's the best news I've heard in a long time," Carter murmurs, then winks my way, melting my heart.

I clear my throat and grasp for anything to redirect this conversation before I combust. "So. You all ready for the rodeo tomorrow?"

Carter's lips twitch like he knows exactly what I'm doing, but he plays along. "Born ready, darlin'."

"I've been riding horses for too long," Seth adds, his deep voice rumbling beside me. "One more competition isn't going to shake me."

Kai throws a pillow at Seth's head, which he catches without even looking. "The man's made of granite."

I find myself grinning at their easy banter, the way they rib each other. This is nice. Normal.

Seth pushes to his feet, and the other two follow suit like they're operating on some unspoken signal. "We hold a ritual before each rodeo. We need to head out."

"A ritual?" I sit up straighter.

The three of them exchange looks, smirking. Seth's expression remains stoic, but there's something playing at the corner of his mouth that might be amusement on anyone else.

"Can't tell you," Kai says. "Sacred tradition."

"Very hush-hush," Carter adds.

I stand from the couch. "Well, seeing as I'm meant to chaperone you three..."

"Yeah?" Kai's voice dips, and he takes a step toward me. "You want to join us, doll?"

My knees wobble. Just slightly. I lock them in place and lift my chin. "Someone has to make sure you don't end up in jail before tomorrow."

"Such confidence in our judgment." Kai is close now. The glint of his eyebrow piercing catches my attention, the individual strands of dark hair escaping his tie, the bold lines of tribal ink disappearing under his sleeve. "I like that."

"Kai." Seth's voice cuts through like a blade as he heads for the front door and opens it. "Give her room to breathe."

Kai steps back, hands raised, but his grin doesn't fade. "Just getting to know our Omega."

Our Omega.

I've spent years hiding from the world, running from the truth, building walls against others. And yet, the words coming from his mouth, from all of them... it doesn't feel like a trap but more of a homecoming.

Which is absolutely terrifying.

I grab my jacket from the hook by the door, mostly because I need something to do with my hands that isn't reaching for one of them. "Let's go before I regain my common sense."

"Can't have that," Carter adds, falling into step

beside me, close enough that I catch traces of his tempting scent.

"For the record," he murmurs, quieter. "I'm glad you're coming. It'll be better if you're there."

I don't know what to say to that, so I just tuck a curl behind my ear and follow Seth out into the night.

We pile into Carter's pickup truck, the massive red beast that looks like it could survive an apocalypse and still have gas left over. I end up in the back with Kai, while Seth claims shotgun and Carter takes the wheel. The space feels smaller than it should, Kai's broad shoulder warm against mine, his presence filling up all the air in the cab.

"Comfortable, doll?" He stretches his arm along the seat behind me. Not touching. But close enough that I feel the heat of him like a brand.

"Perfectly."

His low chuckle vibrates through me.

Carter pulls onto the road, and the ranch disappears in the rearview mirror, swallowed by the endless Montana darkness. Out here, there's nothing but open land and sky so big it makes you feel small in the best way. Stars scattered across the black like someone spilled a bucket of glitter and decided to leave it there.

Twenty minutes later, Carter pulls off onto a dirt path I would never have noticed. We wind through a cluster of trees until the road opens up to reveal a river, its surface gleaming silver under the bright moon. A few streetlights dot the area farther up, but here, we're tucked into shadows and starlight.

"It's beautiful," I breathe. I step out of the truck with the guys, cool night air washing over my heated skin. The river stretches before us, its surface gleaming silver under the fat full moon. The water moves lazily, catching light in ripples of white and gray. It smells like pine and clean earth. An owl calls out somewhere in the darkness. Fireflies blink along the far bank like tiny green stars.

"An amazing spot." The moonlight catches Carter's face, softens his edges. "Found it during our last circuit. It feels right to come back."

"I love it," I admit, and I mean it with my whole heart.

Kai appears at my side, his presence like standing next to a furnace. "Glad you approve." His fingers brush my lower back as he passes, brief, barely there, and electricity crackles through my veins.

Something warm curls through me at his touch.

Get a grip, June.

I'm so focused on getting my body under control that I don't register what's happening until Kai's already pulling his shirt over his head.

Tanned skin. Sculpted muscle. The bold black lines of his tribal sleeve stark against his arm. The other guys are doing the same.

Then his hands go to his belt.

"Um. What's—"

Seth is working his own belt buckle. Carter is kicking off his boots.

Jeans hit the ground. Then more jeans. The moonlight is doing things that should probably be illegal, painting shadows across ridges of muscle and planes of skin.

"The ritual, doll." Kai grins at me, thumbs hooked in the waistband of his boxers. "You said you wanted to know."

"The ritual is *skinny-dipping*?"

"Cleansing in the river before competition." Carter unbuttons his shirt with deliberate slowness, revealing a chest that looks carved from marble and kissed by moonlight. "Washes away bad luck."

"Very spiritual," Seth adds, deadpan, as his boxers join the pile. And I don't know where to look now.

I spin around so fast I nearly give myself whiplash. "You could have *warned* me!"

"Where's the fun in that?"

My imagination fills in the details with devastating accuracy from when I saw him naked the night I picked him up from jail—broad shoulders and narrow hips, muscle and shadow and miles of bare skin. Heat floods through me, pooling between my thighs, and I press them together like that'll help.

It doesn't.

"Come on, June." Kai's voice is closer now, rough silk against my nerve endings. "Strip down and get in."

A laugh escapes me, slightly strangled. "You know that's illegal, right? Public nudity?"

"Only illegal if someone catches you," Carter says, chuckling.

"Nope. Absolutely not." I shake my head, still facing away from them. "I'll leave the skinny-dipping to you three. Some of us have a healthy relationship with consequences."

"Suit yourself."

Splashing behind me. Bodies entering water.

Don't look. Don't look. Don't look.

I twist around.

All three of them wade into the river, water rising to their waists, moonlight painting their backs in silver and shadow. Muscles shift and flex as they move. Droplets catch the light like scattered diamonds. Seth's broad shoulders. Carter's lean lines. Kai's powerful build.

My mouth dries while my body temperature spikes high enough that I'm surprised I don't steam. Between my thighs, slick gathers, my biology screaming, *Hello, yes, those three, please, immediately.*

But my body doesn't give a damn about boundaries. It only cares about the three gorgeous Alphas currently putting on a show that would make Renaissance sculptors weep.

"Enjoying the view?" Kai calls, glancing back with a knowing smirk. Water drips from his dark hair.

I should deny it. Pretend to be fascinated by the trees. The stars. Literally anything else.

Instead, I plant my hands on my hips. "Well, if you're going to parade around like that, I might as well appreciate the effort."

Carter throws his head back and laughs, bright and uninhibited. The sound bounces across the water and settles somewhere warm in my chest. Even Seth's mouth curves into something dangerously close to a real smile.

"That's our girl," Kai says.

Our girl.

I drift closer to the water's edge and find a tree to lean against. The bark is rough through my jacket, grounding me when everything else feels like fever and fantasy.

The river runs chest-deep at the center, and they're splashing around, laughing and calling out to each other. Kai dunks Carter's head, who retaliates with a tackle. Seth watches them with the long-suffering patience of someone who's seen this exact scene play out a thousand times.

Every nerve ending is lit up, humming, desperate for more of them. The desire is overwhelming. Intoxicating. The kind of sensory overload that makes you understand why Omegas used to lock themselves away during heats.

I've been on suppressants for years. But without them,

it's just a bone-deep attraction toward compatible Alphas. The way my body recognizes theirs on some primal level and screams, *Yes, them, those ones, take us home.*

I've never felt it this strongly before. Not once. Not with anyone.

Underneath the fear is something reckless and giddy, like standing at the edge of a cliff knowing you're about to jump.

"So," I call out, desperate for a distraction, "does this ritual actually work? Does it guarantee a win?"

Seth turns to look at me, water dripping down his chest, and I forget how my lungs function. "Every single time."

"Wow." My voice comes out breathier than intended. "Bold claim."

"It's not a claim." His blue eyes hold mine. "It's a fact."

"We're kind of a big deal," Kai adds, surfacing from underwater and shoving wet hair from his face. Droplets cling to his lashes. "Thought you'd have figured that out by now."

"The collective ego in this river could power a small city."

"And yet here you are, watching." Carter floats on his back, and the water hides absolutely nothing. I jerk my gaze up to the sky, cheeks burning.

"I'm chaperoning. It's my job."

"Sure it is."

They roughhouse some more. Diving and surfacing. Every time one of them emerges, I catch glimpses of things I definitely shouldn't be staring at. Broad shoulders. Defined abs. The V of muscle disappearing below the waterline, and even more...

I fan myself with my hand before I can stop myself. It's not even that warm out. My body is just staging a full mutiny.

Carter catches me. "Getting a little flushed over there?"

"It's a... warm night."

"It's fifty degrees."

"I run hot."

His grin says he knows exactly why I'm running hot, and he's enjoying every second of it.

Damn Omega biology. I've spent years hiding what I am, building a life where my designation doesn't define me. And now three cowboys show up with their perfect scents and their perfect faces and their perfect naked bodies, and my carefully constructed control crumbles like wet tissue paper.

Carter wades closer to the bank, water sheeting off his shoulders. "You sure you don't want to come in?"

"The water's freezing, and we both know it."

"Builds character."

"My character is fully built, thanks."

He laughs, then dives, giving me an excellent view of his backside before he disappears. I press my palm to my chest like I can physically hold my heart inside my body. Seth is watching me the whole time, quiet but noticing my reaction.

"So you're chaperoning us," Kai says, treading water in the shallows. "But now that you're out as an Omega, who's going to chaperone you?"

The question lands differently than he probably intended.

See, in most places, Omegas don't go anywhere alone. It's baked into the culture, old as time—unmated Omegas need supervision, protection, an Alpha or Beta escort until they've got a mate's mark and a bond in their chest. Some towns enforce it with actual laws. Curfews. Travel restrictions. Papers you have to carry proving you have permission to be where you are.

Our town isn't like that. It's one of the reasons I love it here, why I've fought so hard to stay even when my parents wanted me to join them in Dallas. Here, things are more relaxed. Two of my closest friends are both Omegas, and they live their lives freely—working, traveling, making choices the old guard would clutch their pearls over. The traditional families still whisper about it, call it improper and dangerous and *asking for trouble*, but nobody actually does anything.

Most of the time.

Carter winks at me under the silvery moonlight. "Guess we'll have to volunteer."

"I've been taking care of myself just fine."

"Never said you couldn't." Seth's low voice carries

across the water. When I glance his way again, there's something soft lurking behind his usual hardness. "Doesn't mean you have to anymore."

Before I can untangle what that means—before I can process the way those words make my chest ache—I hear the crunch of tires on gravel. Headlights cutting through darkness. And approaching fast.

"Shit." I push off the tree. "Someone's coming. You need to hide."

The three of them exchange looks, smirks playing on their lips like this is all very funny.

I glance at the fast-approaching lights. "I'm serious! *Go!*"

They dive under, swimming toward the far bank where trees hang low and shadows pool deep. I watch them disappear, then sprint for the scattered clothes.

Boots. Jeans. Shirts. Boxers. I scoop everything into my arms and bolt for the truck, yanking open the back door and tossing it all inside. I slam the door shut just as the vehicle pulls onto the grass, headlights blazing so bright I have to shield my eyes.

The engine stays running, a low hum in the quiet. I squint past the glare, trying to see who's behind the wheel.

The door of a police cruiser opens, and Tanner steps out in his brown deputy's uniform.

Of *fucking* course.

He strolls toward me with that swagger I used to find attractive, back before I learned what lived underneath. One thumb hooked over his belt buckle, flashlight in his other hand. The cruiser's engine hums behind him, lights still blazing.

Once upon a time, I thought he was everything. Tall, broad-shouldered, sharp jaw, deep blue eyes. The way he looked at me like I was the center of his universe.

Turns out I was. Just not in the good way. I was the center of his universe because he wanted to own it.

"What do you want, Tanner?" I keep my voice flat. "Stalking me now?"

He doesn't look at me, just scans the area with his flashlight. "Got complaints about shouting. Someone thought there might be trouble out here."

"It's just me. As you can see, I'm fine. You can leave."

His light lands on Carter's truck. "Since when do you drive that thing?"

"Fuck off, Tanner."

He ignores me, walking toward the river. "Skinny-dipping is public indecency. That's an offense."

"Last time I checked, I'm fully dressed." I gesture at myself. "Don't you have real crimes to investigate? Jaywalkers to ticket?"

He turns back to me, and his flashlight catches me right in the eyes. Spots explode across my vision.

"You *asshole*—"

When I blink the glare away, he's right there. Too close. Invading my space like he always used to.

"Heard you're babysitting those rodeo idiots," he says, voice low. "What the hell are you doing with them? If they give you any trouble, you let me know. I'll handle it."

"I don't need you to do anything." I retreat. He follows. "Just leave, Tanner."

His hand shoots out, grabbing my wrist. The grip is too tight, fingers digging in.

"You can't keep pushing me away, June."

"Let. Go."

His nostrils flare suddenly. I see the moment the breeze shifts, carrying my scent to him. His nose scrunches up, confusion and something darker crossing his face.

And I *hate* that he's scenting me, that my body, still wound up from watching the guys, still humming with Omega hormones, is probably broadcasting signals I can't control. He has no right to smell me. No right to any part of me. But here he is, sniffing like he owns what he's finding.

"Why do you smell like that?" He leans closer, inhaling deeply, and revulsion crawls up my spine. "So damn strong. You going into heat? Betas don't—"

I rip my wrist from his grip. "What I do is none of your business. We haven't been together in over a year. *Leave.*"

He stares at me with that calculating look I know too well. The one that says he's filing information away for later, that says he's not done, will never be done, because in his mind, I still belong to him.

I turn and walk toward the truck. My legs shake, but my stride stays steady. The guys left it unlocked. I just need to get inside. Put a barrier between us.

The handle gives. I slide into the driver's seat, slam the door, and hit the lock. Then I sit there with my phone out, trying to look casual while my heart threatens to crack my ribs.

Through the window, I watch him move to the riverbank, flashlight sweeping the water. My knees bounce.

Just leave. Come on. Just leave.

He moves farther down the bank. Closer to where the trees hang over the water. The guys are somewhere in those shadows, and if Tanner takes two more steps—

Movement catches my eye.

Not from the river. From the cluster of trees near the cruiser.

I blink. Sure that I'm imagining things.

But no. That's definitely a very naked Kai, sprinting across the grass like his life depends on it.

And he's holding a white paper bag in his hand and shoves it over his head. It has holes torn out for eyes.

Where in the world did he even find that?

He reaches the cruiser while Tanner is still facing the water, and slides into the driver's seat. Starts backing up quietly, door still hanging open, that ridiculous bag bouncing on his head like some kind of deranged ghost.

Kai. What the absolute fuck are you doing?

The door slams shut. Engine revs. And then Kai is tearing across the grass, tires spinning, leaving a dust cloud in his wake.

Tanner whips around. Flashlight swinging wildly. "STOP! STOP THE VEHICLE!"

He takes off running after his own cruiser, screaming, and I'm frozen in place with my heart in my throat.

So much for chaperoning and keeping these three out of trouble. We're all going to prison because Kai just stole a cop car.

The cruiser disappears around a bend. Tanner sprints after it, his shouting getting fainter.

Something bangs against the truck, and I nearly scream.

Seth and Carter are at the doors, pulling handles, water streaming down their bodies. I slam the unlock button.

Carter yanks open the driver's side. "Move."

I scramble over the console, hip catching the gearshift, landing awkwardly in the passenger seat. Both men are soaking wet and very, very naked.

Don't look.

I catch a glimpse of water-slicked skin and muscle and—

Windshield. Stare at the windshield.

"Kai just stole a cop car." My voice sounds strangled. "While naked. With a bag on his head. A bag he found—where?"

"Who knows with Kai?" Carter starts the engine. "That's just who he is."

Seth is in the back, water dripping everywhere, and tosses boxer shorts at Carter's head. "Get dressed. Move."

Carter pushes his seat back and wrestles into the boxer shorts while driving, which seems like it should be physically impossible. My peripheral vision catches every flex of muscle, every shift of bare skin, every drop of water trailing down his chest.

Eyes forward, June. Forward.

Seth's low voice comes from the back. "That was close. Goddamn Tanner." A pause. His tone drops, turns dangerous. "He was lucky he left you alone. We were ready to come out of that water and put him on his ass."

I risk a glance back. Seth is pulling on jeans, water dripping from his dark hair.

"You three are making this chaperoning thing a nightmare," I say.

"Never promised we'd be easy." Carter guns the engine. "Let's go find our idiot."

"Where did he even go?"

Seth leans forward between the seats, wet hair plastered to his forehead, a grin cracking through his usual severity. "He had a plan. Couldn't talk him out of it."

"What kind of plan involves stealing a cop car while naked?"

"A Kai plan."

We tear down the dirt path and hit the main road. A few minutes later, movement in the trees—

Kai bursts from the darkness, sprinting toward us, paper bag clutched over his groin, the biggest grin I've ever seen splitting his face.

Carter slams on the brakes. Kai yanks open the back door and throws himself inside next to Seth.

"WOO-HOO!" He's breathing hard, grinning like a maniac. "That was *insane!*"

"What happened?" I twist around. "Where's the cruiser?"

He shoves wet hair from his face. "Drove the cruiser to that hill past the bend, jumped out, then gave it a nice push toward the river. Rolled into some bushes, then watched Tanner chase after it screaming. After that, I ran."

"You rolled a cop car into the river."

"Might've made it in. Might not. Either way, his problem now."

Carter is laughing, shoulders shaking. Seth is chuckling. And somehow, despite the felonies, despite Tanner, despite everything, I'm laughing too.

It bubbles up from somewhere deep. The kind of laugh that takes over your whole body. All the tension releasing at once—Tanner's grip on my wrist, the fear of getting caught, Kai sprinting across the grass with a bag on his head.

"I wiped down everything before I jumped out," Kai adds. "Wheel, door handle, gear stick. Saw cleaning wipes on the dash."

"Convenient," Carter manages.

"We're all going to jail." I wheeze, wiping my eyes.

"Nah." Kai sprawls across the back seat, still naked, utterly unbothered. "No way Tanner has evidence that it was us. There was no camera in the Charger like the modern cop cars, so we're good. But imagine the paperwork: 'Some naked guy with a bag on his head stole my cruiser, and I couldn't catch him.' They'd laugh him off the force."

He has a point. Tanner's ego would never survive that story.

"Still." I catch my breath. "Let's never do that again."

"Agreed," Seth says, but he's smiling.

"Here, Kai," Seth orders. "Put pants on."

There's lots of shuffling behind me, and my seat keeps getting bumped.

Carter glances my way. He's managed to get fully dressed while driving—still slightly damp, hair curling at his neck.

"You okay?" Voice softer now. "That got intense."

"Yeah." I nod, meaning it. "I'm good."

"Tanner didn't hurt you?"

I think about the grip on my wrist, the way he

leaned in to scent me, and the revulsion still crawling under my skin.

"Nothing I couldn't handle."

Seth makes a sound. "He touches you again, and I'm destroying him."

"I can take care of myself."

"Yeah. You can." His eyes meet mine in the rearview mirror, blue and steady. "Doesn't mean you're on your own anymore."

My heart stutters to hear those words that embrace me.

"This kind of chaos normal for you three?" I ask.

"Usually just Kai," Carter says.

Kai is chuckling. "Doesn't matter. You're stuck with us now, doll."

Stuck with us.

I glance back at them. Kai, finally dressed. Seth, watching me with those too-seeing eyes.

Something dangerous unfurls in my chest.

I like them. God help me, I really do, and a damn lot. Not just my body responding to their scents, though that's definitely happening, every nerve still humming from proximity. I like *them.* The banter. The loyalty. The way they'd steal a cop car to protect each other without blinking.

And that's the scariest part. Because I know how this story ends.

They're rodeo men. Traveling circuit. Here for a few weeks, then gone, next town, next competition, next horizon. And I'll still be in Honeyspur Meadow, pretending my heart isn't scattered across three hundred miles of Montana highway.

I've always been practical about this stuff. Smart. Protective of myself in ways that Tanner made necessary.

But sitting here, laughing with them, feeling more alive than I have in months… I'm not sure I know how to protect myself from this.

"For the record," I say quietly, "Tanner deserved every second of that."

The truck fills with laughter.

Outside, the moon hangs full and silver over the hills. Some old country song crackles through the radio, and Kai hums along, off-key.

I lean my head against the window and watch shadows blur past.

These men are going to break my heart. I can see it coming, clear as the road ahead.

But tonight, wrapped in their warmth and laughter and the electric current of their presence, I can't bring myself to care.

Tomorrow, I'll be smart.

Tonight, I'm just going to let myself fall.

14

CARTER

The hallway is dark and quiet, the house settling into that deep-night stillness where every creak sounds like a gunshot. I've got my phone's flashlight on low, angled down at the notebook balanced on my knee, and I've been sitting here for... hell, I don't even know how long. Enough that my ass is numb against the hardwood floor and that I've scratched out the same line four times.

She tastes like—

No. Erase.

When she laughs, I—

Garbage. Cross it out.

I drag my hand through my hair and exhale slowly. This is pathetic. I'm a grown man sitting outside a woman's bedroom door at two in the morning, trying to write poetry like some lovesick teenager. Kai would laugh his ass off if he could see me now.

I've never been good at saying the important things out loud. Words get stuck somewhere between my chest and my throat, tangled up with all the jokes I use to keep people from looking too close. But on paper, maybe I can be honest. I can tell her what she does to me without tripping over my own tongue or deflecting into humor.

I read what I've got so far, and it's not enough. It's never enough. How do you capture the way someone rewires your whole damn brain just by existing? How do you explain that you've spent years feeling like you're running on fumes, and then this woman shows up and suddenly you remember what it feels like to want something?

I scratch out another line.

The soft creak comes from behind me.

I freeze.

June's door eases open, and she steps out in a thin sleep shirt and shorts, hair mussed, eyes half closed. She's clearly aiming for the kitchen, moving on autopilot, and she doesn't see me until her bare foot connects with my outstretched leg.

She squeals and grabs the doorframe to catch herself. I lunge up instinctively, hands hovering near her arms, terrified I've somehow hurt her.

"Shit—are you okay? Did you hit anything? June—"

"Oh my God." She's clutching her chest, breathing hard, blinking down at me like I'm a hallucination.

"Carter. You scared me to *death*."

"Sorry, sorry—" I keep my voice low, mindful of Seth and Kai sleeping down the hall. "I didn't mean to. Are you hurt?"

"I'm fine." She laughs, shaky and breathless. "Just... what are you *doing* out here?"

Good question. Excellent question. One I don't have a good answer for.

"Couldn't sleep," I say, which is technically true. "And I figured, if you were in pain again, I'd be here if you needed help."

She stares at me with these heartfelt eyes. "Thank you, that's so sweet." Then her gaze drops to the notebook in my hand. The pen. The scratched-out lines are visible even in the dim glow of my phone's light.

"What's that?"

"Nothing."

She's waking up now, curiosity replacing the sleepy fog. A smile tugs at her lips. "Is that... Are you *writing* a poem?" She says it like an accusation, delighted and teasing. "You're writing poetry outside my door in the middle of the night. Do you know how romantic that is?" She grins, and it tugs at my heart.

She's already leaning closer, trying to get a better look, and her scent hits me like a wave. Lemon zest and honey and wildflowers, stronger than usual, wrapping around me until I can barely think straight.

"Did you write something for me?" Her voice drops

softer, the tease gone. There is something unguarded behind her eyes, like she forgot to lock the door on it.

I crouch back down in the dark hallway outside her bedroom with the notebook in my hand, feeling ridiculous for even having it out. I glance toward her door, then back to the floor.

"I'll be here," I say, careful. "If you need me." I mean it as an escape hatch for her, a way to let her step back without making it a thing. I mean it for me too.

I don't add anything else or try to joke it away. The silence takes over.

June doesn't move.

"Can I read it?"

"It's not finished. It's crap, honestly. I was just messing around."

"I was going to get water," she says, quietly.

I wait for her to head down the hallway. Instead, she lowers herself to the floor beside me.

Not across from me. Not safely distant. Beside me, close enough that if I moved, our shoulders would touch.

My chest pulls tight, and I keep my eyes forward because I don't trust what my face will do if I look at her too long.

"But now," she adds, settling in like she belongs here, "I want the poem more."

The hallway seems to narrow. The air feels different. Not loud, not dramatic, just... charged, like the house noticed we stopped running from each other.

Her bare knee is a few inches from my thigh. I can make out the freckles across her nose even in the dim light. Her lashes shadow her cheeks.

"It's really not good," I say.

"Let me decide that."

I swallow, and slowly I angle the notebook toward her and hold up my phone so she can see.

The poem is short so far. Just a couple of lines. A blank space where I couldn't find the right words. It isn't clever or polished. It's just the truth I couldn't say out loud.

You make the quiet louder—the kind I used to drown out.

Now I want to sit in it, if you are sitting there too.

June reads it once. Then again, slower. Her lips move with the words like she's trying them on, like she wants to know how they feel.

When she glances up, something in her has shifted. Softer. Open. Like she made a decision and it scared her a little.

"Carter," she whispers.

"I told you it was crap."

"It's not." Her voice catches on the last word. "This is how you see me?"

I shrug because I can't do anything else with my hands except hold on tighter. I can't hold her, so I grasp the notebook.

"It's just words," I say, even though we both know that's not true.

"No." She shakes her head, small and certain. "No, this is you. You see me."

And she stays there beside me in the dark, like she's saying it back without needing to.

"Look at me," I say.

June's eyes lock on mine like she's been waiting for permission to stop pretending she isn't burning up. There's no timid hesitation in her. No backing away. Just that sharp, bright need that makes my pulse jump hard in my throat.

A beat of silence. Not uncertainty. Decision.

I reach for her.

Not gentle. Not careful in the way that keeps space between us. I catch her by the waist and pull her in close, dragging her into my body like the distance has been the problem all along. She comes willingly, knee sliding in, breath catching, and the moment her weight shifts toward me, it feels like something in the room finally clicks into place.

My mouth finds hers.

This is the kind of kiss that makes the air disappear, like the hallway has been sealed shut and all that exists is her mouth and mine and the sound she makes when I take it deeper. Her hands grab at my shoulders, then my hair, and then the front of my shirt like she is trying to pull me closer than physics allows. She kisses me back greedily, as if I am the only thing that tastes like relief.

I tilt my head and keep going, slowing down only

long enough to make her feel it, to make her chase it. Her lips part, her breath turns uneven, and she makes this soft, wrecked sound right into my mouth that shoots straight through my spine and down to my cock. I slide my hand up her back, firm, anchoring, not letting her drift away from me even by an inch. The phone's light throws shadows across her cheekbones, across the curve of her mouth, and I swear I could kiss her forever and still not get enough.

She shifts again, restless, impatient with the hallway floor and the way we are positioned. Her thigh slides over mine, then her other leg follows, and suddenly she is moving onto me like it's the most natural decision she has ever made. She straddles me there in the dark, close and warm, breath shaking, mouth still on mine like she refuses to let the connection break for even a second.

I groan against her lips. My hands find her hips, then lower to her ass, holding her there with a grip that makes it clear I am not letting her go. She rolls her body forward even more, needy, and I can't get enough. This is her, unapologetic, losing control in a way that feels like a gift.

I break the kiss only to drag my mouth along her jaw, to the corner of her lips again, then back to her mouth, because I can't decide where I want her most. She tips her head, giving me access like she knows exactly what she's doing, and when I return to her mouth, it's deeper, slower, the kind of kiss that ruins your ability to pretend this is nothing. Her fingers curl at the back of my neck like she's holding me in place, claiming her turn.

"Carter," she breathes, not a warning, not a plea. Just my name.

"I'm right here," I murmur, and I kiss her again, swallowing whatever she was about to say.

She rocks against me, impatient, and I tighten my hands on her hips to steady her. Not to stop her. To keep her with me. To keep her exactly where I want her. Her forehead drops to mine for half a second, her eyes half lidded, mouth swollen from the kiss.

"I'm stunned that you can do this to me," she whispers, like she's accusing me of a crime she is happy to be guilty of.

I brush my mouth over hers, barely there, a cruel little touch that makes her chase it.

"I'm not doing anything," I say quietly. "You came to me."

Her smile is all heat, all challenge.

"Then keep up," she adds. And she kisses me again, harder, like she has decided she's done waiting.

I let her set the pace for a few breaths, just to watch her take what she wants. Then I take it back, because she wanted confidence, and I have plenty of it. I slide one hand up to cradle the back of her head, guiding her mouth where I want it, holding her there while the kiss turns into something that feels too big for the space we're in.

She makes another sound, soft and wrecking, and it hits me right in the gut. I pull her closer, until she is pressed fully against me, until there is no room left for doubt or distance or anything except the way she is shaking with it.

"This," I murmur against her mouth, "is what you need?"

June's eyes flash. She leans in, lips brushing mine when she answers. "Yes, please."

My thumbs press into her hips, the fabric of her sleep top and shorts thin as paper. "Good," I say, low. Certain. "Because I know exactly what to do with you."

June makes a sound against my lips—a soft, desperate whimper—and my cock throbs in response. I'm already hard, aching, every nerve ending on fire. She pulls me closer like she's trying to climb inside me.

Fuck. I love the way she's grabbing at me, hungry and unashamed. Love the way her body arches into mine, seeking friction, seeking heat.

I break the kiss just long enough to breathe, and she chases my mouth like she can't stand the distance.

I stand, holding her still wrapped around me. She gasps, then laughs, keeping her arms around my neck as I carry her through the open doorway into her room. I push the door shut behind us, and the click of the latch makes everything feel suddenly, dangerously private.

Her room is dark except for the moonlight filtering through the curtains. I set her on the edge of the bed, and she stares up at me with those wide hazel eyes, chest heaving, skin flushed.

"I'm on fire," she whispers.

"I know. I can feel it, and it's beautiful." I kneel in front of her, cupping her face in my hands.

She pulls me down, and our mouths crash together again.

This kiss is different. Hungrier. Her hands are everywhere—my arms, my chest, tugging at the hem of my shirt, at my sweatpants—and I match her desperation with my own. I kiss her like I'm starving for it, because I am. She pulls at my shirt again, and I break the kiss just long enough to yank it over my head. Her palms land flat on my chest, fingers spreading across my skin, and the touch sends sparks racing through my bloodstream.

"You're so warm," she breathes.

"So are you." I gently push her back onto the mattress, following her down, bracing myself above her on one arm while my other hand traces down her side. "God, June. You're burning up."

I kiss her jaw, her throat, the sensitive spot below her ear that makes her gasp.

Her hands fumble with the drawstring at the waistband of my sweatpants while I tug at the hem of her sleep shirt. We're a tangle of limbs and desperate movements, both of us trying to get closer, to get *more*. Her shirt comes off, and I have to stop, have to breathe, have to just *look* at her for a moment—all that soft skin and those perfect curvy breasts, the dusty pink nipples calling to me, laid out before me.

"Stunning," I murmur, and she shivers under my gaze. "You're so fucking beautiful, June." My hands are already reaching for her shorts, needing them off. I peel them down her legs and toss them aside, and I waste no time sliding my hands up to her bent knees and spreading them. I pause, taking in what I've been craving... Her sweet pussy, all shaved and glistening for me. I can't wait, so I lean in, my mouth to her lips like my life depends on it.

On the stroke of my tongue, pressing between her folds, and she's moaning, thrashing. My cock is so hard it fucking hurts with the need to be inside her. But not yet... First, I need to show her what an Alpha's mouth can do to ease that Omega ache.

I absolutely adore the way her hips rock against my face, and how I can't get enough of having my mouth around her offering, sucking, licking, driving her insane. She tastes like honey, her scent intoxicating. I take long strokes while pushing two fingers into her, knowing she's craving that stretch, while my teeth gently bite down on her swollen clit.

She shudders beneath me, her soft thighs cradling on either side of my head, and I fucking love being trapped between her legs, drowning in her scent, devouring her delicious pussy.

Pumping into her faster, I reach down with my other hand and push down on my sweatpants, needing to release my cock. It's strained, dripping with precum. I'm so fucking ready to rut her—that crazy, wild sensation wraps around me, the one where I am about to lose all damn control very soon.

I stroke myself a few times, growling with agony for release, while sucking on my sweet Omega, fingering her relentlessly. She's writhing, moaning for me, her hands in my hair, tugging, and I'm all for her desperation.

It's in that moment when she freezes for a second that I feel her body tensing and about to climax. So I finger her harder, suck down where she can't push me away, and ride her orgasm with her. She's shuddering, her voice loud enough to wake up the other two, but I don't give a damn. Not when I'm in heaven and nothing can pull me away from her.

I lick her pussy, her inner thighs, taking all of her offering, adoring how she tastes, while her hips are bucking. Once she settles, I lift my head to find her collapsed on the bed, breathless, and she's gorgeous.

She hauls me up her body, and our bare chests press together, skin to skin, the sensation almost too much. Her legs wrap around my waist, drawing me closer, and when I settle between her thighs, we both groan at the pressure. My sweatpants slide to my ankles, and I kick them off.

"Carter—" Her voice is wrecked, needy. "I loved that so much."

I smile, adoring her words. "That makes me so

happy." And as she shifts her hips, I press my cock to her entrance. She's staring up at me, arousal in her eyes, and I love seeing her this way. I push into her, slowly at first, not wanting to shock her. Her face is concentrated...

"Deep breaths, and let me know, gorgeous."

She exhales, and I sense her muscles easing around my cock, so I go in a bit farther. "I had no idea you were so large."

"Is it a problem?" I tease.

"Not at all." She grins like she's found gold, and I'm chuckling at her reaction. Then I thrust into her deeper, harder, and she lets out a small cry, her hands clutching the bedsheets around her until I'm buried in her down to the hilt. And I stare at her as she's gasping for air.

"Fuck me, June, you have no idea how insane it feels to be deep in your tight little pussy. I could live here, never wanting to come out."

She giggles, and her wriggling only squeezes my cock more, and I hiss at the growing arousal thundering through me. "It's never felt this big or this good before."

"You've never had me," I brag, then I rock against her slowly, giving her the friction she's desperate for, and build up to a faster tempo because I can't fucking help it. She cries out. "I've got you—"

The sounds she makes are going to kill me. Little gasps and moans that slip out between kisses, breathy repetitions of my name like a prayer. Every single one goes straight to my cock, making me throb and ache with a desperation I've never experienced.

"More," she whispers against my mouth.

I growl like some kind of animal and capture her lips again. My hips roll, and I slam into her faster now, and she matches me thrust for thrust, her body moving on pure instinct. The heat between us is unbearable, building and building toward something inevitable.

Her hands slide down my back, and I shudder at the sensation. She tips her head back, giving me access, and I take full advantage, kissing and nipping down the column of her neck, tasting the salt of her skin, inhaling her scent until I'm drunk on it.

"God, Carter, I've never—it's never felt like this before—"

"Good." I suck gently at her pulse point, and she arches beneath me with a cry. "You're mine now."

We fuck on the sheets, her breathless and needy. She's radiant in the moonlight—all tousled hair and flushed skin and bright eyes—and I have to pause just to take her in. This impossible, beautiful woman who crashed into my life and turned everything upside down.

Her expression softens. She reaches up, traces her fingers along my jaw, my cheekbone, the curve of my ear. The tenderness of it makes something crack open in my chest.

This isn't just want. It's deeper than that. It's a

bone-deep recognition, a certainty that settles in my chest like a key sliding into a lock.

Mine. She's mine. My fated mate.

The realization puts everything into place. This is why her scent drives me crazy. Why I can't stop thinking about her, can't stop writing terrible poetry in the middle of the night, can't stop positioning myself between her and any threat like my body knows something my brain is just catching up to. The thought of walking away is like physical pain.

Her legs tighten around my waist as I plunge into her over and over. She's soaked, and I love her this way. She's clawing at me, crying out my name, and I know she's building up... Fuck, I am barely holding on myself. And the second I feel her squeezing me, soaking me in the gush of her climax, I lose my control.

I growl, shoving deep into her, and I unleash, unable to hold back even if I tried. I'm hissing, eyes shut, lights blinking behind my eyelids as I pulse into her, filling her, needing every last drop to flood her. The pressure at the base of my cock intensifies, the swelling of the knot already kicking in. Grunting as I pump into her, lost in the pleasure of her tight pussy walls constricting me as I grow inside her, the knot locking me in.

"Oh, shit, is that...?" She gasps.

I flip open my eyes, staring down at her surprise, and realize I am her first knot. Fuck. "Baby," I groan, still spilling into her. "My cock's knotting now, claiming you, locking us together. Are you okay?"

She's flushed, head tipped back against the pillows, and the sound that comes out of her is half moan, half laugh, like she can't believe her own body.

"Oh my God!" Her breath stutters. Then she starts laughing for real, soft and bright and wrecked. "Why didn't anyone tell me it feels so amazing and intense and slightly ticklish?"

The laugh shakes her. It shakes me too. Something in my chest gives way, the tightest part unclenching, because it's her. Even like this, overwhelmed and glowing and undone, she's still June. Still sharp, still funny, still refusing to be delicate about what she wants.

I laugh with her, and I lower to lie on the bed, turning her with me so we land face-to-face. Our bodies fit in a way that feels inevitable, like we have been trying to find this exact shape since the first day we met. Heat rolls off her in waves. Her hands cling to me, fingers digging into my shoulders.

Her eyes are glassy, but not lost. Present. Hungry. Fixed on my mouth.

I kiss her again, slower this time, savoring her, letting the moment deepen instead of just burn. Her sigh spills into my lips, and she shudders, her whole body reacting as if the kiss travels straight through her. I feel it too, that ripple of connection, that humming pulse under the skin that's not just desire. It's closeness. It's attachment forming in real time, braided together with everything we have been holding back.

Her cheek brushes mine, her breath warm at my jaw.

"I can't believe you," she whispers, like it's an accusation and a compliment at once.

"I'm right here," I murmur, and I keep my forehead to hers. "I've got you."

June's lashes flutter. She drags her mouth along the side of my throat, a dazed little kiss that turns into something more deliberate, like she's following a craving she has finally stopped denying. Her voice is still soft, still roughened by everything she's feeling.

Then she pauses.

Her gaze lifts, taking me in like she's suddenly noticing a detail she missed.

"You didn't bite me," she says.

The question is so simple, so blunt. I still, watching her face and seeing the surprise there, the curiosity, the aching want underneath it.

My hand slides up her back, firm and steady, keeping her close without pinning her.

"Do you want me to mark you?" I ask.

June's mouth parts. For a second, she just stares at me like she can't believe how calm I am about saying it out loud, how easily it exists between us. Then she shrugs, but it's not casual. It's an attempt at casual that doesn't quite land.

She leans in, kissing the side of my neck again, soft

and messy, still riding whatever high is moving through her. Her lips linger there, and the tenderness of it makes my vision go sharp around the edges.

"I keep thinking a mark would make me being an Omega real," she whispers against my skin. "Secure it permanently."

My throat tightens. I force myself to slow down, to make space for the one thing that matters more than how badly I want it.

"Yes," she says again, clearer this time. "I want it."

"June." I cup her jaw, making her look at me. "Are you sure? Right now, you're flooded with me. Your hormones are zapping. Everything feels bigger. I need you to be certain this is what you want, not just what your body is demanding."

Her eyes hold mine, steady and bright. She isn't timid or wavering.

"I'm sure," she states. "Do it. I want it so badly."

A tremor runs through me. Want and awe and something fierce and protective. I inhale, and her scent fills my lungs, wraps around my ribs, makes my head feel light. The bond between us is already there, humming. The thought of making it permanent, of knowing she will carry my mark, makes something in me go quiet and absolute.

I move slowly, giving her every chance to stop me.

June tips her head, offering her throat with a deliberate tilt that makes my control strain. My mouth grazes her skin first, a kiss that's almost reverent. Then another, lower, where she has presented herself. My hands settle at her waist, holding her close while I breathe her in, while I try to be steady enough to do this the right way.

She shifts against me, impatient, and it sends a shock of want through my body.

"Carter," she whispers, and there's need in it, but there's also choice. "Do it."

I hesitate for one heartbeat, the last thin line of restraint.

June's fingers thread into my hair, and she nudges me closer, a small push that's all permission.

"Please," she repeats, voice rough with wanting. "I want to finally feel real."

That does it.

I press my mouth to her neck and sink my teeth into her flesh, drawing blood.

She gasps, and her whole body goes taut beneath me, a sharp sound caught in her throat, then a low, shaky exhale that turns into a groan. She doesn't pull away but clutches at me instead, holding tighter, as if the sensation roots her deeper into the moment, into me.

And I feel something locking into place. The connection between us surges, thickens, settles like it has finally found its home. My chest goes tight, then expands, as if I've been living with a missing piece and only now realized how much air I was denying myself.

Forever is a terrifying word.

Right now, it feels like the only one that fits.

I lift my head just enough to look at her, licking the blood from my lips. June is gasping for air, mouth parted like she's trying to understand what she feels.

Her fingers trace my shoulder, then my neck, almost dazed.

"There," she whispers.

"Yeah," I manage, voice rough. "There."

She smiles, slow and stunned, like she can feel the change too. And like I'm her world, which melts me.

I kiss her forehead, then her mouth, gentle and possessive all at once.

"It was real before," I tell her. "But yeah. Now it's permanent."

15

JUNE

Sunlight filters through the curtains, warm across my face, and for a moment, I just lie here, suspended in that hazy space between sleep and waking. My body feels heavy and satisfied. There's a comforting ache between my thighs that has me blushing even though no one's watching.

I reach out instinctively, palm pressing against cool sheets beside me, and my stomach dips. Carter is gone. Again. Just like before, I've woken up alone without—

My fingers brush paper.

I roll over, squinting against the light, and find a folded note propped against my phone on the nightstand. I grab it and push up onto one elbow, sheets pooling around my waist.

The paper is slightly creased, like it's been handled too many times. When I unfold it, I recognize Carter's handwriting immediately from last night, messy and slanted.

But this isn't the same poem from last night. He finished it.

You make the quiet louder—the kind I used to drown out.

Now I want to sit in it, if you're sitting there too.

Before you, I was running from a silence that felt like drowning.

Now I think I could stay still forever, if staying still meant staying with you.

My heart flutters in my chest, beating faster, harder, a rhythm that seems to pulse his name. *Carter. Carter. Carter.*

I press the paper to my chest and just breathe for a moment, inhaling the lingering scent of him in my sheets, as though he's somehow seeped into the fabric, into the mattress, into me. I'm smiling so wide my cheeks hurt, and I don't even care that I probably look ridiculous lying here grinning at a piece of paper like it contains the secrets of the universe.

Maybe the secret is just this—someone really seeing you, and putting it into words you'll carry forever.

The last thing I remember is falling asleep in his arms, his body still buried deep inside me, knotted together in a way I'd only ever read about. I'd never experienced knotting before. Never let anyone close enough to try. I always assumed it would be painful, clinical, some biological function to endure rather than enjoy.

I was so wrong.

It was intimate in a way that made me feel cracked open. Vulnerable and safe at the same time. The stretch and fullness, yes, but more than that—the way our bodies locked together, the bond humming between us, connecting us so deeply that I felt his heartbeat as if it were my own.

Even now, hours later, I feel him as if he's still part of me somehow.

Which is when the panic hits.

My hand flies to my neck, fingers pressing against the tender skin just above my collarbone. The bite mark is there—raised and slightly warm, unmistakable. Carter's mating mark.

Oh, shit.

I sit up so fast the room spins. The sheet falls away, and I'm suddenly very aware of being naked, of the evidence of last night scattered across the floor in the form of clothes and the lingering scent of sex.

Not only did I sleep with him, but I also asked him to bite me.

What was I *thinking*?

My fingers trace the mark again, and even that light touch sends warmth flooding through me. A tug in my chest, an awareness that tells me exactly where he is even though I can't see him. Downstairs, maybe. The bond stretches between us like an invisible thread.

A low hum of want has me pressing my thighs together.

Our bond is permanent.

A mating mark isn't something you can undo. It's not a tattoo you can laser off or a ring you can remove when things get complicated. But a bond that ties you to someone for the rest of your life, soul-deep and unbreakable.

And I asked for it. Begged for it, actually, if I'm being honest. I remember the words tumbling out of my mouth between kisses, desperate and certain: *Do it. I want it so badly.*

At the time, it felt right. Inevitable. Like we were always going to end up here.

But now, in the cold light of morning, reality crashes in.

What happens when the rodeo circuit moves to the next town?

Carter, Seth, and Kai—they don't stay anywhere for too long. That's the whole point of the circuit. They travel from place to place, chasing competitions and prize money and the open road. In two or three weeks, they'll pack up and move on to the next arena, the next adventure.

Will they expect me to go with them? Leave Honeyspur Meadow behind, the town I love, the business I've built, the life I've fought to keep even when my parents tried to drag me to Dallas?

Or will they just... leave me?

My chest squeezes, the bond seeming to buzz with something that feels like distress. Can Carter feel this? Can he sense my panic bleeding through our connection?

I didn't move with my parents, because I'd made a life here. Sweetwater Creek Realty might have started as their agency, but I've poured my heart into it. The photo binder of every sale. The keys I've collected. The properties I've nicknamed and loved and fought to preserve. This town is my home in a way Dallas could never be. And I realize now how much that job means to me and how much resentment I'm holding on to that they want to just sell it.

Even as the panic spirals, memories surface. The way Carter stared at me as if I was precious. The way he worshipped every inch of my body, whispered my name like a prayer. How he held me after I experienced my first knot.

I was thinking that I wanted more, that I didn't want it to end, and for the first time in my life, I felt like my real self—an Omega, desired and cherished—instead of the carefully controlled Beta I've pretended to be.

And now he writes me poetry.

I've made things so much more complicated, haven't I?

Add it to the pile. My parents want to sell my business, and I'm just waiting for them to announce that they want to sell the house too, the house I grew up in, the house that holds more memories than I can count.

Maybe joining the circuit is my best solution. Follow Carter and the others, leave everything behind, start fresh.

Well, that's if they even want me to come. Seth's father owns the circuit, and to him, I'm just the chaperone. Just some small-town person who got too close to his star riders. Would he even allow it?

And is that what I want? To give up everything I've built for three men I've known for a handful of days?

Okay. Stop. Stop thinking about it, or you will spiral into a full-blown panic attack.

I force myself out of bed, legs wobbly, and head for the shower. The hot water helps, loosening the tension in my shoulders, washing away the lingering traces of last night. I let myself just stand there for a few minutes, face tilted up to the spray, trying to find my equilibrium.

Today is the first day of the rodeo. I agreed to take photos for Belle, who's out of town for a few days, and I have my camera ready and waiting. A full day of work means no distractions by bites and marks and impossible decisions about my future.

Theoretically, anyway.

I dry off, get dressed in my favorite cherry-print vintage dress and comfortable flats, and comb my hair into something resembling order. The mating mark peeks above my neckline, impossible to hide completely. I consider changing into something higher-necked, then decide I'm being ridiculous. It is what it is.

My reflection stares back at me, flushed cheeks, bright eyes, a woman who looks thoroughly ravished and not nearly as panicked as she feels.

Fake it till you make it, June.

I grab my camera bag and head downstairs.

The three of them are in the kitchen, talking quietly over coffee, and they all go silent the moment I appear in the doorway. Six eyes swing toward me. Three sets of shoulders straighten.

I raise an eyebrow. "Well, that's not suspicious at all."

Carter's mouth twitches. Kai grins outright. Seth just watches me with those intense blue eyes, unreadable as always.

God, they're gorgeous. All three of them, dressed and ready for the rodeo, looking like they stepped out of some cowboy fantasy designed specifically to destroy me. Seth is in a dark chambray shirt with the sleeves rolled to his elbows, forearms on display, his favorite hat already on his head. Carter is wearing a green-and-white-checkered button-up that brings out his eyes, blond hair still damp from the shower. And Kai is in a fitted black T-shirt that clings to every muscle, his tribal sleeve bold against his tanned skin, hair pulled up in that messy knot that makes me want to yank it loose.

It's my second day without suppressants, and I feel

it. Their scents crash over me the moment I'm close. My body buzzes with awareness, nerves lighting up like someone flipped a switch. I want to touch them, and I keep thinking about hands and mouths and skin against me, and it's taking every ounce of willpower to stand here and act normal.

But Carter. God, Carter.

The bond between us hums, warm and insistent, and I'm drawn to him like a magnet. I want to cross the kitchen and press myself against his chest, bury my nose in his neck, inhale until I'm drunk on his scent. I want those arms around me again, that sense of safety and belonging that made everything feel simple last night.

Instead, I stay where I am and pull myself together, smiling as if my whole world isn't tilting on its axis.

"We should head to the rodeo," I say brightly. "I have photos to take, and you three have competitions to prepare for."

Carter moves toward me, concern softening his features. "How are you feeling?"

"I'm fine." The lie tastes like ash on my tongue. All three of them stare at me with identical expressions of *We can tell you're bullshitting us.*

"And you slept well?"

Heat floods my cheeks. Before I can answer, Kai coughs into his fist, and I definitely hear the words "bed creaking" and "screaming" hidden in there somewhere. "No one slept last night," he adds with a wicked grin. "Just saying."

I might actually combust. My face is on fire, spreading down my neck, probably reaching my chest at this point. Of course they heard. The walls in this house aren't soundproof, and I wasn't exactly... quiet.

"I—that's—" I sputter, unable to form actual words.

Seth breaks the awkward silence, pushing off the counter and moving toward me with that slow, deliberate stride. "It was bound to happen," he adds. "We're scent matches. Our bodies were always going to find each other." His lips curve into something between a smile and a smirk. "And those sounds you were making were hard to ignore."

I laugh, fake and slightly hysterical. "Yeah, well. I'm sure Carter gave you all the details." I shoot Carter a pointed look. He crosses the remaining distance between us, stopping close enough that his scent wraps around me like a blanket.

"I don't kiss and tell." His green eyes hold mine, serious underneath the charm. "What happened between us stays between us. Unless you want to share."

"Oh my God, when you say it like that—"

"Like what?"

"Never mind." I press my hands to my burning cheeks. Kai and Seth have drifted closer too, all three of them circling me like I'm the center of their orbit. I know they're staring at my neck. At the bite.

"He definitely told you about the mark," I say quietly.

"How could I not?" Carter reaches out, fingers gentle against my jaw, tilting my face up to show them. "I have you on my mind constantly. My body craves you endlessly. And our bond..." He traces the mark, and I shiver. "It makes you mine for eternity. You have no idea how happy that makes me."

He pulls me into his arms before I can protest, and I should push back, should maintain some kind of distance while I figure out what I'm feeling. But his scent floods my senses the moment I'm pressed against his chest, and I melt, lifting myself onto my tiptoes, my face finding the curve of his neck like it belongs there.

I breathe him in. Deep. Deeper. The bond purrs with satisfaction, and I'm already floating, already lost. "You're dangerous," I mumble against his skin.

"That's what a bond does," Seth explains from somewhere behind me. "Connects you so deeply that you instinctively crave each other. It's biological and unavoidable."

"Yep." Kai's voice is closer now. "And I'm ready for it whenever you are."

I pull back from Carter to find Kai puckering his lips comically, making exaggerated kissing sounds, and a surprised laugh escapes me.

"Okay." I hold up my hands, stepping back. "There's way too much to unpack here, and I'm not ready to deal with it. Can we please not talk about it right now? You three need to focus on your day."

They exchange looks, some silent communication I can't decode, and then nod.

"Fair enough," Carter says softly. "But we're not done talking about this."

"I know." I grab my camera bag from the counter. "I know."

In no time, we're piled into Carter's red pickup truck, country music blasting from the speakers as we wind through the Montana countryside. Kai is in the back with me, and he has one arm stretched along the seat behind me, fingers occasionally brushing my shoulder like he can't help himself.

I should mind. I don't.

Seth rides shotgun, tapping his fingers against the edge of the window to the music. Carter is singing along under his breath, slightly off-key, and it's so endearing that I want to kiss him again.

This right here, the easy comfort of being with them, the way they don't push when I need space, the way they seem to communicate without words, it's the sweetest thing they do. Well, one of many.

We drive past golden fields and rolling hills, the morning sun painting everything in shades of amber. By the time we reach the rodeo grounds, my nerves have settled into something manageable.

The arena is massive, an outdoor stadium that's been set up in the wide-open fields just outside town. A huge banner stretches across the entrance: WILD-FIRE STAR RODEO in bold letters, with the dates underneath and photos of the star riders.

Including three very familiar faces.

Seth on horseback, hat tipped low. Carter in mid-motion, reins in hand, grinning at the camera with that golden-boy charm. Kai, all muscle and intensity.

And here I am with them in their truck, wearing one of their mating marks.

Heat creeps up my cheeks again, and I catch Carter watching me in the rearview mirror. He grins, slow and knowing, and mouths a single word: *Mine.*

I duck my head, fighting a smile. Okay. What is wrong with me? I am completely, utterly lost.

Kai is already out of the truck, and in seconds he's on my side, pulling open the door with a flourish and offering his hand. "My lady," he says with mock gravity.

I take his hand, letting him help me down, and my smile is probably too wide, but I don't care. "Such a gentleman."

"Only for you, doll."

Seth chuckles as he rounds the truck, and before I can say anything, he's right there in my space, fingers brushing hair from my face and tucking it behind my ear with surprising tenderness.

"Don't worry," he murmurs. "There's no rush to

make any decisions. We're a pack now. You and us." Then he leans in and kisses me.

I freeze on the spot. It's not a quick peck, not a chaste brush of lips. It's a real kiss that's deep and claiming, his hand cupping the back of my head, his mouth moving against mine with a hunger that makes my knees buckle. And I'm gripping his shirt just to stay upright.

When he finally pulls back, I'm breathless. Dazed. My lips are tingling, and there's a very good chance my underwear needs changing.

"That's—" I manage. "That was—"

"Unfair is what it was." Kai is right there, practically in our faces, and I laugh despite myself. Seth doesn't seem bothered, just smirks at him.

"Back up, buddy," Seth says.

"Fuck no." Kai's pale eyes are fixed on me, hungry and a little petulant. "Carter gets to make her scream, you get to kiss her like that, and what do I get? Left behind? Forgotten?" He pouts, and it's dangerously adorable on a man built like a weapon. "I'm feeling very neglected here."

Something reckless surges through me. I've already gone this far. Already let Carter mark me, already kissed Seth in a public place where anyone could see. What's one more kiss?

I grab the front of Kai's shirt and pull him down to me.

He makes a surprised sound against my mouth,

then his hands are on my cheeks, cradling my face like I'm something special, and he's kissing me back with everything he has. It's different from Carter, different from Seth—Kai kisses like he's showing me the stars and he's trying to make sure I'll remember this moment for the rest of my life. His tongue sweeps into my mouth, tasting, exploring, and I moan softly before I can stop myself.

When we finally break apart, he's inches from my face, gray eyes blazing. "You have no idea what I have in store for you," he whispers.

An excited shiver runs down my spine. "You worry me, Kai, when you say things like that."

He grins and gives my rear a playful smack that makes me yelp. Then his arm loops around my back, pulling me close.

"Let's go, doll. We've got a rodeo to win."

I glance over and catch Seth's father watching from across the lot. He's standing near one of the equipment trailers, arms crossed, expression unreadable. Our eyes meet for a split second before he turns away, and I have no idea what he's thinking.

To him, I'm just the chaperone. Just some Beta they hired to keep his son and the other riders out of trouble. If he saw those kisses, saw the way they're touching me...

I push the thought aside. Today is not the day to worry about it.

And here I am, walking into a rodeo with three star

cowboys at my side, life speeding up in ways I never expected. Everything seems to be telling me they're meant to be in my life. But things in my life have never been simple or perfect. Quite the opposite. And I'm terrified of what the future holds.

Today is not the day to think about it, I remind myself, echoing Seth's words.

I'm such a terrible liar. Even to myself.

Once we're inside, the guys peel off toward the stables where the other performers are gathering. I've got a pass around my neck, courtesy of Belle's photography credentials, that gives me behind-the-scenes access, so I figure I'll start there.

The arena is even more impressive from the inside. Rows and rows of seating surrounding the central ring, a massive Wildfire Star Rodeo sign spinning overhead, banners featuring the star riders—including my three Alphas—rippling in the breeze. My heart races at the sight of their faces blown up twenty feet tall.

I snap a few photos of the empty arena, the early morning light casting long shadows across the dirt. Then I wander toward the back, where the real action is happening.

Riders warming up, horses being brushed and saddled, equipment being checked and double-checked. I capture it all, candid shots of stars, the beautiful, powerful animals, the worn leather and polished buckles.

I'm adjusting my lens near the main-office trailer

when I spot Seth's father. He's deep in conversation with someone I recognize: Holden, the town committee's finance guy who works closely with Pete. But it's odd to see him out here, because Holden is usually glued to his desk at the town hall. I've never seen him at community events, let alone chatting up rodeo owners.

They haven't noticed me yet, and I inch closer, pretending to photograph a nearby horse.

"... last chance for the town." Seth's father's voice is gruff, irritated. "If you don't bring in decent numbers for me this year, I'm pulling the circuit from Honeyspur Meadow permanently."

"We're just not attracting the attendees we used to," Holden replies, sounding defensive. "The economy, the competition from other events—"

"I don't want excuses. I want results."

I lower my camera and step forward, plastering on a friendly smile. "Morning!"

Both men turn. Seth's father recognizes me immediately, his eyes flicking from my face to my camera to the pass around my neck.

"Miss Calloway." He nods. "Photography and chaperoning. That's quite the workload."

"Keeping those boys in line is definitely a full-time job," I agree with a laugh.

He almost smiles. "Ain't that the truth."

Holden's nostrils flare as he studies me, something dismissive in his expression that immediately gets my back up. "June. Shouldn't you be focused on your… duties?"

"Just taking photos. But I couldn't help overhearing—" I gesture vaguely between them. "You're worried about attendance numbers?"

"That's not really your concern," Holden says sharply.

"It's just odd." I keep my voice light, casual. "I booked out every rental property in town for this week. Every single one. Plus the B&Bs and the motel on Route 7. If the town is full of visitors, why wouldn't they be coming to the rodeo?"

Seth's father's eyes narrow, fixing on Holden. "She's got a point. If the town's booked solid, where's my money going?"

Holden's jaw tightens. "There are a lot of factors at play here. Ticket sales, concessions, merchandise—it's complicated. June, you should focus on the chaperoning job and leave the finances to the professionals."

He puts a hand on Seth's father's arm and steers him away, already launching into some explanation I can't quite hear. I watch them go, something uneasy settling in my stomach.

That was weird, but I walk in the opposite direction and continue taking photos.

By the time the arena starts filling up, I've taken hundreds of images. My memory card is going to be stuffed, but Belle will have plenty to choose from for the town's promotional materials.

I spot a familiar head of reddish hair in the crowd and wave frantically.

"Sophia!" She was meant to come meet me today so we can watch the event together, especially since her Alphas are participating.

She turns, green eyes lighting up when she sees me, and we meet in a crushing hug that probably looks ridiculous, but I don't care. She's wearing light-blue jeans, a silk blouse, and sandals.

"I've been looking for you everywhere! Cash said he saw you with the Benton crew earlier, and I was like, 'Oh my God, I need details immediately.'"

"First of all, hello to you too." I laugh, looping my arm through hers as we head toward our seats. "Second, how are you? How are the guys?"

"Amazing. Perfect. Exhausting." She rolls her eyes dramatically. "Cash has been insufferable about some new horse he bought, Walker won't stop reorganizing the ranch office, and Ridge is on a sourdough kick, which means I've gained five pounds in bread alone."

"Sounds rough."

"The hardest life." She grins, and there's so much happiness underneath her sarcasm that it makes my heart swell. Sophia found her fated mates last year when she inherited Wild Hearts Ranch, and watching her fall for them was like watching a romantic movie in real time—complete with miscommunication, dramatic gestures, and a happy ending.

We settle into our front-row seats, and she immediately twists to face me.

"Okay. Spill. What's going on with you and the rodeo trio? I've been hearing some gossip through the town vine."

Heat floods my face.

"Babe, everyone's already talking about spotting you kissing two of them out in the parking lot this morning." She's grinning ear to ear. "So? What's happening?"

I open my mouth to deflect, then stop. This is Sophia. My friend. The one person who might actually understand what I'm going through.

"Actually," I say slowly, "I do have news."

Her eyebrows shoot up. "Oh?"

"But you first. You look like you're about to explode, needing to tell me something."

She bites her lip, practically vibrating with excitement, her hand settling on her stomach. "Okay, okay. So, this has been in the works for a while, and it shouldn't be a surprise really, but—"

"Oh my God." I gasp, my gaze dropping to her stomach and back. "Sophia. Are you—"

She's nodding before I can finish, tears springing to her eyes even as she laughs. "I'm pregnant."

I shriek, loud enough that people turn to look, and I don't care even a little bit because I'm pulling her into a hug so tight she squeaks.

"That's *amazing!*" I release her just enough to look

at her face, both of us grinning like idiots. "Oh my God, Sophia. I'm so happy for you. For all of you!"

"Cash, Walker, and Ridge have been talking about babies forever," she says, wiping at her eyes. "And I always thought I wasn't ready, you know? But then something just... clicked. Like I could suddenly see all of us together, a little one running around the ranch, and it felt *right*."

"You're going to be such a good mom."

"You think?" She laughs, a little wobbly. "I'm terrified."

"The best parents always are." I squeeze her hands. "Do you know what you're having?"

She shakes her head. "We want it to be a surprise. But I know it's only one right now, which means the guys are already placing bets on who it looks like most so they know which one 'got me pregnant.'" She makes air quotes. "And then the other two need to 'do their part' too, so we're apparently having at least three kids."

"Oh my God."

"I know." Her hand drifts to her still-flat stomach, something soft in her expression. "I had no idea I'd want this so much. But yeah. So much yes."

I hug her again, holding on tight. "That's the best news I've heard in forever. And I'm going to spoil that baby rotten. You know that, right? Auntie June is going to be insufferable."

"I'm counting on it."

When we finally separate, I glance around the arena. It's filling up, but not as much as I expected. There are gaps in the seating, some small sections that look sparse. Was Holden right about the attendance issues, or is the first day slow, as it includes a lot of parades? If the rodeo isn't profitable, Seth's father might pull the circuit from Honeyspur Meadow entirely. So many local businesses depend on the annual influx of visitors...

"Okay, your turn." Sophia elbows me. "What's your news? And why do you keep touching your neck?"

I drop my hand guiltily. I hadn't even realized I was doing it.

"So." I take a deep breath. "You know I'm chaperoning the Wildfire Star guys. Seth, Carter, and Kai."

"The insanely hot ones plastered all over the entrance banners, yes."

"Well." Another breath. "They're... we're... scent matches. All three of them. And please don't judge me, but I've been hiding the fact that I'm an Omega for years. It's a long story, as I know I told you I was a Beta."

Sophia's eyes go wide. "June. I would never judge you, no matter what, and you don't owe me anything, as long as you're safe and happy."

I grin. "You're amazing."

She nods and I laugh. "That's huge news about the scent matches, by the way!" She grabs my arm.

"That's... that's fate, babe. That's the universe screaming at you."

"The universe needs to lower its voice." I slump in my seat. "And that's not even the biggest part."

"What could be bigger than that?"

"Last night, Carter marked me, bonding us forever." I cover my face with my hands. "He even wrote me this poem, and I was feeling all these things, and he asked about my heat, and one thing led to another and I literally *asked him to bite me*, Sophia. I begged him to."

"Holy shit."

"I know."

"So you're mated. Like, *permanently bonded* mated."

"Yep."

"To one of the hottest men I've ever seen."

"Appears so."

"And you're upset about this because...?"

I drop my hands to my lap and stare at her. "Because they leave town soon! The circuit moves on, and they go with it. What am I supposed to do? Leave everything behind and follow them?"

Sophia says, gently, "Didn't you tell me something similar once?"

"What do you mean?"

"When I was panicking about Cash, Walker, and Ridge. When I kept making excuses about why it couldn't work, why I should go back to Chicago." She tilts her head. "You told me to stop being scared. That they obviously adored me. That sometimes you have to take a leap and trust that someone will catch you."

I groan. "I hate it when my own advice gets used against me."

"Tough." She grins. "The point is, maybe it's time to take your own advice. Why are you holding back?"

The grand-entry music starts, cutting off my response. Riders begin pouring into the arena on horseback, flags waving, the crowd cheering. I spot Seth first, leading the pack on a gorgeous bay horse, then Kai on a chestnut mare, then Carter bringing up the rear on a black stallion.

Seth's father stands in the center of the arena with a microphone, welcoming everyone to the Wildfire Star Rodeo. He explains the five-day event, the various competitions—bull riding, saddle bronc, bareback, roping events—and the process of elimination leading to the final showdown.

"Big congratulations to our defending champions," he announces. "Seth Benton in bareback riding, Carter Storm in saddle bronc, and Kai Kahele riding the bulls!"

The crowd roars. I lift my camera, snapping photos as the riders circle the arena. Seth catches my eye and tips his hat in my direction. Carter blows me a kiss that's probably visible from space. Kai winks, slow and deliberate.

I'm blushing so hard my face might catch fire.

Sophia laughs beside me. "Yeah, they're definitely not into you at all."

"Shut up."

"Just calling it like I see it." She bumps her shoulder against mine. "So? What's the answer? Why are you holding back?"

The riders exit, preparing for the first events. I watch them go, my three cowboys, my fated mates, disappearing behind the scenes.

Why *am* I holding back?

Because I'm scared, and I've been hurt before. Last time I trusted someone completely, it nearly destroyed me, not to mention my trust in others. And loving people means giving them the power to leave, and everyone always leaves eventually, just like my parents did.

Sophia is watching me, waiting.

"I don't know," I finally admit. "I'm just... scared."

"I get it." She takes my hand, squeezes. "But sometimes the scary thing is the right thing. Trust me on that one."

I look back at the arena, at the massive banners featuring the men who've turned my entire life upside down.

Maybe she's right.

Maybe it's time to stop running and start falling.

16

KAI

The smoke from the big metal BBQ pits drifts across the patio, thick and rich with the smell of brisket and burnt ends and something sweet—probably the honey glaze they use on the ribs here. My stomach has been growling since we pulled into the parking lot, and now that I've got a plate piled high with meat, I'm a happy man.

Well. Mostly happy.

June is sitting across from me at one of the long wooden tables, wedged between Carter and some barrel racer from Wyoming who won't stop talking about her horse. The sunset paints everything gold and amber, catches the red highlights in June's hair, makes her freckles stand out against her flushed cheeks. She's laughing at something Carter said, head tipped back, and the sound cuts through the noise of the crowd and the twang of country music playing from the speakers mounted on the patio posts.

I want to be the one making her laugh like that.

Down, boy. You'll get your turn.

The place is packed tonight—half the rodeo circuit crammed onto these benches, mixing with locals who came out for the food and the spectacle. It's the kind of scene I usually love: loud, chaotic, everyone a little drunk and a lot competitive. But my attention keeps drifting back to the woman with the hazel eyes and the mating mark on her neck that isn't mine.

Not yet, anyway.

"You gonna eat that or just stare at it, Kai?" Seth's voice cuts through my thoughts. He's working on a rack of ribs, sauce smeared across his fingers and lips, looking more relaxed than I've seen him in weeks. Probably because our Omega is sitting close, safe and claimed, even if technically she's got Carter's mark on her skin.

Pack, I remind myself. We're a pack. What's his is ours.

Doesn't make the hunger any less sharp.

"Just pacing myself," I say, tearing into a chunk of brisket. The meat falls apart on my tongue, smoky and perfect. "Unlike some people, I don't need to inhale everything in front of me."

"Big words from the guy who ate an entire pizza by himself last Tuesday," Carter pipes in.

"That was different. That was strategic carb-loading."

"For what? Sitting on the couch watching TV?"

I laugh out loud, and June catches my eye from across the table, grinning. Fuck me, she's beautiful.

The barrel racer finally takes a breath, and June uses the opening to lean forward, elbows on the table. "So I've been thinking about the attendance today. Despite a bunch of empty seats, I noticed the stadium was reasonably full."

Seth nods, reaching for his beer. "My father mentioned a few days back that ticket sales are down, especially the multiday passes. But you wouldn't think that by today's turnout. Unless the next few days sell fewer tickets?"

June's brow furrows in that way it does when she's working through a problem. "The town is booked solid. I handled most of the rentals myself. Why is your dad being told sales are down?"

"Maybe the tourists are here for something else," Carter suggests. "The scenery?" He gestures vaguely at the Montana landscape beyond the patio. "Fresh air? The dubious pleasure of small-town charm?"

"Doubt it," she answers.

"You'd be surprised what people do," Carter adds.

I tune out their speculation and let my gaze wander across the patio. Past the crowded tables and the waitresses weaving through with trays of food, past the big smokers billowing their fragrant clouds, to the corner where something catches my eye.

A mechanical bull.

It's set up under a covered area, surrounded by thick padded mats for landing. The thing is built like a tank, all chrome and leather and mechanical joints designed to throw riders on their asses. A small crowd has gathered around it, watching some guy in a too-tight shirt try to hang on. He lasts maybe three seconds before he's eating mat.

But that's not what interests me.

It's the name painted on the bull's side in bold red letters: BRUTUS.

"Hey." I nod toward the corner. "Why's the mechanical bull called Brutus? That mean something around here?"

June follows my gaze and laughs. "Oh, that. It's named after a real bull in town. Total legend."

"You don't say?"

"Brutus." She says the name like it's a curse and a blessing all at once. "He belongs to old Farmer Crawford, but 'belongs' is a strong word. That black bull does whatever he wants. He's escaped his enclosure more times than anyone can count. Just shows up in people's yards, on the main street, wherever he feels like. Terrorizes the locals on a regular basis."

Carter and I exchange looks.

"No fucking way," I say slowly, thinking back to the night we both swore we were going to die.

"I bet it was him," Carter adds.

June's eyes go wide. "Wait—you've *seen* him?"

"The bastard chased us down in the pickup." The

memory surfaces, vivid and visceral. That massive black shape appearing out of nowhere, hooves pounding the dirt road, those murderous eyes locked on our truck. "We thought he was a demonic bull sent straight from hell to murder us."

"It was fucking terrifying," Carter confirms with a chuckle.

June is laughing so hard she's wiping tears from her eyes. "Oh God, everyone in town has a Brutus story. He's part of the local experience. Farmer Crawford believes in letting him have his freedom, which is a nice way of saying he can't keep the damn thing contained. Brutus knows how to break through gates, fences, anything. He's basically a four-legged escape artist with anger issues."

Seth chuckles around a mouthful of ribs, sauce glistening on his lips. June is watching him with that look —the one where her eyes go soft and hungry at the same time, like she wants to devour him but also maybe climb into his lap and never leave.

I know the feeling. I'm pretty sure we all have that look when we watch her.

She catches herself and looks away, a blush creeping up her cheeks. Reining it in. Always reining it in.

"So why put his name on that?" I jerk my chin toward the mechanical bull. "Closest anyone can get to him without dying?"

June takes a sip of her drink. "Brutus used to be a

champion rodeo bull. Retired now, obviously, but back in the day, he was legendary on the circuit. Not many people know that part. Most of the stories around here are about him showing up at the elementary school during a fire drill or crashing the Fourth of July parade. There's even one about him breaking into the mayor's house and eating his prize-winning rose bushes."

"You're joking."

"I wish." She grins. "Small-town life, baby. Never a dull moment."

Carter nudges her with his shoulder, and she leans into him automatically, like gravity. The jealousy that spikes through me is irrational—I know she's ours, know we're building something together—but my instincts don't give a damn about logic.

I want her leaning into me like that.

"Dad's been grumbling about pulling the circuit from smaller towns if the numbers don't improve," Seth says, dragging the conversation back to serious territory.

"He can't do that." June sits up straighter, alarm flickering across her face. "So many businesses here depend on the rodeo. The restaurants, the hotels, the shops, this is their biggest month of the year. If the circuit stops coming..."

"Then they lose a major revenue stream." Seth's jaw tightens. "I know. He knows. But at the end of the day, it's a business decision."

"That's bullshit," I say flatly. "The circuit was built

on towns like this. Real rural communities with actual farms and ranches, people who live this life every day. Not those bougie fake-country towns full of rich people playing cowboy."

Seth nods. "I've said as much. He's... considering his options."

The worry in June's eyes concerns me. This town matters to her, not just as a business opportunity or a place to live, but *really* matters—the kind of deep-rooted connection that becomes part of your identity.

I get it. The circuit is like that for me. The only home I've ever had that didn't hurt, but I know at the core, it's my pack with Seth and Carter that keeps me grounded.

"I'll talk to him more," Seth says, reaching across the table to squeeze June's hand. "See what's really going on with the numbers. There might be something we can do."

She gives him a grateful smile, but I can see the tension she's carrying in her shoulders. The fear she's trying to hide.

We eat for a while in comfortable silence, the conversation around us ebbing and flowing. The mechanical bull keeps drawing my attention, my brain turning over possibilities. A champion rodeo bull. Retired. Legendary. And currently terrorizing the locals for fun.

I nod toward it with my fork. "You ever wonder if

people think they're riding the real Brutus when they climb onto that thing? Like it's some kind of tribute."

Carter snorts into his beer. "If you're so obsessed with Brutus, why don't you go ride him yourself and get it out of your system?"

I shoot him a look. "He wouldn't stand a chance with me."

June makes a small sound that might be a laugh, and when I glance over, she's smiling like she's trying not to. "You're way too good for Brutus," she says, then reaches across the table and brushes her fingers over my hand.

Just that. Bare skin to skin.

My whole body lights up. I turn my hand slightly so our fingers fit together, like it's the most natural thing in the world, and the way she watches me while I do it ruins me.

I hold her gaze, letting my voice drop. "For you, I'd do anything."

Her lashes flutter, and her mouth parts like she's about to say something she shouldn't. The heat in her eyes is quiet but real, and I mean every word.

Carter clears his throat like he's not listening, even though he absolutely is. He finishes his beer and stands. "Anyone need a refill? I'm heading to the bar."

Orders fly at him from around the table, and he wanders off to collect drinks. Seth's father appears a few minutes later, weaving through the crowd with the slightly loose gait of a man who's had a few whiskeys.

"I need to—" I gesture vaguely. "Be right back."

Seth gives me a suspicious look, but I'm already moving.

It takes me twenty minutes to track down the old farmer. He's holding court at a table near the bar, surrounded by other weathered ranchers trading stories and giving each other shit. When I approach, they all go quiet, sizing me up with the particular wariness rural folks reserve for outsiders.

"Mr. Crawford?" I keep my voice respectful. This is his home turf. "I'm Kai Kahele. I ride for the Wildfire Star circuit."

"I know who you are, son." His voice is gravelly. "Seen your picture on those big banners."

"That's me." I grin. "Mind if I ask you something about Brutus?"

The old man's eyes sharpen with interest. "What about him?"

"I heard he used to compete. Back before he retired."

"Best damn bull there was." Pride straightens his spine. "Threw most riders who tried to stick him. His retirement record was a ninety-seven percent buck-off rate. Only three people ever made the full eight seconds on him."

"And now he just... roams around?"

"He's earned the right." Farmer Crawford shrugs. "Spent his whole life performing for crowds. Now he gets to do whatever he wants. If that means escaping his pasture to scare the hell out of tourists, well, that's his choice."

I like this man.

"What would it take," I say carefully, "to get him back in the arena? One more ride?"

Farmer Crawford stares at me for a long moment, as do his buddies nearby. Then he starts laughing—a deep, wheezing sound that shakes his whole body. "Boy, you've got a death wish."

"So I've been told."

"Brutus hasn't had a rider attempt him in years. No one's crazy enough to try."

"I'm crazy enough. I'm not saying I'll stick to the full eight seconds."

He studies me, something shifting in his expression. "Then why would you want to?"

"Because the circuit is thinking about pulling out of this town." I lay it out straight, no bullshit. "Towns like Honeyspur Meadow are the first to get cut. But if we could offer something special that people would travel to see, it might change the equation and get more attendees."

"And you think riding Brutus would do that?"

"A legendary bull coming out of retirement for one final challenge? A rider willing to take him on when no one else will?" I spread my hands. "That's not just a rodeo event. That's a spectacle. That's the kind of thing people talk about for years."

Farmer Crawford is quiet, chewing over my words, his buddies whispering about how it might work.

"You know he could kill you," Farmer Crawford says finally.

"I take that risk with any bull I ride."

"He's not like those practice bulls you're used to. He's got instincts honed from years of learning exactly how to destroy riders."

I nod.

"And you still want to do this?"

I think about June's worried face when she talked about the businesses that depend on the rodeo. I think about Seth, whose father built this circuit from nothing and is watching it slowly shrink in this town that used to be a huge earner for us. I think about Carter, who rides to honor his dead brother and can't afford to lose another piece of the life they shared.

"Yeah," I say. "I do."

Farmer Crawford stares at me for a long, measuring moment. Then he nods slowly. "All right. Give me a sec."

Before I can even answer, he's already stepping away from the edge of the table, phone out, turning his shoulder to the crowd, and lifts it to his ear.

I stay where I am, hands tucked behind my back so I don't look like I'm hovering. Doesn't stop the nervous energy from buzzing under my skin anyway.

I keep my eyes on Farmer Crawford, but I can't hear a word he's saying with the chatter around us.

He ends the call after a decent chat and looks at his screen for a beat, thumbs moving like he's firing off a quick message. Then he turns back toward me, and this time he's smiling like he's been waiting to.

"Well," he says, slipping the phone back into his pocket, "Pete's in. Town committee will want the paperwork and some promotional materials, but that's normal." He reaches out his hand. "You got yourself a deal."

Relief hits me so fast it's almost dizzying. I shake his hand, grip firm. "Appreciate it."

Farmer Crawford's grin widens, a little boyish now that the hard part is done. "Will be good to see Brutus in the arena again."

"That's the idea," I say, and it's the easiest I've felt all day.

By the time I get back to the table, Carter's still got his spot next to June like he's claimed it in blood. Seth's father is there now, sitting across from him, and the conversation looks like it could crack glass.

I hang back, not wanting to interrupt.

"... just remember when you were younger," John is saying, his voice rough. "Back in Amarillo, with your mother. Everything felt perfect then. Like nothing could ruin what we had."

Seth's jaw is tight, but he doesn't pull away when his father reaches across to grip his hand.

"I want that for you, son. That same chance to build something real. A family. A home." John's attention drifts to June, who's watching the exchange carefully. "You can't be a rodeo legend forever. Sometimes it's best to leave when you're on top; that's what I've always said."

"Is that what you're telling me to do?" Seth's voice is carefully neutral.

"I'm saying not to let the good things slip away while you're chasing buckles and trophies." John squeezes his hand once, then releases it. "The circuit will sort itself out. You focus on what you want in your future."

A woman appears at John's elbow, his new wife, Marlene. She's maybe thirty-three, thirty-four, wearing a pretty sundress and heels that seem impractical for a BBQ joint. He's in his late fifties. Her smile is bright and a little artificial as she touches his shoulder.

"Dear, come on. There's someone I want to introduce you to, and you've been gone forever." Her gaze flicks to Seth. "Oh, you did amazing today. I'm rooting for you."

Seth nods, expression carefully blank. "Thanks, Marlene."

John lets himself be led away, throwing one last look at his son over his shoulder, then he's gone.

June reaches across the table and takes Seth's hand. "Family is complicated."

"You have no idea." He laces their fingers together. "But one thing I know is that I don't want a strained family like I had growing up after my mom passed. Whatever we build, it's going to be solid. Real."

June's gaze softens. "Seth…"

"You're my world, June. Our world." His voice drops low, meant just for her, but I'm close enough to hear, as is Carter. "Even if you're not ready to accept it yet, I'm going to make you ours forever."

"You mean it?"

"Every word." She looks as though she might cry, and I've never wanted to hold someone so badly in my life.

I drop onto the bench beside her, seeing as the woman sitting there earlier is gone, making my presence known. "Miss me?"

The moment breaks, but not in a bad way. June laughs, swiping at her eyes. "Where did you disappear to?"

"Had to take care of something." I reach for my beer, keeping my expression casual.

"Nothing important."

Carter narrows his eyes at me. "Why do I feel like you're lying?"

"Because you have trust issues."

"I have *Kai* issues."

Before he can push further, June turns to look at me properly. Her hand finds my thigh under the table, and the touch sends electricity racing up my spine.

"You okay?" she asks quietly.

"Perfect." I cover her hand with mine. "Just thinking."

"About what?"

I glance at the mechanical bull in the corner, then back at her face. Those hazel eyes are always doing too much, like she's trying to hold herself together.

"About what comes next," I say. "And what I'm willing to do to make sure you don't regret saying yes to any of this."

We're most of the way through our second round when I decide it's time.

"So," I say, loud enough to slice through the table's chatter. "I have a solution to the attendance problem."

Carter makes a pained noise. "Why do I already hate this?"

"Because you lack imagination. Anyway, I talked to Farmer Crawford, and he spoke with Pete from the town committee. They agreed to let me ride Brutus at the rodeo."

Silence.

"Are you out of your mind?" Carter's beer hits the table hard enough to slosh. "Did you miss the part where the demon bull tried to put a horn through my door? And now you want to climb on him like it's a carnival ride?"

"It'll be fine."

"It'll be your funeral."

June's hand is on my thigh again before she even realizes she's moved, fingers tightening like she's anchoring me in place. Her face goes pale, but her eyes are locked on mine.

"Kai." Her voice drops, softer than the noise around us. "Are you sure? Brutus isn't just any bull. He's—"

"A retired champion with a ninety-seven percent buck-off rate. I know." I turn fully toward her, because she's the only part of this that matters. I take her hand and bring it up between us, holding it like I'm reminding both of us that we're real people and not just adrenaline and plans. "Doll, look at me."

Her gaze flicks to my mouth, then back to my eyes like she's fighting herself.

"The circuit is thinking about dropping this town," I say. "That's businesses losing money. People losing jobs. A place that actually cares getting left behind. I don't want that. And I don't want you feeling like you walked into a mess you can't fix."

"I didn't say that," she whispers.

"You didn't have to." My thumb brushes slowly over her knuckles. It's a small gesture, but it's deliberate. "I'm not doing this because I want attention. I'm doing it because I want you to stay."

Her face freezes in a surprised expression for half a second. Then she swallows.

"But the risk," she says, voice unsteady.

"Every bull is a risk. That's the point." I hold her eyes while I say it, letting her see the truth. "The difference is people will pay to see this. Brutus coming out of retirement for one final ride. That's headlines. Tickets.

The kind of stunt that makes the whole state look at this town again."

Seth has been listening, expression tight, and now he shakes his head once, slow. "Your heart's in the right place, Kai. It always is. But you have a talent for throwing yourself into the fire."

June's fingers squeeze mine again, like she's silently agreeing with him.

"I know my limits," I say.

Carter scoffs. "Do you? Because from where I'm sitting, this looks like you volunteering to get launched into the bleachers."

I don't look away from June. "If I get thrown, I get thrown."

Her lips part. "Kai."

I dip my head a fraction closer, voice going low so it's just for her. "I'm not reckless. I'm motivated."

Her cheeks flush at that, like she hears the second meaning in it. Like she knows exactly who my motivation is.

I lean back and address the table again. "Pete's already working on flyers and advertising. We raise ticket prices for the Brutus event, make it a special attraction. The revenue might be enough to convince your father that this town is worth keeping on the circuit."

"And if you get hurt?" Seth asks, flat.

A beat.

June's eyes stay on mine. Worried, yes. But there's

something else too. Something that looks a lot like she cares more than she wants to admit.

"The plan isn't for me to do the whole eight seconds, but to show people Brutus, and in all honesty, I'm happy for Brutus to win here," I say. "I'm not doing it for glory but for ticket sales."

Carter drags a hand down his face. "This is my fault. I made that stupid joke about you riding Brutus, and now you're doing a whole civic project with your skull."

I grin at him. "You gave me the idea. So really, this is on you."

"That's not how any of this works."

June lets out a small, shaky laugh, and my chest loosens. Like even scared, she's still here. Still with us.

I lift her hand to my mouth and press a quick kiss to her knuckles. "Pretty sure it is," I say, eyes on hers. "Trust me. I'm not an idiot."

"Debatable," Carter mutters.

I ignore him. "I only do what I know I can handle. I wouldn't have agreed to this unless I was confident I could pull it off. And I'm one mean bull rider. I've been doing this for years. Brutus is a challenge, yeah, but he's not impossible."

Her gaze drops to the ink peeking from under my sleeve, then back to my face. Like she's trying to read the parts I keep locked down. "You always sound like you're fighting something," she says softly.

I huff a breath, half laugh, half truth. "Old habit."

Carter tilts his head at my arm. "Tell her, Kai."

Seth leans closer from across the table. "He's not big on talking about his past," Seth says, like he's covering for me instead of calling me out.

I glance down at my sleeve of ink. "This," I say, keeping my voice low, "is my family's heritage from Maui. I got it so I don't forget who I am... beyond everything I left."

Her fingers hover, then lightly trace the linework. "Everything you left," she repeats, gentle.

I nod once, throat tight. "I didn't grow up with the kind of family you miss."

Her brows pinch.

"My old man drank," I add, blunt and small. "When he got mean and raised his fist, I learned to get out of the way. Then I learned to get gone." My fingers brush the edge of my sleeve like it's an old scar. "I took off young. Didn't have much besides whatever I could carry and a chip on my shoulder the size of Texas."

Her hand closes gently over my wrist, steadying instead of pitying.

Carter clears his throat, suddenly less of a smartass. "He ran with nothing and still ended up the most solid one of us."

Seth's hand taps my shoulder—quick, like he's got my back. "He's the reason this pack works," he says. "Even when he pretends he doesn't need any of us."

"I didn't do it alone," I say, and it comes out rougher than I mean. My gaze flicks away for half a second, long enough to see a memory I don't usually let in. "I got lucky. I was sixteen when John took a chance on me," I add. "Dragged my sorry ass into the rodeo world, put a roof over my head, and gave me rules that didn't come with fists. Gave me a way out."

I look back at them—at her—and the truth sits steady in my chest. "Without that... I don't know where I'd be."

Seth's mouth quirks, eyes steady on mine. "And you're the reason you're still standing, Kai—don't forget that."

My thumb brushes her knuckles again as I give Seth a nod of appreciation, then I'm focused back on June. "So yeah," I say quietly. "Brutus isn't impossible."

And for a beat, with her looking at me like I'm already worth keeping, I don't feel impossible either.

She searches my face for a long moment. I don't know what she's looking for, but whatever it is, she must find it, because some of the tension leaves her shoulders.

"I do trust you," she finally admits. "But I'm still going to worry like hell."

"I'd be disappointed if you didn't."

She laughs, and I pull her against me. She fits there perfectly, her head tucked under my chin, her hands fisting in the back of my shirt. I breathe in her scent and let it ground me.

This is what I'm fighting for. Not just the town or

the circuit or the abstract idea of doing something good.

Her. Them. Us.

A pack. A family. Something worth protecting.

When I finally let her go, Seth and Carter are both watching us with heartfelt expressions. We're all in this together, and they know it as well as I do.

"So," I say, stealing a rib from Carter's plate just to annoy him. "Anyone else got any terrible ideas they want to share? No? Just me? Cool."

Carter flips me off, but he's smiling.

The country music shifts to something slower, and the evening settles into that golden-hour warmth where everything feels possible. Somewhere out there, a legendary bull named Brutus is probably terrorizing some poor bastard's garden, completely unaware that his retirement is about to get interrupted.

And me?

I'm sitting with my pack, my Omega pressed warmly against my side, and for the first time in a long time, I feel like I'm exactly where I'm supposed to be.

Whatever comes next, we'll face it together.

Even if *what comes next* involves an angry bull with a grudge and a ninety-seven percent success rate at destroying anyone stupid enough to climb onto his back.

But hey.

What's life without a little danger?

17

SETH

I t's past midnight, and I'm standing over June's bed like a goddamn creep.

The door is shut behind me. Has been for... I don't even know how long. Enough that my legs should be cramping, but I can't make myself move or leave. Can't do anything except stand here in the dark and watch her breathe like that's somehow going to fix the gnawing hunger under my ribs.

She's asleep and has been for hours. I'm losing my fucking mind.

It's not just the scent match. I keep telling myself that, but I'm not sure it's true anymore. The connection between us is electric. But it's more than biology. More than instinct.

It's *her*.

The moonlight streams through the curtains, painting silver stripes across the bed. She's sprawled out in the center, one leg thrown over Kai's full pillow with his body printed on it, hugging the damn thing like it's a teddy bear. Half on her side, half on her back. Hair fanned across the pillow, dark against the white cotton. Her lips are slightly parted, and every exhale is a soft sound that shouldn't make my cock twitch but absolutely does.

Her skin looks almost shimmery in the pale light. The sleep shirt rides her breasts in the most innocent way, and those miniature shorts... they've got my attention locked so hard it's embarrassing. I rake a hand over my jaw and blow out a breath, steadying myself, because if I keep looking, I'm going to forget how to behave.

Twenty-nine years old and I'm watching a woman sleep in the middle of the night. My father would have something to say about that. Probably something about not wasting time, about seizing what you want, about how Benton men don't hesitate.

I think about my life before her. The circuit. The competitions. The endless road stretching out in both directions, no beginning and no end, just movement. I was good at being in motion, never staying anywhere long enough to get attached. My father raised me on arena dust and motel rooms, taught me that home was wherever we parked the trailer during the circuits.

But I'm tired.

That's the truth I haven't said out loud. I'm

exhausted from running, chasing, waking up in different towns throughout the year.

I want what my parents had before everything went to shit, a time when it was good. I remember it in flashes. Sunday mornings with pancakes. My mother laughing at something my father said. The way they looked at each other like the rest of the world didn't exist.

I've always wanted that, even when I pretended I didn't. And now there's June.

She shifts on the bed, murmuring something unintelligible, and my whole body tightens. Her scent drifts toward me, lemon zest and honey and wildflowers, threaded through with something warmer now. She's my Omega. The one I've been waiting for without knowing I was waiting and the one who's going to give me everything I've been too scared to admit I craved.

The soft click of the bedroom door freezes me.

Someone's easing it open, slipping through the gap, closing it behind them in the shadows. I don't move. Don't breathe. Just watch from my spot near the bed as the figure turns around—

And locks eyes with me.

Carter.

His whole body jerks. For a second, we just stare at each other across the dark room, both of us caught doing exactly the same creepy thing.

He recovers first. Points at me with an aggressive

finger, then throws both hands up, palms open, shoulders rising.

I have no idea if he's asking why I'm here, or telling me to explain myself, or just expressing general disbelief. I point back at him, then jab my thumb over his shoulder toward the door.

He squints. Shakes his head. Points at himself, then at the floor, then crosses his arms.

I try again. Point at him. Point at the door. Make a walking motion with two fingers.

He shakes his head.

Christ. I make a shooing motion with both hands.

He copies the motion right back at me, adding an eye roll.

Real helpful. Then he walks farther into the room. Great.

I'm about to just physically drag him out when the door clicks again.

We both pause.

Kai slips through the gap, easing the door shut behind him with the same careful silence. He turns around, takes two steps into the room, and stops dead when he sees both of us standing there like guilty teenagers.

His eyebrows shoot up. He glances at me, then at Carter, and lastly at June sleeping peacefully in bed.

Then a slow, shit-eating grin spreads across his face.

He doesn't bother with silent communication. Just

strolls right past us, bare feet silent on the carpet, and stops at the foot of the bed to gaze down at June. When he sees her hugging his pillow, his grin widens.

He turns back to us. Points at June, then at the pillow, and taps his own chest. Then gives us both a double thumbs-up, eyebrows waggling.

Carter throws up his hands in exasperation. I'm pretty sure my eye is twitching.

Kai points at the pillow again, then at himself, then makes some kind of gesture I can't interpret—cradling his arms like he's rocking something, then pressing his hands to his cheek like he's sleeping, and then pointing at June again.

I have absolutely no idea what that means. Neither does Carter, based on the look on his face.

Kai tries again. Points at pillow. Points at himself. Makes a heart shape with his hands.

Oh, for fuck's sake.

I grab his arm and jerk my head toward the bathroom door in June's room, as it's right there. Carter is already moving in that direction, and the three of us crowd into the small space, shutting the door as quietly as possible before retreating to the far corner near the shower.

"What the fuck are you two doing here?" I hiss.

"What are *you* doing here?" Carter fires back, keeping his voice to a barely audible whisper.

"I asked first."

"I was awake before you," Carter says.

"Bullshit. I've been standing in here for at least twenty minutes."

Kai snorts. "That's not the flex you think it is."

"Shut up. And why are you here?"

"Same reason you are, probably." Kai leans against the tile wall, arms crossed. In the dim light filtering under the door, the tension in his shoulders flexes with the restless energy he's barely containing. "Can't sleep. Can't think. Can't do anything except think about her."

"That's two *can'ts* about thinking," Carter points out.

"Grammar police at one a.m. Wonderful."

"I'm just saying—"

"Both of you, shut up." I pinch the bridge of my nose. "We can't all stand around watching her sleep. That's serial killer behavior."

"And yet here we all are," Kai adds cheerfully.

"Because we're losing our minds." Carter runs a hand through his hair. "I marked her, and instead of making it better, it's made it worse. The bond is... it's like a constant pull. I feel her even when she's not in the room. And when she is in the room..."

"You want to climb inside her and never leave," Kai finishes. "Yeah. Feels like we're the ones going into heat for her."

I don't say anything, but they both stare at me.

"I get such hard-ons right in my room that it's actually painful," Kai admits without an ounce of shame. "I just need to be close to her. Touch her. Something. I'm going insane."

"It's the scent match," I say, even though I know it's more than that. "Being near her without being *with* her."

"So what do we do?" Kai's voice is rough with frustration. "Because I can't take another night of lying in my room, staring at the ceiling, knowing she's twenty feet away and I can't—"

"We stay with her, then," I admit.

Both of them glare at me.

Kai's eyebrows shoot up. "Just... get in bed with her?"

"She's asleep. We're not going to do anything." I feel the need to clarify that, even though we all know it's true. "We just... stay close. Let our scents calm her. Let her presence calm us."

"That's surprisingly soft for you," Carter says.

"Fuck off."

"No, I mean it." He's almost smiling. "Mr. 'I Don't Do Feelings' wants to cuddle."

"I will end you."

"I'm in," Kai says quickly. "I'm absolutely in. I call dibs to lie in front of her."

"Well, it's technically my room," I point out. "My bed. So I should get first pick of position."

"That's not how it works," Carter protests, stiffening.

"It sure the hell is."

"Since when?"

"Since I said so."

"Okay, but Carter already spent a night with her." Kai's eyes gleam. "Two nights, actually. So he should get the worst spot."

"What's that position?" Carter sputters.

"It's only fair. You got to knot her. You can take the feet."

"I'm not sleeping at her *feet* like some kind of dog."

"Woof, woof. Then on the floor."

He sneers at Kai.

"Rock, paper, scissors," I cut in before this turns into a whole thing.

Carter pauses mid-argument, brows lifting. "Seriously?"

"You got a better idea?" I ask.

Kai's grin flashes, quick and easy. "Three people don't work. Do it like a bracket. One round each."

"Good," I say. "Fast. Quiet. No drama."

Kai and Carter square up first. "Ready?" Kai asks, already smiling like he's about to win.

Carter holds his fist out. "Try not to cry when you lose."

They throw.

Kai flashes rock.

Carter chooses scissors.

Kai whoops under his breath quietly, pleased with himself. "Ha. Winner."

Carter points at Kai. "Don't get cocky. It was one attempt."

"It was a victory," Kai says, turning toward me. "All right, big guy. Me and you. Winner gets first pick."

I roll my shoulders like I'm stepping into a damn title match. "Fine."

Kai's eyes gleam.

We go.

I pick rock.

Kai does paper.

He freezes for half a second, then grins like the devil himself just handed him a prize. "Got you."

I stare at my hand like I can bully it into changing. "Of course you did."

Kai points at the bed like it's a trophy. "I'm in front of her. That's settled."

"That leaves us two," I tell Carter, nodding toward him. "Which means we play one more round."

Carter and I square up. We throw.

Carter flashes paper.

I choose scissors.

Carter's face lights up anyway. "YES. Feet avoided —" He stops, blinks down at our hands, then groans. "Oh, for fuck's sake."

Kai grins, delighted. "Congratulations, buddy. You get the feet."

Carter glares at him like he's deciding where to bury the body. "You're the worst."

"I'm the best," Kai corrects, still smiling, then he

turns his attention to me with that satisfied, feral little look. "All right, big guy. What's your pick?"

"I'm behind her. That's a given."

Carter exhales, then mutters, "If I get kicked, I'm kicking you both back."

Kai grins. "If you get kicked, it means she likes you."

"Settled," I say. "Everybody shut up and let's go to sleep."

Carter gives me one last glare, but it's already turning into a reluctant smile. "Yes, sir."

Kai laughs under his breath, pleased. "Damn right."

We crack open the bathroom door, still bickering in whispers. Slowly, carefully, we approach the bed.

It's a California king, plenty of room for three large men and one small Omega. The mattress barely dips as I ease onto the right side, settling behind her in the big-spoon position I won. Kai takes the left, facing her, close enough to share breath.

And Carter is at the foot of the bed.

As we settle onto the mattress, Junes makes a small murmuring sound.

"Easy, doll," Kai murmurs as she stirs. "Just us. Go back to sleep."

She burrows closer to Kai, her hand finding his chest, palm pressing flat against his heart, and I shift in behind her, pushing closer to her, my chest to her back, my arm firm around her waist. When I lift my head to check on Carter at the end of the bed, I catch her foot sliding against his forearm, toes curling once before he settles his hand over her ankles.

Something in my chest unknots.

This is what we needed, her touch and closeness. The simple reality of being near her.

June shifts again, a small sound escaping her lips, and we all go still. But she's just getting comfortable.

"She's perfect," Kai whispers, barely audible.

No one disagrees.

My eyes are already closing, my face buried in her hair, engulfed by her scent.

I think about what my father said at the BBQ about leaving when you're on top and not letting the good things slip away.

He's not wrong. Much as I hate to admit it, the old man knows something about regret. He lost my mother in an accident, and it changed everything—twisted his priorities, hardened him in places that used to be soft, left a hole he never figured out how to live with. And now he's got Marlene, pretty, young, surface-level Marlene, and I see the way he looks at her sometimes. Like he's trying to convince himself it's enough, like if he keeps it light, he can't lose it the way he lost Mom.

I don't want that. I want the messy, complicated, all-consuming real thing.

And she's right here, sleeping in a bed surrounded by three men who would burn the world down for her. She has no idea how much power she holds.

I let sleep finally pull me under, one hand curved around her like an anchor. And for the first time in years, I don't dream about the road or the circuit or the endless empty horizon.

I dream about home.

JUNE

Something's different.

I surface from sleep slowly, awareness seeping in like water through cracks. The room is still dark, that deep, heavy darkness of the hours before dawn, but something has changed. The bed feels different. Warmer. More... crowded.

My eyes flutter open.

And I freeze.

There are men everywhere.

Kai is in front of me, close enough that I feel heat radiate off his bare chest. He's on his side, one arm stretched out above my head, his face slack and peaceful in sleep. The moonlight catches the dark lines of his tribal tattoo, the sharp angle of his jaw, the way his hair has come loose and spills across the pillow.

I glance over my shoulder to find Seth pressed

along my back. A solid wall of his chest fits against me, the slow rise and fall of his breathing soothing me. His arm is draped over my waist, heavy and possessive even in unconsciousness.

And something is at my feet—I shift slightly to confirm—yes, that's Carter. He's curled at the foot of the bed, one hand wrapped around my ankle, his cheek pressed against my calf.

When did this happen?

My heart hammers against my ribs as I try to piece it together. I went to bed alone. I'm certain of that, and I recall falling asleep hugging Kai's pillow, missing the scent of them, wishing—

Oh.

They snuck in and climbed into bed with me like it was the most natural thing in the world.

I should be upset. I should be furious. But I take a breath, then another.

And I realize that I'm not upset at all.

The panic I expected to feel isn't there. Instead, there's something warm and settled, like a knot in my chest finally loosening after being pulled tight for years.

I feel... safe, calm in a way I can't remember feeling since my parents moved away and I had to fend for myself. I love my independence, but having that family vibe and support is everything.

The Alphas' scents surround me, and I grin each time I inhale them deeply. I lie there for a long moment, just letting myself exist in this strange new reality. Three Alphas. All of them wrapped around me.

My bladder, unfortunately, doesn't care about emotional revelations.

Moving carefully, I start the delicate process of extracting myself from the tangle of limbs. Seth's arm tightens briefly when I shift, but I pause, holding my breath, and after a moment, he relaxes again with a soft exhale.

Kai doesn't stir when I ease out from under his outstretched arm. Carter mumbles something and releases my ankle, rolling slightly to one side.

I slip out of the sheets, pulling myself up over the pillows and off the bed, then pad to the bathroom on silent feet, easing the door closed behind me before I dare to turn on the light. The sudden brightness makes me squint.

I use the bathroom quickly in the moonlight from the window, deliberately not flushing to avoid waking them. Then I crack the door open.

They haven't moved. Three large men sprawled across my bed, taking up most of the mattress, leaving a June-sized gap in the middle where I'd been sleeping.

It looks like a nest.

The images have my heart fluttering in my chest, a distinctly Omega sensation that I've spent years suppressing. And now I crave my nest, built from Alpha bodies and warmth and the mingled scents of the men who are apparently mine now.

I climb back into bed because I'm tired and cold, trying to find my spot in the tangle of limbs.

The moment I'm close enough, Kai moves.

His arm shoots out, wrapping around my waist, and suddenly I'm being pulled down to him. My body lies against his chest, hip to hip, and his eyes are still closed, his breathing still deep and even, but his grip is firm and sure.

"Sleep now," he mumbles, the words barely audible.

My head settles onto his outstretched arm, my face pressing into the warm skin of his bare chest. His scent floods my senses. I breathe him in, and my whole body relaxes.

His leg slides over mine, heavy and possessive, pinning me in place.

Before I can even process that, Seth shifts closer behind me. At my feet, Carter repositions, his hand finding my ankle again. He's completely unconscious, but even in sleep, he's reaching for me.

I'm surrounded. Cocooned. Trapped in the best possible way.

Never in my life have I felt so complete, safe, and utterly, perfectly comfortable.

I close my eyes, letting their warmth seep into my bones. The fear and uncertainty are still there, waiting at the edges, but right now, they feel far away.

Sleep comes quickly, pulling me under like a gentle tide.

18

JUNE

"Oh, meant to tell you, I spotted her," Hazel says.

I glance up from my phone, where I've been pretending to scroll through emails while actually staring at a photo of Carter, Seth, and Kai from yesterday's grand entry inside the rodeo arena. "Who?"

Hazel finishes snapping the lid onto her takeaway coffee and turns to face me, her dark eyes gleaming with the particular intensity she gets when she's onto something good. "The chick from the video. The one who spiked Seth's drink at the Spur. She's here. At the rodeo."

My stomach drops. "Wait—she's here? Right now?"

"Saw her about fifteen minutes ago near the food stands when I went to get my phone I left in the car." Hazel takes a sip of her coffee, casual as anything, like she hasn't just dropped a bomb in my lap. "Figured maybe we could chat with her. See if she says anything about that night."

I glance around the arena automatically, as if the mystery woman might materialize out of thin air. Day two of the rodeo is gearing up to be busier than day one. The stands are already filling with early birds claiming the best seats, and the smell of coffee and breakfast burritos drifts from the vendor stalls set up along the perimeter.

"We can't just walk up to her," I say, my mind already racing through possibilities. "If she thinks we're onto her, she'll bolt. And then we've got nothing."

"Yeah, true." Hazel frowns, chewing on her bottom lip. "So what's the play? Because I'm not exactly trained in interrogation techniques. My skill set is more aggressive flirting and being really good at Wordle."

"Both valuable life skills."

"Thank you for acknowledging that."

I lean against one of the support pillars, trying to think. The video from the Spur showed someone reaching toward Seth's drink, but the footage was grainy enough that we couldn't see clearly if she spiked the drink. But maybe she'll let it slip? Highly unlikely.

"Here's the thing," I say slowly. "She's not going to admit to anything if we just confront her. Why would she? She knows how much trouble she'd be in because spiking someone's drink is serious. We're talking potential felony charges."

"So we need leverage."

"We need proof, but first we just need to find her. And then we can work something out." In truth, I'm not sure yet how to convince her to talk.

Finding one woman in a crowd of rodeo enthusiasts shouldn't be this hard, but ten minutes later, Hazel and I are still weaving through the growing throngs of people without any luck. I'm starting to wonder if she left, or if Hazel imagined seeing her in the first place, when Hazel suddenly grabs my arm.

"There." She jerks her chin to the left. "Behind the funnel cake stand."

I follow her gaze and immediately spot a woman there.

She's standing near one of the vendor stalls, looking around like she's waiting for someone. Early twenties, maybe. Long, dark hair. Low-cut jeans that sit well below her hip bones and a cropped top with long sleeves that shows off a strip of tanned stomach. She's clutching a disposable coffee cup, one of the ones from the arena café with names written in Sharpie on the side.

Even from here, I can make out the letters: B-R-O-O-K-E.

"Brooke," I murmur. "At least now we have a name."

"What's the plan?" Hazel asks, her voice low and eager.

I quickly outline an idea in my head and relay it to Hazel, keeping my voice barely above a whisper. Hazel's grin grows wider with every word.

"That's devious," she says when I finish. "I'm so proud of you."

"Save the praise for after it works."

We approach from different angles, me hanging back while Hazel circles around to come at Brooke from the side. I watch as Hazel lifts her own coffee cup to her lips, taking a long, casual sip like she's draining her cup, looking like she's just another tourist wandering through the crowd.

Then Hazel adjusts her trajectory and walks directly into Brooke's path.

The collision is perfectly executed. Hazel's shoulder catches Brooke's arm, hard enough to send the other woman stumbling sideways. Brooke's cup goes flying, hitting the ground and bouncing once, the last dregs of coffee splattering across the dirt.

"Oh my God!" Hazel's hand flies to her mouth. "I'm so sorry! I wasn't looking where I was going. Are you okay?"

"What the hell?" Brooke steadies herself, glaring at Hazel. "Watch where you're—"

I'm there in seconds, swooping down to grab the cup before Brooke can react. I'm careful to hold it only by the base, keeping my fingers away from where hers would have gripped.

"Here, let me help," I say brightly.

Brooke's eyes narrow. "I can pick up my own—"

"I feel terrible," Hazel cuts in, already rummaging in her oversized bag. "Here, I have a—let me just—" She produces a plastic shopping bag, the kind you get from the grocery store, and holds it open.

I drop the cup inside before Brooke can protest.

"What the fuck?" Brooke reaches for the bag. "Give that back—"

Hazel zips the bag into her purse with a smooth motion, stepping back out of reach. I move to stand beside her, and together we form a wall between Brooke and any escape route.

"What the fuck are you two doing?" Brooke's voice rises, attracting a few curious glances from nearby spectators. "Why did you put my cup in a bag?"

"Brooke," I say calmly, "we need your help with something."

Her eyes slip between us, suspicious and increasingly alarmed. "Yeah? What's that? And I'm not inclined to help you after whatever the fuck that was. Why did you take my cup?"

Time for the gamble.

"Look," I say, keeping my voice low enough that the people around us can't hear. "We saw the video. Of you spiking Seth Benton's drink at the Spur a few nights ago."

The change in her expression is instantaneous. Her face goes pale, her eyes widening for just a fraction of a second before she schools her features back into defiance.

But that fraction of a second is all I need to see the truth.

I exchange a quick glance with Hazel, a silent confirmation that we're on the right track. She gives me an almost imperceptible nod.

"I don't know what the fuck you're talking about," Brooke says, but her voice has lost its edge. "I'm not from this town. I don't know any Seth."

"Funny, as his face and name are plastered all over this arena," Hazel says, pulling out her phone and scrolling to something. "And I have a picture of you stalking his friends at the carnival. You were in the background of their photo booth pictures, taking photos of them on your phone. Super subtle, by the way."

She turns the screen to show Brooke. I can't see the image from this angle, but I see Brooke's jaw tighten.

"You've got the wrong girl."

"No, we really don't." I step closer, lowering my voice further. "See, the cops already have the video. They also have the glass you touched at the bar, the one with your fingerprint on it. The only reason they haven't arrested you yet is because your prints aren't in any database." I'm lying through my teeth about most of this. The cops only have the video, and I have no idea if they collected the glass or if fingerprints are even viable evidence at this point. But Brooke doesn't know that.

Brooke's face goes from pale to almost gray.

"But now we have this." I gesture toward Hazel's bag, where the cup is safely stashed. "Your name. Your prints. All we have to do is hand it over, and they can match it to the glass from the Spur. After that?" I shrug. "Well. Spiking someone's drink is a felony in Montana. You're looking at serious time."

Judging by the dread blooming across her features, she believes every word.

"Look," Hazel says, her tone shifting to something almost sympathetic. "If you just confess, they might go easier on you. Cooperation counts for a lot with prosecutors. But if they have to track you down, drag you in, do all the work themselves?" She shakes her head. "That's when they throw the book at you."

"Why do you even care?" Brooke's voice cracks. "What's it to you?"

"Because of that video, Seth is facing drunk and disorderly charges," I say. "He could face worse depending on what happened that night while he was drugged. If he can't clear his name, his career is over. His reputation is destroyed. And all because someone decided to slip something into his drink without his knowledge or consent."

I let that sink in.

"So yeah," I continue quietly. "We care a lot."

Brooke glances around like she's calculating escape routes. Hazel and I shift slightly, closing ranks. We're not physically blocking her, but we're making it clear that running isn't going to solve her problems.

"So," Brooke finally says, her voice dropping to barely above a whisper. "It wasn't my decision. I didn't want to do it, okay? Someone paid me. I needed the money."

The air between us goes electric. That's new.

"Who?" Hazel demands.

Brooke shakes her head frantically. "He told me to spike the drink because Seth's the star of the rodeo. Said if Seth got bad publicity, the town would lose the circuit after this year. I don't know why he wanted that —I didn't ask questions. I just needed the cash."

My mind is racing. Someone who wanted the rodeo to fail in Honeyspur Meadow paid her.

"Who paid you?" I press.

Brooke's eyes dart between us. "If I tell you, you give me back the cup. And you let me go."

"Depends on the name."

"Fuck." She drags a hand through her hair, looking like she might cry. "If I get caught later, he's going to deny everything. He'll hang me out to dry. But I'll tell you if you promise to give me the cup and not turn me in right now. If you catch him with actual evidence, I'll confess that he made me do it. I'll testify or whatever. Just... not like this. Not with nothing to protect me."

Hazel and I exchange a look. It's a risk, letting her

go without concrete assurance that she'll follow through. But right now, the bigger fish is whoever orchestrated this in the first place.

"We need your phone number," Hazel says. "And your address."

Brooke hesitates.

"We need some guarantee before we decide not to report you," I add. "Insurance. You understand."

"Fuck me." She laughs bitterly, a hollow sound. "Everything's gone to shit since I came to this crappy town. Fine. Fine."

She rattles off a phone number and an address. Hazel types it into her phone, then sends a quick text. A moment later, Brooke's pocket buzzes.

"Check it," Hazel says. "Show me the text."

Brooke pulls out her phone and turns the screen toward us. The message is there—Hazel's number, a simple "Hi."

"Okay," I say. "Now tell us who paid you."

Brooke takes a shaky breath. "Some guy called Holden Pierce."

The world tilts.

Holden. Who works in the committee with Pete as the financial director.

The same guy I saw yesterday, talking with Seth's father about the rodeo's poor performance. Who got defensive when I pointed out that the town was fully booked with visitors and who is supposed to be managing the finances for the committee that works with the rodeo circuit. What the hell is he doing?

"You're sure?" My voice comes out steadier than I feel. "Holden? That's the name he gave you?"

"Yeah. Skinny guy, kind of nervous-looking? Said he worked for the town. Paid me half up front, promised the other half after the rodeo." She laughs again, that same bitter sound. "Guess I'm not seeing that money now, huh?"

"Probably not," Hazel agrees.

"Are you going to give me the cup or what?"

I nod at Hazel. She reaches into her bag and pulls out the plastic-wrapped cup, holding it out to Brooke.

"Holden still owes me five hundred dollars," Brooke mutters, snatching it from Hazel's hand. "But I guess staying out of prison is worth more than that." She gives us both one last wary look. "If you find real evidence and need me to back you up, you have my number. But I'm not sticking around this town for another second."

She turns and disappears into the crowd, moving fast, shoulders hunched like she's afraid we might change our minds.

I watch her go, my thoughts spinning in a dozen directions at once.

"Holden," I say slowly. "He's the financial director at the town committee that oversees all events."

"Okay..."

I tell her what I saw and heard yesterday. "So why

would he be trying to sabotage the rodeo on purpose. Pete is working so hard to keep the rodeo in our town. And I think there's something a lot bigger going on here than one girl spiking one drink." I stare out across the arena, at the crowds gathering for day two of the rodeo, at the massive banners featuring Seth and Carter and Kai. "And I think Seth was just collateral damage. A way to create scandal, drive down attendance, give Holden a cover story for why the numbers don't add up. Except, I have no idea why."

"Maybe the next town over paid him?"

I shrug. "Something I'll tell the guys and see if they know anything else."

Hazel loops her arm through mine, squeezing tight. "For now, let's go and enjoy the shows."

And together, we walk back into the arena to watch the rodeo, and I can't get it out of my head as to why Holden would orchestrate this, seeing as he's been living in Honeyspur Meadow most of his life.

19

The Mustang's engine purrs as I downshift, turning off the main road onto a dusty side lane that cuts through open farmland. Late afternoon sun slants through the windshield, and the Montana sky stretches out in front of us like something out of a painting.

But I'm not looking at the sky.

I'm glancing at my Omega.

June has her window cracked, letting the warm air tangle through her hair. She's wearing a short skirt and a shirt with buttons down the front, as it's an extra warm day, and every time she shifts in the passenger seat, I catch a fresh wave of her scent wrapping around me in the enclosed space of the car until I can barely think straight.

"Thanks for coming with me," I say, my hand working the gear shift as we navigate a curve. "I know checking out a psychotic bull wasn't exactly on your afternoon agenda."

She laughs, that bright sound I fucking love. "Are you kidding? I wouldn't miss this for anything. I'm very interested to see how this goes."

"Yeah?" I glance over at her, catching the smirk playing at the corner of her lips. "You think I'm crazy, don't you?"

"Never." She holds up her hands in mock innocence. "But it's definitely terrifying. I think it's great you're coming to see him first, though. Maybe you can make a connection. He's just an animal, so you never know how he'll respond to someone who takes the time."

"That's surprisingly optimistic."

"I remember when he was born." She settles back in her seat, a nostalgic smile crossing her face. "I was in high school, and we were doing practical experiences at local farms. I got placed at the farm where Brutus was born, and I helped bottle-feed him because his mother wasn't producing enough milk."

I stare at her. "You're telling me you bottle-fed the demon bull?"

"He was adorable back then." She giggles, and fuck me, the sound goes straight to my cock. "Feisty, even as a calf. Always headbutting everything, trying to escape his pen. But he'd get all soft and snuggly when it was feeding time."

"So he wasn't always a psychotic menace intent on terrorizing an entire town?"

"Apparently that developed later." She grins.

I bark out a laugh, shaking my head. The road curves again, and I ease the Mustang around a bend, taking in the view. Rolling hills dotted with horses. Cows grazing in the far distance. It's beautiful out here, quieter than the arena, more peaceful, but my attention keeps drifting back to the woman in my passenger seat.

Her scent is everywhere, caught in the leather, clinging to the air, sinking into me like it has teeth. Being boxed in with her like this is heaven and hell at once, because there is nowhere for it to go and nowhere for me to hide from it. Every breath drags her deeper into my chest, warm and sweet and sharp enough to make my pulse kick hard, and my control frays around the edges. She is close enough that the heat of her skin keeps brushing mine, that one bad decision would have me hauling her into my lap just to breathe her properly, and the thought hits like a craving I can't swallow down. I grip my knee, jaw tight, forcing myself to stare out the windshield instead of at her mouth, because if I look too long, I'm going to do something reckless, and part of me is already smiling at the idea.

I shift in my seat, adjusting my cock as subtly as possible.

Last night didn't help. Crawling into bed with her—feeling her warmth, breathing her in while she slept—was supposed to calm me down. Instead, it just made everything worse. I spent half the night hard as a rock, trying not to wake her or roll her over and bury myself inside her.

And then there's the knowledge that Carter already has. That she screamed for him, begged for him, let him mark her as his.

I'm not jealous. Not exactly. I'm genuinely happy for them, but knowing how she tastes, how she feels? That's information I don't have yet, and it's driving me fucking insane.

"So," I say. "That's fucking wild about the financial guy. Holden or whatever."

June's expression sobers. "Yeah. Seth's going to dig into it more. I had to tell you guys as soon as I found out."

"Any idea what his angle is? What he gets out of sabotaging the rodeo?"

She shakes her head, brow furrowing. "I keep wondering the same thing. What does he have to gain? I can only imagine that maybe someone's paying him. Someone who wants the circuit to pull out of Honeyspur Meadow."

"Or he's the one stealing," I add, glancing over at her. "You'd be surprised what people will do for money. I've seen guys on the circuit do some shady shit when they got desperate. Throw their events, rig equipment, sell information to competitors."

She's quiet for a moment, clearly processing. "It's going to look terrible for the whole committee. For the town, even. Pete's going to be devastated when he finds out one of his own people did this."

My chest twists at hearing the agony in her voice. I reach over without thinking, settling my hand on her thigh. The moment I make contact, I know it's a mistake.

Her skin is warm through the thin fabric of her skirt, and my hand fits against her leg like it was made to be there. She tenses for a second, then relaxes into the touch, and that tiny acceptance has my blood running hot.

I should move my hand back to the gearshift and focus on the road like a responsible adult.

I don't.

Instead, I watch her from the corner of my eye as her breath catches. Her scent deepens, taking on that honeyed warmth that tells me she's as affected as I am.

"I've got a surprise for you tonight," I hear myself say.

She stares over at me, eyebrows raised. "Oh? Tell me more."

I flash her a grin. "I'm taking you somewhere after we finish here. You'll see."

"That's very mysterious of you."

"I'm a mysterious guy."

She snorts. "You literally cannot keep a secret to save your life, Kai."

"Okay, that's fair." I laugh, and I let my hand stay where it is on her thigh a beat too long, thumb tracing slow, lazy circles like I'm marking time. Like I'm testing how much she'll let me get away with. "But I'm keeping this one. You'll just have to trust me."

Her eyes narrow like she's pretending to be suspicious, but then she smiles. Soft, genuine, lighting up her whole face like the sun decided to pick favorites. Fuck me, she's beautiful. She's the kind of stunning that makes you forget to blink, the kind that digs in deep as though it has claws.

"So," she says, voice turning teasing, as if she knows exactly what she's doing to me. "What was with you all coming to my bed last night?"

The question catches me off guard, but I don't let it show. I keep my grin in place. "Did it bother you?" I ask, casual, like I'm not watching her mouth every time she speaks.

"Actually..." She pauses, and I watch her think, her lashes dipping as she searches for the right words. "It was so calming. I had the best night's sleep of my life."

Something hot and satisfied spreads through my chest at her response. Possessive too.

"It's the growing bond," I explain, keeping it light even as my gut tightens. "Alpha and Omega pull. It's building and drawing us in."

"Kai..." Her voice does that soft warning thing, like

she wants me to stop and also doesn't want me to stop. I move my hand away to change gears, already missing her touch, and she's tugging down on her skirt.

"You do know you're ours now, right?" I say, and I let the joke fall away, let her see what's underneath. "There's no going back from this. Not for any of us."

"Let's not talk about—"

"You can't keep dodgin' it, June. You can pretend you don't feel it, but your body's not faking it. You melt right into us."

Her throat moves when she swallows. "It's not that." She bites her bottom lip, and I have to force my attention back to the road, because if I stare at her mouth too long, I'm going to crash. "I just... I still don't know what I want. Or what I'll do. My parents want to sell my real estate business, and—"

"Then perfect," I cut in, because the idea hits like lightning and I'm the kind of man who grabs lightning with both hands. "You come with us. Be our on-tour photographer. You're already taking pictures for the rodeo anyway, so why not make it official?"

She just stares at me. "But what if I don't want to leave this town? What if I want to settle down?"

My hand stills for the first time, fingers on the steering wheel. I glance over, meeting her eyes, and my smile turns slow and serious.

"Then we settle down," I say, like it's obvious. Like it's already decided. "You think I can't plant myself somewhere if it means I get to wake up with you every morning? You want roots, doll, we'll grow 'em. You want a home, we'll build it. You just gotta stop talking like you're doing this alone."

Settle down. She said "settle down." A house most likely in town. Sharing her bed. Kids running around with her curly hair and my eyes, or Seth's jaw, or Carter's smile. A family. A real one, not the broken mess I came from.

I've thought about it before. Mentioned it to Seth and Carter in those late-night conversations where we got too drunk and too honest. But to hear her say it and know she's thinking about it too—

Fuck, for June, I'd give it all up. The circuit, the competitions, the constant movement. All of it.

I reach over and take her hand, lifting it to my mouth and pressing a kiss against her fingertips. She doesn't pull away. Her breath catches, and when I look over at her, her eyes are wide.

"We would give you the world if you asked for it," I say quietly. "All three of us. So there should be no doubts. We're meant to be together, and nothing is going to come in our way."

She smiles, but there's still doubt there, and fear, and I wish I could kiss it away. But she glances up, and I follow her gaze to the open farm gate we're approaching. A sign reads CRAWFORD FARM in faded letters.

Later, I promise myself. Tonight, I'll show her.

I ease the Mustang through the gate and up the long driveway toward a weathered ranch house surrounded by outbuildings. The property is sprawling with acres of pasture, a big red barn, various animal pens scattered across the landscape. Movement catches my eye near the back of the house, and I spot a figure in the distance.

I park near the main house and kill the engine. The sudden silence feels heavy after the rumble of the motor.

"Ready to meet your old friend?" I ask.

June takes a breath. "As ready as I'll ever be."

We climb out of the car, and I round to her side, taking her hand automatically. Her fingers lace through mine, and the simple gesture warms me.

"This way," I state, leading her around the side of the house. "When I called Farmer Crawford earlier, he said Brutus is usually in the back pasture this time of day."

"What if he's out?" She's scanning the area nervously. "What if he's escaped again?"

"Then you run inside and I deal with him."

"That's not comforting, Kai."

"Wasn't meant to be, doll."

She laughs despite herself, squeezing my hand.

We round the corner and find Farmer Crawford near a vegetable garden, watering some crops with a hose. He's an older guy, maybe sixty, with sun-weathered skin and a trucker cap pulled low over his eyes.

"Hey there!" I call out. "Appreciate you letting us come by."

He straightens up, nodding in greeting. "Brutus is back that way, grazing behind the fence." He gestures toward a large paddock about fifty yards away. "Head on up, and I'll join you in a minute."

June and I make our way toward the paddock, and I spot him immediately.

Brutus is huge, even bigger than I remembered from our terrifying encounter on the road. Black as midnight, with a chest like a barrel and horns that could impale a man without effort. He's grazing near the far side of the enclosure, seemingly peaceful, but the moment we get close, his head snaps up.

His nostrils flare. His hooves stamp the ground. A low snort escapes him, a warning.

"Yep," June says quietly. "Doesn't look like he's happy to see us."

I step closer to the fence, keeping my movements slow and deliberate. I've worked with bulls my entire career. I know their body language, their signals, the subtle cues that tell you when they're about to charge versus when they're just posturing.

"Easy, boy," I murmur, using the same calm tone I use in the arena. "Nobody's here to hurt you."

Brutus eyes me with what can only be described as contempt. Another snort. Another stamp.

And then, slowly, he starts moving toward us.

My heart rate picks up, but I hold my ground. This

is what I wanted, to see him up close, to get a read on him before I have to climb onto his back in front of thousands of people.

But Brutus doesn't come to me.

He walks right past the section of fence where I'm standing and moves instead toward June.

She freezes.

"Hold still," I say, watching, fascinated, as Brutus stops directly in front of her. He tilts his head, nostrils flaring as he inhales the air. His demeanor has changed, the aggression fading into something almost... curious.

June takes a tentative step closer to the fence. "Hey, Brutus." Her voice is soft, gentle. "Do you remember me? Because I remember you."

Brutus lowers his head. A soft sound escapes him, not a snort, but something gentler. Almost a huff.

"That's a very passive move," I say, impressed despite myself. "He likes you."

She moves a bit closer, still wary. "You're not tricking me, are you? Luring me in so you can take my arm off?"

Brutus doesn't move. His head lowers further, and he makes that soft sound again.

Very slowly, very carefully, June reaches out and touches the top of his head. I'm tense, ready to move in a split second if needed.

Nothing happens.

She strokes his massive skull, and Brutus just

stands there, accepting it. If a bull could purr, I swear he would be.

"Holy shit," I breathe.

"Well, I'll be damned." We both turn to see Farmer Crawford approaching, his eyes wide with disbelief. "That's a first," he says, stopping a few feet away. "That bull doesn't let anyone touch him but me. Tries to kill most folks who get within arm's reach."

"She bottle-fed him when he was a calf," I explain. "Guess he remembers."

"Must be." Crawford shakes his head, still looking stunned. "Thirty years of working with animals, and I've never seen anything like it."

I grin at June. "Well, he has a new favorite person. And honestly? I can't blame him. She is pretty amazing."

June shoots me a look, half embarrassed, half pleased, before turning back to Farmer Crawford. "I helped take care of him when he was just a few weeks old. We bonded, I guess."

"It seems so."

Brutus suddenly pulls his head back, and June quickly steps away from the fence. The bull's attention swings toward me, and all that gentleness vanishes in an instant.

His nostrils flare, hooves stamp. He snorts so aggressively that spittle flies from his mouth, and his eyes lock on to me with unmistakable murder.

"Sure hope this fence is going to hold," June says

nervously. "Because he has definite murder in his eyes for you."

I move toward her instinctively, wrapping my arms around her from behind and pulling her against my chest. She fits perfectly, her back against my front, and I rest my chin on top of her head.

Brutus goes absolutely still.

"Damn," I say, watching him. "He's giving me the worst stink eye I've ever seen. And I've been kicked by a bronco, so that's saying something."

"I think he wants you dead." June holds on to my arms where they're wrapped around her waist. "Maybe reconsider riding him?"

"Nah. Where's the fun in that?"

"The fun is in not being gored to death."

I laugh, pressing a kiss to the top of her head, and Brutus snorts so hard his whole body shakes, nostrils flaring wide, hooves striking the ground like he's trying to dig his way through the earth. His head tosses, horns catching the fading light.

"Maybe he doesn't like me touching you," I muse, kissing her head again just to see what happens.

Another furious snort. Brutus takes a step toward the fence.

June elbows me. "Stop antagonizing the murder bull!"

"What? I'm just giving you affection."

"You're going to get us both killed!"

Farmer Crawford is laughing so hard he's bent

over, slapping his knee. "Oh, that's rich. Never thought I'd see the day Brutus got jealous over a woman."

"Jealous?" June raises an eyebrow at the bull.

"You got a crush, big guy? Sorry to tell you, but she's taken," I state.

Brutus tilts his head to the side, and I swear he's trying to figure out how to get through the fence.

"Okay, okay." Crawford straightens up, still chuckling, and grabs a big bucket from nearby. "Let me go calm him down before he has a heart attack."

He carries the bucket into the paddock—Brutus tracks his movement but doesn't charge—and dumps the contents into a wooden feeding bay. Brutus hesitates, clearly torn between his desire to murder me and his desire for food.

Food wins.

He moves to the bay and starts eating, though he keeps shooting me dirty looks between mouthfuls.

Farmer Crawford comes back out and latches the gate behind him. "Tell you what," he says to me. "If you come by every day before the event, it might help him get used to you. Make the ride a little less deadly."

"Appreciate it." I shake his hand. "Thanks for letting him compete."

Crawford snorts like it's nothing. "Hell, I'm just glad someone's brave enough to try." His grin widens. "Good luck, son. You're going to need it."

The sky is streaked pink and orange by the time we climb back into the Mustang. I start the engine and pull out, tires crunching on the gravel as the farm falls behind us and the main road opens up ahead.

June goes quiet for a minute, eyes on the rolling fields.

Then she turns to me. "You're really going to do this, aren't you? Ride him."

"Yeah." I glance over, catching the worry in her face. "Does that bother you?"

"It terrifies me." She doesn't soften it, doesn't joke it off. "He looked at you like he wanted to tear you apart, Kai."

"Most bulls do," I say. "That's the job."

"This felt different."

"Maybe." I reach over and rub my thumb over her knuckles, because I can feel her tension sitting right under her skin. "But I've been around bulls my whole life. I know what they do right before they blow. I know what the shift looks like when they're about to try to kill you. Brutus is mean, but mean doesn't scare me. Mean is predictable."

Her gaze stays on me, sharp, like she's trying to decide if I'm full of it.

"I don't take stupid risks. Not anymore."

That gets a tiny change in her expression. Not relief, not yet, but she hears me.

"And," I say, letting the corner of my mouth lift, "now I know his weakness."

She blinks. "What's that?"

"You." I look at her long enough to make her cheeks

warm. "He clocked you the second you walked up. Tried to act like he didn't. He did."

She frowns. "That's not comforting."

"It should be." My grip tightens just a little, a reminder. "I'll keep you out of his way at the event. You can be near, but not close enough for him to get ideas."

Her eyes narrow. "You're talking like you're in charge."

"I am in charge of my ride." I pause, then add, more bluntly, "And I'll keep you safe while I do it."

June exhales like she wants to argue, but her fingers curl around mine instead. "You're impossible."

"Yeah," I say, and my gaze slides to her mouth before I force it back to the road. "You still like me."

She makes a disbelieving sound, but I catch the twitch at the corner of her lips.

I lift her hand and press my mouth to her knuckles, slowly enough to make it feel deliberate, before I let go and take hold of the gear stick. It takes effort not to turn my head and drag her into a kiss that would make her forget what we're talking about.

"Where are you taking me?" she asks, and there's a cautious curiosity in her voice. "You said something about a surprise."

I turn at the next intersection, heading across town instead of back toward the town. "It's time."

"Should I be worried?"

"Depends." I glance at her again. "Do you hate fun?"

She giggles, and I love seeing her so laid-back and happy, like she belongs in the passenger seat of my life.

"I don't know how to answer that coming from you," she says.

I grin. "You'll figure it out. And you're going to look real pretty when you do."

20

JUNE

The night has settled around us, stars scattered across the Montana sky as Kai's blue Mustang eats up the road.

Being this close to Kai is impossibly hard. So much warmth pouring off him, raw energy contained in that body, not to mention his scent that turns me on constantly. I stand no chance. No matter how much I tell myself I'm in control, I lost that battle long ago with these rodeo stars.

This is why I agreed to come with him tonight. As their chaperone, I figured it was my responsibility to make sure nothing crazy happened. And out of the three men currently turning my life upside down, Kai is the most unpredictable. The one most likely to do something reckless, impulsive, dangerous.

I adore that about him. I shouldn't, but I do.

We're scent matches. All four of us bound together,

and now that I'm an Omega in the open with no more hiding or pretending to be a Beta, my body seems determined to remind me of that fact at every possible moment.

My default is still to hide. To tell myself I can't have things, that wanting is the first step toward disappointment. But maybe my body is going to prove me wrong. If our bodies are calling to each other this strongly, does that mean I'll go into heat with them soon?

The thought sends a shiver down my spine.

I've never had a heat. The suppressants I've been taking made sure of that, but I stopped taking them several days ago, and already I can feel the difference. The ridiculous attraction, the way my body burns whenever they're near, the way my panties don't survive more than an hour in their presence...

It's not full heat yet. I don't know exactly what that feels like, but I imagine it's more than this constant, simmering need. This is just the prelude to something bigger, more overwhelming, waiting just around the corner.

Will I be enough for them when it happens? Three Alphas, one Omega. Can I satisfy all of them?

"What are you thinking about so heavily?" Kai's voice cuts through my spiraling thoughts. I glance over at him, one of his hands on the steering wheel, the other resting on the gearshift, looking like the poster boy for every damn sexy cowboy fantasy ever imagined.

His face is all sharp angles and soft curves in the dashboard light. Those pale gray eyes that seem to see right through me. The strong jaw, the full lips that curve so easily into a grin. That small kiss we shared, the one at the rodeo parking lot, was enough to burn me up for hours. I know those lips would be magic against my skin.

"Just probably overthinking as usual," I say lightly. "Like, why am I getting a surprise? What did I do to deserve special treatment?"

He laughs. "Well, I feel like we need to spend more time showing you why we're made for one another. Get to know us well enough that you know you can't bear to be without us."

"That's very confident of you."

"That's me."

"I've noticed."

His grin widens, and my heart races.

We keep driving, leaving the lights of town in the distance. The road curves through open countryside, past fields and fences and the occasional farmhouse glowing in the darkness. I have no idea where we're going, and the anticipation is almost unbearable.

Then I see a sign illuminated by soft lights: HONEYSPUR FESTIVAL GROUNDS.

The fairgrounds are supposed to be closed at night,

but as we pull closer, I notice lights beyond the gate. And someone standing there, waiting.

Kai parks the Mustang and comes around to open my door. I slip out, my hand finding his automatically, curiosity burning through me.

"What's going on?" I ask.

"You'll see." His eyes are bright with excitement. "It's a surprise."

"I do love surprises," I admit.

He squeezes my fingers and leads me toward the gate. A man I don't recognize hands Kai a set of keys, exchanging a few words I can't quite hear. Something about everything being set up, about locking up when we're done.

Then we're through the gate, and it swings shut behind us, and—

Oh.

Oh.

The fairgrounds have been transformed.

Fairy lights are strung everywhere, draped across the rides, wound through the trees, outlining the paths in a soft golden glow. The main lights are off, leaving the grounds bathed in shadow and sparkle, like something out of a dream. It's beautiful and eerie all at once, a fantasy world created just for us.

"Are we completely alone?" I whisper.

Kai nods, his smirk illuminated by the twinkling lights. "You're all mine."

Something flutters in my chest. "You know this is the setup for about a hundred horror movies, right?"

He chuckles, nudging me with his side. "Trust me, doll. If anyone shows up, I'll be the monster they should be terrified of for spoiling a night meant just for you."

We stroll deeper into the fair, and I can't stop looking around. Every ride is outlined in fairy lights, creating silhouettes against the dark sky. The Ferris wheel rises like a glittering crown. Shadows pool between the attractions, adding depth and mystery to the scene.

It's magical, like stepping into a snow globe filled with stars, and I absolutely love it.

Then I hear the faint tinkle of merry-go-round music drifting through the night air. We round a bend, and the carousel comes into view.

It's huge, one of those two-tiered antique kinds, with a sweeping staircase leading to the upper level and ornate horses prancing on both floors. Every light on the carousel is blazing, turning it into a beacon in the darkness. The music is coming from within, that old-fashioned carnival melody that sounds both nostalgic and slightly haunting.

And in front of the carousel, there's a table with a proper dining setup, two high-backed chairs that look as though they belong in a palace. A golden tablecloth. A vase of flowers in the center. Silver domed covers over what I assume are plates of food.

"Oh, Kai…"

He's grinning now, that infectious smile that lights up his whole face. He takes my hand and leads me closer.

"I wanted to take you out to dinner tonight," he says. "Just you and me. But it had to be special. Not some ordinary restaurant, that wouldn't do for you. So I created something you'll never forget."

My throat is tight. My eyes are stinging.

No one has ever done anything like this for me. Not Tanner, who thought romance was letting me pick the movie. Not anyone before him. I've always been the one making the effort, planning the surprises, trying to make other people feel special.

And here's Kai, this wild, reckless cowboy with a reputation for trouble, creating a literal fairy tale just because he wanted our first real date to be memorable.

"I feel like I should have dressed for the occasion," I manage, laughing to keep from crying with happiness. "Something like a gown."

He pulls out my chair for me, his hand warm on my lower back. "You are spectacular exactly as you are. This is about us. There's no one here to judge us having a quiet moment together."

I sink into the chair, still overwhelmed. The place setting in front of me is elegant with white porcelain plates that have gold trims, crystal glasses, golden cutlery that catches the light.

Kai moves around the table, lifting the silver domes one by one, and my breath catches.

It's not a traditional meal. It's a feast.

The entire table is covered with what looks like the most elaborate charcuterie spread I've ever seen. Plates of aged cheeses in every variety. Crackers and crusty bread. Clusters of deep purple grapes. Chocolate-dipped strawberries, their coating gleaming. Heart-shaped sandwiches on silver trays. Curled meat slices arranged into the shapes of roses. Fresh figs split open to reveal their pink centers. Honeycomb dripping with golden sweetness. Pink rose petals scattered like confetti.

And that's just the beginning.

There are sushi rolls arranged in neat rows. Pastel macarons stacked in a tower. Sliders with tiny tooth-pick flags. Miniature pizzas with crispy edges. Meat-balls speared with fancy picks. Tiny jelly candies in every color of the rainbow. Cheese-stuffed dates. Prosciutto-wrapped melon. Things I don't even recog-nize but desperately want to try.

I'm salivating.

"My mouth might have fallen open," I say, "because I can't find my words."

Kai laughs, taking the seat adjacent to mine so we're close enough to touch. "I wasn't sure what you liked, so I tried to get a bit of everything."

"Kai, I'm..." I shake my head, genuinely struggling.

"I'm blown away by how incredible this is. I want to eat literally everything, and you did this for me."

"That's the goal, and I need to convince you that I would do anything you want. Ask me the wildest thing, and hand on heart, I'll do it."

My breath catches, and I hate how fast my chest tightens with it. I love hearing it. I love the promise in his voice, the certainty, the way he says it like it's already done. And that's the problem. Kai does not say things lightly. When he offers something, he means it literally. It should make me feel safe. Instead, it leaves me feeling a little shaky, because I know what men like him do when they decide they're all in. They crash in like a wave and drag you under with them.

"You're saying that like you don't have a limit," I manage, trying to keep it teasing when it comes out softer. "And that's... insanely sweet. Also terrifying. Because I can tell you actually mean it."

He reaches across the table and takes my hand, and the contact sends warmth flooding through me. "I mean it."

"No one has ever done anything like this for me before," I admit quietly. "You're going to make me cry."

He lifts my hand to his lips and presses a kiss to the back of it, his gray eyes holding mine. "Then this is just the start of what I'm going to give you."

"I never took you for such a romantic."

He just grins at me.

I laugh, because I can't help it, and something in my chest loosens as if it's been bracing for impact.

He reaches for one of the serving plates, sliding it closer to me. "Now eat. I'm starving, and I know you are too."

He's right. I'm famished.

We dig into the feast, and it's even better than it looks. The cheeses are sharp and creamy and perfect. The strawberries burst with sweetness. The sliders are juicy, the sushi fresh, and the macarons melt in my mouth like they were made for this exact moment.

"Most of this is locally made," Kai tells me between bites. "I wanted to support the town as much as I could."

"That's…" I shake my head, still a little overwhelmed by him, by the effort, by the way he watches me like my reactions matter. "That's really thoughtful."

"I have my moments," he says, and the grin he gives me is pure trouble, like he's already planning the next one.

We eat and talk and laugh, the fairy lights twinkling around us, the carousel music providing a gentle backdrop. He tells me about growing up in Colorado, about his grandmother who taught him to ride a bike and about their

Hawaiian heritage, about the first time he got on a bull and knew it was what he was meant to do.

I tell him about Honeyspur Meadow, falling in love with this town as a teenager, how I fought to stay here when my parents wanted me to leave. About the properties I've sold and the people I've helped find homes.

He listens like everything I say matters and as if I'm the most interesting person he's ever met.

"I could get used to this," I admit, accepting a grape he holds out to me. "You're setting the bar very high."

His smile is slow and warm, softening his sharp features. "That's the plan."

"What if the others can't compete?"

"They'll figure it out. We all will." He feeds me another grape, his fingers brushing my lips. "Besides, I'm pretty sure Carter already claimed the poetry angle. And Seth will probably just grunt at you meaningfully until you fall for him."

I burst out laughing. "That wouldn't surprise me."

"I know my pack."

We've been grazing for a while now, the moon rising high overhead, when he says, "I was deciding between this and a picnic in a field somewhere. But honestly, the thought of Brutus breaking out and finding us in the middle of a romantic moment worried me."

"Oh God." I press a hand to my mouth, trying not to laugh. "Can you imagine?"

"I'd rather not. That bull already wants me dead. If

he caught me with you under the stars?" He shakes his head. "Carnage."

"Good call on the fair, then."

"I thought so."

He refills my glass with sparkling juice. "I wanted you clearheaded for the surprises," he says with a wink, and we talk more. About everything. About nothing. The conversation flows easily, naturally, like we've known each other for years instead of days.

At some point, I realize I'm not nervous anymore. The anxiety that usually lives in my chest, that constant buzz of worry about saying the wrong thing or being too much or not enough, is quiet. Kai makes me feel like I can just... be.

When we've eaten our fill and have been just sitting here talking, he stands and offers me his hand.

"Follow me."

I take it, letting him pull me to my feet. "I'm not sure how many more surprises I can handle without my heart giving out from all the swooning."

He laughs, his arm sliding around my back. "This is a night all about you, doll. I'm just getting started."

He leads me toward the carousel, and now that we're closer, I can see every detail. The horses are painted in bright colors, white and gold and rose, with flowing manes and jeweled bridles. The mirrors on the center column catch the lights and scatter them like diamonds.

Kai guides me up onto the platform, and I grip one

of the brass poles as he moves toward the center mechanism.

"Hold on," he calls back.

I hear him fiddling with something, hear the grunt of machinery coming to life, and then the carousel starts to move.

Slowly at first, then picking up speed until we're spinning at a gentle pace, the horses rising and falling on their poles, the music swelling around us. The fairy lights outside blur into streaks of gold, and I'm laughing, gripping the pole, feeling like a kid again.

"This is insane!" I shout over the music.

Kai reappears, grinning. "Pick your horse, my lady. Which one should we ride?"

"Us? Together?"

"Obviously."

I tap my chin, pretending to consider, then start walking through the rows of horses. They're all beautiful, prancing stallions and gentle mares, each one unique. But then I spot a carriage, tucked between two horses, designed for two passengers. It's going up and down with the rest of the ride, painted white with gold scrollwork.

I climb in quickly, the momentum making me slightly unsteady, and I flop onto the padded bench with a laugh.

Kai is there in seconds, sliding in beside me. It's a tight fit, as he's a big man, all broad shoulders and long legs, and we end up pressed together, his thigh against mine, his arm brushing my shoulder.

I turn to face him, to give him more room, and suddenly his hand is on my jaw, tilting my face up.

"You have no idea what you do to me, June." His voice is rough, low, barely audible over the carousel music.

"Maybe I have some idea," I breathe. "Considering what you do to me."

He kisses me.

Not gently. Not tentatively. He kisses me like he's been starving for it, as if he's been holding himself back for days and finally can't anymore. His mouth claims mine with a need that steals my breath, his hand fisting in my hair, angling my head exactly where he wants me.

The carousel carries us up and down, the motion making us bump against each other, but neither of us cares. I grab on to his shirt, pulling him closer, and he groans against my lips, a sound that vibrates through my entire body.

He tastes like strawberries. His tongue sweeps into my mouth, claiming, tasting, demanding, and I give him everything. Every hesitation I've been clinging to, every wall I've built, they crumble under the passion of his kiss.

We're moving with the ride now, rising and falling, and somehow that makes it better. More urgent. Like we're suspended in our own world where nothing else exists.

He breaks the kiss just long enough to shift us, his hands gripping my hips and lifting me like I weigh nothing. Suddenly I'm on his lap, my legs between his spread thighs, and he pulls me flush against him, feeling him hard and thick against my hip, and I'm gasping for air.

"Better," he murmurs, and then his mouth is on mine again.

This kiss is different. Deeper, more desperate. His hands are everywhere—sliding up my back, gripping my waist, tangling in my hair. I'm drowning in him, in his scent and the solid heat of his body against me.

The carousel keeps spinning, the music keeps playing, and I stop thinking entirely.

When his mouth finally leaves mine, it's only to trail down my neck, teeth grazing my skin. I cling to his shoulders, my head falling back, and a moan escapes me that I couldn't stop if I tried.

"Fuck," he breathes against my skin. "The sounds you make. I've been imagining them for days."

"Kai..."

His hand slides up my thigh where my skirt has ridden up. "Do you know how hard it's been? Lying next to you last night, breathing you in, knowing you were right there and I couldn't touch you how I wanted to?"

"Yes." My voice is shaky.

"I could smell how much you wanted us." His hand inches higher, slipping under the hem of my skirt. "Could feel it when Carter marked you, when you came for him. You have no idea what that did to me."

I shiver, his words twisting my insides. "Then show me."

Something shifts in his expression. It's darker, more intense, bleeding through the playful charm, and his grip on my thigh tightens.

"Stand up for me," he says quietly.

My heart stutters. "Oh?"

"On your feet in front of me, doll."

I don't know why I obey. Maybe it's the command in his voice, the Alpha authority bleeding through. Maybe it's the desperate need building between my legs, demanding satisfaction.

I climb off his lap on shaky legs and stand before him, gripping the brass poles on either side of the carriage for balance. The carousel is still moving, making me sway slightly, and Kai stares up at me with eyes gone dark as storm clouds.

His gaze travels down my body. My breath is coming too fast, my skin flushed. He sits back on the carousel carriage, all relaxed confidence, while I stand there in front of him, pretending I'm not one inhale away from losing my mind.

His hand lifts, knuckles brushing the front of my

shirt. "Let me," he murmurs, and it isn't a question. He undoes my top button with maddening patience, then the next, tugging the fabric open more and more to show him what he wants. Cool air slips in. Heat explodes everywhere else. I suck in a breath, and my whole body reacts as though it's been waiting for permission.

His gaze fixes on the skin he's exposed, the lace bra, and the look on his face turns feral. He leans forward and cups my breasts through the fabric. I moan before I can stop it, and his mouth curves.

"So damn gorgeous," he says softly as he peels down the lace of my bra, completely exposing my breasts while I'm holding on to the poles.

He drags his thumbs over my erect nipples, teasing just enough to make my breath hitch again, then he looks up at me through his lashes, completely focused. "Look at you," he murmurs, voice rough. "Absolutely fucking beautiful."

Then his hands are on my thighs again.

They slide up, pushing my skirt higher as they go. I suck in a breath when his fingers find the waistband of my panties.

"Kai, we're—anyone could—"

"There's no one here but us." His eyes hold mine as he hooks his fingers in the fabric.

"No one's going to see you but me."

He tugs my panties down, slow and deliberate, all the way down my legs until they pool at my feet.

"Step out," he orders.

I do, on a moving carousel in the middle of an empty fairground, and some distant part of my brain is screaming that this is insane, but the rest of me doesn't care.

Kai picks up my panties and brings them to his face.

He inhales deeply, his eyes rolling back, and the sound he makes is almost pained. "Fuck," he groans. "I need to drown in your scent."

He casually tucks my panties into the pocket of his jeans like they belong there, and then his hands are on me again. Sliding up my bare legs. Pushing my skirt up around my waist, his gaze lowering, taking in all of me.

His lips pull into a wicked grin. "So pretty, so wet for me," he murmurs, seeing everything. I'm completely exposed to him, standing on a carousel in the moonlight on display.

It should be mortifying.

Instead, it's the most turned on I've ever been.

"I need you," I hear myself say. "Kai, please—"

His hands guide my legs wider, and his fingers find me instantly, cupping my offering, his middle fingers flicking across my length, pushing between my folds, and I cry out.

He doesn't tease or make me wait. He slides two fingers inside me with one smooth motion, his thumb finding my clit, and the dual sensation weakens my knees. I grab the poles harder, barely staying upright.

"That's it," he says, his voice gone rough and dark. "Let me hear you."

He works me expertly, fingers curling, thumb circling, his free hand gripping my hip to keep me steady. The carousel rises and falls, the motion adding to every sensation, and I'm gasping, moaning, completely lost.

"You're going to beg me," he tells me, his eyes hazed over with lust. "Going to wear my mark right next to Carter's. Going to scream my name so loud the whole damn town hears."

"Yes," I pant. "For you."

"You feel like silk on my fingers, dripping down my hand. So tight and wet and perfect." His thumb presses harder, his fingers thrusting deeper. "I want to devour you. Want to bury my cock in your tight pussy and fuck you until you're sobbing. I want to feel you come on my dick."

The orgasm hits me like a tidal wave. I cry out, loud and uninhibited, my whole body shaking as pleasure crashes through me. Kai doesn't stop but keeps working me, drawing it out, until I'm gasping and trembling and dangerously close to collapsing.

"That's my girl," he murmurs, finally slowing his movements. "So beautiful when you come."

I'm still trying to catch my breath when he withdraws his fingers. He holds them up, glistening in the carousel lights, and brings them to his mouth.

He sucks them clean, holding my gaze, and the sight burns itself into my mind.

"Even better than I imagined," he says.

My legs are shaking, my whole body buzzing. I don't know if I can stand much longer—

But Kai is already rising, already taking my hand.

"Now that you're ready for me," he says. "Let me show you something. Take a seat."

I lower onto the spot where he was moments ago, palms braced like I need something solid to hold on to, and the second I look up, he's already turned to face me. He steps in close until all I can see is him, until his scent fills my head and my thoughts start to slide out of order. My breath catches, my pulse turns loud, and he watches every reaction like it's his favorite kind of entertainment.

He leans over, one hand tipping my chin up so I have to meet his eyes. His voice is calm, but there's a harder edge under it now. "All that fight you like to put on, and you're sitting there pretty as sin, waiting for me."

"Kai, you're teasing me," I manage, and it comes out softer than I want.

He smiles as if he likes that too. Then his hands drift to his waist, not rushed, not clumsy. It's the confidence that gets me, the way he moves like he already knows I'm going to let him do whatever he wants. He keeps his attention on my face the whole time, watching me, making sure I'm still with him.

"Do you want to see what all the fuss is about?" he asks quietly. "Because I'll show you. But you've got to tell me you want it."

I swallow hard. "Show me."

"That's my girl," he says, voice rough with approval, and then he unbuckles his pants, lowers his zipper, and pushes them down to his thighs, along with his boxers. A huge cock bounces out, and I gasp at how thick, how long, it is. He grips it with his hand like he's trying to tame an anaconda and shows me the line of small metal beads of his Jacob's ladder.

My eyes widen before I can stop it. "Oh…"

He grins, loving it. "Yeah."

I stare, stunned and wildly curious in the same breath. "Does it hurt?"

He gives a low laugh. "At first."

I lift my hand before I fully decide to, fingers hovering, then brushing the cool metal carefully. The contrast of how soft and hot the skin of his cock is has my breath hitching. "And now?"

His grin turns slow, satisfied, and his voice drops. "Now it's just pleasure." He leans in a fraction closer, eyes locked on mine, watching my face as I touch him. His erection hardens further against my fingers, throbbing. "You keep lookin' at it like that and I'm gonna lose the last bit of patience I've got. Why not take it for a spin?"

My cheeks burn, but I don't pull my hand away. I

can't. Curiosity and heat tangle together in my chest until they're the same thing. I wrap my hand around the base and push my lips over his tip, instantly tasting him, salty and something sweet.

He hisses. "Fuck me!" he howls.

Kai's gaze flicks down to me as I glance up at him. "Show me how much you can take into that pretty mouth of yours."

I push him deeper into my mouth, loving the feel of the cool metal, taking him deeper, my tongue running his length, teasing him as I suck him in and out.

He's growling, his hand on my head, gently guiding me to move faster, and I give him everything he wants. I glance up to see him staring down at me with his cock buried in my mouth, the tip reaching my throat. I hold back the gagging, tears forming at the edges of my eyes as I suck him deeper. Something possessive passes over his gaze, an untamed sexual hunger.

"How is it, doll? My cock as good as Carter's, or am I the first you've sucked between us three?"

I grin as much as a full mouth allows, then pull out, licking my lips. "I haven't tasted his," I admit truthfully, then slide my lips over him, tightening them around his size, wanting him to feel it. And he groans, his hips grinding.

"Fucking right, I'm the first."

I love seeing him on the verge of losing control, how a growl vibrates in his chest as I take him deeper once more, lost in the motion of having him at my mercy. I pull out slightly and go deeper as he rumbles, his body trembling.

"You're driving me insane. Your mouth feels so fucking good."

I continue drawing him in and out, letting it stroke the curve of my throat, feeling him getting harder, closer to bursting.

"That's it, June, take more of me into your throat." He pushes his hips forward, and when I run my tongue under his shaft once more, he roars. His fist tightens in my hair, his cock throbbing and spilling into my mouth. I work my throat, lapping it all up, swallowing everything he gives me, not wasting a drop.

"I can barely hold back when I need to take over." His entire body shudders as I keep working to swallow everything because there's so much.

When I finally pull back, I wipe my mouth with the back of my hand and grin up at him.

"You're absolutely amazing," he groans. "I'm never going to be able to get that image out of my head of you sucking me off."

"So, you have something new for your jerk-off memory box, hey?" I tease him, but I can tell he's not finished. His cock is so huge and hard, and he pulls me up onto my feet, his other hand pushing his pants down to his ankles, and he steps out of them.

"Don't need it when I have the real thing." He winks my way, guiding me to the biggest horse on the carousel, a magnificent white stallion with a golden mane, its head tossed back mid-gallop. It has no saddle, making it easy for us to sit there together.

He helps me up onto the horse backward, then swings up on it as well, facing me, his chest to mine. Hands on my hips, he lifts me easily onto his lap, my legs wrapping around him, his cock already pressing against me.

"If you really want to ride a cowboy," he murmurs, his hands settling on my hips, guiding me closer, "then let me show you how it's done."

The carousel keeps spinning, the horse going up and down. The fairy lights keep twinkling, and as his hands slide under my skirt again, pulling me against the hard length of him, I stop thinking about anything except this moment.

Then he pushes into me, that thick monster of a cock knowing where it wants to be buried, and I'm holding on to Kai as he pulls me down on him, spreading me. I whimper as the sensation of his width and the pressure of the metal studs press into me. I arch as he drives deep, his hips rocking forward.

I meet Kai's gaze, and his eyes are rolling back, jaw tense, muscles under my hands stiff. "You're so tight," he hisses. "I can't get enough."

With him all the way in, me gasping for air, he lowers his attention to me, grinning. This is where I want to be, always. Then he's kissing me, our bodies pressed tight, his hands on my hips, helping me as I ride him, stroking his cock with each push back down on him. Our breathing picks up, that earlier urgency rekindling as we fuck like we can't get enough. I wrench my head back as he kisses my neck, my chest.

God, he's so big. Every time he thrusts into me, it's like the first time, spreading me wider. He fucks me faster, and I cry out, me bouncing on him, both of us going up and down on the merry-go-round horse, which adds something to the whole sensation. In truth, the arousal and the pressure of his size clash just so beautifully that it's almost indescribable.

His lips find my ear, breath hot against my skin. "You have no idea how long I've wanted this and you."

I'm trying to catch my breath, and smile at him. I notice his gaze dipping to my exposed and bouncing breasts, then he pulls me against him faster, harder.

"Mine," he growls against my skin, and the possessiveness in his voice heats up my insides.

I feel like I'm floating. Suspended between the earth and the stars, held only by Kai's strong arms and the magic of this gorgeous night.

This man.

This wild, reckless, impossibly romantic cowboy who created a fairy tale just to make me feel special. To know that someone like Kai is there to catch me.

The carousel dips through another lazy turn, lights smearing into soft ribbons at the edge of my vision. Kai tightens his hold for a beat, then eases me back just enough that I feel the loss of his heat, the withdrawal of his cock, and immediately want it again. He studies my face, eyes bright with that wicked patience he always wears when he's about to ask for something.

"Turn around for me," he asks.

My breath stutters. "Are you sure?"

He nods but doesn't rush me, though his hands are already ready at my waist, steadying me as the horse rises and falls. I start to shift because my body understands the instruction before my brain catches up. He guides me up, lifting me just enough that I can swing one leg over without wobbling. My hands grip the pole for balance, and I laugh softly, half nerves, half exhilaration, as I swing my leg back over so I'm facing the front of the horse. Then I shuffle back toward him, the top of the horse feeling cool and hard against my burning pussy.

"Easy, now lean forward for me," he murmurs, close to my ear, voice warm and certain.

I lean against the painted horse's head, holding on to the handles, steadying myself. Then Kai shifts behind me, knees bracketing mine, one hand settling at my hip to keep me anchored as the carousel carries us around.

"There," he says, satisfaction threading through his voice while he lifts my hips slightly as he shuffles closer, and instantly I feel his cock at my entrance. "That's better."

"You really like giving orders," I whisper.

Kai's breath brushes my neck. "Only when you

listen." Then he pushes into me without ceremony, just claiming me as if being inside me is normal and where he belongs. I'm holding on to the horse, and he's holding on to my hips, lifting me to meet him as he rocks into me. It's only when I glance over my shoulder that I realize he's partially off the horse, his legs in the brackets on either side of the horse, taking his weight as he claims me, over and over.

"This is so fucking incredible," he murmurs. "Fucking you on a horse... Maybe one day we'll try it on a real horse."

I laugh, almost choking on my breath. "I don't think the horse will appreciate it." My words turn into a loud moan from the depth of his cock, the speed with which he's thrusting into me.

"Fuck," he hisses. "June, I fucking love your pussy."

I can't deny that hearing him say my name, telling me how much he loves my body, sends delicious shivers through me. He's picking up his pace, somehow going with more force, and the brutish thrusts have him slamming into me. I'm crying out, hoping this horse can take our brutality on its back.

"Please don't stop," I beg.

"You sound so unbelievably sexy when you plead."

The carousel creaks beneath us, lights blurring at the edge of my vision, the cold outside making the heat inside me feel even sharper. I can barely breathe. All I can do is hold on, to the horse, to the pole, to the sound of his voice, and let him take me apart piece by piece.

"Kai, God..." I whisper again, broken, and he answers with a low growl that moves straight through me. His mouth finds my neck, my shoulder, anywhere he can reach, and the way he moves behind me makes it feel impossible that we are out here under the stars where anyone could look up and see us. The danger of it only makes my body tighten faster, climbing higher, the edge turning vicious and sweet until I can't tell where I end and the night begins.

"That's it," he murmurs, voice rough, breath coming hard against my ear. "Let go. Give it to me."

His grip tightens at my waist, like he's holding me together because he's barely holding himself back. He trembles against me, and his mouth brushes my skin.

"June," he breathes. "I need to mark you." His hand flexes like he's fighting the urge to take more. "Please don't tell me no."

It should scare me. Instead, it strikes something deep and reckless inside me, because like with Carter, I crave a bond with Kai. A laugh slips out of me, half breathless, half broken, and it turns into a moan when he shifts behind me, when his mouth finds the line of my shoulder.

"You're driving me wild," I whisper, shaking.

His teeth graze my skin, a promise. "Say yes."

My head falls back against him, my whole body already tipping over the edge. "Do it," I manage, and it comes out like a plea.

Everything in me snaps open in that second as my

orgasm bursts free. The release comes over me so hard that my vision whites out and a sound tears from my throat that I don't recognize as mine. For a second, I'm weightless, floating, suspended in cool air and spinning lights, my body trembling as pleasure rolls through me in waves I can't control.

Kai makes a broken sound behind me, pure need, and his hold turns possessive, solid. His mouth presses to my shoulder again, hot and intent, and I feel him lose the last of his restraint.

He bites down, tearing skin, marking me.

I scream out as he shudders hard, breath ragged against my skin, and then he finally lets himself go too, shaking and throbbing inside me, filling me with his cum. His cock thickens, and that unique sensation of being stretched from the inside out, just as Carter had done, repeats itself. He's knotting inside me, his arms around me possessively.

For a heartbeat, the impossible sweetness of being wanted consumes me completely. It isn't just pleasure; it's the way my chest loosens like I've been bracing my whole life and somebody finally caught me before I hit the ground. I feel wrecked in the best way, dazed and full of him, full of us, and the night air makes it sharper, more real, like the stars are witnesses and the whole world can do nothing but keep turning while I cling to him and decide, in the middle of this madness, that I don't want to be careful anymore.

"You're mine, June," he hisses, his mouth on my

neck, his body shaking as he fills me, making me his permanently.

He stays there, both of us trying to find our breathing again, while the carousel keeps turning as if nothing happened, like the whole world didn't just narrow down to us bonding on a carnival ride.

21

SETH

The boardroom smells of stale coffee and bullshit.

I'm sitting at a long wooden table in the Honeyspur Meadow Town Hall, a jug of water and a plate of untouched pastries between me and Holden, who I'm fairly certain tried to destroy my reputation. My father is on my right, Pete, the committee head, across from us.

"Nice to have you attend, Seth," Holden says, shuffling through a stack of papers. He's a thin man, nervous-looking, with the kind of smile that makes him seems wary. "I don't think I've ever seen you at one of these meetings."

I lean back in my chair, keeping my expression neutral. "Figured it was time to start paying attention."

"Well, that's a pleasant surprise."

I bet it is.

My father glances at me, something like approval behind his eyes before his usual gruff mask settles back into place. "Good to see you taking an interest."

"I will be from now on." My gaze stays fixed on Holden. "Seems like an important part of the business I should understand better."

Holden shifts in his seat. It's subtle, just a small adjustment, a barely perceptible tension in his shoulders, but I catch it. Good. He should be uncomfortable.

Because right now, sitting across from him, all I can think about is the girl at the bar. The one who slipped something into my drink because this piece of shit paid her to do it. The night I lost hours of my life, the charges I'm still facing, the way people looked at me the next morning like I was some out-of-control animal.

All because of him.

I want to reach across this table and break his jaw. To watch fear replace that smug confidence in his eyes as I make him confess everything right here, right now, in front of my father and Pete and anyone else who might be listening.

But I can't. Not yet.

We have the girl's confession, but Holden will deny everything. He'll claim she's lying, that she's trying to shift blame, that he's never seen her before in his life. Without proof, real, concrete proof, it's her word against his.

And a town committee finance director carries a lot

more weight than some out-of-towner desperate for cash.

So I sit here and play nice while pretending I don't know that this man tried to ruin me.

"Let's get started, shall we?" Holden clears his throat, pulling out more papers. "I've compiled the intake figures from the first two days of the rodeo, broken down by category—ticket sales, concessions, merchandise, and ancillary revenue from local businesses."

He passes sheets to my father and Pete, pointedly not giving me one. My father slides his copy between us, and I lean in to look at the numbers. "If I'd known you were coming, Seth, I would have prepared an extra copy of the financials."

I just stare at him, then down at the figures.

They're not good.

According to this report, day two brought in only marginally better numbers than day one. Ticket sales are down nearly twenty percent from last year. Concessions revenue is flat. Merchandise is barely moving.

I frown. That doesn't match what I saw yesterday. The stands were packed. The lines at the food vendors stretched around corners. People were buying shirts and hats and programs left and right.

"Strange," I say, keeping my voice casual. "It looked pretty busy yesterday."

Holden's smile tightens almost imperceptibly.

"Appearances can be deceiving. The numbers don't lie."

"I was there." I tap the paper. "Day two had way more people than this suggests."

Pete nods, stroking his chin. "I thought the same thing, actually. The crowd seemed much larger than on the first day. And with the Brutus event flyers going out, we've had a lot of excitement building. People are already talking about buying tickets for the final day specifically."

"That's encouraging," my father adds, though his tone suggests he's not encouraged at all. "But these figures tell a different story."

"Unfortunately, perception doesn't always match reality." Holden spreads his hands in a gesture of helpless resignation. "I can only report what the data shows. And the data suggests that perhaps this town is... growing tired of the rodeo circuit."

My father's jaw tightens. I know that look. It's the one he gets right before he tears someone a new one.

He sets down the paper with deliberate care. "The circuit has been coming to this town for years. We've brought millions of dollars in revenue to local businesses. We've put Honeyspur Meadow on the map."

"Of course, of course." Holden holds up his hands. "I'm not diminishing the value of your business. I'm simply presenting the facts as they are."

"Facts." My father practically spits the word. "You know what I think? I think if you're just going to sit there and tell me we're failing, then you clearly aren't serious about our relationship. I've had interest from other towns, bigger ones, with committees that actually seem to want our business."

Pete shifts in his seat, his face going pale. "Now, now, that's not what Holden means at all." He shoots a sharp look at the finance director. "Your business is crucial to Honeyspur Meadow. Absolutely so. Without the rodeo circuit, so many local businesses would suffer. The hotels, the restaurants, the shops, everyone depends on the revenue this event brings."

"Then why does it sound like your finance man is trying to push us out the door?"

"He's not." Pete's voice is firm, trying to smooth over the tension. "Holden is a numbers person. Not the best with words, perhaps, but excellent with data. What he means is that we need to find ways to boost attendance, not that we're giving up."

Holden nods quickly, seizing the lifeline. "Exactly. And I'm convinced the Brutus event will help tremendously. A legendary bull coming out of retirement? That's the kind of spectacle that brings people in droves."

I watch him as he talks. The way his eyes dart around, never quite meeting anyone's gaze for long, and the slight tremor in his hands as he shuffles his papers again.

He's nervous. Hiding something.

But he's also smart, as he knows exactly what to

say to keep Pete on his side, to make my father doubt his own instincts. He's playing a long game here, and I'm only just starting to see the shape of it.

After a few more minutes of back-and-forth, Pete smoothing feathers, my father grumbling, Holden deflecting, the meeting wraps up. I stay quiet for most of it, just watching. Filing away every nervous twitch and evasive answer.

When we finally stand to leave, Holden extends his hand to me. "Good to have you involved, Seth. I hope we'll see you at more of these meetings."

I shake his hand. Grip it maybe a little harder than necessary. "Count on it."

The morning air hits my face as we step out onto the sidewalk, and I take a deep breath to clear the stench of Holden's bullshit from my lungs.

My father walks beside me, his boots heavy on the concrete. We're both quiet for a moment, processing.

Then he says, "You don't trust him."

It's not a question.

"No." I glance over at him. "Do you?"

He's silent for a long moment, his weathered face unreadable. Then he sighs. "In business, you deal with a lot of people you don't trust. It's part of the game. The key is knowing how to keep on top of them, watching everything, verifying the numbers, never taking anything at face value." He pauses. "But no. I don't trust him. Something about that man has always rubbed me wrong."

"Then why do you work with him?"

"Because Pete vouches for him. The committee handles all the financial logistics for events in this town, and Holden is their finance director. And sometimes you don't have a choice but to work with people you'd rather never see again." He glances at me, something sharp in his eyes. "So why the sudden interest in the business?"

I consider how much to tell him. "I don't know anything concrete, yet," I say carefully. "But I'm going to dig around because I think he's pulling some shit behind the scenes. I'll see what I can find."

My father nods slowly. "Good. Keep me updated." A pause. "I'm glad to see you taking an interest in this side of things, son. It's something I've always wanted, for you to understand the business beyond just the competitions."

The sincerity in his voice catches me off guard. My father isn't the type for heart-to-heart conversations. He shows his affection through criticism and high expectations, through pushing me to be better even when I want to tell him to go to hell.

"I know the riding won't last forever," I admit. "Figured I should start learning the rest."

He's quiet. "You know, your mother always said you'd be the one to build something lasting. Even when you were just a kid, she saw it in you. The way you paid attention to everything, not just the flash, but the details. She said you had the heart of a provider."

I stop walking.

My father almost never talks about my mother. She died in a car accident that took her faster than anyone could process. One moment she was there; the next she was gone. And after that, it was like he sealed that part of his life away. Locked it in a box and buried it deep. The circuit came after, something he built from the ashes of his grief, pouring all that loss into motion and competition and the endless road.

"I didn't know she said that," I say quietly.

"She was right about a lot of things." He clears his throat, looking uncomfortable with his own vulnerability. "Anyway, this June girl." He keeps his gaze fixed ahead, hands shoved in his pockets. "The chaperone. You serious about her?"

I tense. "Why do you ask?"

"Saw you boys getting pretty intimate with her the other day. In the parking lot at the arena." He glances at me sideways. "Hard to miss."

Heat creeps up my neck, but I don't look away. "More serious than I've ever been about anything."

He nods slowly, processing that. "She seems nice. Strong, from what I've heard. Runs her own business, doesn't take shit from anyone." A pause. "You want a partner who can stand up for herself. Someone who won't crumble when things get hard."

"She's all of that and more."

"Nothing wrong with wanting to settle down, son." His voice has gone gruff, but there's something softer underneath. "Have a family. Put down roots somewhere."

I stare at him. In twenty-nine years, I have never heard my father talk about settling down. Never about anything beyond the next competition, the next town, the next challenge to conquer.

"Would be nice to have some grandkids running around someday," he adds, almost offhandedly. "Before I'm too old to chase them."

I genuinely don't know what to say. The man who raised me on arena dust and motel rooms, who taught me that home was wherever we stopped, is now talking about grandchildren?

"Dad..." I start, but he waves me off.

"Don't make a big thing of it." He clears his throat again, the vulnerability obviously making him uncomfortable. "Just saying. If she's the one, don't let her slip away. That's all."

I think about June, about her laugh, her fire, the way she fits against me as though she was made for exactly that purpose.

"I don't plan to," I say quietly.

He nods once, sharp and decisive, and that's the end of it.

"Anyway. Let's get to the rodeo. Lots to do."

We walk to his truck in silence, but it's a different kind of silence now. Heavier. More meaningful.

The drive to the rodeo grounds takes about fifteen minutes. My father keeps the radio on low, some old country station, and I stare out the window at the Montana landscape rolling by.

Golden fields. Distant mountains. The occasional farmhouse or barn.

He's right that the riding won't last forever. Eventually, every cowboy has to hang up his hat and figure out what comes next.

Maybe my *next* is closer than I thought.

When we pull into the rodeo grounds, the morning is still early. A few crew members are setting up, checking equipment, preparing for the day's events. The stands are empty, waiting to be filled.

"Gonna go get ready," I tell my father as I climb out of the truck.

He nods. "Good luck today."

"Thanks."

I watch him drive toward the main-office area, then turn and head in a different direction.

I have a stop to make first. I spot Carter's pickup truck and Kai's car, so they're already here. But first, I have something to do.

Joshua is exactly where I expected to find him, in the ticketing booth near the main entrance, organizing his station for the day ahead. He's a local and has always helped with the circuit when we're in town, handling admission. He's always been good to us.

"Seth!" His face breaks into a grin when he sees me. "Been meaning to grab a drink with you. How long you in town?"

"Couple more weeks at least." I shake his hand, clapping him on the shoulder. "We'll make it happen. Got some things to sort out first."

"I heard about the Brutus thing." He whistles low. "Kai's either brave or crazy."

"Little of both."

We make small talk for a few minutes, catching up on circuit gossip, complaining about the travel schedule, the usual. But eventually, I need to steer the conversation where it has to go.

"Hey, I need a favor," I ask.

"Name it."

"Can you pull up the sales numbers in the system? For the last two days."

Joshua raises an eyebrow but doesn't ask questions. He turns to his computer, types in a few commands, and swivels the screen toward me. I pull out the figures from Holden, as I'd taken my father's handout.

The numbers match exactly what Holden showed us this morning.

I frown. "Who has access to this data?"

"Just management and committee leadership. Why?"

"No reason." I study the screen, thinking. Would Holden alter these numbers to cover his tracks?

The question is, are these numbers accurate, or has he been cooking the books from the start?

"I need you to do something for me," I say,

lowering my voice. "Today, as you process sales, keep a manual record. Paper. Write down every ticket you sell, every transaction that goes through your station. Get the other booths to do the same if you can."

Holden's expression shifts from curious to serious. "You think something's off?"

"I don't know yet. That's what I'm trying to figure out." I meet his eyes. "Keep this between us, yeah? I don't want anyone knowing I'm looking into this until I have something concrete."

"You got it."

"Thanks, Joshua. I owe you. And if you can email them to me when you get a chance..." I lean over and jot down my email on a notepad on his desk.

Joshua nods. "Buy me that drink and we're even."

I leave the ticketing booth and head toward the stables, my mind churning. If the manual count matches the system's numbers, then maybe I'm wrong. Maybe Holden is just incompetent, not corrupt. I highly doubt that.

I'm almost to the stables when I spot her.

June is standing near the media tent, phone pressed to her ear, her expression intense. Whatever conversation she's having, it's serious. I can tell by the way she's pacing back and forth.

Even worried, she's beautiful. That dark, curly hair glinting in the morning light. Her gorgeous legs in those tiny denim shorts. The anger I've been carrying all morning softens at the sight of her. It's like she has some kind of magic over me, the ability to take the sharp edges of my mood and smooth them into something bearable.

I want to go to her. Want to pull her into my arms and bury my face in her hair and breathe in that lemon-honey scent until the world makes sense again.

But she's busy. And I have work to do.

So I turn toward the stables instead, stealing one last look over my shoulder.

How the fuck did I get so lucky?

An Omega like her, smart, fierce, beautiful, and she's mine. Ours. The woman I've been waiting for without knowing I was waiting.

Whatever Holden is planning, whatever scheme he's running, I'm going to uncover it. For the circuit. For my father. For this town.

But mostly for her.

Because June loves this place. And anyone who tries to hurt something she loves is going to have to go through me first.

22

JUNE

A Few Minutes Earlier

The phone buzzes in my pocket, and when I pull it out, my mother's name flashes across the screen.

I hesitate. Part of me wants to let it go to voicemail, as I'm still raw from everything that's happened, still processing the whirlwind my life has become. But guilt wins out over self-preservation.

"Hey, Mom."

"June, sweetheart!" Her voice is warm, bright, achingly familiar. "How are you? I've missed you so much."

Something in my chest loosens. Despite everything, I've missed her too. "I'm okay. Busy with the rodeo."

"Oh, that's right—the big event. How's it going?"

"Good. Lots of stuff going on, but the good kind. How's Dad?"

"He's fine. Working too hard, as always." A pause. "Actually, sweetie, that's part of why I'm calling. We have some news."

The tone of her voice shifts, just slightly, but I catch it. My stomach tightens.

"What kind?"

"Well, we found a potential buyer. Someone who's ready to make a deal for Sweetwater Creek Realty."

I knew this was coming, but hearing it stated so plainly still feels like a punch to the gut.

"Okay," I manage.

"The thing is, June..." Another pause, longer this time. "They want the business and the house. It's a package deal. And it's such a good offer, better than we expected, honestly."

The world tilts.

"Wait." My voice comes out strangled. "The house too?"

"I know it's a lot to take in—"

"Mom, do I mean nothing to you?"

"June, that's not fair. You know we love you."

"Then how can you sell my home out from under me?" I'm shaking now, my free hand clenched into a fist at my side. "I thought, when you moved to Dallas, that you were giving me the house. That was the plan. That's what we discussed."

"Plans change, sweetheart. We're in a difficult situation, and this deal solves everything. You can move to Dallas with us and start fresh. All your ties to that small town would be cut, and we'd help you build something new. You wouldn't be alone."

"You know I don't want to move to Dallas!" The words burst out, and a few people nearby glance in my direction. I turn away, lowering my voice.

"The business will belong to someone else soon. You have to let it go."

"That's not—" I press my fingers to my temple, trying to think through the panic. "Can't you just sell the business? Keep the house separate?"

"The buyer wants both. And honestly, June, the house is worth more than the business at this point. We need both sales to cover all the debts."

"So I'm homeless," I say flatly. "That's what you're telling me. I'm losing my business and my home in one fell swoop."

"You're not homeless. You'll come live with us—"

"I want to stay here, in the town I love, running the business I've poured my heart into for years."

My mother sighs heavily. "June, please don't be angry with us. We're doing the best we can with an impossible situation. If your father and I end up on the street, we can't help anyone."

"Then move back here." I'm grasping at straws and I know it. "Both of you. Live in the house, help me run the business. We could make it work."

"We've outgrown that town, sweetie. And moving

back doesn't solve the debt problem. We'd still owe the money, and soon."

I'm silent, tears pricking at my eyes. Everything I've worked for. Everything I've built. Gone.

"Who's the buyer?" I ask, keeping my voice level through sheer force of will.

"What?"

"Who's buying the business and the house?" My throat tightens. I swallow hard, like I can push the panic back down if I do it fast enough. "Do I at least get to know that?"

There's a small pause on the line. I blink hard, staring at the dirt by my sneakers, willing the sting behind my eyes to behave.

"A local man," she says finally, as if she's trying to remember who it is. "Holden Pierce. And he works for the town committee."

The world stops.

Holden.

Fuck.

The sound in my ears goes hollow, like the arena noise has been turned down to nothing. Holden Pierce, the financial director with his too-clean spreadsheets and his polite little questions in meetings. I see him so clearly that it makes me sick. The way he'd linger after committee sessions, hands shoved in his pockets, asking me how Sweetwater Creek Realty was doing. Whether business stayed lucrative through winter. If I was managing all the listings on my own. I always laughed it off. Thought he was awkward and trying to be friendly in that stiff, numbers-guy way.

And now he's buying my home, my business, my entire life like it's a neat little acquisition he can file away and feel proud of.

My jaw locks. Anger flares hot enough to burn the tears right back for a second. What the hell does he need it for? And where did he get the money? The last time I saw Holden, he was still renting that sad little place at the edge of town, still showing up to meetings with coffee stains on his sleeve like he couldn't even keep himself together. This doesn't make sense.

"June?" my mom says, sharper now. "Sweetheart, are you still there?"

I open my mouth, and nothing comes out except a breath that sounds wrong. My ribs start to hurt, like my body is trying to hold everything inside and it's failing.

"I have to go," I manage, and my voice cracks on the last word.

"June—"

"I'll call you later." I don't even wait for her answer. I stab the screen and end the call before she can hear me break.

For one second, I just stand here, phone clutched in my hand so tightly my knuckles ache. I tell myself not to cry here. Not now. Not in front of anyone. I've held it together for years, so I can hold it together for five more minutes.

Then my throat collapses around a sound I can't stop, and the tears come anyway, hot and fast, spilling down my face like my body has finally decided it doesn't care what I want. My chest heaves, my vision blurs, and the sobs punch out of me hard enough to make me fold at the waist.

I'm crying in earnest now, ugly and uncontrollable, like something inside me has cracked clean through at the fact that everything I've worked for is gone, that the one place I called home, taken.

"June," a faint male voice calls.

I frantically wipe my face.

Strong hands catch my shoulders.

I look up through the wet haze and find Seth's face. The second he sees my tears, something changes in him, the concern sharpening into something darker, harder. The kind of expression that belongs on a man who breaks things for a living and doesn't lose sleep over it.

"What happened?" His voice drops, tight and urgent. "Who did this? Give me a name and I'll take care of it."

I try to answer. I do. But the words won't form around the sobs. All I can manage is a broken shake of my head before I crumple forward into his chest like my body has given up trying to keep me standing.

He doesn't hesitate. His arms wrap around me, and he lifts me clean off the ground like I weigh nothing, cradling me against his broad chest. I clutch at his shirt, shaking, and he starts walking, long, purposeful strides pulling us away from the arena like he's moving me out of danger.

"I've got you," he murmurs into my hair, voice rough and steady. "I've got you, darlin'. Whatever it is, we'll fix it."

I bury my face in his neck and let myself fall apart.

When I finally surface, blinking against the sunlight, we're in the parking area. He's approaching Carter's red pickup truck, fishing keys from his pocket.

"You have Carter's keys?" My voice is hoarse, wrecked.

"We all have keys to each other's vehicles." He unlocks the door and sets me gently on the passenger seat, then stands in front of me, hands on my knees. "I don't have my own car. I usually drive the livestock trucks between towns, so I share with Carter and Kai."

I nod, wiping my face with the back of my hand. I must look like a disaster.

"Talk to me," Seth says quietly. "Seeing you cry is shredding my heart."

So I tell him. All of it. My mother's call, the sale, the house, the devastating realization that Holden, of all people, is buying it.

"And my parents are selling it all because they're desperate for money. But where the hell did Holden get so much money from?"

Seth's expression turns cold. "That motherfucker," he murmurs under his breath.

"So I'm homeless," I whisper, and it comes out thin and ugly, like the word has teeth. "I'm a nobody. A loser without a business or a place to live, and if you guys don't want—"

"Hush." Seth's hands tighten on my knees, firm and steady, like he can physically stop the spiral if he holds me in place. His eyes burn into mine. "Don't you dare finish that sentence."

I swallow hard, throat raw. My chest keeps doing that awful collapsing thing as if my body is trying to fold in on itself. I hate that I'm shaking and that everything I built can be taken with a phone call and a signature I never saw.

"You have us," he says, slower now, like he's making sure every word lands. "You're pack. Wherever we are, that's your home. Do you understand?"

"Seth..." My voice wobbles on his name.

"I mean it, June." His jaw flexes. "This changes nothing except the logistics. You're ours, and we take care of what's ours."

The tears slide down my face again, but they don't feel like the earlier ones. Those were from panic. These are from relief so intense it hurts.

I blink fast, trying not to fall apart again. "I don't want to be a burden."

Seth's expression shifts, softer around the edges but no less serious. "Darlin', you don't get to decide you're a burden. Not to me."

I let out a shaky laugh that turns into a sob halfway

through. It's humiliating and honest. I wipe at my face with the heel of my hand and fail to stop the tears anyway.

He exhales. "I think what we need is some time away. Right now."

"You have the rodeo," I manage, because my brain is still clinging to responsibilities like they're life rafts. "You can't just—"

"I have one act," he cuts in, and the confidence in his voice is absolute. "Not until later. The others can cover for me." He's already pulling out his phone, thumb moving fast. "Give me a sec."

He walks a short distance away, shoulders squared, phone to his ear. Even from here, I can see it in the way he stands. Seth doesn't ask for permission; he tells the world what's happening and expects it to fall in line. He says a few things I can't hear, pauses to listen, then speaks again, low and firm. Another call. Another pause. His hand lifts once, a sharp gesture like he's cutting off an argument before it starts.

I sit there, watching him, trying to breathe like a normal person while my whole life rearranges itself around his certainty. A part of me wants to protest, to insist I can handle this alone, to cling to the stubborn independence I've worn like armor for years.

But the bigger part of me is so tired of carrying it all.

Seth returns, shutting my door with me inside, and then sliding into the driver's seat with a smile that hits me right in the ribs. It's not cocky, but a satisfying move.

"Done," he says. "Carter and Kai will handle things." He reaches across, brushing his knuckles lightly along my cheek as if he can't help checking that I'm still here. "Come on. I want to show you something."

I stare at him, blinking. "You… you just fixed it."

"I didn't fix it," he corrects, and his voice softens. "I bought you breathing room." His gaze holds mine. "Let me take care of you for a bit."

My throat tightens again. I nod before I can talk myself out of it.

We stop at a gas station on the way out of town. Seth disappears inside and returns with a bag stuffed with snacks and several bottles of water, grinning as he tosses it into the back seat like we're about to drive across the country instead of just escaping for a few hours.

"Road trip essentials," he says, like it's obvious.

I manage a weak smile, still watery. "You're very thorough."

"Yep." He starts the engine, then glances at me, and his expression softens just a touch. "But you're fed and hydrated under my watch."

I huff out a laugh and wipe at my cheek again. "Where are we going?"

Seth's grin returns, warm and a little wicked. "You'll see."

. . .

I recline in my seat and watch the landscape change outside the window. The town gives way to an open highway, which stretches out to rolling hills and distant mountains. Seth drives with confidence, one hand on the wheel, the other occasionally reaching over to squeeze my knee.

We've been driving for nearly two hours when the road starts to climb. The paved highway becomes a narrower track, then a rocky path that makes me grip the door handle.

"Is this safe?"

Seth laughs. "There are so many incredible places in Montana. After every rodeo, we go exploring to find somewhere new. Carter found this spot on our last trip."

The path levels out eventually, and he parks near a cluster of trees. We get out, and I follow him along a winding trail through the woods until suddenly the trees fall away and—

Oh.

The canyon stretches out before us, vast and ancient, carved by millennia of wind and water. A river snakes along the bottom, glinting silver in the morning light. The walls are striped in shades of red and gold and amber, and beyond them, three distant mountains rise against the blue sky.

I stand at the edge, breathless. "Seth, this is..."

"Beautiful, right?"

I turn to find him watching me, not the view. His blue eyes are soft, warm, completely focused on my face.

"Yes," I whisper. "Beautiful."

He spreads a thick blanket on the stone a safe distance from the edge and sits, patting the space beside him. I join him, tucking my legs beneath me, and for a long moment, we just sit in silence, taking in the view.

"Feel better?" he asks finally.

"Getting there." I lean back on my hands, letting the sun warm my face, but my chest still feels tight, like it forgot how to unclench. "Is this your way of putting things in perspective? Showing me how big the world is and how small my problems are?"

"Not at all." Seth shifts to face me, bending one knee between us, close enough that his shadow cuts across my legs. "It's to remind you that when everything around you goes to shit, the world hasn't fallen apart. It's still here, still breathtaking and standing." He holds my gaze like he's anchoring me to something solid. "And whatever comes at you, you're going to get through it. Not because you have to. Because you can."

Something in my throat pricks. I blink hard and look away for half a second, embarrassed by how fast emotion consumes me when he talks like he's already decided I'm worth fighting for.

I glance back at him, and he's watching me with that serious, intense focus that twists my stomach.

"Besides," he adds, nodding toward the horizon, "see those three mountains in the distance?" He pauses until I follow his gesture. "That's me, Carter, and Kai. Overlooking everything. Watching over you." His mouth curves slightly, but his eyes stay fierce. "Reminding you that you'll never be alone again."

I laugh, loving the notion.

"Whatever you're facing, all four of us face together. So you aren't homeless. You have us and will be with us wherever we are."

"I don't even know where you really live."

"Colorado, technically." He shrugs as if it barely matters. "But we've been living like nomads for years." His gaze stays on mine, unflinching. "I'm ready to find somewhere permanent for my pack, for my Omega."

The butterflies in my stomach go wild, stupid and bright. My chest aches in a way that isn't pain, not exactly. More like something opening.

I reach over and brush the longer strands of hair away from his eyes. My fingers linger because I can't help it. He's so handsome it almost hurts to look straight at him, and the way his whole body angles toward me leaves me swooning.

"I don't think you realize how committed we are," he says quietly. His hand lifts and closes over mine. "You're more important to us than the rodeo. Than any win. Than any damn expectation anyone's ever put on us."

My throat tightens. "I'm starting to see that," I whisper. "It's just... new for me. Being wanted without it coming with strings."

Seth's expression shifts, something protective tightening in his jaw. He doesn't look away. "You won't lose us."

I swallow, the old fear trying to rise anyway. "You can't be sure. Nothing in life is certain."

"Then I'll spend every day convincing you." His thumb rubs over my knuckles, slow and steady. "I'll show you. Over and over, if I have to." He leans closer. "I'm not promising you perfect, June. I'm promising you me. And I don't let go of what's mine."

The possessive edge in his words should make me bristle. Instead, my eyes sting again, and tears are building up.

I nod once, because I can't quite speak, and Seth's hand tightens on mine.

I stare at him, this grumpy, intense man who keeps showing up at the exact moment my world cracks, and something in me finally gives. So I lean forward and kiss him.

My mouth brushes his in soft presses, waiting for him to pull back or tease or make a joke to break the tension. He doesn't and just stays still, letting me set the pace and be the one to choose it.

That alone nearly undoes me.

When I shift closer and deepen it, he answers. Not with frenzy, not with desperation. With certainty. His hand comes up, cups my jaw, and angles me where he wants me, taking control without stealing the choice. My stomach tightens, fire burning between my thighs because Seth does not do anything halfway. Even a kiss from him feels like being claimed.

We sink down onto the blanket, the mountains and sky turning into a blur at the edge of my vision. Seth settles beside me, not crushing me, just close enough that his shoulder and hip line up with mine, his weight braced on one arm as he leans over me and blocks the wind with his body. His palm slips under my shirt, flattening against my stomach, and my breath catches at the simple intimacy of it. He's just holding me there, steady, reminding my nervous system what safe feels like.

He breaks the kiss and drags his mouth down my throat, teeth grazing the spot that makes my pulse jump. "I saw it this morning," he says against my skin. "Kai's mark."

Heat rushes up my neck. "Jealous?"

"You don't want the honest answer if you're trying to keep this sweet."

I huff a laugh, breathless. "Try me."

His head lifts, those bedroom eyes fixed on me with a hard-focus attention that makes it impossible to pretend I'm unaffected. "I've been thinking about it since Carter gave you one," he admits out loud.

"Thinking about you wearing his bite while you look at me with those innocent eyes."

I should be embarrassed. Instead, my body responds with a sharp, hot pull, and I press my thighs together.

The pieces in my head keep clicking into place. Carter's mark. Kai's mark. Once Seth adds his, once the bond locks in the way my biology has been resisting for years, my body won't be able to keep playing dead. The suppressants, the dormant diagnosis, all the control I've clung to will finally stop mattering.

And the wildest part is that I want it.

I want him.

So I bring my mouth to his ear. "Then make it happen."

A sound rumbles out of me before I can stop it, low in my chest, vibrating up my throat. It shocks me so much I almost pull back, but Seth freezes above me, his whole body going still as if my instincts just spoke a language he understands better than words.

His gaze drops to my mouth. "You want this now?"

I hold his stare and lift my chin. "We're alone. You got me out here to breathe again." My fingers slip into his hair, tugging gently, not a plea, not a test. An invitation. "Don't make me go back to pretending."

Something in his face hardens into decision.

He kisses me again, deeper, hungrier, and it's not messy. It's controlled hunger, the kind that tells me he could ruin me and still keep me safe while he does it.

His leg slides between mine, pressing in with just enough friction to leave me gasping, and he doesn't let me hide the reaction. His hand moves under my shirt, fingers splaying along my ribs, mapping me as if he's memorizing every inch he plans to protect.

I meet him for once, drag my nails lightly down his shoulder over his shirt, and he groans in approval.

He draws back just enough to stare at me properly, gaze sweeping my face, my mouth, the way I can't stop breathing too fast. His thumb brushes my cheek, gentler than a man this fierce has any right to be. "You're unreal," he says. "You've got no idea what you do to me."

I swallow. "Go on," I tease.

His gaze flares, approval and possessiveness tangled together. "Careful, darlin'. You ask me for that and I'm going to give it to you exactly the way I want."

"And what way is that?"

His mouth tilts, pure cowboy arrogance, but his hand stays warm on my skin. "The way that makes you forget anybody ever had the nerve to make you feel disposable."

He kisses his way down my stomach, pushing my shirt higher as he goes, and the warm afternoon air brings every nerve to life. When he reaches my bra, he doesn't fuss or ask twice. He pushes it up and out of the way with the same quiet confidence he brings to everything, leaving me exposed to the sun and the open sky, and the fact that we are out here makes my pulse trip even faster.

"You don't even know what you're doing to me." The words land hard, like he's warning me and himself.

Then his mouth finds my hardened nipple, and my whole body arches, the sound that slips out of me unfiltered and agonizingly desperate for more. I clutch at the blanket, trying to keep myself grounded, but Seth is not interested in me staying composed. His mouth sucks, that devious tongue flicking, and just when I'm about to burst, he lets go and moves on to my other nipple, adoring it with the same affection.

His hand slides to the waistband of my shorts and works them open, tugging them down over my hips, along with my panties, in slow strokes that make me squirm. I lift my hips, helping, and they slide down to my knees. The air kisses my skin. His attention stays fixed on me, reading every reaction, tracking the way my breathing changes, as I reach down to push them lower.

"Impatient," he murmurs, and it sounds amused, not scolding. "You always this needy, or is it just me?"

I try to answer, but my voice breaks as I grin. "I'm going to blame you." I'm shuffling my legs and manage to kick off my shorts and panties.

He glances down, and his gaze goes sharp, hungry, taking in the completely shaved offering I've left for him. "Hell," he murmurs, eyes lifting back to mine. "You're trying to make me lose my mind."

He shifts closer, sliding his other leg between my thighs until he has me spread, steadying me in place and blocking any chance of escape. One firm hand presses into the blanket beside my hip, the other settling at my inner thigh with a quiet warning of control. Then he pushes himself back onto his knees, his hands running down the length of my thighs, sliding them wider.

I gasp as he just stares down at me. When his fingers trace the seam of my lips, I tremble from the touch, then he presses them open.

"Let me see all of you," he murmurs, pulling me open, revealing it all.

That shaking intensifies from a combination of arousal and nerves. He grins, his finger teasing around my entrance. I moan, my hips arching already. "You're so wet. I love seeing you like this."

He's undoing his belt and jeans, pulling them down enough so the huge cock that I know hides there pops out. I gasp at the sight as he palms it a few times, then uses the tip to rub me the full length, then to lightly smack me.

"She's such a greedy little pussy, isn't she? I see her clenching already for me."

"And are you going to feed her?" I ask.

His gaze lifts to mine, an eyebrow arching so sexily I almost melt. "Hands," he demands.

It's one word. No softness around it. My hands lift without argument.

Seth catches my wrists, kisses the palm of each, and guides them up above my head, pinning them to the blanket with one firm hand. Not painful or cruel. Just absolute. My breath catches hard, and I expect fear to show up.

It doesn't.

What shows up is heat, a deep, startling thrill that rolls through my stomach and lands between my thighs, because he is holding me still and I trust him enough to let him.

"You're safe," he says, as if he can see the thought flicker through me. His thumb strokes the inside of my wrist once. "You're not in trouble. You're exactly where I want you."

My throat tightens. I nod, because words feel too small.

His gaze drops to my mouth. "Now say it," he tells me. "No pretty lies. Tell me what you're asking for when you beg."

I swallow, cheeks burning, body trembling. The truth rises sharp and unstoppable. "I want you to take control."

Seth's expression shifts, something dark and satisfied settling into place. "That's my girl."

He adjusts his grip, keeps my hands where he put them, and lowers himself closer, his heat, his strength, the steady pressure of him caging me in without crushing me. He kisses the side of my throat, then my jaw, then the corner of my mouth, taking his time in a way that feels like ownership.

"You don't get to run," he murmurs. "You don't get to hide what you feel. You stay right here, and you let me see it all."

A shiver tears through me, half fear, half hunger, and I realize with a dizzy rush that this is what I've wanted without knowing how to name it. Being held, directed, and allowed to let go while someone else carries the weight. Something I feel with each of my three Alphas.

Seth watches the moment I stop fighting myself. Instead, I give myself to him while my body shakes with need, my pussy fluttering, and excitement seeps out of me.

Then he smiles. "Good," he says. "Because I'm not letting you go until you believe you belong with us."

He pushes his hips forward, his cock finding me instantly, driving into me without hesitation. I arch back, moaning, never able to get enough of being fucked by these Alphas, who all have massive cocks and know exactly how to wield them.

Seth is above me, holding my hands over my head with one hand, and the other he scoops underneath my thighs, lifting my hips to better meet his thrusts. When he's got me where he wants me, he grins almost evilly.

"That's it, beautiful. Now scream for me."

The moment he drives the point home, my whole body jolts, the world tilting under me as if the mountains themselves shift. Air punches out of my lungs. My hands are still pinned above my head, his grip firm enough to keep me right where he wants me, and I realize with a rush of heat and awe that Seth isn't holding back. Not even a little.

I try to form words, but all that comes out is a broken sound. My hips lift on instinct, chasing more, and Seth makes a quiet, satisfied noise that goes straight through me.

"There you are," he murmurs, close, approval threaded through every word. "Quit thinking. Quit fighting. Just take it."

My pulse is everywhere. My skin is too hot for the cool air. Every movement sparks friction, fire, and I can feel myself tipping too fast, losing control in the best possible way.

"I want you to…" I gasp, swallowing hard, cheeks burning with the honesty of it. "I want you to do anything you want. I want you to use me. I don't want gentle."

Seth stills just enough to look down at me, eyes dark, expression fierce and intent, as if he's making sure this is real and not panic talking.

"Say it again," he tells me, quiet and commanding. "So I know you mean it."

"I mean it," I breathe. "All of it. Take what you want."

Something in his face shifts. Satisfaction, possession, and the kind of restraint snapping that he's been holding for my sake.

"Good," he states, and the word lands heavily. "Because I've been picturing you like this. Hands above your head. Nowhere to go. Nothing to do but feel me."

My body shudders at that, a sharp tremor that turns into a helpless moan when he moves again, when he sets a pace that steals my breath and makes my mind go blank. I can't keep up with it. I can barely breathe through it.

He leans down, mouth at my ear. "You'd look real pretty tied up," he murmurs, filthy and soft at once. "Would you like that, darlin'? Me taking my time. You being forced to hold still while I do whatever I want."

My throat works, vision going glassy. The idea nearly undoes me right there, just from the words.

"I've never..." I gasp, the confession jagged. "Never tried it."

Seth's grip tightens, not punishing but claiming. "With me you can," he says, certain as law. "You trust me, and I'll show you what you like and what you've been missing."

I nod breathlessly, barely able to think past the way he's spreading me with each plunge, deepening the pressure inside me, how he's dragging me closer to the edge and not letting me hide from it. Every time I try to pull away from the intensity, he holds me there, makes me stay with it, makes me take it.

"Shaking already. That's what I want. You falling apart for me."

I make a broken sound, my back arching, my whole body trembling as the peak rushes up too fast, too big. The open sky, his strength over me, his hands keeping me exactly where he wants me. It's overwhelming. It's perfect.

"I'm close," I choke out.

"I know. I feel your sweet little pussy squeezing my cock," he says, calm and brutal, like he owns the moment. "Give it to me. Let me hear it."

The pressure coils tighter, tighter, until I can't hold it back. I can't even form words properly. I just cling to him with every shaking breath.

And then I break.

His name tears out of me, raw and helpless, like it's the only thing I know, like it's prayer and surrender all tangled together.

Seth's mouth curves, satisfied, and his eyes stay locked on mine as if that sound is exactly what he's been chasing the whole time.

"Yeah," he murmurs, dark and pleased. "That's it. That's what I wanted." Then his rhythm turns ruthless, clearly chasing his own release.

He gasps aloud, the control in him finally cracking. He buries his face against my neck and curses through his teeth, whole body tightening as he hits the end too, and I feel the change in him instantly. The way he holds himself there. The way he doesn't pull away.

A sharp, helpless sound slips out of me.

Because I know what that means.

That deep, claiming finish I've been bracing for. The pressure of his knot swelling within me, holding him locked inside of me, as he spills his seed into me, more and more. The bond connecting us in the way my body has been waiting for, the final proof that this isn't just want anymore. We are meant to be together.

Seth's grip stays tight around me. The cool air brushes my skin, and the world beyond us is nothing but open sky and jagged rock and wind, but inside his arms, it's strangely quiet. The aftermath is still humming through both of us while we're locked together.

He lowers his face into my hair, and for a second, I think he's just catching his breath, that he'll say something rough or teasing to cut the intensity.

"I love you, June," he whispers, then lifts his head to stare down at me, releasing my wrists from his grasp.

I go completely still because, my whole life, I've dreamed of an Alpha saying that to me.

Seth—saying it as fact, as promise, as something he's willing to stand up for.

My eyes burn. I swallow, but it doesn't help. All I can think is how he carried me when I fell apart, how he made space for my fear without letting me ignore it, how he keeps reminding me that I'm his.

I lift my hand to his jaw, thumb brushing along the edge of it, needing to touch him.

"I love you too," I whisper, and it comes out shaky and honest, the kind of truth you don't get to take back.

He lifts his head and stares down at me, the wind gently tugging at his hair. "I'm the happiest man in the world," he says quietly, like he can't quite believe he's allowed to say it. His gaze drops to my chest again, then returns to my eyes. "And I'm about to make sure I don't lose it."

My breath catches. I nod, then force the words out past the lump in my throat. "I want this."

Seth's expression tightens. "Say it again."

"I want it," I whisper. "Secure it, Seth."

He leans in, presses a slow kiss to the top of my breast first, a steadying touch, then he bites me with the final mark, firm and undeniable. I gasp, my body going taut for a heartbeat, and he holds me through it until he lets go and licks the wound and I can breathe again.

Seth lifts his head, eyes locked on mine. "Now you're mine forever."

The sun is starting to set by the time Seth and I make it back to town. My body is pleasantly exhausted, the kind of tired that comes from emotional release, from crying and then being held, from letting someone see you fall apart and trusting them to help put you back together. Not to mention, being railed by a hunky cowboy who knows how to bring me to orgasm.

"Mind if we stop by my office for a minute?" I ask as Seth navigates Carter's truck through the familiar streets. "I just... I need to see it."

He glances over at me, understanding in his blue eyes. "Of course."

Sweetwater Creek Realty sits on the corner of the main road, next door to the Wildflower Bakehouse & Café. It's a small building with just three rooms and a bathroom in the back, but it's mine. Or it was mine. The thought sends a fresh pang through my chest.

Seth parks in front, and once I'm out, I unlock the front door and go inside. My hands tremble slightly as I switch on the lights.

The familiar scent of vanilla candles and old paper finds me, the combination that's become synonymous with this space. I breathe it in, letting it settle in my lungs, trying to memorize it.

The office is exactly as I left it. My desk sits near the window, cluttered with files and sticky notes and the vintage typewriter I bought at a flea market because it looked professional and quirky. A plush armchair in deep burgundy faces the desk, the one where clients sit while I walk them through listings and contracts. The walls are covered with framed photographs of properties I've sold, interspersed with travel brochures showcasing gorgeous locations around the world. Places I've dreamed of visiting someday.

A small couch sits against the side wall, upholstered in worn leather that's softened with age. I drift toward it almost unconsciously, sinking down onto the cushions and pulling my knees up to my chest. I've been keeping up to date with any emails on my phone, so I know I'm all caught up, but sometimes just sitting here calms me. Except, I'm now going to lose this place.

"June?" Seth asks softly.

I shake my head, wrapping my arms around my legs. "I just need a minute."

He doesn't push, just stands there, watching me, waiting.

The tears come before I can stop them.

"This is me," I whisper, my voice cracking. "This place, this business, it's everything I've worked for. Everything I thought I was." I press my forehead to my knees, shoulders shaking. "And my parents are just… selling it. Without asking me. Without involving me at all. They're selling my entire life to a man who's trying to destroy this town, and I don't even get a say. Geez, I'm sorry. I know you already saw me crying today over this, but I'm struggling to accept it."

I feel the couch dip as Seth sits beside me. Then his arms are around me, pulling me against his chest, and I let myself collapse into him.

"I'm trying so hard to be okay," I manage between sobs. "But it hurts so much to know that everything I thought I had, who I thought I was, means nothing to them."

"Hey." His voice is low, rough with emotion. "That's not true."

"It feels true."

He holds me tighter, one hand stroking my back in slow circles. His lips press against the top of my head, and his heartbeat thumps beneath my cheek.

"You're amazing," he murmurs against my hair. "You took a dream and made it real. And just because this place is being sold doesn't mean you can't do it again."

"I don't know if I have the energy to start over."

"You won't be." His hand moves to cup the back of my head, fingers tangling gently in my curls. "What's different now is that you have us. And if you want to open another office, here or somewhere else, we'll help you do it. We'll be there every step of the way."

I pull back just enough to glance at him, my vision blurry with tears. "You mean that?"

"I mean everything I say to you." His thumb brushes across my cheek, wiping away the tears. "I'm sorry your parents did this to you, put you in this impossible situation. But you're not alone anymore, June. You never will be again."

I wrap my arms around his neck and hold on.

We stay that way for a long time. Him stroking my hair, pressing kisses to my temple, murmuring words of comfort and reassurance. The mating mark on my breast hums with warmth, a constant reminder of the bond between us.

This is what it means to have a pack, I realize. What I've been missing my entire life without knowing it. Not just romance or attraction or even love, but belonging. Being claimed and cherished and protected. Having people who will catch you when you fall, who will hold you together when you're breaking apart.

I press my face deeper into his chest, breathing in his scent and calming slowly.

"Thank you," I whisper. "For not letting me fall apart alone. I just wanted to come in here, feeling like I'm going to lose it soon, and... I don't know."

His arms tighten around me. "Taking care of you isn't a favor, June. It's a privilege."

Eventually, Seth shifts against me. "How about we go meet Kai and Carter? Get some food and drinks. I bet they're wondering where you are."

I manage a small smile despite the tear tracks on my face. "That would be nice."

"Then let's go." He helps me to my feet, and I take another glance around the office. The vintage typewriter. The burgundy armchair. The wall of photographs showing all the happy families I've helped find their homes.

This chapter of my life is ending.

I turn off the light and lock the door behind us.

The BBQ joint is already lively when we arrive, the parking lot packed with trucks and the air thick with the smell of smoked meat and mesquite. Country music drifts from inside, and strings of fairy lights cast a warm glow over the outdoor seating area.

Seth leads me through the restaurant to the back courtyard, where picnic tables are scattered beneath a canopy of more fairy lights. The effect is almost magical, transforming the simple space into something cozy and intimate.

I spot them immediately.

Kai and Carter are at a corner table, drinks already

in hand, deep in conversation. But the moment Kai sees us approaching, his whole face lights up.

"There she is!" He's on his feet in an instant, crossing the distance between us in three long strides. His arms wrap around me, lifting me clean off the ground, and I laugh despite myself.

"Miss me?" I ask when he finally sets me down.

"Every second." He cups my face in his hands and kisses me, not deeply, but thoroughly, making sure I feel it. "You smell incredible, by the way. Did you roll around in a meadow or something?"

"Something." I can't help the blush that creeps up my cheeks.

Carter is there before I can say anything else, pulling me into his own embrace. His kiss is softer, more lingering, his hand sliding up to cup the back of my neck. "You okay?" he asks quietly, searching my face. "Seth messaged us that you were having a rough day."

"Better now."

He smiles that slow, warm grin that hypnotizes me. He guides me toward the table with his hand on the small of my back. We settle into our seats, and suddenly I'm surrounded by them. Kai is on my left, his thigh pressed against mine beneath the table, radiating warmth even through the fabric of our clothes. Carter is across from me, reaching over to take both my hands in his, our fingers interlacing in a way that feels natural now—inevitable, even. His legs tangle with mine beneath the table, ankles hooking together, a constant point of contact that sends little sparks up my spine.

"We're starving," Seth announces, standing at the table. "Have you two ordered anything?"

"Nope." Kai takes a swig of his beer. "Figured we'd wait for you."

"Good man. I'm getting us food." Seth rises and heads toward the counter, leaving me alone with the other two.

The moment he's gone, Kai leans in closer, his nose brushing against my neck. I feel him inhale deeply, and a shiver runs down my spine.

"Fuck," he breathes against my skin. "You smell so good. But there's something else under there..." He inhales again, and his breath tickles me. "Seth. You smell like him."

My cheeks flush hotter. "Well, he did mark me today."

Carter's eyebrows shoot up, a grin spreading across his face. "Finally pulled his head out of his ass, did he?"

"He was very romantic about it, actually."

"Seth? Romantic?" Kai pulls back, looking skeptical. "Are we talking about the same guy? Tall, grumpy, communicates primarily through grunts and scowls?"

I giggle, loving how relaxed they make me feel. "He took me to this canyon outside town. Laid out a blanket, gave me this whole speech about how the mountains represent you three watching over me..."

"Holy shit." Carter squeezes my hands. "That's adorable. I'm almost jealous."

"You gave me poetry," I remind him. "And Kai rented out an entire fairground."

"True." Carter doesn't look particularly humble about it. "We are pretty amazing, though I need to lift my game, by the sounds of it."

"So incredibly modest too," I say.

"Modesty is for people who don't have anything to brag about."

Kai's hand finds my thigh under the table. "So all three marks now," he says, his voice low and intimate. "Love knowing that you're ours for good."

My stomach flutters. "I guess my heat will come soon, then."

They both nod, their expressions shifting to something more serious. More intense.

"We'll take care of you," Carter promises, his hands lightly squeezing mine. "When it happens. Whatever you need."

"I know." And I do. For the first time in my life, I actually believe it.

I glance around the courtyard, trying to compose myself, and catch a couple of girls at a nearby table staring daggers at us. Or perhaps only at me. They're young, early twenties, probably, dressed in the kind of revealing outfits that scream *rodeo tourist hoping to catch a cowboy*. Their glares are focused entirely on me, and I can practically see the jealousy radiating off them.

Three rodeo stars. Three gorgeous, devoted men who can't seem to stop touching me.

Too bad for them. These ones are mine.

I turn back to my Alphas with a satisfied smile, but it freezes on my face when I see who's approaching our table.

Tanner.

He's out of uniform, wearing jeans and a T-shirt that's seen better days, and he's swaying slightly as he walks. His eyes are glassy, his movements uncoordinated.

Drunk. Great.

He stops at the edge of our table, one hand slapping down on the wood to steady himself. "June."

"Tanner." I keep my voice flat. "Go away."

"I can't." He's trying to sound earnest, but it comes out sloppy and pathetic. "I still love you, you know that? It fucking destroys me to see you with these... these dicks." He gestures vaguely at Carter and Kai. "You deserve better than them. You deserve me."

Kai's hand tightens on my thigh. Beside him, Carter has gone perfectly still, his jaw set and his eyes hard.

I laugh. "Which is exactly what I have now—better than you. So do yourself a favor and walk away before you make this worse."

"They're using you." Tanner leans in, his breath rank with alcohol. "Can't you see that? The second the rodeo leaves town, they're gone. You'll be nothing to them."

"Wrong." Carter's voice cuts through the noise of the restaurant, sharp as a blade. "She'll be everything to us for the rest of our lives."

Tanner's attention swings to him, his lip curling. "Oh, fuck off. I know what you did. You and your little friend here"—he jabs a finger at Kai—"stole my cruiser the other night. By the river."

"Can't prove it," Kai says with a shrug.

"I'll fucking find proof. And when I do, I'm getting all of you tossed in prison. See how much she loves you then."

"Tanner, you're drunk," I say. "Go home. Sleep it off. Stop embarrassing yourself."

He reaches for me, and suddenly Kai is on his feet, moving with a speed that seems impossible for someone his size. He positions himself between me and Tanner, his broad shoulders blocking my ex from view.

"Don't." Kai's voice has dropped to something low and dangerous, a growl lurking beneath the words. Every muscle in his body is coiled tight, ready to strike. "Don't touch her. Don't look at her. Don't even think about her."

The transformation is startling. Gone is the playful, reckless cowboy who jokes about everything. In his place is something primal, an Alpha protecting his Omega, and God help anyone who gets in his way.

Tanner tries to peer around him. "June—"

"She's not yours anymore." Kai steps forward, forcing Tanner to stumble back. His voice is quiet now, almost conversational, which somehow makes it more terrifying. "She's our Omega now. Our pack. And you? You're nothing but roadkill we haven't bothered to scrape off the pavement yet."

"Big talk from a guy who steals police vehicles. You left water everywhere. You better not have been fucking naked in my car."

"At least I have something worth showing off naked." Kai's grin is all teeth. "Can't say the same for everyone."

Carter snorts out a laugh.

Tanner's face goes red. "Fuck you. I'm huge. Every woman I've been with has cried from my size."

I can't help myself. "Yeah, cried with disappointment."

The people at the surrounding tables are starting to pay attention now, conversations dying as they tune in to the drama unfolding at our corner.

Tanner sputters, looking between us. "You—I—that's not—"

"The true measure of a man," Carter continues, his tone philosophical, "isn't what's in his pants. It's how much he can drink."

Tanner blinks, thrown by the change in direction. "What?"

"You heard me." Carter leans back in his seat, arms crossed, completely at ease. "Anyone can brag about size. But it takes a real man to hold his liquor."

I see what he's doing. Tanner has always been competitive, always needed to prove himself, and alcohol has always been his weakness. Carter is dangling bait, and Tanner, drunk, angry, humiliated, looks like he's going to take it.

Sure enough, Tanner puffs up his chest. "I can outdrink any of you clowns."

"Prove it." Carter's smile is slow and dangerous. "You and me. Shot for shot. Right here. We'll see who the real man is."

"Not tonight," Tanner states.

"Why not?" Kai answers.

"Because I'm not a fucking idiot. I've already had a head start. Wouldn't want anyone to say you cheated."

"Fine, then you won't have any problem showing up sober tomorrow." Carter's eyes glitter with challenge. "Unless you're scared."

"I'm not scared of shit." Tanner's chest is heaving now, his face mottled red. "Shot for shot. And when I win, you admit, publicly, that you stole my police car."

"I can't claim something I never did," Carter adds.

"Fuck you."

"Look, I'll admit you're the better man," Carter states. "How's that?"

"And when you lose," Kai interjects, "you leave June alone. Forever. No more talking to her, no drunk confrontations or pathetic attempts to win her back. You stay away from her and from us. Deal?"

Tanner's gaze jumps to me, something ugly passing across his face. Then he nods sharply. "Deal."

"Excellent." Carter raises his beer in a mock toast. "See you tomorrow, Tanner. Try not to piss yourself thinking about it."

Tanner opens his mouth—probably to deliver some devastating comeback—but nothing comes out. He just stands there for a moment, jaw working, before finally turning and stumbling away toward a table in the far corner where a group of his buddies are waiting. A girl I don't recognize drapes herself over his arm, shooting me a smug look.

You're welcome to him, honey.

"Fucking prick," I mutter under my breath as I sink back into my seat.

Kai slides in beside me and drapes an arm around my shoulders. "You okay?"

"I will be once he's gone." I glance at Carter and shake my head. "You don't have to do this. Seriously. He's not worth it."

His grin stays bright, almost cheerful, which is unfair considering he is about to start a war with a man he doesn't even respect. "Oh, I know he's not worth it. That's why it's going to be fun."

Kai snorts. "If anyone can win a drinking contest,

it's Carter. I've seen him put away a whole bottle of whiskey and still recite poetry."

I laugh despite myself, despite Tanner and the tight coil of anxiety that has been living in my ribs all day. These three make it hard to stay scared. They keep dragging me back into the moment, into breath, and into something that feels survivable.

That's when Seth returns, balancing a tray stacked with food. He sets it down in the middle of the table, and the smells hit me all at once—brisket, ribs, pulled pork, cornbread, coleslaw, beans. He slides into the seat beside Carter, scanning our faces.

"What did I miss?"

Kai, Carter, and I exchange glances, a shared silent agreement, then we all start laughing again.

Seth's eyes narrow, already suspicious. "All right. What did you two do now?" His gaze lands on Kai and Carter, because of course it does. He knows where trouble lives.

"Nothing," Carter says, too innocent to be believable.

"Absolutely nothing," Kai agrees, the picture of sincerity, if sincerity had dimples and a criminal record.

I press my lips together, trying not to laugh harder, and fail.

Seth stares at them, unimpressed. "Well, you all look suspicious."

Kai spreads his hands. "We are offended that you would accuse us."

Carter nods solemnly. "Deeply offended."

Seth doesn't blink. "Because I know you both."

Kai leans closer to me, stage-whispering, "See? He has trust issues."

Carter whispers back, "He was born with them."

This time it's Seth who laughs out loud, and I love the sound so much. It's intoxicating and contagious. And somehow, even with Tanner sitting nearby and my nerves still buzzing under my skin, my shoulders loosen a fraction, because this is what my Alphas do. They crowd in, feed me, and then joke until I can breathe again.

24

I've read my father's text message three times now.

Meet me after the morning meeting, out in front of the town hall. You don't need to attend today since you got a bit heated yesterday, but we can go through the numbers together and talk through anything you found.

Heated. That's one word for it. Another might be *justified, furious,* or *ready to tear Holden's throat out with my bare hands.* But sure. *Heated* works.

I stand on the sidewalk outside the town hall, shoulders hunched against the morning chill, and pull up the email Joshua sent an hour ago. The subject line is simple: *Yesterday's count.* I open the attachment on my phone and scroll, thumb moving fast over rows of handwritten totals turned into neat columns.

Tickets. Concessions. Merchandise. Every sale tracked in real time.

The numbers look right.

Not perfect, not polished, but right in that gut-level way you learn after years of running events. They match what I saw yesterday: the packed stands, the constant lines, the vendors barely keeping up. And much closer to the kind of revenue we've pulled in at past stops on the circuit when things are running clean.

Which is exactly why my jaw tightens.

Because Holden's story about the first two days has been one of underperformance. Lower totals. Smaller margins. A steady drip of disappointment that never quite turns into a crisis, just enough to keep everyone resigned and distracted. If yesterday was this strong, then day one and day two should not have been as weak as Holden made them sound.

That missing chunk of money did not evaporate. It had to be redirected.

I keep scrolling, double-checking categories, scanning for any obvious mistake, any reason to doubt it. There isn't one. The pattern is too consistent, too clean, and it lines up too well with my memory of the day.

Footsteps crunch behind me on the pavement. I look up and spot my father coming down the sidewalk, hands in the pockets of his pants, expression set in that hard, unreadable way he gets when he's already bracing for bad news. He slows when he sees my face.

"Seth," he says, stopping in front of me. "Thanks for waiting."

"Do you have the numbers from Holden?"

He pulls a folded sheet from his pocket and passes it over.

I take it, scan it once, and the anger in me sharpens. Even without going line by line, it's what I suspected. Underreported. Neat. Convenient.

I lift my phone. "Joshua tracked yesterday by hand. Proper count. Every ticket, every food sale, every piece of merch."

My father's eyes narrow. "Joshua who?"

"Local guy running the tickets at the rodeo," I say. "He's not on Holden's payroll, and he has no reason to lie to me."

My father takes the phone from my hand and scrolls, then looks down at Holden's printout, and then back to my screen. He does it again, slower this time. His face doesn't change much, but his jaw sets harder with each pass.

When he finally looks up, the air between us feels heavier.

"It's short," he says, voice flat.

"About a third," I reply.

My father stares back toward the town hall, then back at me, and his jawline clenches. "That son of a bitch," he says quietly. "He's been skimming money from us."

• • •

My father snatches the printout back, staring at it as if the numbers might rearrange themselves into something less damning. They don't.

"Are you certain about this? Your contact is reliable?"

"Joshua has worked for the circuit for as long as we've been coming to this town. He has no reason to inflate or change anything. These are actual sales, Dad. Real transactions recorded as they happened. So why don't they match what Holden's reporting? Even if there was some margin for error, it shouldn't be this wide."

"Hell." My father's voice stays low, but there's steel in it. "That bastard has been playing us. I trusted him and the committee's systems, their processes."

"Holden has full access to the financials," I say. "Joshua confirmed it. If he adjusts the totals after the fact and skims the difference, it looks clean on paper. Nobody questions it because nobody thinks to."

My father's jaw flexes. Then he starts walking again, faster, boots striking the sidewalk in sharp, angry steps. I fall in beside him.

"This isn't pocket change," he mutters. "That gap's too damn consistent." He glances down at the sheet in his hand, then away, as if looking at it might make him angrier. "If it's running about a third short and it's been happening since day one, you multiply that across the full run, and we're talkin'..." His mouth tightens. "A hell of a lot."

"At least half a million," I say.

He stops so abruptly that I nearly run into him. He turns to face me, anger in every line of him, cheeks flushed, fists clenched at his sides.

"All that money is ours," he says, each word clipped. "I should've seen it. The excuses. The disappointing reports. The way he kept pushing that story about the town losing interest. He was setting expectations low so nobody went looking."

"You couldn't have known," I tell him, because I mean it. Holden played it carefully. He fed everyone just enough truth to make the lies believable.

My father shakes his head, sighing. He drags a hand across his mouth, breath harsh. "I got complacent. Trusted the wrong people. But not again," he says quietly. "Not on my watch."

We stand there for a moment, both of us processing. Then I nod toward a building up ahead. Sweetwater Creek Realty. June's office.

"Come on. We need to bring the others up to speed."

The morning light catches the windows of the real estate office as we approach. Through the glass, I spot movement inside. June, Carter, and Kai. My pack. My family.

Something warm spreads through my chest despite the anger still simmering beneath the surface.

We push through the door, and three heads turn toward us simultaneously. June is perched on the edge of her desk, looking effortlessly beautiful in a short skirt and a loose blouse that keeps slipping off one shoulder. Every time I see her, the pull gets stronger. The bond humming beneath my skin, demanding more. Carter is sprawled in the burgundy armchair, long legs stretched out in front of him, looking annoyingly comfortable for a man about to compete in front of thousands. Kai is leaning against the wall near the window, arms crossed, radiating the kind of restless energy that usually precedes him doing something monumentally stupid.

"Morning, Mr. Benton," Carter says, rising to shake my father's hand. "Good to see you this morning."

"Carter. Kai." My father has known these two for years now. Watched them grow from promising young riders into the stars of his circuit. Bailed them out of trouble more times than I care to count. "How are you boys holding up?"

"Ready to cause some trouble," Kai says with a grin. "As always."

"Try to keep it legal."

"Where's the fun in that?"

My father almost smiles. Almost. "I don't doubt you'll find a way."

His attention shifts to June, and his expression softens noticeably. The change is subtle but unmistakable. "June. I hope these three aren't giving you too much grief."

"Nothing I can't handle." She smiles.

I move to stand beside her, my hand finding the small of her back automatically. The contact settles something in my chest, even as the rest of me stays coiled tight. "The numbers are in, and it's worse than we thought," I tell the pack. Then I go through and explain what Dad and I were chatting about earlier.

"That piece of shit." Kai pushes off the wall, his whole body going tense.

I spread Joshua's printout and my phone on June's desk, and everyone gathers around. "Look at the comparison. Actual sales versus what Holden reported to my father."

Carter lets out a low whistle. "Jesus. And I bet the difference is disappearing into his pocket."

"None of this would have come to light without June," I say, addressing my father but keeping my eyes on her. "She's the one who started pulling at the thread."

June meets my gaze, and I give her a small nod.

"Go on," my dad asks of her.

"I discovered something at first," she explains. "From the night Seth got arrested. He wasn't drunk."

My father's brow furrows. "I don't understand."

"Someone spiked his drink," she says. "We found security footage from the bar showing a woman likely slipping something into Seth's glass. An out-of-towner. A friend and I tracked her down and got a confession."

"Who the hell is she? Why?" My father's voice rises.

"Holden paid her," I say. "He wanted me to look drunk and out of control. If everyone's whispering about the Benton boy's public meltdown, then maybe fewer people will attend and nobody will ask why the numbers don't add up."

The room goes quiet.

My father sinks into the chair behind June's desk, and for the first time in my life, he looks... older. He drags a hand down his face and lets out a heavy breath through his nose, the kind that sounds too controlled to be anything but anger.

June leans forward with her palms on the desk, eyes sharp. "He paid a woman to spike Seth's drink," she says, blunt as a hammer. "My friend and I got her to admit it. She thought it was just a prank, that it would make him look reckless. She didn't know Holden was using it to cover a financial mess he created."

My father's head snaps up, and his gaze locks on her.

"I told you I didn't get drunk that night," I add. "I knew something was wrong. I just couldn't prove it."

My father's jaw twitches. He stares in my direction, and there's something raw in his gaze I'm not used to seeing. "I should have believed you," he says. "I'm sorry, son."

The apology is new. My father doesn't apologize, not ever, so hearing it now, in front of everyone, tells me exactly how deep this cut goes.

My father turns to June. "June, I can't thank you enough. You've saved this circuit more than you know." His gaze shifts to me, then to Kai and Carter, and a faint smile tugs at his mouth. "And I can see exactly why my boys are so taken with you."

June's cheeks color, her lips curling upward at the corners. "They're not the only ones with good taste," she replies, dry and bold, and it's enough to make Kai choke on a laugh behind me.

My father's smile sharpens, pleased by the spine. "Good," he says simply. Then the warmth drains and the businessman returns. "I'm contacting my lawyers immediately. Get Joshua to do another account, and if today's numbers come back similar when compared to Holden's, we move fast before he gets wind and tries to disappear."

"He's not running," June says, voice edged now. "He just agreed to buy my house and my business from my parents. He's planting roots. He thinks he's about to set himself up permanently with money he stole."

My father's expression turns dark. "Then we'll make sure he doesn't profit from any of it." He stands, and the air shifts with him. "We'll burn his whole plan to the ground."

He claps my shoulder on his way out, grip firm. "Good work, Seth. All of you. I'll be in touch."

The door swings shut behind him. For a beat, none of us move.

Then Carter exhales and breaks the silence. "Well. That was fucking great progress."

"Understatement of the century," Kai says, pacing, restless energy spilling out of him. "So we've got initial proof he might be stealing and proof he tried to frame you. What now?"

"Now we go to the police to see what they need in order to start searching," I state. "We get official charges, see if we can lock down the records, and we force an audit of everything he's touched." My mind is already shifting into problem-solving mode, anger turning into action. "I'll speak to the sheriff this morning. We get it on record before Holden realizes we're onto him and he has time to spin a story."

"I'll come with you," June says, already moving.

"No." I step in front of her. I cup her face in my hands. "You go to the rodeo with Carter and Kai. Carter's up soon, and I won't be long." I press a kiss to her forehead and breathe her in. I pull back, then steal a real kiss. Short, no nonsense, enough to put the taste of her on my tongue and remind her she is ours.

Carter stands and stretches, all long limbs and confidence. "Come on, beautiful. You can watch me be incredible on horseback. It'll change your life."

June snorts.

Kai slips an arm around June's shoulders and steers her toward the door. "Let's go before Carter starts turning into a greeting card. I want to check on the Brutus setup anyway. Make sure Crawford's got everything ready for tomorrow."

We all head out, June locking the door and then being flanked by Carter and Kai. She glances back over her shoulder at me. The smile she gives me is captivating, and all mine.

25

KAI

I have no idea what's happening in the arena.

Somewhere in the distance, an announcer is saying something about the saddle bronc championships. The crowd is cheering, and cowboys are risking their necks on thousand-pound horses bred for violence.

I missed the entire introduction and the first rodeo star. The man could have been trampled for all I know, and I wouldn't have noticed.

All I can focus on is the woman sitting next to me.

June is pressed against my side in the stands, her body warm and soft and impossibly distracting. My arm is draped around her back. Her scent wraps around me with every breath I take, and I swear it's getting deeper. Richer. More intoxicating by the hour.

She insists she feels normal, says nothing has changed, but I know better.

"Kai." Her voice cuts through the fog in my brain. "Are you even paying attention?"

"Absolutely," I lie.

"Really? What just happened?"

I glance toward the arena, where a cowboy is climbing off a horse to scattered applause.

"That guy rode. Did okay. Not as good as Carter will do."

She laughs, shaking her head. "You didn't watch any of it."

"I watched the important parts."

"Which were?"

I lean in closer, letting my lips brush against the shell of her ear. "The way your thighs look in that skirt."

Her breath catches, just slightly, and satisfaction curls through my chest. She's wearing this tiny denim thing that barely covers anything, and with her legs crossed beside me, the hem has ridden up to dangerous territory. I've been staring at those legs for the past twenty minutes, imagining what it would feel like to have them wrapped around my head.

"Kai." Her tone is warning, but I can hear the smile underneath it.

"June." I match her inflection perfectly.

"We're in public."

"I know." I breathe her in again, letting my nose trail along the curve of her neck.

"Doesn't change what I want to do to you."

"You're such a tease."

"I want to eat you." The words come out low and rough, barely audible over the noise of the crowd. "Want to spread you out and taste every inch of you until you're shaking."

She shivers against me, and I feel the tremor all the way down my spine.

"How do you hold on to any control?" she asks, her voice slightly breathless now.

"Who says it's working?"

"You're still sitting here, aren't you?"

"Barely." I press a kiss to her cheek, lingering there, letting my lips drag across her skin.

"So you enjoy teasing me, is that it?"

She turns her head, those hazel eyes sparkling. "I admit, I do enjoy seeing you all worked up."

"You know this is just going to make me crazier."

"More than you already are? Impossible?"

I nod slowly, holding her gaze. "You have no idea. Right now, I'm so hungry for you I could do anything."

She laughs, bright and warm, and her hand lands on my thigh. It's a casual gesture. Friendly, even. But the moment her palm makes contact with my leg, every nerve ending in my body lights up.

"You'll be fine," she says.

I will absolutely not.

Her fingers are just sitting there. Not moving, not stroking, just resting against my thigh, and somehow that simple touch has my cock throbbing, straining against my jeans, desperate for attention it's not going to get. Not here, anyway.

I try to focus on the arena and watch the next cowboy settle into the chute. But my attention keeps drifting back to June, to the curve of her shoulder where I left a mark not long ago, to those goddamn legs that are going to be the death of me.

She shifts beside me, uncrossing and recrossing them, and the movement causes her skirt to ride up another inch. I catch a glimpse of smooth inner thigh, the shadow where the fabric ends, and my imagination goes into overdrive.

What is she wearing under there? Those little lace things she seems to favor? Something simpler? Nothing at all?

The last thought makes me groan out loud.

"What?" June glances at me, confused.

"Nothing." Everything. "Just thinking."

"About?"

"Things that would get us both arrested if I said them out loud."

She blushes, that pretty pink color spreading across her cheeks, and I want to strip her out of that top and watch the flush spread across her chest, her stomach, lower.

The announcer's voice booms through the speakers, snapping me back to reality. "Next up, ladies and gentlemen, from the Wildfire Star Rodeo is Carter Storm!"

June immediately perks up, clapping her hands together. "Carter's next!"

She's bouncing in her seat now, excited and eager, and I can't stop staring at the way her breasts move with each bounce. Her top is thin, doing very little to hide anything, and I'm fairly certain I can see the outline of her nipples through the fabric.

Christ. I need to get a grip.

"Kai." She's staring at me now, eyebrow raised. "Don't look at me. Carter's right there."

Right. Carter. My best friend. The reason we're here.

I force my attention to the arena, where Carter is settling into the chute, positioning himself on the back of a massive bronc. Even from here, I notice the tension in the horse, the way it's already fighting against the confined space, eager to explode.

Saddle bronc is one of the classic rodeo events, and Carter has been dominating it for years. The goal is simple in theory, brutal in execution: stay on the horse for eight seconds while it does everything in its power to throw you off. The rider holds on to a thick braided rein attached to the horse's halter, keeping one hand in the air at all times. Touch the horse with your free hand, and you're disqualified. Get thrown before the buzzer, and you get nothing.

Points are awarded based on the rider's form, the horse's performance, and the overall difficulty of the ride. Judges look for smooth, controlled spurring, a strong grip, and the ability to match the horse's rhythm without fighting it. The best riders make it look effortless, and the horse's power works with them rather than against them.

It sounds manageable when you describe it. It's not. The horses used in saddle bronc are specifically bred and trained to buck, and they're incredibly good at it.

Carter makes it look effortless. That's his gift. He's one of the most naturally talented riders I've ever seen, with an instinct for movement and balance that borders on supernatural. Where other cowboys fight against the horse, Carter seems to flow with it, anticipating every buck and twist before it happens. He reads the animal beneath him with uncanny precision, shifting his weight and adjusting his position in real time.

It's beautiful, in a violent sort of way. Poetry written in dust and adrenaline, just his thing.

June is on her feet now, blowing him a kiss from the stands. Carter's head turns toward us, that familiar grin spreading across his face. I give him a nod: *You got this*.

The gate swings open.

The horse explodes out of the chute, all strength and fury. Its back legs kick high, launching Carter's body upward, then its front end drops and twists, trying to throw him sideways. The motion is violent, jarring.

Carter doesn't even flinch.

He rides with his free arm high, his body moving in perfect counterpoint to the horse's bucking. Back and forward, up and down, a brutal rhythm that he makes look almost graceful. His form is textbook, spurs marking forward and back with each buck, his center of gravity low and stable.

"He's a fucking show-off," I mutter, but there's pride in my voice. The bastard really is something else.

Beside me, June is gushing. Melting. Her eyes are locked on Carter, and I feel a flash of something that might be jealousy if I were a different kind of man. Instead, it's just heat. Arousal. The knowledge that she looks at all of us that way, that we all get to experience her awe and her passion and her complete, undivided attention.

The buzzer sounds. Eight seconds.

Carter lets go and tumbles off, landing on his feet and immediately moving away from the still-bucking horse. Pickup riders move in to help the bronc, while Carter jogs to the arena fence, climbing up to wave at the roaring crowd.

But his eyes find us first. Find June, who's cheering and clapping and whistling through her fingers so loudly that the people around us are staring.

Carter blows her a kiss, and she pretends to catch it, pressing her palm to her heart.

I lean in close to her ear again. "You wait until I'm on Brutus. Much more dangerous than that."

She glances at me, concern flickering across her features. She kisses me quickly.

We settle back into our seats, her hand finding mine and squeezing tight.

Fuck me, she's beautiful. "You have to be careful on Brutus." Even worried, even scared for me, she's the most stunning thing I've ever seen.

"I will," I promise.

But June is restless now, shifting in her seat, glancing around the arena.

"I want to grab a drink," she says. "Come with me?"

"Absolutely."

We make our way out of the stands, navigating through the crowd until we emerge into the area behind the arena. It's quieter here, the roar of the audience muffled by distance and concrete walls. Vendors are selling food and souvenirs, and groups of spectators mill around, taking a break from the action.

June starts toward one of the drink stands, but I catch her hand.

"Come on. Let me show you something."

She raises an eyebrow. "What?"

"You'll see." I tug her away from the crowds, leading her down a corridor that most people don't know exists. It's where the rodeo crew have their private spaces, rooms reserved for the performers and staff who work behind the scenes.

I find the door I'm looking for and push it open,

ushering June inside before following and kicking it shut behind us.

The room is basic but functional. A couch along one wall, a few chairs, a mirrored wall, a rack for gear. Nothing fancy. But it's private, and right now, that's all that matters.

"This is where all the magic happens," I say, spreading my arms wide. "Well, the behind-the-scenes stuff, anyway. Where we rev ourselves up before events, decompress after. Carter, Seth, and I share this one."

June looks around, taking it in. "It's nice."

"It's private." I adjust my cock over my jeans, trying to relieve some of the pressure that's been building since we sat down in the stands. My dick is rock hard, has been for the better part of an hour, and I'm about two seconds away from losing my mind completely.

June's eyes drop to where my hand is adjusting, and something shifts in her expression. She starts walking toward me, hips swaying with each step.

"Why did you bring me here, Kai?"

"Because I need to kiss you or I'm going to implode."

She giggles, but it cuts off when I grab her, hauling her against my chest. My mouth finds hers, and I pour every ounce of desperation into the kiss. Days of wanting, hours of teasing, minutes of watching her bounce in that goddamn skirt while my cock begged for attention.

She moans against my lips, and the sound goes straight to my groin.

Her hands are everywhere suddenly, grabbing at my clothes, tugging at my belt, fighting with my zipper. I pull back just long enough to grin at her.

"Oh, June. Here I thought I was the only one losing my mind."

"Shut up." She yanks my belt open, the buckle clanging. "You can't whisper all that sexy stuff to me back there and expect me to feel nothing. I'm on thin ice with how burning hot I am around you three, and then you push and push, and I'm easy to break."

"Is that so?"

"Yes." She smiles up at me, and it's the most beautiful thing I've ever seen. "So are you going to do something about it, or are we just going to stand here?"

I answer by spinning her around and walking her toward the far wall. It's a floor-to-ceiling mirror.

I press her against it, her face and body flattening against the cool surface. She gasps at the contact, and I bury my face in her hair, breathing her in.

"Don't worry. I've got you." My hands find the hem of her skirt, yanking it up around her waist. Underneath, she's wearing a tiny scrap of lace held together by strings at the hips. I hook my fingers through one of the strings and pull.

It snaps.

June gasps again, louder this time.

"Oops." I don't move from my position, my chest

pressed against her back, my hips pinning her in place. "My bad."

"Did you just break my underwear?"

I pull the ruined fabric away, tossing it aside. "I'll buy you new ones."

"You'll buy me several new ones, at the rate you're going."

I laugh against her neck, one hand sliding between her thighs. She's wet. Soaking. The evidence of her arousal coats my fingers instantly, and the groan that tears out of me is almost animalistic.

"Spread your legs, doll."

She does, widening her stance, and I stroke through her heat, pressing past her lips, and teasing her entrance. She pushes back against me, seeking more, and the needy sound she makes nearly undoes me.

"I can't hold back much longer," I warn her.

"Then don't."

That's all the permission I need.

I free my cock from my jeans, position myself behind her, pushing the tip inside her, and then thrust home in one smooth motion.

June cries out, her palms slapping against the mirror. The sound echoes in the small room, mixing with my own groan of relief. She's tight and hot and perfect, and being inside her feels the way I imagine heaven would.

"Fuck," I breathe against her ear. "You feel incredible."

"Move," she demands. "Kai, please, move."

I start to thrust, setting a rhythm that's probably too hard, too fast, too desperate. But I can't help it. I've been wound tight for hours, wanting her, needing her, and now that I have her, I can't hold anything back.

Her moans grow louder with each plunge, bouncing off the walls, filling the room with the sound of her pleasure. I watch our reflection in the glass, the way her face contorts with ecstasy, how my hands grip her hips hard.

"That's it," I growl. "Let me hear you."

"Kai... Oh God, Kai..."

The door suddenly swings open behind us.

I glance in the mirror, not slowing my pace, and spot Carter standing in the doorway. His eyes widen, then narrow, a grin spreading across his face.

"You fucker." He steps inside, letting the door swing shut behind him. "Of course you're in here with her."

June moans, either not hearing him or not caring. I thrust harder, deeper, chasing the building pressure at the base of my spine.

"Scream for me, doll," I tell her. "Let him hear you."

She does, loud and uninhibited, her whole body shaking as she gets closer to the edge. Carter approaches until he's standing beside us. He reaches out and brushes the hair back from June's face, forcing her to look at him.

"You're doing so well," he murmurs, his voice low and approving. "So beautiful when you're falling apart."

"Carter…" She's gasping, barely coherent.

"Hope you're ready," he continues, his eyes meeting mine over her shoulder. "Because I'm next. We're going to keep taking turns."

The words push her over the edge. June comes undone with a scream that probably echoes down the entire corridor. I feel her clenching around me, milking me, and it takes every ounce of willpower I have not to follow her over. Not until we're both done with fucking her senseless.

I work her through it, slowing my thrusts to long, deep strokes that draw out her orgasm until she's trembling, barely able to stand.

For a moment, none of us move. June is pressed against the mirror, held up only by my body behind her. Carter is watching us with dark, hungry eyes, his cock already out and in his hand. And I'm trying to remember how to breathe.

"Well," Carter says finally, his voice rough. "That was quite a show."

June laughs weakly. "Glad you enjoyed it."

"Oh, I did." He steps closer, sliding a hand up her back, nudging me out of the way. "But now it's my turn to make you scream."

I pull out carefully, steadying June when her knees threaten to buckle. She glances at us through the mirror, her cheeks flushed and her eyes glazed with satisfaction.

Carter grins, staring her up and down. "Just beautiful. Now bend over for me a bit more."

I tuck myself back into my jeans and move to the couch, sprawling out to watch. June catches my eye and shakes her head, a smile playing at the corners of her lips. She's bent over, her hands on the mirror, and Carter is shoving that monster into her. She cries out, and the sound sends a thrill right through me and to my balls.

"You two are going to be the death of me," she moans.

"What a way to go, though," I say.

She laughs again, and the noise of Carter slapping into her wraps around me, sexy as fuck. This incredible, perfect woman who somehow chose us. Chose me.

Carter is pounding into her like a maniac.

I settle deeper into the couch and enjoy the view, waiting for my turn.

Some things are worth watching.

And some women are worth sharing.

That's the thing about being a pack, I realize as I watch Carter please our Omega. There's no jealousy here. No competition. Just three men who all love the same woman, who all want to see her happy and satisfied and screaming with pleasure. Whether it's me making her fall apart or Carter or Seth, the result is the same. She's ours. We're hers.

And this is just the beginning.

26

The neon sign above the BBQ joint flickers twice before settling into a steady glow, casting red and orange light across the parking lot. Inside, the evening crowd is building, laughter and country music spilling out every time the door swings open. The smell of smoked brisket and hickory hangs in the air, mixing with the sharper scent of spilled beer and anticipation.

Tonight is going to be fun.

Kai drops into the chair beside me, his grin so wide it threatens to split his face in two. "You ready for this?"

"Born ready."

"That's my boy." He slaps me on the shoulder hard enough to make me wince. "You're going to destroy that fucker. Absolutely annihilate him. I want to see tears. I want to see him crawl out of here on his hands and knees."

"That's the plan."

We deliberately didn't tell Seth about tonight. He would have found some way to shut it down, lecture us about responsibility and consequences and not making things worse. The man means well, but sometimes you just need to let chaos reign. Besides, June distracted him perfectly. She has a book club meeting tonight with Sophia and somehow convinced Seth to tag along.

The thought still makes me laugh. Seth, grumpy Alpha cowboy extraordinaire, sitting in a circle of women discussing romance novels. I would pay good money to see his face when they start analyzing the spicy scenes.

The door swings open, and Tanner strides in, flanked by two of his buddies. He's sober tonight, I can tell. Clear eyes, steady gait, that infuriating smirk plastered across his face. He's wearing a tight shirt that shows off muscles he probably thinks are impressive and jeans so new they still have creases.

"Carter." He stops at our table, arms crossed. "Didn't think you'd actually show."

"Wouldn't miss it for the world."

His friends fan out behind him, trying to look intimidating. One of them is a skinny guy with a patchy beard, the other built more solidly but with the vacant expression of someone who peaked in high school. Real threatening crew he's assembled.

"We need rules," Tanner announces, pulling out a chair and straddling it backward. "Can't have you cheating your way through this."

"Agreed." I lean back, keeping my posture relaxed. Confident. "Lay them out."

"Simple enough. We each take a shot. After every round, we each throw one dart at the board." He gestures toward the dartboard mounted on the far wall, currently unoccupied. "You miss the board entirely three times, you're out. You lose. I win."

"Yeah, you'll always be the loser," Kai interjects, that smug grin spreading across his face.

Tanner's expression sours. "This doesn't involve you."

"I'm moral support. Deal with it."

I can practically see Tanner's blood pressure rising. Good. The more agitated he gets, the sloppier he'll be. "Fine. Let's relocate to the dartboard, get ourselves set up."

We all migrate to the corner of the room where the dartboard hangs, commandeering the nearby tables. A few regulars shoot us curious looks but don't interfere.

"So we go until one of us misses three darts," I confirm. "Got it."

Kai clears his throat loudly. "Hold on. This seems way too easy. We need to up the stakes a bit."

Tanner narrows his eyes. "What did you have in mind?"

"Every ten rounds, both of you have to ride the mechanical bull." Kai jerks his thumb toward Brutus. The mechanical monstrosity sits in its own roped-off area, currently dormant but waiting. "Shake things up. Add some physicality to the mental game."

I keep my expression neutral, but inside I'm grinning. Kai knows damn well that riding a mechanical bull is second nature to me. I could do it blindfolded, hungover, and missing a limb. Tanner, on the other hand, is a desk jockey who probably hasn't been on anything more challenging than a bar stool.

"Not sure that's necessary," Tanner hedges, and I catch the flare of uncertainty in his eyes.

"I think it's essential," I counter. "Otherwise, this is way too simple. Come on, don't chicken out before we've even started."

His buddies immediately start in on him, clapping his shoulders and talking him up. "You got this, man. Don't let these rodeo pricks intimidate you."

Peer pressure is a beautiful thing.

"Fuck it. Fine." Tanner straightens up, squaring his shoulders. "Let's do this."

Kai catches my eye and winks. The man is an evil genius sometimes.

The bartender appears with two trays loaded with shot glasses, amber liquid inside. Whiskey. Good stuff too, from the smell of it. Kai must have ordered while I was watching Tanner posture.

"Twenty shots' worth to start," Kai announces, arranging ten glasses in front of each of us. "Should make things interesting."

I pick up my first glass, studying the liquid inside. The smell hits my nose, sharp and smoky, with notes of caramel underneath. Tennessee's finest, ready to do battle.

"You first," I tell Tanner.

He snatches up his glass and throws it back without ceremony, slamming the empty container down on the table with more force than necessary. A few drops splash onto the wood.

I follow suit, letting the whiskey burn a trail down my throat. It's smooth going down, warmth blooming in my chest almost immediately. One down. Who knows how many to go?

We approach the dartboard together. Tanner goes first, squinting at the target with intense concentra- tion. His form is decent; I'll give him that. The dart flies true, embedding itself in the center ring with a satis- fying thunk.

"Bull's-eye." He smirks at me over his shoulder.

I step up, barely aiming, and let my dart fly. It lands a millimeter from his, perfectly centered.

"Looks about even to me," Kai observes from his seat, legs stretched out in front of him. "This is gonna take a while before it gets interesting."

He's not wrong.

We settle into a rhythm. Glass after glass disappears, the whiskey warming my blood, loosening my limbs. By the fifth round, there's a pleasant buzz humming through my system. By the eighth, the edges of the room have started to soften.

Tanner is feeling it too. His throws are getting wilder, his stance less steady. He's managed to hit the board every time so far, but the precision is gone. His last dart landed in the outer ring, barely qualifying.

Round ten. Kai clears the remaining glasses and gestures toward the mechanical bull. "Gentlemen, your chariot awaits."

Tanner stares at the bull the way a man might look at his own grave.

"You first," I offer magnanimously.

Tanner climbs over the rope anyway, approaching the mechanical beast with obvious trepidation. One of the staff members appears to operate the controls, barely suppressing a grin.

"Five seconds to qualify," Kai announces, appointing himself as official referee. "Anything less and you forfeit the round."

"That wasn't part of the original rules," Tanner protests.

"Consider it an amendment. All in favor?" Kai raises his own hand. "Motion passes."

Tanner mutters something under his breath and mounts the bull. The machine whirs to life, and immediately he's clinging on for dear life as it bucks and spins. His body jerks back and forth, completely out of sync with the motion, his arms windmilling for balance.

The five seconds that pass might be the longest of his life. When the bull finally stills, he slides off with all the grace of a wet noodle, stumbling several steps before catching himself on the railing.

"And he survives!" Kai commentates. "Barely. Very, very barely. Looking a bit green around the gills there, buddy."

"Fuck off." Tanner is definitely swaying now, his face taking on a distinctly pale hue. He makes his way back to our table and drops into his chair, reaching for the next round of amber liquid with a shaking hand.

My turn.

I approach Brutus and mount up, give the operator a nod, and let my body find the rhythm automatically.

Five seconds pass in a blur of motion. The bull bucks and twists, but I'm with it the whole way, my hips moving in counterpoint, my core keeping me centered. When the time is up, I dismount smoothly and hop over the railing.

The room spins slightly when I land. Just slightly. I'm fine.

"And that's how a professional does it," Kai crows. "Take notes, Deputy Dipshit."

We return to the table where fresh rounds await. The whiskey is starting to taste less like alcohol and more like water, which is either a very good sign or a very bad one.

Round eleven. Tanner manages to hit the board, though barely. His dart wobbles in flight and catches the very edge of the target.

I pick up my dart, weighing it in my hand, and make a decision. I've been matching him throw for throw, but where's the fun in that? Time to show this asshole exactly how outclassed he is.

"You know what?" I toss the dart without looking, deliberately aiming for the wall. It embeds itself in the wood paneling a good foot from the dartboard. "I don't need the security blanket. Too easy otherwise."

Tanner actually cheers, pumping his fist in the air. "Ha! One miss for the cowboy!"

Kai bursts out laughing. "You realize he did that on purpose, right? He's spotting you points."

"Bullshit. Nobody throws a game on purpose."

"I do." I retrieve my dart and return to the table. "I'll beat you even with a handicap. Makes things more interesting."

Tanner's face cycles through several emotions, uncertainty winning out over indignation. He grabs his next glass and downs it aggressively, amber liquid dribbling down his chin.

We push through rounds twelve, thirteen, and fourteen. The whiskey is really hitting now. My vision has that pleasant underwater quality, everything soft and slightly delayed. Tanner has started leaning heavily on the table between throws, his aim deteriorating rapidly.

Round fifteen. His dart goes completely wild, sailing past the board and embedding itself in the wall a full two feet to the left.

"That's one legitimate miss!" Kai announces gleefully. "Two more and you're done, my friend."

"I fucking got this," Tanner growls, but the words slur together into something closer to

"I fuggin godthis."

Round sixteen. Another wild throw, another miss. This one actually bounces off the wall and clatters to the floor, nearly hitting a woman walking by. She yelps and shoots us a dirty look.

"Sorry about that!" I call out, charming as ever. "Drinks are on him."

Tanner doesn't even register the exchange. He's too busy staring at the dartboard with the intense focus of a man trying to will the universe to cooperate.

It doesn't.

I purposely miss my own throw, evening us up at two misses each. "See? Now it's fair."

"Stop fucking doing that," Tanner snaps. "Stop pretending you're better than me."

"I'm not pretending anything. I am better than you. At this, at riding, at everything that matters." I step closer, lowering my voice so only he can hear. "And I'm especially better for June."

Something dark flashes across his face, and for a

second, I think he might take a swing at me. Instead, he just grabs another glass, throws it back, and misses the dartboard entirely.

The dart sails past the target, past the wall, and embeds itself in some poor bastard's forearm.

The man screams.

Tanner takes one step forward, his eyes rolling back in his head, and pitches face-first onto the floor. He's snoring before he hits the ground.

Chaos erupts. The stabbed man is clutching his arm and shouting profanities. Tanner's friends are scrambling to revive their fallen champion. The restaurant staff is rushing over with first aid supplies and apologetic expressions.

Kai is on his feet, grabbing my hand and thrusting it into the air like I just won a championship bout. "We have a victor! The loser is unconscious! Carter remains undefeated!"

"Slowly," I manage, my stomach lurching. "Do that slowly."

"You did fucking amazing." Kai's grin is manic, triumphant. "Absolutely crushed him. Did you see his face when he went down? I wish I'd gotten video."

I'm pretty sure someone did get video, but I'm too busy concentrating on not vomiting to comment on it.

Tanner's friends have managed to roll him onto his back, where he continues snoring peacefully, completely oblivious to the havoc he's caused. The dart victim is being attended to by staff, still furious, gesturing wildly at the unconscious deputy while his companions try to calm him down.

"Our cue to exit," Kai decides, wrapping an arm around my shoulders to steady me. "We came, we conquered, we created chaos. Mission accomplished."

We slip out the back door as voices behind us rise in argument and accusation. The cool night air hits my face, and I take deep gulping breaths, trying to settle my spinning head.

"That was incredible." Kai is practically bouncing as we walk, high on victory and secondhand adrenaline. "The look on his face. The way he just collapsed. I'm going to remember this for the rest of my life."

"Glad you enjoyed the show." I lean against him more heavily, the ground feeling slightly unreliable beneath my feet. "Take me home. I need to go snuggle June."

"The book club should be wrapping up soon. She'll be back."

"Good. She always makes things better." The words come out mushier than intended, affection bleeding through the alcohol haze. "Everything's better when she's around. Her smell. Her laugh. The way she looks at us."

"Yeah." Kai's voice softens. "Yeah, she does."

We walk in companionable silence down the sidewalk to Kai's car, the sounds of the BBQ joint fading behind us. Stars are scattered across the Montana sky, impossibly bright, and the air smells clean and fresh.

Kai squeezes my shoulder. "You're a good man, Carter. Underneath all the pretty-boy bullshit."

"Thanks. I think."

"You're welcome." He pauses. "Also, you should probably vomit before you get into my car. Better out than in."

He's not wrong. I detour behind a convenient dumpster and lose everything I've consumed over the past several hours. It's not dignified, but it's effective. When I emerge, wiping my mouth on the back of my hand, I feel marginally more human.

"Better?" Kai asks.

"Getting there." I take one careful breath through my nose and immediately regret it. The alley smells like stale beer, garbage juice, and bad decisions. My decisions. I wipe my mouth again, even though it doesn't help, and try to stand with some dignity.

Kai checks his phone as the screen lights up his face for a second, and then his mouth twitches.

"What?" I squint at him. My eyes feel gritty. Everything feels gross.

He scans it, then makes a strangled sound that turns into a hollering laugh.

"Oh, what is it?" I rasp.

Kai holds the phone up so I can see that it's a message from Seth.

Where are you guys? Do you know what those women made me discuss at the book club? Do you have any idea the things I've heard tonight?

Then another message pops up.

I've learned things. Horrifying things.

My laugh bursts out of me, and it makes my stomach clench in warning. "Jesus. He's going to need therapy."

Kai wipes his eyes. "He's going to need holy water." He shakes his head, still grinning. "I've heard romance book clubs get wicked. Apparently, the men in those books do the most unhinged stuff—stalking, breaking in, growling about 'mine'—and readers eat it up." He snorts. "Half of it sounds illegal, and the other half sounds exhausting. Who has time to do all that?" He pauses, then shrugs, grin turning sly. "Although... if she's into it and it makes her happy, I can see the merit. I'm just saying."

I try to laugh again, and my body immediately threatens mutiny. I clap a hand over my mouth and gag once, hard.

Kai's grin turns vicious. "Oh, you are absolutely going to be sick again."

"Do not speak it into existence," I warn, voice hoarse.

Kai starts walking, still laughing, and hooks an arm around my back to steer me toward the car. "Come on, let's get you home before you end up making friends with another dumpster."

I stumble after him, boots scraping, head spinning in slow circles. "If Seth's traumatized, tell him I'm sorry I wasn't there to suffer with him."

Kai types as we walk, thumbs flying. "I'm telling him you're currently praying for forgiveness behind a dumpster."

"That is not what I'm doing."

Kai looks at me. "You literally just did."

The cool air hits my face when we step out of the alley and into the open lot. His car sits under a street-light, and it might be the most beautiful thing I've ever seen.

Kai hits the unlock button. The lights flash.

I take two steps toward it, confident for half a second, and then my stomach rolls again, mean and sudden.

I freeze.

Kai stops and watches me with the calm of a man who has seen this movie before. "You okay?"

I swallow hard. "Yep."

He raises his brows. "That's a lie."

I point at the Mustang. "Just get me in the car."

Kai opens the passenger door, then pauses, phone buzzing once more. He glances down and starts laughing all over again.

"What now?" I wheeze.

Kai reads, then looks up at me, eyes bright with evil. "Seth says if he has to hear one more woman explain why monsters are the superior choice, he's driving into the woods and living off-grid."

I bark out a laugh and immediately gag. "Son of a

—" I clamp a hand over my mouth and bend at the waist.

Kai pats my back, still laughing. "You laugh, you lose, Carter."

I glare at him, eyes watering, and manage one last thought before I ruin another patch of pavement.

If I survive tonight, I'm never drinking again.

Which is exactly the kind of lie a man tells right before he throws up.

27

JUNE

Sunlight streams through the curtains, pulling me slowly from sleep. I stretch beneath the covers, my body pleasantly heavy, limbs loose and relaxed in a way I haven't experienced in years. The bed is empty beside me, but the sheets still hold traces of warmth, of scent, of the man who held me through the night.

Seth.

I smile at the ceiling, remembering last night at the book club, which somehow turned into a book club with Seth awkwardly perched on the edge of the couch, looking as if he'd rather be wrestling an actual bull than discussing the romantic entanglements of fictional characters.

"That's not how any of this works," he'd muttered at one point, arms crossed, brow furrowed. "No Alpha would ever say that. It's ridiculous."

The room had gone quiet for a beat, then erupted in giggles and questions and demands that he explain exactly what he meant. By the end of the night, Seth was being asked to rate fictional Alphas on a scale of one to ten.

He'd been mortified.

It was incredible.

Carter and Kai hadn't made it home by the time we crawled into bed. I remember Seth pulling me against his chest, his heartbeat steady beneath my cheek, his arm heavy and warm across my waist. I was asleep within minutes.

All week we've been sharing the bed, the four of us tangled together in various configurations. They take turns on who gets which position, and there's an entire unspoken hierarchy about what constitutes the best spots. Kai insists that being in front is superior. Carter claims that being behind is the real prize. Seth just wants to be wherever he can wrap himself around me most completely.

Their dedication to the sleeping arrangement is oddly endearing.

I push myself up, swinging my legs over the edge of the mattress, and that's when I spot the folded note on my bedside table.

My heart stutters, then picks up speed. For days now, I've been waking up to these little gifts of words, carefully crafted, left where I'll find them. Carter's poetry.

I eagerly snatch the paper up, unfolding it with trembling fingers.

When the world goes quiet and the stars blink out,

When the weight of tomorrow makes you want to shout,

Remember you are my dawn,

The light I reach for when the dark feels too long.

I've wandered through storms and slept under rain,

I've buried my heart to outrun the pain,

But you, wild girl, with your laugh like a song,

You make me believe I can finally belong.

Tears prick my eyes. I read it again, then a third time, letting each word sink into my bones. He writes as if he can see inside my soul, as if he knows exactly what I need to hear before I even know I need to hear it.

I rise from the bed and cross to my chest of drawers, pulling open the top drawer. Inside sits a small wooden box I found at a thrift store, its surface worn smooth with age. I lift the lid and add Carter's latest poem to the growing collection inside.

Just reading them sometimes makes everything in the world seem less stressful.

I close the box gently and grab some clothes before heading into the bathroom. The shower is hot and soothing, washing away the last traces of sleep, but it does nothing to calm the anxiety that's been building in my stomach for days.

Today is the final day of the rodeo and when Kai rides Brutus.

The thought tightens my chest.

I try to push the fear down as I dress, but it clings to me. All I can do is be there for him. Support him and maybe, somehow, use whatever strange calming effect I have on Brutus to help.

When I finally emerge from the bathroom, fully dressed, Carter is leaning against the doorframe. He looks rough, hair disheveled, eyes slightly bloodshot, a shadow of stubble darkening his jaw. He's wearing clean jeans, a button-up checkered shirt, his hair still partially wet as if he just recently stepped out of the shower.

He's gorgeous.

"Hello, handsome," I say, unable to suppress my smile.

"Hello, sexy girl." His voice is raspier than usual, but his grin is the same. Warm. Genuine. "I missed you."

"I know." I close the distance between us, reaching up to cup his face. "I read your poem."

Something shifts in his expression, eyes narrowing.

"You make me so happy when I read them," I continue. "You know that, right? Every single one. I keep them all."

"You do?"

"Yep, I read them when I need to remember that good things exist in this world."

His hands find my waist, pulling me closer until our bodies are flush. The scent of him wraps around me. "Then my job is done," he murmurs, but his eyes are serious, searching my face.

"Carter, I..." I pause, suddenly overwhelmed by everything I'm feeling. The fear about today. The gratitude for his words. The bone-deep certainty that I am exactly where I'm supposed to be. "Your poems mean everything to me. You mean everything to me."

He smiles.

"I love you," I whisper, revealing the truth.

"June."

I'm blushing furiously now, looking away, unable to meet his eyes. "I'm sorry. I don't want to scare you off, as I know we're still getting to know each other and—"

His finger hooks under my chin, tilting my face up until I have no choice but to look at him. His expression steals my breath.

"You have no idea how much I wanted to hear that."

"Oh..."

"I love you." Carter's voice cracks on the words, raw and honest and utterly without pretense. "I love you so fucking much, June. I know this feels fast and it seems crazy, but what I feel for you is unlike anything I've ever experienced."

A tear escapes down my cheek. He catches it with his thumb, gentle as a whisper.

"I spent years running from anything real after I lost my brother in a rodeo," he continues, swallowing hard like the memory still has teeth. "Hiding behind pretty words and easy smiles. Telling myself I was fine and it didn't matter that I was hollow as long as I could keep moving."

His hand shifts, settling at my jaw like he needs the contact to keep himself steady, and my heart breaks for him.

"I thought my job in this world was simple," he says. "Ride the circuit the way he did. Win what he never got to win and be there where he can't be, so he's never forgotten. Like if I stayed on that road long enough, if I kept throwing myself into it, I could keep him alive in the only way that made sense."

He lets out a shaky breath, and his eyes shine like he hates that they do. I hold on to him. "You have been doing amazing."

"So I stayed," he murmurs. "Part of me believed quitting would mean letting his love for it die twice. And part of me... I didn't know who I was without the circuit in my blood. I kept showing up, kept doing the work, kept chasing that promise. Some days it felt noble. Some days it felt like I was using the arena to punish myself."

His thumb strokes my cheek again, slower now.

"But you..." His gaze locks on mine. "You make me want more than survival. You make me want a future, a home I come back to, a family. Something that isn't just me trying to outrun grief."

"Oh, Carter, I am always here for you."

His forehead drops to mine. "You make me want to stay for real, June. You make me want to be the man those poems describe instead of just the man who writes them."

I cup his face, steadying him the way he's been trying to steady himself all this time, and I don't let him look away like this is something he has to carry alone.

"Carter, you don't have to keep riding just to prove he existed. Do it for yourself," I say. "Your brother isn't a promise you have to bleed for, and you're not doing him justice by punishing yourself in his name." I lean in and hug him. "I love you, Carter," I say. "You don't have to forget him. Just don't leave yourself behind to keep him alive."

He embraces me, and we stay like that for a long time. "You mean everything to me, June." Then his lips find mine, and the kiss is sweet and slow and perfect. It tastes faintly of whiskey too. I sink into him, letting myself be held, because I deserve this and I never knew love could actually feel this good.

"Okay, enough of that or we're never leaving this house," Kai blurts out.

We break apart to find him standing in the door-way, grinning. He looks slightly better than Carter.

"Morning," I manage, wiping my eyes.

He strides into the room and physically pries me out of Carter's arms, swooping me up and planting his lips on mine before I can protest.

Not that I would.

His kiss is different from Carter's. Hungrier. More urgent. His hands grip my waist, pulling me tight against his chest, and I melt into him the same way I melt into all of them. Completely. Helplessly. Happily.

When we finally separate, I'm breathless and probably flushed and definitely not thinking about rodeos or bulls or anything except the three impossible men who have claimed my heart.

"So," I say, trying to collect myself. "Did you two even sleep last night? I don't remember seeing you before I fell asleep."

Carter snorts. "I'm pretty sure Kai deposited me on the couch after we got home. Woke up around five, still in my boots. Let's just say I had a bit to drink," he adds. "But in my defense, it was all worth it. Tanner won't be annoying you anymore."

I look between them, suspicious. "What did you two do last night? Did Tanner actually show up for your challenge?"

"Oh, he was there." Carter's grin is angelic and completely untrustworthy. "No fights or property damage. Just the agreement between gentlemen."

"The idiot lost colossally," Kai adds gleefully. "And his loss means he leaves you alone for good. That was the deal."

"Really?" Hope blooms in my chest. "He's going to honor that?"

"He agreed to it in front of witnesses."

"Oh my God." I throw my arms around Carter, then Kai, and then Carter again because I can't contain my joy. "I love that so much. Thank you. Both of you."

"Speaking of witnesses..." Kai pulls out his phone, his grin turning downright wicked. "Someone recorded the whole thing. It's going viral."

We crowd around the screen as he pulls up a video. The quality isn't great, clearly filmed on someone's phone in a dimly lit place, but the content is unmistakable.

Tanner, swaying on his feet, draws his arm back to throw a dart. He releases. The dart goes wildly sideways. Someone screams, then Tanner pitches forward, face-first onto the floor, and starts snoring.

The video has half a million views.

I'm laughing so hard I can barely breathe. "Oh my God. This is the best thing I've ever seen."

"No one will ever let him forget this," Kai says with deep satisfaction. "Best karma ever."

"I sure hope you don't plan to drive today, Carter," I manage, still giggling. "That alcohol is probably still in your blood."

"Nope. Kai is our designated driver." Carter drapes an arm around my shoulders. "Which means you can snuggle in the back seat with me today."

Kai is already bouncing toward the door, energy

radiating off him. "Come on, come on. I made coffee for the road. Those big travel mugs that keep everything hot. One for each of us."

I catch his arm as he passes. "Hey. Are you ready for today? With Brutus?"

"Yeah," he says, and there's a steadiness there even if his eyes give him away. "You have no idea how ready I am, but I know it's going to be a great day."

He tugs me in for one more kiss, and I let myself melt into it. For a moment, I allow myself to forget everything that could go wrong.

Carter clears his throat, loud, dramatic, and completely unnecessary. "Okay. Seriously. We need to leave."

Carter is guiding me toward the door, while Kai thrusts coffee cups into our hands, laughter echoing through the hallway.

And just for a moment, I forget everything.

The anxiety about Brutus. The uncertainty about my future. The loss of my home and my business and everything I thought I knew about my life.

When I'm with these Alphas, none of it matters.

There's only the four of us against whatever the world decides to throw at us.

I take a sip of my coffee, let Carter's hand find the small of my back, and watch Kai practically skip toward his car with boundless energy. I'm starting to believe that change doesn't have to be something to fear.

It might just be something to embrace.

28

SETH

The rodeo grounds are slowly coming alive around us—crew members setting up equipment, vendors preparing their stalls, the distant sounds of horses being led to their pens. It's the last day of the rodeo shows, followed by a week of carnival fun, but our job will be done.

My father and I stand near the livestock area, a sprawling section of the grounds dedicated to housing the animals that make the rodeo possible. Large outdoor stalls stretch in rows before us, constructed of sturdy wooden posts and metal railings.

"The numbers don't lie," my father says, pulling my attention back to the papers in his hands. He's comparing Joshua's count from yesterday against the official report from this morning's committee meeting. The discrepancy is similar to that of the previous day.

"A third of our revenue. Gone. Just disappeared into that bastard's pocket."

I look over his shoulder at the figures, my jaw tightening. Every category shows the same pattern, with actual numbers significantly higher than what Holden reported.

"We've got him," I say quietly. "There's no way he can explain this away."

"No, there isn't." My father folds the papers and tucks them into his jacket pocket, handing me back my phone. "I spoke with Pete this morning. Before the meeting."

"And?"

"He was horrified." My father's expression is grim but satisfied. "Genuinely shocked. The man was shaking and terrified that this was going to ruin the town's reputation, furious that he trusted Holden with so much responsibility." He shakes his head. "In hindsight, leaving all the financial oversight to one person was a massive mistake, but Pete had no idea what was happening. I believe him."

I nod slowly. Pete has been a fixture in this town for decades, a man whose entire identity is wrapped up in Honeyspur Meadow's success. The idea of him being complicit in embezzlement never sat right with me anyway.

"So what happens now?"

My father's smile is the cold, satisfied expression of a man who has his enemy exactly where he wants them. "My lawyer is here. So is Sheriff Cade. Holden was supposed to come down to the rodeo right after the committee meeting, so we timed everything perfectly."

"They're going to finally arrest the asshole?"

"The police have already started looking into his finances. Turns out our friend Holden has had a sudden influx of cash recently." My father's eyes meet mine. "Hence his buying June's parents' house and business. No loan. No mortgage. Just a straight cash purchase."

My stomach clenches at the mention of June.

"So that was enough to get a warrant?" I ask.

Dad nods. "Combined with the discrepancies in the financial records and the testimony from the woman who spiked your drink, yes. They have enough to arrest him and conduct a full investigation. A complete audit of every transaction he's touched since he took over the position."

"Thank fuck for that."

"Speaking of which," my father continues. "I have more good news."

"Go on."

"The lawyers have been working with the sheriff's office. Your charges have been dropped. You don't need to go to court this afternoon."

For a moment, I just stare at him. The weight I've been carrying for days, the looming specter of a criminal record, the humiliation when I knew that something was wrong that night. All of it, gone.

"That's exactly what I needed to hear."

My father's expression softens slightly. "No son of mine is going to be dragged through the dirt for another man's crimes."

I don't know what to say. After years of feeling like I could never quite measure up to his expectations, after all the arguments and disappointments and silences that stretched too long, this feels like progress.

"Thank you," I manage. "For making that happen."

He waves off the gratitude with a gruff gesture. "It's what any father would do. Besides, the evidence was on our side. That woman went to the station yesterday on her own and gave a full statement. Confirmed that Holden paid her to spike your drink." He snorts. "She even brought the bag he gave her the money in. It had a stamp of the town hall logo on it." My father shakes his head in disbelief. "Can you imagine? The man uses official town stationery to pay off someone for drugging a drink, then leaves it with her as evidence."

"How dumb is this guy?" I mutter.

"Arrogant. He thought he was untouchable. Thought no one would ever look closely enough to catch him." My father's smile returns. "He had no idea what was coming his way."

"And the money he took? Is there any chance of getting it back?"

"Already in discussions with the lawyers about recovery options. If the audit confirms what we suspect, we'll pursue full restitution. It'll take time, but we'll get there."

The sound of approaching footsteps draws our attention. I turn to find Sheriff Cade strolling toward us, his badge glinting in the morning sun, his expression all business.

Behind him, looking like death warmed over and then microwaved for good measure, is Deputy Tanner.

I have to suppress a grin at the sight of him. His face is pale, almost green around the edges, and there are dark circles under his eyes that suggest he didn't sleep last night. He's walking stiffly, each step clearly causing him discomfort, and there's a general air of misery radiating off him that's deeply satisfying to witness.

Kai told me everything this morning about their drinking competition, the darts, and the grand finale, where June's pathetic excuse for an ex-boyfriend accidentally stabbed a bystander with a wayward dart, face-planted onto the floor, and started snoring.

It's fucking glorious.

"Mr. Benton." Sheriff Cade extends his hand to my father, and they shake. "Everything is in place. My deputies have eyes on every exit."

"Excellent." My father dips his chin, then angles his attention toward me like I'm a bullet point on his agenda. "Seth here has been instrumental in uncovering this whole mess. He and his... pack."

The sheriff's gaze slides to me, and he nods his thanks.

While my father and the sheriff continue trading logistics, I let my attention drift to Tanner. He's standing a few feet away, trying to look professional and failing spectacularly. His uniform is wrinkled, his hair is a mess, and he winces every time someone speaks above a whisper.

I catch his attention and let the smug satisfaction show.

He glares back, but there's no real threat behind it. The man is too busy trying not to vomit to muster anything convincing.

"Rough night?" I ask, keeping my voice just loud enough to carry.

"Fuck off, Seth."

I laugh and glance around, only to spot Holden Pierce walking around the corner of the livestock area, coming in our direction. He's dressed casually today, jeans and a button-up shirt, with a cowboy hat perched on his head that he clearly bought for the occasion. He looks relaxed. Confident. The king of his little empire, surveying his domain.

Until his gaze lands on us.

The transformation is instantaneous. His easy smile freezes, then crumbles. His confident stride stutters to a halt. I watch the color drain from his face as he takes in the sheriff, my father, the officers positioned around the perimeter.

He fucking knows.

"Holden Pierce!" Sheriff Cade's voice booms across the grounds. "I need a moment to speak with you!"

But Holden is already moving, spinning on his heels and bolting toward the livestock stalls. His fancy cowboy hat flies off his head, landing in the dirt, forgotten. He doesn't look back.

"Tanner!" The sheriff's voice is sharp with command. "Go get him, for fuck's sake!"

Tanner grunts something and takes off after Holden, his movements stiff and uncoordinated. He's not running so much as lurching, each step a clear struggle against whatever his body is trying to expel. As I watch, he steps directly on Holden's discarded hat, his foot sliding on the brim, and nearly goes down. He catches himself at the last second, arms windmilling, but the damage is done.

The sheriff pinches the bridge of his nose. "Christ Almighty."

We all move after them, following the chase at a more measured pace. Holden has a decent lead, but he's not exactly in peak physical condition. Tanner, despite his compromised state, is slowly closing the distance.

Then Holden scales the fence into an enclosure.

"I wouldn't go in there if I were you!" I shout, but

it's too late. Holden is already over the top, dropping down into the stall with the kind of desperation that overrides common sense, and running, except he freezes halfway across the corralled area.

Brutus is standing at one end of the enclosure, massive and motionless, watching this new intruder with the cold calculation of a born predator. The bull's head is lowered slightly, his dark eyes fixed on Holden, nostrils flaring with each slow, deliberate breath.

The silence stretches.

Well, fuck...

Then Brutus stamps one enormous hoof against the packed dirt, and the sound is like a gunshot in the morning quiet.

"Fucking idiot," my father breathes beside me.

We reach the fence just as Tanner climbs it, huffing and puffing, his face now a concerning shade of gray.

"We have to get him out of there," Sheriff Cade says urgently. "That bull will kill him."

Tanner, apparently having a death wish, attempts to get into the stall, starts wobbling, and, without warning, begins hurling up his breakfast.

Everyone groans and looks away.

"Tanner, you fool!" The sheriff grabs his deputy by the back of his collar and hauls him down. He lands on his side, coughing.

He wipes his mouth with the back of his hand. "Cade, I'm not—"

"Enough!" The sheriff's voice could cut steel. "You

show up to work in this condition, barely able to walk straight, and you can't even do your job. Consider yourself suspended. Immediately. We'll discuss the details later."

Tanner sputters a protest, pushing himself to his feet, but the sheriff has already dismissed him, turning to face the rest of us with desperate urgency.

I'm already moving along the stall before I consciously decide to act. Not that this asshole Holden deserves saving, but he does need a healthy dose of humiliation, as well as having everything taken from him. "I've got an idea."

I circle around to the side of the enclosure, away from where Holden is frozen in terror. Brutus tracks my movement with those calculating eyes, but his attention remains primarily fixed on the intruder in his territory.

"Hey!" I vault onto the lower rung of the fence, making myself visible. "Over here."

Brutus's head swings toward me, and for a heart-stopping moment, we lock eyes. This close, I can see every detail of the animal that's haunted this town for decades. The scars from past battles. The powerful muscles bunched beneath his hide. The intelligence in those dark eyes.

"That's right," I call out, keeping my voice steady. "I'm the one you want. Not that pathetic sack of shit in your stall."

The distraction works because Brutus takes a step

toward me, then another, his attention shifting away from Holden.

"Run!" I shout at him. "Get to the fence! Now!"

Holden doesn't need to be told twice. He breaks into a desperate sprint toward the far side of the enclosure, legs pumping, arms flailing, pure terror propelling him forward.

But Brutus is no fool, because the moment Holden moves, the bull's head whips back around. In less than a second, he calculates the angles, dismisses me as the lesser threat, and launches himself with terrifying speed at the fleeing man.

"Oh, fuck."

I drop down from the fence inside the enclosure and scan the area frantically. There, near the gate, a stack of plastic barrels used for various training exercises. I don't think. I just move.

I sprint toward the barrels and grab one just as Brutus closes the distance on Holden. The man is screaming, high-pitched and hysterical, his hands reaching for the fence that's still too far away.

Brutus is inches from him when I hurl the barrel with everything I have.

It connects with the bull's side, bouncing off his massive frame with a hollow thunk that sounds pathetically inadequate. Brutus stumbles slightly, his momentum disrupted, his attention momentarily diverted.

Holden hits the fence and climbs with the

desperate strength of a man facing death. He's at the top in seconds, but not quite fast enough.

Brutus recovers and charges.

The bull slams into the fence just as Holden clears the top, his horns catching the man's calf as he tumbles over the other side. Holden screams, a raw sound of pain and terror, and crashes to the ground outside the enclosure.

I don't have time to celebrate the save. Brutus has turned on me now, those murderous eyes fixed on the idiot human who dared to interrupt his hunt.

I run.

The fence seems miles away. I hear Brutus behind me, feel the thunder of his hooves through the packed dirt. My lungs burn, my legs pump, and every instinct screams that I'm not going to make it.

I leap for the fence.

My hands catch the top rail, and I haul myself up with a strength I didn't know I possessed. Brutus crashes into the fence beneath me, the whole structure shuddering, but I'm already over the top, dropping down on the safe side, rolling to absorb the impact.

Behind me, Brutus bellows his frustration and turns his attention to the plastic barrel I left behind, goring it with his horns and tossing it around the enclosure with violent satisfaction.

That was fucking close.

"Son." My father is at my side, his hand gripping

my shoulder. "That was either the bravest or the stupidest thing I've ever seen."

"Probably both." I'm breathing hard, my heart hammering against my ribs, adrenaline still flooding my system.

We make our way to where Holden is lying on the ground, surrounded by rodeo medical staff who materialized seemingly from nowhere. He's wailing, clutching his leg, blood seeping through his fingers from where Brutus's horn caught him.

Sheriff Cade is standing over him, expression hard as granite.

"Holden Pierce," the sheriff says, "you are under arrest for embezzlement, fraud, and conspiracy to commit assault. You have the right to remain silent. Anything you say can and will be used against you in a court of law."

Holden's wails increase in volume. "I need a doctor! I'm dying!"

"You're fine." One of the medics is examining the wound, already wrapping it with practiced efficiency. "It's a surface laceration. You'll need stitches, but you'll live."

"I've had worse," I mutter.

"You have the right to an attorney," Cade continues, ignoring Holden's dramatics. "If you cannot afford an attorney, one will be provided for you. Do you understand these rights as I have explained them to you?"

"This is ridiculous!" Holden's voice has gone shrill with panic. "I haven't done anything wrong! This is all a misunderstanding!"

"The financial records suggest otherwise." The sheriff nods to a nearby officer. "Cuff him."

I watch as they secure Holden's hands behind his back, the reality of his situation finally seeming to sink in. His face crumbles, the arrogance and confidence replaced by naked fear. He looks smaller somehow, diminished, just a pathetic man who thought he could cheat his way to success and got caught.

"I want a lawyer," Holden whimpers.

"That's certainly your right."

They haul him to his feet, supporting him on either side, as his injured leg can't bear weight. Blood has soaked through the bandage already, leaving dark stains on his jeans.

"Take him away," the sheriff states. They drag Holden toward the parking area, where a police cruiser is waiting. His protests fade into the distance, becoming just another part of the morning noise. Tanner chases after them.

My father claps me on the shoulder. "Well done. Now, I need to speak with my lawyers. Make sure everything is in order for the next steps." He pauses, his expression uncharacteristically warm. "You did good today, son. Real good."

"Thanks, Dad." He nods once, gruffly, and walks away.

The rodeo grounds are fully awake now, buzzing with activity as the final day's events approach. Vendors are hawking their wares, spectators are finding their seats, and the air is electric with anticipation. This is what I love about the circuit. The energy. The excitement. The sense that anything can happen.

I make my way toward the main staging area, weaving through the growing crowds, my mind already shifting to the day ahead, to the future that's suddenly looking a lot brighter.

And then I spot Carter, Kai, and June heading toward me through the crowd. Carter is still looking a bit rough around the edges, but he's grinning from ear to ear. Kai is practically bouncing with contained energy, his nerves about the upcoming ride manifesting as restless motion. And June is beautiful.

Her smile when she sees me is like watching the sun rise, and everything else falls away. The stress of the morning, the confrontation with Holden, the lingering adrenaline from my encounter with Brutus. None of it matters.

There's only her.

I meet them halfway, my hands finding June's waist and pulling her close. She melts into me, her arms wrapping around my neck, and I kiss her. Right there, in the middle of the rodeo grounds, in front of everyone.

"Well, hello to you too," she says with a laugh when we finally break apart.

"Holden just got arrested."

Her eyes go wide. "What? When? Tell me everything."

I give them a complete rundown.

Carter lets out a low whistle. "You went into the pen with Brutus?"

"Wasn't my finest moment in terms of self-preservation," I admit, "but yeah."

"Dude." Kai studies me with something dangerously close to awe. "That's either insanely brave or insanely stupid. You need to leave that stuff for me to do." He smirks my way.

June's hands slide up to my chest, her face quickly shifting from shock to worry. "Are you okay? You're not hurt?"

I catch one of her hands and press a kiss to her palm. "More than okay, actually. I'm just glad my charges got dropped. I don't have to go to court."

She throws her arms around me again, squeezing hard. "That's amazing."

"And my house and business?" The hope in her voice lands like a strike to the ribs.

"That's with the lawyers now while they investigate, but I'm guessing it won't go forward," I say.

She smiles, and I tighten my hold, breathing her in like I've been starved for it.

Carter and Kai crowd in, and suddenly it's a pack embrace, all four of us tangled together in the middle of the bustling rodeo grounds. And with June tucked into my chest and the guys braced at my sides, I know exactly what I'm doing next.

First, I get Kai through Brutus's ride without a disaster, and then I make the next move, one that ends with June in my home and a family around our table.

29

Thousands of voices rise and fall in waves, crashing against the metal rails, reverberating off the bleachers, filling the air with an electricity that has every hair on my body standing on end. Dust motes dance in the afternoon sunlight, golden and glittering, suspended in the charged atmosphere. The smell of dirt and sweat and animals fills my lungs with each breath.

Not a single seat is empty. People are standing in the aisles, pressed against the railings, craning their necks for a better view. I've never seen the arena this packed, this alive, this hungry for what's about to happen. The energy is different from that of every other event today. Heavier. More primal. Like the crowd knows they're about to witness something that only comes around once in a generation.

And beneath it all, a chant is building...

"BRUTUS! BRUTUS! BRUTUS!"

The crowd isn't here for me. Not really. They're here for him, the legend. For the black mountain of muscle and fury who's been terrorizing this town for over a decade. And this is his moment, his comeback.

I'm just the idiot who volunteered to be his dance partner.

My hands grip the top rail of the chute as I position myself above Brutus's huge back. The metal is warm from the sun, slick with sweat from the handlers who helped wrangle him in here. Below me, two thousand pounds of pure destruction waits, black hide gleaming, muscles rippling with barely contained violence.

The helmet on my head feels heavier than usual, the protective gear mandatory for bull riding, but right now it's a reminder of exactly how dangerous this is. How many ways this can go wrong. How one bad buck, one mistimed twist, could end with my skull cracked open on the packed dirt.

I lower myself onto Brutus's back.

The sensation is immediate and overwhelming. There's no saddle between us, just my jeans against his coarse hide, and I can feel everything. The heat radiating off him, furnace-hot, the constant movement, the shifting of massive muscles, the coiled tension of an animal preparing to explode. It's not sitting. It's balancing on an earthquake that hasn't started yet.

Brutus grunts, low and deep, a sound I feel more than hear. His head swings to the side, one dark eye rolling back to look at me. There's intelligence in that gaze. Recognition. He knows who I am, remembers me from the visits this week, from the times I stood outside his pen while June worked her calming magic.

I set my rope hand, wrapping the braided leather around my gloved palm, testing the tension. The burn starts immediately in my forearm, a preview of what's coming. I lock my wrist, adjust my grip, and feel the first real spike of adrenaline hit my system. Those around me are watching, ready if anything goes haywire.

Brutus bumps against the side of the chute, metal rattling, the whole structure shuddering with the impact. I absorb the jolt through my hips and knees, keeping my upper body stable, forcing my breathing to stay steady even as my heart tries to punch its way out of my chest.

"Easy," I murmur, more to myself than to him.

The handlers around me are tense, ready to move.

"Time," I call out, my voice steadier than I feel. "Give me a minute."

The arena grows somehow louder, the anticipation building.

I focus on breathing. In through the nose, out through the mouth. Slow. Controlled. I force my heart rate down, force my muscles to relax, force my body to remember that panic is the enemy. Brutus will exploit every moment of tension, every second of fear. If I want to survive this, I need to be loose. Fluid. Ready to move with him instead of against him.

So I lean forward slightly, bringing my mouth closer to Brutus's ear.

"All right, big guy," I say quietly, my voice lost beneath the roar of the crowd. "Here's the deal. I'm not here to hurt you. I'm not here to prove anything at your expense, but I'm not here to lose either."

Brutus's ear flicks. He's listening. Maybe not understanding, but listening.

"Eight seconds. That's all I'm asking. You give me eight seconds of your worst, and then you get to run around this arena while ten thousand people scream your name. Sound fair?"

The bull responds in the only language he knows. A deep grunt and shift of his large head. A stomp of one enormous hoof that shudders through my entire body, rattling my teeth, vibrating up my spine.

It feels like acknowledgment, and like a promise to make those eight seconds the longest of my life.

"Kai." June's voice cuts through everything. The crowd, the announcer, the thundering of my own pulse. June is there, pressed against the rails behind the chute.

"Hey, beautiful. Come to wish me luck?"

"Something better." She leans in, not looking at

me, but at Brutus. The bull's eye tracks her movement, and I feel some of the tension in his body shift. Not disappear, but change. Redirect.

"Hey, Brutus," she says softly, her tone completely different from how she speaks to anyone else. "Remember me? I used to feed you bottles when you were just a baby."

Brutus huffs, a sound that might be recognition or might be contempt. It's hard to tell with him.

"I need you to do me a favor," June continues. "Don't be too rough with this one, okay? He's kind of important to me. Bring him back in one piece."

The bull's response is another huff, this one longer, almost offended. His body shifts beneath me, coiling tighter, and I feel it as both a warning and a dare. He's going to give me everything he has. June or no June.

But maybe, just maybe, he'll let me survive it.

"Thank you," I tell her, and I mean it for so much more than this moment.

She meets my eyes, and everything she's feeling is right there on the surface. Fear. Pride. Love. Trust. "I love you so much. Please, come back to me," she says.

My heart pulses at her words. "I love you, and I'll always be back for you."

Seth is at the rails too, his expression hard and focused. He gives me a single nod, the kind of silent communication we've developed over years of friendship. Carter stands beside him, looking slightly green around the edges, probably still suffering from last night's drinking competition. But he manages a grin anyway, flashing me a thumbs-up.

My pack. My family. I turn back to focus on the event.

I adjust my posture one final time. Legs clamped against his sides, knees bent, core engaged. My free hand rises, ready to keep balance, ready to stay away from his hide no matter how much my instincts yell to grab on. My rope hand is locked, wrist turned in, forearm already screaming.

This is it.

I lean forward slightly, signaling the gate operator.

"Let's go."

The gate swings open.

Brutus explodes.

There's no other word for it. One moment he's coiled power and contained fury, and the next he's a black tornado of muscle and violence, launching out of the chute with enough force to snap my head back and steal the breath from my lungs.

The first buck is brutal. His back end kicks up, higher than should be possible, and I'm thrown forward, my face almost meeting his neck. I wrench myself back, overcorrect, and nearly lose my balance in the opposite direction.

Brutus doesn't give me time to recover.

He twists. A savage corkscrewing motion that tries to throw me off-center, to spin me loose, to send me flying into the dirt. I feel my body rotating, feel my grip slipping, feel the rope burning through my glove.

I clamp down harder. Hold. Breathe. Lock.

The world becomes a blur of motion and sensation. Coarse black hide rough against my thighs. Heat rising off his body, almost burning. The rope biting into my hand. Dust filling my mouth, coating my tongue, making each breath a struggle.

Every muscle in his body is dedicated to one purpose: getting me off his back.

He bucks again, a massive vertical surge that lifts me clear off his spine before gravity slams me back down. My tailbone screams in protest. My teeth click together so hard I see stars.

Then I find a rhythm. For one glorious heartbeat, I think I've got him. My body moves with his, anticipating the next buck, rolling with the motion instead of fighting it. This is what the good riders do. This is how you survive.

Brutus changes the pattern.

The drop and twist comes out of nowhere, a combination I've never felt from any bull in all my years of riding. He drops his front end, kicks his back end up and sideways simultaneously, and twists his entire body in a direction that defies physics.

I'm yanked forward. My rope hand nearly tears free. For one terrifying moment, I'm airborne, connected to Brutus by nothing but a fraying grip and pure stubbornness.

I hear the crowd gasp. A collective intake of breath from all the people who are watching me die.

I refuse.

Something deep inside me, some primal survival instinct, takes over. I re-grip the rope, ignoring the searing pain in my forearm. I throw my weight back, using the momentum of Brutus's own twist to pull myself back to center. My free hand windmills for balance but never touches him.

The crowd's gasp becomes a roar.

I'm still on.

But Brutus isn't done. He never is. The old bastard has decades of experience throwing riders, and he's not about to let some upstart cowboy break his streak.

He spins. A vicious rotation that creates centrifugal force strong enough to peel me off like a loose scab. I clamp my legs tighter, feel the burn spread through my thighs, feel muscles I didn't know I had screaming for mercy.

How long has it been? Three seconds? Four? It feels like hours, as if my entire life has been compressed into this moment, this endless struggle against two thousand pounds of fury and pride.

I can hear June somewhere in the noise. Can't make out the words, but her voice reaches me anyway, a distant anchor in the storm. She's there. She's watching. She believes I can do this.

Brutus bucks again, a massive, earth-shaking motion that rattles my bones and threatens to liquify my spine. I absorb it through my hips, let it roll through my body, and keep my upper half as stable as possible.

My free hand stays up. It has to. Looking confident is part of surviving Brutus, part of the scoring, part of the show.

Suddenly, he drops, plants his front hooves, and kicks his back end so high that for one heart-stopping moment, I'm looking straight down at the ground. I'm nearly vertical, clinging to a living cliff face, gravity trying to tear me loose.

I hold. I don't know how, but I do.

Brutus lands and immediately spins, trying to catch me off-balance from the recovery. I move with him, barely, my body operating on pure instinct now because my brain checked out about three seconds into this nightmare.

The crowd is a distant roar. The buzzer sounds.

Eight seconds.

Eight fucking seconds that felt like eight years.

Relief crashes through me so hard it nearly knocks me loose. My body wants to go limp, wants to collapse, wants to surrender to the exhaustion and pain that's been building with every passing heartbeat.

Not yet. Not until I'm clear.

I wait for Brutus to buck again, use the upward motion to push myself off his back, release the rope I'd been gripping for dear life, and hit the dirt running. My legs feel like they're filled with fire instead of muscle.

My forearm is completely numb from the elbow down. But I'm moving, I'm upright, and I'm getting distance between myself and the animal who just tried to destroy me.

Brutus kicks and struts across the arena, clearly pleased with himself. His head tosses, snorting at the crowd, and I swear he's taking a victory lap even though he lost. That's Brutus. Win or lose, he owns the room.

The crowd is going absolutely berserk. I climb up and over the enclosure and head to the announcer. I grab the microphone from him.

"Ladies and gentlemen!" My voice is ragged, rough, barely recognizable as human. I don't care. The adrenaline is still pumping, the crowd is still roaring, and I have something to say.

"Let me be clear about something." I turn to face Brutus, who's now standing in the center of the arena, watching me with those dark, intelligent eyes. "I didn't win today. He did."

The crowd murmurs, confused.

"This bull right here," I continue, gesturing at Brutus, "is the most incredible animal I've ever had the privilege of riding. Ninety-seven percent buck-off rate. Years of dominance. A legend in every sense of the word."

Brutus snorts, as if agreeing.

"I stayed on for eight seconds. That's all, and let me tell you, those were the longest eight seconds of my life." I laugh, still shaking, still riding the high. "So when you go home tonight, when you tell people about what you saw, make sure you're telling the right story. This wasn't about me conquering Brutus. This was about Brutus letting me survive."

The crowd erupts again, louder than before. They're cheering for the bull now, cheering for the legend, giving him the recognition he deserves.

"Welcome back, Brutus!" I shout into the microphone. "The rodeo has missed you, you beautiful, terrifying bastard!"

Brutus tosses his head, grunts, and resumes his parade around the arena. The handlers have given up trying to wrangle him. They're just letting him have his moment, watching with a mix of amusement and terror as the black menace struts past the cheering crowd.

I drop the microphone and turn toward the rails.

My body is screaming at me now. Every muscle aches, every joint protests, and my forearm is starting to throb as feeling returns to it. I can feel blood soaking through my glove, can feel bruises forming on bruises, can feel the exhaustion trying to drag me down.

But my pack is waiting for me.

June reaches me first. She throws herself over the rail, not waiting for me to come to her, and suddenly she's in my arms, her body pressed against mine, her face buried in my neck.

"You did it," she's saying, over and over.

I hold her tight, breathless. Seth and Carter are there a second later, and then it's all of us, tangled together at the edge of the arena while ten thousand people continue to lose their minds. Carter is slapping my back hard enough to leave marks. Seth is gripping my shoulder with the kind of intensity that says he was more worried than he'll ever admit.

"That was insane," Carter states. "Literally insane. I swear I had three heart attacks watching you."

"Only three?" I manage, forcing a crooked grin. "I had at least seven."

"You're never doing that again," June says, and when she pulls back to look at me, her eyes are wet. Not drama. Real fear. The kind that crawls under your ribs and stays there. "Never. Do you understand me?"

"Yes, ma'am."

"I mean it, Kai." Her voice wobbles on my name. "My heart can't take it."

"I know." I cup her face in my hands, sweat on my skin, and I don't care about any of it. All I worry about is the way she's holding herself together by sheer will, the way she's staring at me as if she was already planning a life and I almost ripped it out from under her. "I know. And I promise you, that was the first and last time. One ride with Brutus is plenty for a lifetime."

Her laugh breaks out, shaky and wet, relief tangled with fear and something softer that makes my chest tighten. I kiss her forehead, then her nose, then her mouth, each one quick and gentle because I'm still keyed up and I don't trust myself not to turn it into something deeper.

"Come on," Seth says. "Let's get you cleaned up before the closing ceremonies."

"And maybe some ice," Carter adds. "Lots of ice. You look like you got hit by a truck."

"I got hit by something worse," I mutter, glancing back at the arena as they lead Brutus toward the gate.

The bull goes with that slow, deliberate swagger of a creature that knows he owns the place. His performance is done, his point made, and even in defeat, he looks untouchable. King of every man who ever thought he could control him.

I tighten my arm around June as we start walking, holding her close so she can feel what I'm trying to say without words.

As we make our way through the crowd, people reach out to clap me on the shoulder, to shake my hand, to tell me what a ride that was. I accept the praise graciously, but my attention keeps drifting back to June walking beside me.

"That is something I will never forget," I say quietly, more to myself than to anyone else.

June squeezes my hand. "None of us will."

And she's right. Years from now, decades from now, we'll remember this moment. The day Brutus came out of retirement. The day I survived eight seconds on the most dangerous bull in rodeo history.

The day that proved, beyond any doubt, that I would do anything for the people I love.

The afternoon sun is warm on my face as we walk away from the arena. Behind us, the crowd is still buzzing, still replaying the ride in their conversations, still chanting Brutus's name.

In front of us, the rest of our lives are waiting.

And I can't wait to see what comes next.

30

JUNE

The bell above my office door chimes as another client leaves, their signed paper-work tucked safely in my filing cabinet. I lean back in my chair and stare at the ceiling.

Seven days since the rodeo ended, when Holden was arrested, his assets frozen, the sale of my child-hood home and business falling through in spectacular fashion. Of living in a strange limbo where everything should feel better, but instead feels like standing on ice that might crack at any moment.

My parents are relisting the properties, as the plumbing issues are all fixed. They're still desperate to sell, drowning in debt, and expecting me to pick up the pieces of their poor decisions. I've stopped answering every call, stopped volunteering to fix every problem. But the weight of it still sits on my shoulders.

The real estate office feels different now. The

vintage typewriter on my desk, the burgundy armchair, the wall of photographs and travel brochures. It's all the same, but I'm not. I've been going through the motions, showing up, smiling, closing deals, because that's what I do when the ground beneath me feels unstable. I work. I move. I pretend everything is fine until it actually is.

Or until it isn't.

Living with Seth, Kai, and Carter is the best thing that's ever happened to me. Waking up tangled in their arms, eating breakfast together in the small kitchen of the rental house, falling asleep to the sound of their breathing. It's everything I never knew I needed, every-thing I was terrified to want.

But lately, there's been a tension under the surface.

Every time I bring up the future, they dodge. Every time I ask about their plans, whether they're staying in Honeyspur Meadow or moving on to the next town, the next rodeo, the next chapter of their nomadic lives, they redirect. They crack jokes. They kiss me. They pull me close and change the subject.

It's not cold. It's not cruel, but it's maddening.

I'm not asking for grand declarations or iron-clad promises. I'm not asking them to map out the next fifty years. I just want to stop feeling like I'm waiting for a trapdoor to open beneath my feet. I want to know that this, us, means something beyond the moment.

The ugly thought keeps circling, no matter how hard I try to push it away.

Maybe they're hesitating because I haven't hit my heat yet.

It's been weeks since I stopped taking suppressants, waiting for my body to do what every Omega's body is supposed to do. And nothing. No fever, no desperate aches or need, no biological confirmation that I'm really what I think I am. Just normal days stretching into normal weeks, my body stubbornly refusing to cooperate. Don't get me wrong, the arousal between the Alphas and me is astronomical, but it's not the heat that even Alphas crave.

Maybe they're waiting to see if I fit. If I'm a real Omega or just a broken woman pretending to be something she's not. Maybe they need that proof before they can commit, before they can plan a future with someone who might not be able to give them what they need.

The thought makes me sick, but I can't stop thinking about it.

I shake my head and gather the paperwork on my desk. I have a handover to do today, a major one. A beautiful ranch property on the edge of town that I just sold to a new family moving to the area. It's one of the biggest sales I've ever closed, the kind of deal that should have me celebrating.

Instead, I just feel tired.

The drive to the ranch takes about twenty minutes, winding through the outskirts of Honeyspur Meadow where the houses thin out and the land opens up into rolling hills and pastures. The afternoon sun is warm through my windshield, casting everything in golden light, but my mind stays loud with worry.

The ranch being sold appears around a bend in the road, and despite everything, my breath catches. It's stunning. A sprawling property with white fencing stretching as far as I can see, an oversized main house with a wraparound porch, several outbuildings, including what appears to be a stable complex, and acres of green pasture dotted with old oak trees. The kind of place that belongs in a magazine.

I pull up the long gravel driveway, feeling professional and prepared.

Until I see the familiar vehicles already parked near the house.

My pulse jumps. Confusion first, then a quick spike of anger, because why are they here, and why do I feel like I'm about to get blindsided again?

I park my car and climb out, file folder tucked under my arm, trying to compose myself. All three of my Alphas are standing on the porch, watching me approach. Seth has his arms crossed, jaw set. Carter is leaning against a post, that easy smile playing at his lips. Kai is practically grinning.

"What are you doing here?" I demand, and I hate how my voice wavers. "This is a client meeting. I'm supposed to be handing over paperwork to the new owners."

Seth pushes off the porch railing and walks toward me. His blue eyes are intense, locked on mine.

"We're here to take our ranch," he says simply. "Our home."

The words don't register at first, and my brain tries to correct them. *Did I mishear him?*

I blink, staring between the three Alphas as though I'm waiting for the punch line.

"What do you mean, *our*—" My voice cracks on the last word because something in my chest is already softening into hope despite my best efforts to protect myself.

It takes a few beats for the pieces to click into place. The paperwork in my hands. The address. The fact that I'm here to do a handover for a sale. And they're standing on the porch like they own the place.

Because they must be the new owners.

My eyes sting, and I hate that my first instinct is still panic.

"Is this why you've been avoiding the conversation?" The words come out shaky. "I thought... I thought you were going to skip town on me."

I try to laugh it off, but the sound is too honest. Too raw.

They just watch me.

"I thought maybe you were waiting," I continue, and now I can't stop, can't keep the fear locked away where it belongs. "Maybe because I haven't hit my heat yet. Perhaps you needed to see if I'm really... if I can really..." I can't finish the sentence.

Seth's face hardens with emotion, something fierce and protective flashing across his features. Carter's eyes go sharp, all the easy humor draining away. And Kai is staring at me with so much love.

They close in on me immediately, all three of them. I'm wrapped in arms and warmth and the scent of them, and it's impossible to pretend I'm fine.

"Listen to me." Seth's voice is low against my hair, steady in a way that doesn't leave room for doubt. "We're not waiting for anything or testing you. Or keeping our options open in case you don't measure up to some bullshit biological standard."

"You're our Omega," Kai adds, arms tight around my waist. His mouth brushes my temple, a touch that feels both soothing and possessive. "Heat or no heat. Now or never. We chose you, June. We're already all in."

Carter's hand cups the back of my neck, warm and grounding. "Your heat will come when it comes," he says. "And if it doesn't, that's okay too."

That's when I break. Proper, ugly crying, my face pressed into Seth's shirt while everything I've been holding inside finally comes loose. All the fear. All the shame. All the stupid thoughts I've let fester in the dark.

"I thought..." I try to speak, and it comes out wrecked. "I thought you were going to leave."

"If you ever think we're leaving again," Kai cuts in, pulling back just enough to look me in the eye, "I'm handcuffing myself to you. Permanently. We'll sort out the logistics later."

Carter snorts.

A laugh slips out of me. I hate how ridiculous I probably look, but the knot in my chest loosens anyway, just a fraction, enough that I can breathe.

Seth tilts my chin up, firm fingers making me meet his eyes. "We bought this ranch for us," he says. "For our pack. For our family. We were trying to keep it quiet to surprise you, but clearly we're terrible at surprises, because you thought we were planning to abandon you."

"In our defense," Carter adds, "we've never planned a surprise in our lives. We're learning."

"You're awful at it," I mutter, wiping my cheeks with the back of my hand.

"Noted," Kai says. "We'll add it to the list."

I pull back and look around the property with new eyes. It's so beautiful that it doesn't feel real but like something you drive past and admire, not something that could belong to me.

To us.

"Wait," I whisper, the truth spreading through me in slow waves. "So this is... our home."

They nod, all three of them watching me closely, faces open in a way that makes my chest ache.

And then the absurdity of it hits so hard I almost laugh again.

"I just sold us our own home," I say, voice cracking.

"You did," Kai confirms, grinning. "Extremely professional. Strong pitch. Ten out of ten. I felt emotionally manipulated in the best way."

"Shut up," I whisper, but I'm smiling through tears.

I flip through the documents with trembling fingers, trying to make sense of what I'm seeing. "But the paperwork was under a different name. A company name."

Seth nods. "Three Kings Group," he says. "It's the business entity we run together. We keep earnings, contracts, and investments under it, and it's different from my dad's."

He pauses, then continues more carefully, as if he's choosing each word for me. "We want to add you to it. Your name on everything. The ranch, the company, the future." His gaze holds mine. "If that's what you want."

My hands shake as I reach for them, touching their arms, their chests, their faces, as if I need proof that they're solid and here and not a dream I'll wake up from.

"I can't believe you did this for us," I whisper. "So does that mean you're settling down here in town?"

"Yep," Seth says, and I want to scream with joy because I love this town.

The sound of a vehicle coming up the driveway

cuts me off. We all turn to watch as a truck pulls up beside my car. It's Seth's father.

"Dad. What are you doing here?"

His father gets out of the truck, giving Seth a smile that appears strange on his face, not because it's fake, but because I haven't seen it often. "You think I'm missing this? I've waited a long damn time to see you settled, son."

Then his attention shifts to me.

The look he gives me isn't soft, exactly. It's assessing, sure. But it's also the kind of approval that doesn't ask for permission. It says he's already decided I belong here, whether I'm ready to believe it yet or not.

"June," he says with a firm nod. "You've been good for him. For all of them. I'm glad they found you."

I wipe my cheeks, still trying to pull myself together. "Thank you. I'm glad too."

He clears his throat and turns back to Seth, the warmth still there, but tucked under that gruff tone he never fully drops. "I've got a gift. For all of you. Call it a housewarming."

Seth's shoulders go tight beside me.

His father reaches into his jacket and pulls out a thick envelope. When he hands it to Seth, it's not casual. It has weight. Intent.

"I'm retiring," he explains.

Seth just stares at him.

"The circuit," his father continues, watching Seth

closely. "It's yours now. Legally, officially, completely. You and your pack run it however you see fit."

Seth opens the envelope with hands that don't shake, but they're not steady either. He scans the paperwork once, then again, his gaze moving faster the second time, as if he's trying to find the catch hidden in the fine print. I watch his expression shift in real time: disbelief, shock.

"You're... giving it to me?" he asks, voice rough.

"I'm acknowledging what's been true for a long time. You've had the vision for this circuit for years. I dug my heels in because, for too long, I wanted it done my way. That stubbornness cost you time."

Seth swallows, blinking hard once. "I don't understand."

"You will." His father gestures toward the ranch around us. "Make this place the home base. Bring riders here. Change the schedule and build a circuit that doesn't swallow your whole life. You've got a pack now." His gaze flicks to me, then returns to Seth. "You've got a family. It's time you stop living out of bags and motel rooms just because I did."

Carter and Kai exchange a look, both of them processing what this means in practical terms, not just emotionally. A life that doesn't require constant running.

Seth glances up from the papers, and for a second, he appears younger than I've ever seen him, caught off guard in a way that strips the armor right off. "Thank you," he manages. "Dad... I don't know what to say."

"Don't say anything." His father's mouth twitches. "Just don't screw it up." Silence. "I'm proud of you, son. I should've said that more."

The quiet that follows isn't awkward but heavy in a different way. Decades of tension shifting, not fixed, not erased, but finally acknowledged.

His father claps Seth on the shoulder and turns toward the house. "Now. Do I get to see your new place?"

Seth takes my hand, and we all step up onto the porch, where his dad says, "And don't take too long giving me grandkids. I'm not getting any younger. I'm not too far away in Colorado if you need me."

"Come on," Seth says, offering me a loving smile. "Let's go inside. We've got it ready."

I let them guide me through the front door, still dazed and emotional. Is this real life?

The inside of the house is stunning, just as I remember it from when I came to take photographs for the sale. High ceilings, exposed beams, huge windows that let in floods of natural light. But it's the living room that gets me every time.

Only it's already set up, as if we aren't the first people to ever set foot in here.

There's a bar cart stocked and ready, bottles lined up, glasses polished, a hand-lettered sign that squeezes my chest. Platters of food cover every surface, the kind of spread you throw when you want people to stay awhile. Decorations in soft colors that somehow perfectly embody me, not generic party-store nonsense, but chosen specifically for this party.

And the walls are covered in framed photos of me with my three Alphas, like we've been living our lives here for months instead of minutes. Me pressed between them in front of the pyramids, perched on someone's knee with a Scottish castle looming behind us, Kai throwing a grin at the camera with the Eiffel Tower over his shoulder, Carter looking annoyingly perfect beside some ancient ruin, Seth riding a horse, as he's been superimposed on all the photos.

Then I finally notice the people.

"SURPRISE!"

I jolt, then laugh, because it's too much and perfect and I don't know what else to do with the swell in my chest. I clutch at all three of my Alphas, overwhelmed and grateful and so impossibly happy that my eyes sting again.

I stare around properly, and my brain scrambles to catch up. Sophia is here with her three cowboys, all of them grinning as if they've been in on this for weeks. Hazel is near the drinks, pink sunglasses pushed up in her hair, looking smug enough to be arrested for it. She's chatting with Belle who's finally back in town. I spot the women from the book club, beaming and waving, and a handful of familiar faces from the town shops, plus neighbors I've lived beside for years, people who have watched me build a life here with scraped knees and stubborn pride.

There are so many of them who matter.

I turn back to Seth, still half convinced I'm going to blink and wake up.

He leans in close, one hand firm at my waist. "Everyone you love is here," he says, quiet but sure. "Everyone you care about. We wanted them with us for this." His gaze holds mine, steadying me. "To celebrate our home, and the start of what comes next."

My throat tightens. I nod, because words won't work, and Kai kisses my temple as Carter presses a hand to my back, keeping me upright while my heart tries to spill out of my chest in every direction at once.

I laugh, clinging to all three of them, overwhelmed and grateful and so incredibly, impossibly happy.

The party flows around us. People hugging me, congratulating us, marveling at the house and the property and the future stretching out before us. I float through it in a daze, accepting drinks and food and well wishes, constantly finding my way back to my Alphas.

At some point, we end up in a quieter corner, and Seth's expression turns serious.

"We need to talk about the business," he says. "Your real estate business."

I tense slightly, the old anxiety creeping back in. "What about it?"

"Whatever you want to do, we'll support you. If

you want to keep running it, we'll help. Buy out your parents' share, protect it from their mess, whatever you need. You don't have to do it alone anymore."

The offer is practical and loving all at once. I hesitate, really thinking about it for the first time, about what I want, and not what I feel obligated to do.

"I think..." I take a breath. "That I might want to let it go."

They wait, giving me space to find the words.

"My parents can sell the business and the house. I'm done tethering my future to their decisions. I've spent so long trying to save something that was never really mine to begin with."

"Is there anything else you want to do instead?" Carter asks gently.

The answer comes easier than I expected. "I want to be your photographer."

A beat of silence.

"Our personal photographer, I love that." Kai's grin is spreading. "Perfect. You can start with us, in the bedroom. Very artistic lighting required."

"That's not photography," Carter says dryly when I lift my camera. "That's straight-up porn."

Kai raises an eyebrow, amused. "And the issue is?"

"You can't go capture the moment and then immediately aim that thing at our asses."

I laugh, shifting my grip. "It's called documenting real life."

Seth's mouth twitches into a smirk. "Real life, huh?

You planning to submit those to a gallery or blackmail us later?"

"Depends," I say sweetly. "Are you going to cooperate and give me new photos for my portfolio, or do I have to work with whatever material you're offering?"

Kai grins. "I volunteer as tribute."

Carter groans. "Of course you do."

Kai tilts his head suddenly, like he's remembering something. "Should we tell her the final surprise?"

I narrow my eyes immediately. "Should I be worried?"

"Yes," Carter answers, deadpan.

They take my hands and lead me through the house, pointing out rooms and plans and little touches they set up for me. A reading nook by a window, a dark room that could be converted to a photography studio.

We step out the back door into the expansive yard. In one of the stalls stands Brutus.

"Wait." My voice comes out strangled. "What's he doing here?"

Carter delivers it like it's the most normal thing in the world. "He's ours now."

"Ours?"

"Farmer Crawford is getting too old to handle him," Kai explains. "He offered us Brutus because we're apparently the only people crazy enough to want him."

Brutus grunts and shifts in his stall, his dark eyes tracking our movement. He looks exactly as terrifying as he did in the arena. Two thousand pounds of muscle and attitude, a living legend of destruction.

He also looks... content? Is that possible?

Brutus huffs, tosses his head, and turns away like we're boring him.

"Oh, things are going to be so much crazier, aren't they?" I ask.

They laugh and pull me in like everything I've ever wanted is wrapped up in three impossible men and one psychotic bull.

"I love you so much, June." Kai's voice is rough with emotion, stripped of his usual humor. "I've never loved anyone the way I adore you."

"You're everything," Carter says, quiet but sure, his arms tight around me.

Seth doesn't speak right away. He just holds me, face tucked into my hair, breath warm against my neck. "I'm going to love you forever, darlin'."

"I love you all," I tell them, and the words feel too small for what I mean, but they're the truest thing I have. "So much it scares me."

"Good scare or bad scare?" Kai asks.

"The best kind," I manage, laughing a little.

We stay there, the four of us tangled together in the yard at the start of a life I never let myself picture too clearly.

"This house is perfect," I whisper, and I mean it. Right now, I have everything.

Even if a small, scared part of me is still waiting for my body to catch up.

EPILOGUE
JUNE

Two Months Later

I wake slowly, drifting up through layers of warmth and comfort like swimming toward the surface of a deep, still pool. The afternoon light filters through the curtains.

The bedroom is enormous. When we first moved in, the guys insisted on custom-ordering the biggest bed I've ever seen, large enough for all four of us to sleep side by side without anyone getting relegated to the foot of the mattress. It dominates the room, draped in soft sheets and weighted blankets and more pillows than any reasonable person needs.

I'm tangled in those sheets now, my body twisted around them like I've been fighting in my sleep. Which, knowing the past few days, I probably have been.

Something has been wrong with me lately. Not

wrong, exactly, but off. Different. I've been exhausted constantly. For the past three days, I've been sleeping more than I've been awake, dragging myself out of bed only when absolutely necessary before crawling back under the covers.

The only thing that seems to help is being in our bed surrounded by the scent of my Alphas, cuddling into every pillow and blanket and inch of fabric. Their scents settle something restless inside me.

I shift slightly, and my arm tightens around Kai's body pillow pressed against my side. There are two others now, one with Carter's image and one with Seth's, all of them arranged around me in a configuration that probably looks ridiculous from the outside.

A nest, I realize suddenly. *I've built myself a nest.*

The thought should surprise me, but it doesn't. It feels right and natural. When the guys come to bed at night, they toss the body pillows aside to make room for themselves. All except Kai, whom I once caught snuggling his own pillow with a completely unashamed grin on his face.

I smile at the memory, even through the fog of exhaustion still clinging to my brain. I stretch carefully.

I'm burning up, my skin radiating heat as though I've been lying in direct sunlight for hours. Even the light cotton of my sleep shirt feels unbearably heavy against my skin.

I kick off the blankets and immediately miss their weight. Then I pull them back up because I'm cold.

Then I kick them off again because I'm too hot. The contradiction is maddening.

"What the hell?" I mutter, pushing myself up to sit. The room tilts slightly before stabilizing, and I reach for the water bottle on the nightstand. Someone has been keeping it filled for me, along with an array of snacks. Chocolate. Cookies. Crackers and cheese. Little things I can graze on when getting up feels like too much effort.

I drink deeply, but the water doesn't help. If anything, it makes the inferno inside me worse, like I'm trying to cool a bonfire with a teaspoon.

Maybe we need another fan in here. Or to turn the air-conditioning down to arctic levels. Or to move to Alaska entirely.

I set the water bottle down and swing my legs over the edge of the bed. A shower, that's what I need. So I get up and make it three steps before the first cramp hits.

It starts low in my belly, a dull ache that blooms into sharp, stabbing pain so quickly I don't have time to brace for it. I double over with a gasp, my hands flying to my stomach, trying to press against the source of the agony.

"What the—"

Another cramp. Worse than the first. It feels like something is trying to claw its way out of me from the inside, and I stumble sideways, my shoulder hitting the wall hard enough to leave a bruise.

I can't breathe or do anything except try to survive each wave of pain as it crashes over me.

"Oh God, what's happening to me?"

I slide down the wall until I'm crouching on the floor, arms wrapped around my middle, gasping for air. The pain is everywhere now. Not just my stomach but my whole body, every nerve ending on fire, every muscle clenched tight against an onslaught I don't understand.

I think this is what dying feels like.

Then a warming buzz spreads up my inner thighs. Hot and slick and unmistakable.

My hand moves without conscious thought, reaching between my legs, and when I pull it back, my fingers are coated in something thick and smooth. Something that glistens in the afternoon light.

Slick.

And suddenly everything makes sense. The exhaustion. The nesting. The fever that won't break. The desperate need to surround myself with my Alphas' scents.

My heat is finally here.

I let out a sound that's half laugh, half sob, still crouched on the floor with my back against the wall. After all these weeks of waiting. Nights of lying awake wondering if I was broken, if I would ever experience what other Omegas take for granted, if my body would ever catch up with my heart.

Another cramp rips through me, and the relief is

swallowed by a fresh wave of panic. Because reading about heats and experiencing one are two entirely different things. Nothing I read prepared me for this. The intensity. The loss of control. The way my body has suddenly become a foreign country with its own laws and demands.

I stumble to the bathroom, leaving a trail of slick on the hardwood floor that I'll be embarrassed about later. Right now, I don't care. Right now, the only thing that matters is cooling down my body enough to function and finding the three men who can make this stop.

The shower is a blur. Cold water that does absolutely nothing to cool the fire under my skin. More slick sliding down my thighs almost as fast as I can wash it away. My hands shaking so badly I can barely hold the soap.

And underneath it all, a craving that's growing stronger by the second. The desperate need to be filled and claimed and marked.

I dry myself as best I can, but my body isn't cooperating. Slick keeps coming, soaking through the towel, and I'm trembling so hard my teeth are chattering. I wrap a fresh towel around myself and grip the bathroom counter, staring at my reflection in the mirror.

My eyes are glazed, cheeks are flushed, and my lips are parted, my breath coming in quick, shallow pants.

I look like a woman on the edge of losing control entirely.

Because I am.

I leave the bathroom and head for the stairs, moving as quickly as my unsteady legs will allow. Each step sends friction between my thighs, and the sensation is almost too much. I have to stop twice, bracing myself against the wall, fighting back moans that want to escape my throat.

"Where are you?" I call out. "You won't believe—"

I don't get to finish the sentence.

The three of them emerge from different parts of the house, converging on the living room with expressions of alarm. Seth from the kitchen, Carter from the study, Kai from the yard. They take one look at me, standing at the bottom of the stairs in nothing but a towel, flushed and trembling and barely holding myself together.

"What's wrong?" Seth demands, already moving toward me. "June, what happened?"

I open my mouth to tell them. To explain that it's finally here, that my heat has arrived, that I'm not broken after all. But what comes out instead is a moan, low and desperate, as another cramp doubles me over and sends a fresh wave of slick running down my thighs.

They're at my side in seconds. All three of them, surrounding me, their hands reaching out to steady me. And the moment their skin touches mine, something inside me ignites.

Their nostrils flare simultaneously. I watch their

pupils dilate as they inhale the scent pouring off me in waves. For a moment, nobody moves. Nobody breathes.

Then Kai's face splits into a grin that's equal parts delighted and predatory. "Oh, doll," he breathes. "You're priming yourself for us. Someone's finally got their heat."

"It's insane," I manage, but the words come out wrong, tangled up with a purr that rumbles through my chest without permission. "I don't... I can't..."

My body moves on its own. One hand fisting in Seth's shirt, the other tangling in Carter's hair, pulling them both closer with a strength I didn't know I possessed. I need them like I crave air.

"Do something," I moan. "Please. Before I die."

"You're not going to die," Carter explains calmly.

"It sure feels like it," I blurt out.

"We knew it would come," Seth adds, his hands finding my waist, steadying me when my knees threaten to buckle. "Just had to be patient."

"Patience is overrated," Kai declares. "And so is this towel."

He tugs at the fabric, and it slips away before I can protest. Not that I want anything except their hands on my skin, their mouths on my body, their cocks inside me.

"Oh my God." The words tear out of me as a fresh wave of need crashes through my system. "If you don't stop talking and take me now, I'm going to explode. Why does my body feel like this?"

The three of them exchange glances as they look me up and down. There's hunger there, raw and undeniable. They're holding themselves back, I realize, waiting to ensure I'm okay.

"It's your first heat," Carter says gently. "Your body is adjusting. The intensity will even out, but right now—"

"Right now, I need you all to fuck me, or I'm going to lose my mind!" I'm reaching for them with shaky hands.

Kai scoops me up before I can say another word. His arms are strong around me, cradling me against his chest, and I bury my face in his neck and breathe him in.

"Let's begin in the bedroom," he instructs, already moving toward the stairs. "Then we can work our way through the rest of the house. Christen every room properly."

Carter and Seth follow close behind, shedding clothes as they go. I catch glimpses of bare chests, defined muscles, cocks already hard and erect. Fuck, I need them now.

"Why would you say that?" I gasp, even as my mouth finds Kai's pulse point and my teeth scrape against his skin.

"Darlin'," Seth drawls from somewhere behind us, "heats can last anywhere from a day to a week. And the whole time, you're going to want one of us inside you. Claiming you."

"I know that," I manage, but even as I say it, I realize I didn't. Not really. I read the words in books and articles and forums, but nothing, *nothing*, prepared me for the agonizing emptiness. The need that borders on pain. The desperate, primal drive to be rutted by an Alpha or die trying.

"What if you hadn't been home?" The thought strikes me suddenly, sharp with fear. "What if I'd been alone when this started?"

We're in the bedroom now. Kai sets me down on the bed, and I immediately reach for him, for any of them, unwilling to lose contact for even a second.

"That won't ever happen," Carter says firmly, leaning down to press a kiss to my forehead. His lips are cool against my feverish skin, and I whimper at the relief. "Not with the three of us. One of us will always be here."

"We'll get you a panic button," Kai suggests, stripping down, making me drool at all those muscles, the erection that glints with the jewelry piercings. "Something you can press that sends an alert to all of us simultaneously. We'll come running."

"Or we just never leave you alone," Seth adds, his hands already working to clear the bed of blankets and pillows and all the nest materials I so carefully arranged. "That works too."

I watch him sweep everything aside, and some

small part of me protests. That's my nest, but the larger part that's consumed by heat and hunger doesn't care about blankets and pillows. It only cares about the three men now surrounding me, their bodies bare, their eyes dark with desire, their cocks ready.

"I have no idea how we're going to do this," I admit, my voice trembling. "But I need you. All of you."

Seth settles on one side of me. Carter on the other, both naked. Kai kneels at the foot of the bed, his gaze traveling up my body with an intensity that makes me shiver.

"Just breathe," Carter says, his fingers tracing my arm even as his own breathing comes faster.

"And if it gets to be too much," Kai says, staring at me with predatory grace, "just tell us. We'll stop. We'll slow down. Whatever you need."

I gasp as another cramp seizes me. "I need you to never, ever stop."

The pain is bad, but the emptiness is worse. It's a void inside me that demands to be filled. Kai's hands are on my knees, and he spreads them. I lift my feet so they balance on the bed's edge, letting my legs drop open. All their stares focus on my offering.

Kai is grinning. "I love how your pussy flutters, how needy it is for us." His fingers are on me, and I cry out from the sensitive intensity of my skin right where I need them.

Seth's mouth finds mine, swallowing my moan as his hand squeezes my breast. Carter presses kisses down my neck, scraping with his teeth until I see stars. Kai, positioned between my spread thighs, leans in and licks me feverishly.

I arch my back, moaning, desperate for more. He's sucking and tugging at my clit, not being soft either, and I fucking love it.

Carter shifts to my breast, sucking hard on my nipple, nibbling on it, driving me to insanity.

Seth releases my mouth and shuffles forward on his knees, his cock suddenly pressing to my lips. He's so huge, and that greedy side of me parts my mouth, and I scoop him in with my tongue. Those hisses he unleashes are music to my ears.

"Remember this moment," he says softly. "Your first heat with your pack in your home."

I want to respond and tell him that I'll remember this forever, that this is everything I was afraid I'd never have. But my mouth is full with him pushing deeper, and all coherent thought becomes impossible.

The first wave hits me like I've been split open from the inside.

I don't just shudder; I *break*. My breath catches, my ribs aching with it, my whole body going tight and trembling as if it can't decide whether to run or melt. My back arches off the bed, and my hands fist in the sheets, Seth's cock still deep in my mouth.

It isn't only pleasure.

It's surrender and trust.

Carter's mouth brushes my shoulder, warm and

steady, his voice low like he's talking me down from the edge of something. "That's it," he murmurs against my skin. "Let go. We've got you."

My eyes sting, but it's not enough. I suck down on Seth, running my tongue under his shaft, sending him quivering with need. "You're so beautiful like this," he says with a hiss.

Kai doesn't say anything at all. He's too busy taking me apart with his tongue, pushing me higher and higher until I'm certain I can't take any more.

Then Kai releases me, and I exhale through my nose, but he's getting to his feet, lifting my legs up to rest against his chest, and he's smirking down at me as Seth works deeper into my mouth.

I watch him and how concentrated he is as he presses his cock into me, and instantly I feel the ribbed pleasure of his piercings. A moan grazes my throat as he pushes into me, reaching down to grab hold of my ass, lifting me slightly off the bed. And he drives into me so harshly I shudder and feel slick squeezing out of me. This is everything I crave, and exactly when Carter lifts himself up from my breasts.

He grins. "Look at me."

I do. He shifts, settling in closer, straddling my waist with his legs before shuffling up. He presses in close, heavy heat pinning me in place, leaving me nowhere to go but under him. That huge cock of his lies between the valley of my breasts, fire burning off him, all while Kai thrusts into me, and my whole body shudders.

Carter's hands slide to the sides of my breasts, bringing them together, sandwiching his erection. He groans as he starts to thrust, pleasuring himself with me. I hold one hand tight on Seth's thigh, and the other I reach over to Carter, gripping his leg as all three of my men are grunting, and I can't get enough of being their object of desire. The bed rocks beneath us as we find our rhythm, and I'm floating in heaven.

"We're not doing this halfway, June," Seth whispers. "Give it to us. All of it."

"You're so fucking beautiful," Carter adds, breathless.

"Does it feel like what you've been craving?" Kai murmurs, leaning to the side from behind Carter so I can see him, a wink flashing like he knows exactly what he's doing to me.

I break contact, releasing Seth just long enough to lick my lips, my pulse skittering. "I've never felt so wrecked and satisfied at the same time in my life," I breathe. "Just... please don't stop."

Every breath rushes in and out of my lungs as I press closer, chasing the friction and the heat, chasing *more*. Seth stares down at me with that grin, the one that got me in trouble in the first place when I picked him up from prison.

And look where it's landed me.

Pinned between three cowboys, unraveling in their hands, and so damn happy about it that I could laugh.

I melt back into the moment, taking Seth's cock into my mouth again, and letting them have everything I'm giving, letting them set the pace and the rules. I love every second, wanting this greedy, unforgettable moment to stretch out until the rest of the world is just noise and all that's real is us.

BONUS SCENE
JUNE

"Remind me again why I agreed to this?" Seth's voice is somewhere between resigned and suspicious as we stand outside The Dust Jacket Bookshop, the evening light casting long shadows across Front Street. The hand-painted sign swings gently in the breeze, creaking slightly, and the window display features lots of romance books around this month's selection: *Claimed by the Beasts*.

The cover features a woman in a torn dress being carried off by two muscular creatures with horns and tails. Very subtle.

"Because you can't resist me," I say sweetly, threading my arm through his. "And because I want to spend time with you."

Seth's eyes narrow as he takes in the window display. "What kinds of books does this club read, exactly?"

"Romance novels."

"That's not very specific."

"You'll see." I tug him toward the door. "Come on, we're going to be late."

What I don't tell him is that Carter and Kai practically begged me to keep Seth occupied tonight while they held their drinking competition against Tanner, because Seth would definitely shut it down if he found out about it. I have my suspicions about what that competition involves, but plausible deniability seems like the wisest course of action.

Besides, the look on Seth's face when he realizes what he's walked into is going to be absolutely priceless.

The bell chimes as I push open the door, and the familiar smell of old paper and fresh coffee wraps around us. Books are everywhere, stacked on every surface.

"June! There you are!" Loretta's voice booms from somewhere in the depths of the shop. She emerges from behind a towering stack of paperbacks. Her silver-streaked hair is piled high, held in place by chopsticks. "And you brought a... Oh my."

She stops dead, staring at Seth like he's a mythical creature who's wandered into her domain by accident.

"Loretta, this is Seth Benton," I introduce. "Seth, this is Loretta. She owns the bookshop."

"Ma'am." Seth tips his hat politely, his ingrained courtesy overriding his obvious discomfort.

Loretta's hand flies to her chest. "Well, slap my face and call me Sally. You brought a real live cowboy to our book club, and not just any cowboy. You're from the rodeo circuit! I've seen you on the posters."

"Yes, ma'am."

"The girls are going to lose their minds. Now, follow me. Everyone's already upstairs."

She leads us toward the narrow staircase hidden behind the bookshelf that swings open, and Seth shoots me a look that clearly says, *What have you gotten me into?* I just smile and give him an encouraging pat on the arm.

The room at the top of the stairs is cozy and warmly lit. Unlike last month's mafia-themed extravaganza, tonight's setup is more subdued. Comfortable mismatched armchairs and a large sectional couch form a rough circle around a coffee table laden with snacks. Wine bottles stand ready for action. Fairy lights twinkle along the ceiling beams.

The only concession to this month's theme appears to be a large poster of the book cover taped to one wall, featuring those muscular, horned creatures carrying off their human prize.

Three familiar faces turn toward us as we enter. Dolly, with her purple-tinted hair, is wearing a T-shirt that reads Monsters Do It Better. Rita sports a headband with fuzzy monster ears. And Karen is draped in a faux-fur scarf.

Their expressions freeze on Seth.

"Sweet merciful heavens," Rita breathes. "June brought a man."

Seth shifts uncomfortably beside me, clearly unused to being discussed like a prized horse at auction. I bite my lip to keep from laughing.

"Everyone, this is Seth," I announce, guiding him toward the sectional. "He's going to join us tonight since Sophia can't make it."

Rita's eyes go wide. "So, he's going to participate in the discussion?"

"Unless you'd prefer I wait in the car," Seth offers hopefully.

"Don't you dare!" Loretta sweeps into the room behind us, already pouring wine. "When was the last time we had a male perspective on our selections? Never, that's when. This is going to be fabulous."

I settle onto one of the double couches, and Seth drops down beside me with the air of a man accepting his fate. He's pressed close enough that our thighs touch.

"Have you all read the book?" Karen asks eagerly, leaning forward in her chair.

Everyone nods. Seth glances at the poster on the wall, then back at the assembled women. "I have not."

"Oh, that's fine." Dolly waves a hand dismissively. "You'll catch on quick enough. The plot's not exactly complicated."

"Okay, so a quick summary for Seth's sake," Loretta says. "Tonight's book is a monster romance. The main character, Julia, is sold to a clan of monsters to keep the peace between humans and their kingdom. She's supposed to be a bride, a sacrifice essentially, but the monsters turn out to be... more complex than she expected."

Rita giggles. "That's one way to put it."

"There are two monster princes," Karen continues enthusiastically. "Brothers. They're supposed to share her as their queen, but there's all this tension about whether she'll accept them or try to escape."

Seth tilts his head to the side, watching her.

"Here." I press my paperback into his hands. "Maybe at least read the back cover to get a sense of things."

He flips the book over and starts reading. When he's done, he glances at me with an expression that clearly communicates, *Where have you brought me?*

"Wine?" Loretta appears at his elbow, bottle in hand. "You're going to need it."

"I don't—"

"Your loss. Let's get started!" Loretta settles into her throne-like chair. "Since we have a newcomer, let's begin with first impressions. What did everyone think of the book overall?"

"I loved it way more than I expected to," Rita says immediately. "I've never read a monster romance before, but this one had me hooked from chapter one."

"The world-building was surprisingly detailed," Karen adds. "I appreciated that the author took time to explain the monster society, their customs and history."

"The spice level was excellent. Chef's kiss," Dolly contributes. "Just the right amount of buildup before things got steamy."

Loretta turns to me. "June? Your thoughts?"

"I thought it was great. The relationship dynamics between Julia and the princes were really well done. Each one had a distinct personality, and you could see why she was drawn to all of them."

"And which prince was your favorite?"

"Orion," I answer without hesitation. "The brooding one. He acts all cold and intimidating, but underneath he's incredibly protective."

Seth makes a small sound beside me. I glance over to find him skimming through the book, clearly trying to catch up with the conversation.

"What about you, Seth?" Loretta asks, her eyes twinkling with mischief. "Any initial impressions?"

"I'm still trying to figure out the basic premise," he admits. "These monsters. They're not... animals?"

"Oh, no," Karen assures him. "They're humanoid. Mostly. They just have some additional... features."

He raises an eyebrow.

"Horns. Tails. Interesting skin textures." She smirks. "Among other things. Okay, let's move on to specific scenes," Loretta suggests. "Which scene stood out to you the most? The one that really stuck with you after you finished reading?"

"The invisible one," Rita, Dolly, and Karen say in near-perfect unison.

I find myself nodding along. "Same for me."

Seth looks between all of us, confused.

"Chapter seventeen," Dolly clarifies. "It's the scene where the princes use their ability to become invisible to... pursue her through the castle."

"Interesting," he murmurs.

"It's one of their monster abilities," Karen explains. "They can phase into this shadow form where they can't be seen. And in this scene, they use it to—"

"Chase her," Rita finishes, her face slightly flushed. "Even through the halls while she's trying to get to her chambers. And they keep catching her and... having their way with her."

"And she can't see them," Dolly adds with a huge grin. "She can only feel them. Their hands, their mouths, their—"

"What chapter did you say that was?" he asks, already flipping through the book.

"Seventeen. About two-thirds of the way through."

He finds the page and starts reading. The room goes quiet as everyone watches the rodeo champion cowboy discover the particular joys of monster-romance literature. I have to press my lips together hard to keep from laughing as his brow furrows, his jaw tightens, and a faint flush creeps up the back of his neck.

"So," Loretta continues, clearly enjoying Seth's

discomfort, "what was it about that scene that resonated with everyone?"

"The anticipation," Karen says dreamily. "The way Julia knows they're there but can't see them. How she can only wait to feel their touch. It's incredibly suspenseful and sexy."

"And the vulnerability," Rita adds. "She's completely at their mercy, but there's this underlying trust. She knows they won't actually hurt her."

Dolly is nodding enthusiastically.

Seth's head snaps up from the book suddenly. "That's not how any of this works."

Every woman in the room turns to stare at him.

"What do you mean?" Loretta asks, clearly delighted by this development.

"I mean—" He gestures at the book, his expression somewhere between baffled and indignant. "No Alpha would ever say that. It's ridiculous."

"Say what, specifically?" Karen leans forward eagerly. "Read it out for us."

Everyone is leaning in now, waiting, and I am on the verge of laughing out loud.

Seth drags his finger down the page and reads, "He doesn't ask or sweet-talk. He just steps in close until her back hits the wall and the room feels too small for breathing. 'Don't give me that look,' the monster growls. 'You came into my room on purpose.' His hand plants beside her head, hard enough to rattle the wall. 'You wanna pretend you're brave? Fine. Be brave while

I tell you how this goes.' He dips his head, mouth near her ear. 'You run, I'll catch you. You fight, I'll make you scream as I fuck you. You stay... you don't get surprised when I keep you.'" Seth jerks the book back like it bit him.

Everyone's just watching him, no reaction, but it's clear they enjoyed that a lot more than Seth anticipated.

"It's romantic," Dolly protests.

Seth closes the book. "So she's okay with not being able to see them as they ravage her in a hallway where anyone could walk by? That's not intimate. That's an exhibitionism kink with extra steps."

The room erupts in giggles. I'm dying beside him, pressing my hand over my mouth to contain my laughter.

"He has a point about the hallway," Rita concedes between giggles. "I always wondered why none of the servants ever interrupted."

"They were probably watching," Karen suggests wickedly. "Enjoying the show."

"That would actually make a great sequel scene," Dolly muses. "The servants' perspective."

Seth looks genuinely perplexed. "She's being chased through a castle by invisible creatures, and she has no idea what they're going to do to her..."

"She knows what they're going to do to her," I say gently. "That's kind of the point. She's anticipating it, wanting it."

"But she can't see them."

"That's what makes it exciting."

Seth stares at me like I've grown a second head. "You too, darlin'?"

I fan myself dramatically. "That scene made me super hot. I won't lie."

His expression shifts from confusion to something of interest, maybe. Then he catches himself and clears his throat, looking back at the assembled women with renewed wariness.

"It's the loss of control," Karen explains. "The idea of being pursued by someone powerful who wants you so badly they can't contain themselves, and ultimately, it's Julia who holds the power. The monsters just don't realize it yet."

"The fantasy of being desired that intensely," Rita adds. "Of being the center of someone's complete focus."

"Multiple feral someones, in this case," Dolly points out with a grin.

The room goes quiet for a beat as everyone seems to go into deep thought, and I'm grinning, knowing exactly how exciting it is to have the attention of multiple men. I glance over at Seth, smiling, and he winks at me.

"So, wait," Karen says, leaning forward. "From an actual Alpha perspective, how would you handle that situation of pursuing a woman you wanted. Making her feel desired."

Seth shifts uncomfortably. "I'd ask permission first."

"See, that's very sweet," Loretta says, "but these are monsters. They don't have the same etiquette humans do. Different cultural norms."

Dolly adds, "You can't apply human courtship rules to monsters."

Seth glances at me again with an expression that clearly says, *These are interesting books you read and discuss.* I just shrug and take a sip of my wine, enjoying his fish-out-of-water flailing far too much.

"Let's put him to the test!" Loretta announces suddenly, clapping her hands. "Seth, we want you to rate the monster princes. On a scale of one to ten. The main ones from the invisible scene."

"Based on what criteria?"

"Hotness," Karen supplies immediately.

Seth actually laughs at that, the sound surprised out of him. "Well, that didn't exactly do it for me. I'm not really in a position to judge male attractiveness, monster or otherwise."

Loretta waves a hand. "Rate them on their... technique. Their approach. As one Alpha evaluating another."

Seth sighs heavily and flips back through the book to the relevant chapter. He skims for a moment, his expression growing more incredulous by the second.

"I'd give them both a three," he finally announces.

"Three?" Rita exclaims loudly. "Orion is at least an eight or nine!"

"He pins her against a wall without warning and just expects her to be into it. That's a communication failure, not a seduction."

"But she was into it," Dolly protests.

"That's not the point. He didn't know she would be. He assumed. In real life, that's how you get slapped. Or worse."

The women exchange glances, clearly not agreeing.

"He does have a point," I say. "There's no negotiation of boundaries at all, but this is fantasy, and that means exploring and pushing limits. Figuring out what could be possible, what you would never do in real life."

"I understand that." Seth sets the book down on the coffee table. "I'm just saying, from a practical standpoint, the techniques on display here would not work in the real world."

"What would work?" I ask, genuinely curious. "In your expert Alpha opinion?"

He turns to look at me as if the joke drops away and something real steps into its place.

"Depends," he says, voice gone a shade rougher. "You want what *works*... or what makes her think about it hours later when she's trying to be normal?"

Dolly makes a small choking sound into her wine.

Loretta's eyes go wide. "Oh my."

I blink, heat rising fast, because he's still looking at me like I'm the example in his head.

"In my expert Alpha opinion," he adds, and the corner of his mouth lifts like he knows exactly what he's doing, "you don't start with hands. You start with *attention.*"

He leans back in his chair, casual, but his gaze stays locked on me. Steady. Possessive in that way that feels like a hand on the small of my back.

"Building anticipation," he says, his voice dropping lower. "Making her aware of your presence. Your intent." His gaze falls to my mouth, then back to my eyes. "Letting her feel your attention on her before you ever make a move. So when you do finally touch her, she's already desperate for it."

My throat tightens.

The room has gone very quiet.

"God," Karen whispers, like she's in church.

"Go on," Loretta breathes.

Seth's jaw tenses, as if he realizes he's wandered into dangerous territory and it's my fault for asking.

But he doesn't glance away.

"If you're smart," he continues, voice softer now but somehow worse, "you make it clear what you want without rushing her. You give her space to feel it. To want it back." His gaze dips—barely—then returns, deliberate. "You let her catch you watching. You let her *wonder* if you're going to do something about it."

Rita fans herself with a flyer. "This is not the brochure version of book club."

Seth's mouth twitches like he's trying not to laugh. "And when you finally do make a move?" he adds, eyes still on me. "You don't grab. You don't perform. You touch her like you've been thinking about it all day."

My stomach flips, and my face is absolutely on fire.

Seth clears his throat and looks away. "That's all. Just... communication. Paying attention to what your partner actually wants."

"Sure," Dolly says. "Communication. That's what that was."

"I think I need more wine," Karen announces faintly.

"Same," Rita agrees.

I'm staring at Seth with what's probably a very obvious expression of appreciation. He smirks slightly, clearly pleased with himself for turning the tables on the room.

"Careful," Karen warns me, delighted. "That's how it starts. Next thing you know, you're highlighting passages and buying... accessories."

"Karen," Loretta scolds, but she's smiling too hard for it to count.

"Well," Loretta says, fanning herself with a paperback, "that was educational. Let's move on to the anatomy discussion."

"The what now?" Seth looks alarmed.

"Oh, this is the best part!" Karen claps her hands

excitedly. "Last meeting, we agreed that everyone would bring their artistic interpretations of... certain aspects of monster physiology."

Seth just raises an eyebrow. "I'm going to need you to pretend I'm not here for this part," he says, and I'm smiling way too much at his discomfort.

"Don't hold back on our account," Loretta says breezily.

Karen reaches under her chair and pulls out a rolled-up piece of poster paper. With great ceremony, she unfurls it to reveal a detailed colored-pencil drawing of what can only be described as a monster's cock. It's purple, ribbed, and appears to have small glowing nodules along its length.

"I figured creatures who can turn invisible would have some interesting light-producing capabilities elsewhere as well."

Seth makes a sound like he's choking on air. "That's... that's quite detailed," he manages.

"Thank you! I took an anatomy class in the eighties. Very useful."

Dolly goes next, revealing her contribution. This penis is green, forked at the end like a snake's tongue, and covered in what appear to be tiny suction cups. "For enhanced sensation," she explains at Seth's horrified expression. "I thought about what would actually feel good from a recipient's perspective."

"I appreciate the consideration," Karen says dryly.

Rita's drawing features an appendage that's bright

red, has what resembles soft spines along its length, and a notation that reads *Vibrates when aroused.*

"The book mentions that the princes purr when they're excited. I thought, what if that vibration extended to other areas?"

Seth is staring at the ceiling, clearly praying for divine intervention.

"June?" Loretta turns to me expectantly. "Where's yours?"

"Oh, I have one." I reach into my bag and pull out my own folded paper. I'd almost forgotten about it in the chaos of the past week, but I'd actually put some thought into this assignment.

Seth is suddenly very interested and watching me.

I unfold the paper to reveal my contribution of a deep blue penis with a slight curve, covered in overlapping scales that I've called *flexible sensory plates.* At the base, there's a knot-like swelling, and I've added small notes explaining the function of each feature.

"I went with a more reptilian interpretation," I explain. "Given that Orion has scales on parts of his body, I figured his... other features might follow suit."

Seth is looking at my drawing with intense interest. "You drew this?"

I nod, laughing, then I point to a section at the side of the huge blue cock. "There's a notation here that says *Increases in girth during climax.*"

"Seems anatomically logical," Loretta says.

Seth stares at me for a long moment, then slowly

shakes his head, a smile tugging at the corner of his mouth despite his obvious shock. "I had no idea you had this kind of imagination, darlin'. But I'm liking it."

"There's a lot you don't know about me, cowboy."

The room erupts in hoots and catcalls.

"This is literally the best book club meeting we've ever had," Karen announces. "Seth, you should come back next month."

"I'm not sure my heart can take it," Seth admits, but he's grinning now, the initial shock giving way to genuine amusement. "But I'm convinced that my close buddy, Kai, would jump at the chance, and you'd have a very different experience with him attending."

I gasp, knowing Kai would revel in this, and Seth leans in closer to me, the warmth of his body leaping over to me. I adore every touch from him.

We spend another hour discussing the finer points of monster romance, with Seth offering increasingly bewildered commentary that has everyone in stitches. He's a good sport about it; I have to give him that.

By the time we finally leave, it's nearly eleven and my face hurts from laughing. Seth looks shell-shocked but also strangely satisfied, as if he's survived a trial by fire and emerged stronger on the other side.

"So," I say as we step out onto the sidewalk, the cool night air a welcome relief after the warm, wine-scented atmosphere upstairs. "What did you think?"

Seth is quiet for a moment. "I had no idea women

talked about this stuff in such detail, or that you wanted to be chased and ravaged." He grins sinfully.

I laugh and nudge him into a walk toward the truck. "Very funny."

He chuckles, the sound warm and genuine in the quiet street. "That scene you all liked so much. The invisible one."

"What about it?"

"I'm not saying I could turn invisible." He's looking straight ahead, but I can see the hint of a smirk. "But I bet I could make you feel pursued. Desired. Desperate."

My breath catches. "Is that so?"

"Just something to think about." He opens the truck door for me, ever the gentleman.

"For later."

I climb in, my mind already racing with possibilities. The second Seth shuts his door and the engine rumbles to life, my gaze slides to him like it's magnetized.

I try to picture him deciding to chase me. Then crowding me back until there's nowhere left but the wall, his voice in my ear as he rips my dress to get to me. Heat creeps up my neck so fast it's humiliating.

I crank the window down an inch, then another, like cold air might knock some sense into me.

Seth glances over, catching the whole thing—my flushed cheeks, my grip on the door handle, the way I'm suddenly too interested in the night breeze. He lets out a low laugh.

"Oh, yeah," he drawls. "I know exactly what you're fantasizing about right now."

I scoff, grateful for the distraction even as my pulse spikes. "Please. Focus on driving."

Seth's grin turns dangerous as he pulls away from the curb, laughter still in his chest. "If you ever want to play make-believe, if you ever need me to be that monster for you… just say the word."

I suck in a sharp breath, my whole body suddenly burning up. I roll my eyes at him. "As if." But the truth sits heavy and wicked in my chest. If Seth ever decided to hunt me for real, I wouldn't run to get away. I'd run to see how fast he could catch me.

ABOUT HARLEY KNIGHT

Hi, I'm Harley Knight! I'm a romance author who's absolutely obsessed with books, writing, and happily-ever-afters. I love creating stories filled with emotion, passion, and unforgettable characters that stick with you long after the last page. When I'm not writing, you'll find me lost in a good book or dreaming up my next big adventure. For me, there's nothing better than crafting love stories that remind us all why love is worth fighting for.

*Contact: **knightharleyus@gmail.com***